THE
LANDLORD

THE LANDLORD

KRISTIN HUNTER

DOVER PUBLICATIONS, INC.
Mineola, New York

Bibliographical Note

This Dover edition, first published in 2020, is an unabridged republication of the work originally published by Charles Scribner's Sons, New York, in 1966.

Library of Congress Cataloging-in-Publication Data

Names: Lattany, Kristin Hunter, 1931–2008, author.
Title: The landlord / Kristin Hunter.
Description: Dover edition. | Mineola, New York: Dover Publications, Inc., 2020.
 | Originally published: 1966.
Identifiers: LCCN 2019050687 | ISBN 9780486843421 (paperback) | ISBN
 0486843424 (paperback)
Subjects: GSAFD: Satire.
Classification: LCC PS3558.U483 L38 2020 | DDC 813/.54—dc23
LC record available at https://lccn.loc.gov/2019050687

Manufactured in the United States by LSC Communications
84342401
www.doverpublications.com

2 4 6 8 10 9 7 5 3 1

2020

For Chester Himes

"Landlord, I like my water hot."
PALADIN
Have Gun, Will Travel

THE LANDLORD

1

Elgar Enders patted the four new, crisp rent books in his pocket with tender satisfaction. At last he had a business: Real Estate. An occupational title: Landlord. A piece of property, described in a deed with fine legal exactness: Three stories, four units, so many square feet on a lot one hundred by fifty, valuation for tax purposes, twelve thousand dollars.

Elgar almost crowed, and leaped, and clicked his heels in the air until he remembered that he was out on the street where Mothaw browsed every Monday for bargains in emeralds, the calm, stately street, surrounded by cool, contained people. On a bright, beamy Monday in August, hint of breeze.

Well, now he would be contained too, for at last he had work, something to do with his continually itchy, troublesome self. There would be locks to replace, drains to unclog, light fixtures to repair. He might, at long last, allow himself the luxury of a few choice gripes, in the fine tradition of all workingmen since the beginning of history. As a hobby, he might even gather a compendium of colorful complaints—the howls of London hod-carriers, the steamy swearings of Roman pasta-makers, the mutterings of hordes hauling stones to the Pyramids.

—By the sickly lusts of our incestuous Queen, you are a sodomous son of a jackal-faced dog, you Nile-moldered hunk of rock, you.

Yes, drains were solid problems, the solving of which produced tangible results, unlike those vague, cloudy daily exercises with Borden, his psychoanalyst, or those metallic dialogues with Levin, his stockbroker:

"Aluminum Alloys, keep, check?"

"Check. It's holding steady."

"Overseas Pipeline, sell, check?"

"Check. It's loosening up now."

1

"Sell Supersoft Mills, too, Levin."

"No, don't sell Supersoft, Elgar. It's firming up. Check?"

"Roger, Levin."

Never, never, "And how are you today, Elgar, my boy? Loosening, steady, or firming up? Loosening? I know exactly how you feel, man, I have those days too. Firming up? Fine, congratulations."

Check. Firming up, thank you, Levin, though you will never ask. With a drain, you knew where you stood. You worked over it long and tenderly, and suddenly there was the satisfying *swump, gurgle, swish* as it cleared, and you lit up with the holiness of accomplishment, knowing you had done your share in the great work of clearing the drains of the world. Sanitation and sanity. *Mens sana et drains sano.*

Mothaw would die if she knew her sensitive youngest, her precious downy blondling, yearned to be a common *plumbah.* And, oh, then he had another happy, eager thought. Maybe Fathaw would die too.

He sang as he swung along, so loudly and tonelessly that a mauvey-tweed matron, one of Mothaw's Monday-afternoon concert friends, probably, stopped dead and stared.

"Swump, gurgle, swish, ma'am," he repeated politely, tipping his hat, and moved on, adding softly, "Go screw. I am happy."

Elgar felt the dotted outline of his ever-fluid identity filling in, growing almost solid. Catching sight of his grin in a reflecting store window, he tilted his head slightly and patted his thick, buttery hair.

Aha, you handsome dog, you.

Then looked away quickly, superstitiously, lest his image disappear in retribution. He always expected it to, since he was far handsomer than he deserved to be.

God's gift to women, no doubt about it. Have to share the wealth, spread it around. Sorry, my dear, but 'tis my mission on earth. Who are you to be so selfish?

Someday he would have the guts to say that to Sally, blonde Sally-from-Smith, with her pained look of sacrifice every time she granted him her elegant favors, and to Rita, angry-social-worker Rita, with her dark, stony, Talmudic spells of brooding, and to Lanie, with her constant, lilting mockery. —No, not to Lanie, who was nicer to him than she had a right to be.

"Lanie, are you an octoroon?"

"No, silly, a macaroon. Want a bite?"

Of course he did, he was always hungry, no matter how bitter a draught of guilt washed down his dinner. And, no doubt about it, the sight of him curled up next to that golden cornucopia would be just the ticket to send his old man to sudden, apoplectic death. The intensity with which this consummation was desired was probably what tightened the knot in Elgar's stomach so viciously, doubling him over on the street. There was nothing organically wrong with him.

"All right, Elgar." Borden, with the goddamn *kindliness* in his voice, puff-puffing on the pipe. "Let's be honest, now."

"Certainly, Borden, though if you insist on playing this like a gentleman's game, a Christly hour of *chess* or something, it won't be easy. But if you want honesty, Borden, to tell the truth, it's a fake, that bit about my spreading the wealth. It's more a case of covering my bets, you see. I have to have lots of women, because if I concentrate on one, when she leaves me, I'll be alone."

"Alone and worthless?"

"Yes, Borden, you bastard." Oh, yes, I'll have a thing or two to tell you *this* afternoon.

But first there was lovely, solid stuff to buy. A two-inch copper joint, weatherstripping, a set of wrenches. —And I'll take a set of wenches, as well. The very best you have.

But how much weatherstripping? Take a chance, guess, or go measure all the windows?

"Waste not, want not, son. Get it right the first time."

"All right, Fathaw, I hear you!" he screamed. "I've been hearing you all my life!"

He stopped and stared fiercely at three startled passersby who averted their eyes, then took up their directions again, jerkily, like frames in a movie reel that had been momentarily frozen. Elgar laughed maniacally— Make way for the madman—and moved on beyond them, beyond weatherstripping, to dreams of his house of the future.

One day, the present tenants gone, he would strip the place of its apartments, remake it into the residence he would by then deserve. By then he would be able to allow himself a pleasure palace arranged to permit the endless play of light on textures and furnished to indulge all the whims of a restless, robust mind. Then he would leave his dank death-cell in the Trejour Apartments, no longer needing Borden in the same building to reassure him, tell him over and over again that he was real, and good, and deserved things. There would be no more screams into the phone in the middle of the night.

"Borden! Borden, are you up there?"

"Yes, Elgar." —Always patient, even when awakened at three in the morning. Couldn't he ever get upset? "I'm here, and you're there, aren't you?"

"Christ, I know I'm here, you incredible idiot."

"Good. Then good night, Elgar. Go to sleep."

The click, and Elgar would let loose a stream of spluttering curses, yet be somehow satisfied by the exchange, and able to sleep at last.

Someday he wouldn't need Borden always handy to shore him up and undermine him at the same time. Steadying him with his right hand, while with his left he was draining Elgar of dreams and memories, making him paler, pushing him toward disappearance. And charging him twenty-five dollars an hour for the bloodletting.

Elgar sucked in his breath, squinted his eyes shut, and concentrated on seeing the house as it would be someday. His house, an extension of himself, in that fine future when he would have a self to extend.

. . . Rip out the stairs and partitions, recess the second story into a gallery bedroom opening on a balcony, give the first-floor living room a three-story cathedral ceiling. One starkly beautiful light fixture that he would commission, a dancing constellation of lights visible at night through three stories of glass. Of course he would have to curtain that fall of glass, at from twenty-five to fifty bucks a yard, and . . .

His father's hand, pinched with penury in the midst of its millions, unable to replace anything until it frayed and fell apart, clamped down clawlike on Elgar's before it could react to the lovely, crunchy feel of that fabric. An unbelievable shade of goldy-green, it slithered away into the dank subterrain of dreams that would never be realized.

Certainly nothing so lush and lovely would ever see the light of day on the cut-rate counters of J. P. Enders and Co., Seven Branches, Never Undersold. From all seven branches a clammy sea of plastic billowed forth endlessly to curtain the world, for J. P. Enders was the Junk Emporium, and he, Elgar Enders, was the son and heir of the Emperor of Junk. Try as he might, he could not abdicate the throne.

Measure he must.

2

E ven at a distance Elgar's house stood out from all the others, rising tall and clean as the Washington Monument from a surrounding shambles of shingled lean-tos and upended brick coffins, with the good balanced architecture that had sold him, wide, well-placed windows, a fanlighted prince of a door.

The real estate salesman had assured him, over and over, that the tenants were good, steady, reliable types. None had lived there less than five years. One couple had been there *twenty-five* years.

He'd added, with odious chumminess, "Can you imagine the ignorance of those people? By now they've paid enough rent to buy the house four times over. Best value on our list, too. I approached them, but they weren't interested. That's why I prefer dealing with a businessman."

—A white man, you mean, had been Elgar's reaction. And I suppose, since slimy reptiles like you also come under that classification, we are expected to have everything in common.

He'd bought on the spot, rather than submit to the rest of the salestalk. No need for dickering, anyway. It was a good buy.

—An excellent buy, he amended, moving closer to admire the gracefully proportioned windows. Congratulating himself on his astute judgment of property values, his shrewd eye for a bargain, Elgar almost overlooked a startling new development.

Each window now contained a large, boldly printed sign.

What the hell?

Elgar kicked the front door open and stormed into the vestibule.

"This property is not zoned commercial, do you understand?" he raged. "It's residential!"

In the vestibule, a brick-complexioned dwarf with a curly black mop regarded Elgar blandly from its perch on a fire-red scooter.

"I Walla Chee Cho Chee," it chirped. "Gimme nickel."

"Who is Madam Margarita?" demanded Elgar. "Where does Fanny live?"

"I Walla Chee Cho Chee," the dwarf repeated sweetly. "Gimme nickel."

"Oho," said Elgar. "An extortionist. I know your type. Just why should I give you a nickel, Walter Shoji? Just because you have the largest, darkest, most lamplike eyes I've ever seen? Don't you know that's the beginning of creeping socialism? Don't you know how bad socialism is? Do you want to grow up without a shred or particle of individual initiative?"

It was a good imitation of Fathaw, even to the rasping whine in the voice. Elgar held up a shiny dime.

"On the other hand," he lectured, "let me demonstrate to you the advantages of earning your bread. You see this? This is worth *two* nickels. And it is all yours if you will tell me which apartment belongs to Madam Margarita and which to Miss Fanny."

"You the new rent man?"

"Never mind who I am. I am your Uncle Sam, if you must know. Who are Margarita and Fanny?"

"Don't know no Marita. Fanny my mama. I Walla Chee Cho Chee."

Or something like that. Then, in a maneuver that would have done credit to an Olympic skiing champion, the kid leaped, plucked the dime from Elgar's fingers, and sailed out of the door on his scooter.

"Gone buy me two green yum-yums," he tossed over his shoulder. "I *love* green yum-yums. Yum-yum man, he go soon. I hurry. 'Bye, rent man."

There was such lyrical sweetness in the voice uttering this foreign-sounding babble that Elgar was suddenly homesick for the South Sea islands he had never seen, until he realized how thoroughly he had been tricked.

He turned helplessly, masticating his rage, and studied the names which were variously scribbled, printed, and embossed on the mailboxes. Copee. Perkins. Cumberson. And, in raised gold script letters, P. Eldridge DuBois. Elgar copied each name onto the cover of a separate rent book, using the laborious block printing that was the only thing he had taken away from his desperate years at day school. That P. Eldridge character. Hmmm. Elgar smelled trouble there.

He went outside again and stared at the signs for a full five minutes, deliberately allowing his fury to build to a molten froth as he read:

Madam Margarita
Readings $2
Ring 2 Bell
(If No Anser Ring 1 Bell)

and:

Fanny Hair Styling
$3 Up
Ring 1 Bell
(If No Anser Ring 2 Bell)

Obviously, there was collusion at work here. A conspiracy among his tenants to ruin him. Elgar went back into the vestibule and rang *all* the bells. Simultaneously, steadily, with the full, unforgiving pressure of his arm.

There was an immediate response that made him jump. It came from the third mailbox, the only one which boasted a tricky little microphone and speaker. Out of this elegant, custom-installed device came a click, the spooky burr of static, and then a crisply insulting, British-style voice.

"State youah business, please."

"What?" roared Elgar. "Who the hell are you?"

"Dubwah heah," the gadget replied silkily. "State youah business."

"Well, Mister DuBois, you'd better state *your* business. I am the new owner. Do you know anything about those signs out front?"

"I do not participate in the vulgar activities of this establishment, suh," was the suave answer.

"Well, do you participate in vulgar money-making activities, like the rest of us? Readings, for instance? Or Hair Stylings?"

"I, suh, am a *Creole*," the device answered, settling the question forever.

"I don't give a damn what you are!" Elgar bellowed. "You better pay your rent American!"

The thing was offended. "Rally!" it exclaimed breathily, and clicked off.

Elgar had still not gained admittance to his own house. And, in a typically Elgaresque blunder, he had left the keys at the real estate office. Biting his lip to contain a really royal flow of curses, he folded his arms and leaned all his weight against the bells.

In response, a blur of crimson like a full-blown anemone exploded into the vestibule.

"Where's Walter Gee? Have you seen him?"

Scarlet silk emblazoned with golden dragons, slippery and, he hoped, precarious, was the only covering of the softest, smoothest expanse of beige skin Elgar had ever seen, and Elgar was a connoisseur of such matters. You could drown in skin like that, and die happy.

As his eyes slowly traveled upward, a rounded knee obligingly peeked out from beneath the robe. Elgar's eyes halted there. It was a long time before he reached the face, but that was satisfactory too. Adorable, in fact, if you had a taste for the exotic. Slightly Mongoloid features, almond-shaped black eyes with a flat, exciting glitter, shaded by lashes that almost swept the floor. Now batting at the rate of eighty bats a minute. Helplessly, fatuously, Elgar smiled.

"Where is Walter Gee?" she repeated crossly. "Mister, have you seen my little boy?"

"There was a kind of a pygmy con man hanging around here when I came in," Elgar replied. "He got a dime out of me and disappeared."

"Ooh!" she shrieked. "You gave him a dime? To buy that nasty green Wop ice cream? A dime's enough for two of those things. He gets sick to death from *one*. If I have to take him to the hospital, I'll sue you."

"How much?" Elgar asked, thinking, Take it all, take everything I've got. It's yours, if you'll just let that robe slide down a little lower on the left side. Ah, there.

She ticked it off on her fingers. "Ten thousand for damages to my child's life and limbs. Ten thousand for court costs and lawyer fees. Ten thousand for medical expenses. Ten thousand for my mental anguish, and ten for my *husband's* mental anguish. That's fifty thousand dollars if he don't die. If he *does*—"

She looked up at Elgar suddenly, the lashes batting like moth wings, the eyes beaming an expression soft and seductive as a Univac's.

"You're kinda cute, though. For a white man. Who are you?"

"I'm the new landlord."

Her eyes widened. "Maybe I won't sue you, then. Maybe I'll just settle for five years' free rent. I'm Fanny Copee."

"Charmed," he said. "Always wanted to meet the Dragon Lady."

She was not smiling. "You go find my little boy," she said. "Walter Gee Copee. He's only four years old. Find him quick, before he eats that nasty, rotten green poison. Then you come in and have a little talk with me."

"Delighted," Elgar said. "I was intending to have a little talk with you anyway. About, uh, the hairdressing."

Her hand darted out and brushed Elgar's hair, sending a jagged shiver to his toes.

"Oh, you don't need nothin', Landlord. Except maybe a little dandruff treatment and scalp massage."

She wiggled her fingers by way of illustration. Elgar giggled helplessly while she looked him up and down, assessing her power. It was complete. Then, by God, she winked.

"I give body massages, too. Real good ones, Landlord."

Just as he reached for her, she whirled and vanished in a storm of crimson petals. Leaving him to speculate on how a tailor in Hong Kong could have known exactly where to embroider a golden dragon to tantalize him so acutely in America.

Oversexed because underloved, that was what Borden said. A common problem. As if that made it better, not worse. Once the love-index rose, the sex-hunger would fall off.

Meanwhile, his blood stirring, his head reeling, Elgar leaned back absent-mindedly against the row of bells and tried to make sense of things that defied all reason. Haughty Creole aristocrats, scheming Samoan midgets, litigious Dragon Ladies—all, obviously, stark staring mad. What had God wrought? What had he bought? The Mental Health annex of the World Health Organization? The official U.N. nut-hatch?

Good, steady, reliable tenants, my foot. Ooh. Wait till he got his hands on that rotten, lying little real estate agent. He'd wrap his crooked incisors around his slimy fangs, by God; he'd make his mouth resemble the rubbish heap at the Royal Doulton factory.

The vivid details of Elgar's plans for the real estate agent were interrupted by a rumbling like a locomotive in the hall.

"Fanny Copee," it boomed, "you get out of the way and let *me* handle this!"

The owner of the voice flung open the door and steamed toward Elgar, full speed ahead.

"You got till I count to ten. Then you better be off these premises."

Elgar stared up at the darkest, most massive woman he had ever seen. About six feet tall and four wide, wearing sinister rimless glasses, trembling even more than he was, and pointing a gun at him.

He had always been afraid of the dark, and at the sight of all that blackness coming at him, narrowing and concentrated to the point of the black steel barrel that would finally diffuse his paleness into atoms, something loosened the stopper that kept Elgar's compartments watertight, and all of his guilty fears flooded down to his knees. He almost desired her to pull the trigger.

"I count fast. I went to the tenth grade in school. So you better move."

"Wh-why are you pointing that thing at me?" he managed.

"My powers told me evil was coming my way this morning. 'Expect evil on your doorstep,' they said, so I was prepared. Get movin' before I call the police on you."

At the word "police" there was a toccata of high heels, and Fanny blazed into the vestibule again.

"Police? Miss Marge, have you lost your mind? My Charlie just got back home from his last sentence!"

"Don't worry, honey," Marge said. "They won't be after Charlie this time. This time they're gonna take away a white man. For breaking and entering." Marge shrugged. "Though why you want that troublesome husband of yours home *anyway* is more than I can see. If you had any sense, you'd of let me dispel him for you long ago."

It had been like this all his life. No one ever recognized Elgar. Everyone refused to grant him an identity.

"But I'm the new owner of this house!" he spluttered.

"Sho," Marge said. "And I'm the First Lady of the United States."

"He is, though," Fanny said. "He's the new landlord."

"How do you know, you simple-minded child? Just because he told you? Did you think to ask him how come he ain't got no door keys?"

Elgar was choking. Gasping for air. "I've got papers," he said. "I can show you." Then he stopped, humiliated because he again had to prove that he existed. And, this time, to an enraged hippopotamus who probably couldn't read.

Sure enough, she said, "Papers don't mean nothin.' I can't read."

"I thought you went to the tenth grade in school," Elgar said.

Fanny said, "Ha ha, Miss Marge, that's a good joke on you!"

Marge tossed her a death-ray and muttered, "Dumb teachers didn't know the right way to teach me. It was their fault, not mine. You better not get smart with me, you loiterer. Not in *my* vestibule."

"It's my vestibule, I think," Elgar insisted weakly.

The large, shadowy menace moved toward him, blotting out what little light remained, and touched the point of the gun to the third silver fleur-de-lis on his blue tie.

"You tryin' to take advantage of me because I'm a woman?"

"Believe me, Madam," he assured her warmly, "it is the farthest thought from my mind."

"Well, don't try it. I've counted to ten three times. By rights you're dead already. You're a ghost. You hear?"

It was far too close to Elgar's actual feelings about himself. He was fading fast when rage, the only strong and dependable emotion he knew, saved him.

"I am no ghost and no loiterer, either. I am the legal owner of this property. And right now I am planning legal steps to evict you, if you don't immediately put away that illegal weapon."

"Take more than a dozen little boys like you to evict *me*," was the serene answer. "I been here fourteen years. I expect to be here another fourteen. And without no constant doorbell ringing to disturb my concentrations, neither. This is *my* house. You'd better be on your way out of it right now."

"It's my house, I own it," he half sobbed. As, once, into Mothaw's ironclad lap. "I paid money for it. Lots of money. That's why I own it. That's why it's mine."

"Oh yeah?" she said with amused tolerance. "What else do you own?"

"Three cars, two motor scooters, five horses, a stable, and five hundred shares of General Motors." Oops, time to call Levin.

"I have to call my stockbroker right now," he said, and lunged towards the hall, where there must surely be a phone.

Marge braced herself and blocked him, screwing the gun into his ribs.

Elgar's jellied knees liquefied completely. He was looking up at her from the cold, hard tiles of the vestibule floor that had seemed so quaint and friendly on the first visit. But calmly, without surprise, because his life up till now had been one long pratfall anyway.

Behind the lenses, Marge squeezed her eyes together in a vain effort to hold back two enormous tears. Apparently he had failed her by not being a proper loiterer after all. She stood over him, pointing the gun with an accusing quiver.

"My, that's sure a lot for one little man to own. Now tell me something else. What did you have for breakfast this morning?"

She'd probably never heard of Librium; better not mention it. "A Coke," he said sheepishly.

"I knew it," Marge said. "You rich people are all alike. Starvin'. I know all about it. I used to cook for people like you. All them artichokes and anchovies and grape leaves. No nourishment in any of it anywhere.— Fanny Copee, stand out of my way. I got to get this poor little landlord upstairs and inject some nutrition in him."

While Fanny cried, "Don't hurt him!" and he pleaded, "I can manage by myself, let me, Mothaw," Marge got Elgar from behind in a lifesaver's grip and, using her knees and the barrel of the gun as pistons, propelled him upstairs.

Decorating one of Marge's kitchen chairs, he felt insubstantial as a pillow loosely stuffed with feathers, for that was how she had treated him, first dumping him there, then plumping him briskly all over to make sure of no broken bones.

In addition to Elgar, the small dark room had other interesting points of decor. Its four walls were a kind of master composition in *collage* and *découpage* by a member of the Fauve school. Plastered over every inch of wall space were hundreds of aging magazine pictures, recipes, newspaper clippings, post cards, record covers, sheet music folders, and photographs. Not a space showed between these products of fourteen years of gleeful scissorswork, which were cleverly layered and relayered over each other so that most were tantalizingly only half visible. But he recognized "A Tisket A Tasket" by Ella; John Barrymore and Jackie Robinson in black and white; Pecan Pie and Glazed Ham in full color; Christ's Agony in the Garden, ditto; "A Guide to Canadian Birds," rotogravure; and one startling newsprint item that held his attention for some time: "Ten Steps to a Dream Figure."

She who dreamed of a dream figure waddled through this decorator's fantasy, ponderous and menacing as a hydrogen bomb, briskly stirring and turning things that bubbled and sizzled and steamed. As she worked she sang, in an incongruously sweet little-girlish voice, accompanied by rhythmic slamming of lids and doors,

> *I was out all night, my revolver in my hand.*
> *Out all night, my revolver in my hand.*
> *Lookin' for that woman who ran off with my man.*

Finally, with angry emphasis in each plop, she set in front of him:

A bowl of grits,
Four slices of toast,
Six strips of bacon,
A piece of fried ham,
Four fried eggs,
A plate of three-inch biscuits,
A pot of coffee,
And a tureen of cunning little dark sausages frolicking in rich brown gravy.

Oh, he'd pay for this, Elgar thought, swabbing up gravy with a biscuit in each hand, gobbling down three eggs. Most assuredly, most royally he would pay for the crisp sweetness of the fat on this ham. His stomach, tender as the insides of a baby's thighs, would soon make him groan, and scream, and twist up in knots like a demented pretzel. All that grease. Ugh. Elgar licked his fingers and dipped another biscuit in gravy.

What else could he do, with her standing there waving that weapon at him?

"Eat that other biscuit. Don't waste it. When my old man said he was tired of my biscuits last week, I knew it was all over with him and me. Next day he was gone."

Elgar hoped he was not destined to be her next old man.

"Don't waste that gravy, neither. Sop it all up."

"I might get sick," he pleaded.

Fire sparkled behind the rimless bifocals. "Why you puny little thing, you got a nerve. Insulting the first good meal you ever had in your life."

"Oh, but ish excellens," he said, and hastily restuffed his mouth.

"Men," Marge said heavily, and sat down in the chair opposite Elgar. "The more you try and please 'em, the more they mistreat you.

"Fourteen men," she keened. "Fourteen men in fourteen years. I treated each one a little bit better than the last. And each one left me a little bit sooner."

It could almost be set to music. It had a lilt and a beat. And the features buried in the swollen dough of her face had once been small and neat and pretty.

"I'm sorry," Elgar said, and reached out to console her hand.

She jerked it away from him. Her wiry gray hair, bursting its pins and springing loose from its braids, stuck out in angry spikes.

"I've had a hard life, mister," she said as she caressed the butt of the gun. "I'm through trustin' people, especially people in trousers. You want some molasses?"

He didn't, but nodded; better not refuse any more of this gunpoint hospitality.

Without taking her eyes from his face, Marge reached out to a shelf behind her, plucked a molasses bottle from it, and slammed it down in front of Elgar. He wondered what he was supposed to do with it: put it on the eggs? the sausages? He also wondered if Marge might be that mythical creature Borden was always describing, the Loving Person. Maybe she just had an angry style of loving.

"Ummm, thank you," he said noncommittally, and let his eyes wander back to the shelf, hoping to avoid both issues, molasses and men, since he could not win at either.

The curiously assorted contents of the shelf did not make him feel any better. It held a long, black, very dead-looking hairpiece, a human skull and several teeth (her next-to-last old man?), standard bottles of corn oil, vinegar and mustard, and, next to them, some distinctly evil-looking bottles labeled Compelling Oil and Dispelling Oil.

She caught the direction of his gaze and said, "See what men have done to me? For fourteen years I only practiced white arts, mister. Now I practice black arts too."

Plucking one of the nastier bottles from the shelf, she emptied it into a teacup and began to stir.

"What's that?" he asked in alarm.

"Clarifying oil," Marge said somberly. "I read the morning wrong. First time in three years."

"Don't worry," he said, patting her hand gently. "I'm sure it'll clear up soon."

This time she let his hand remain. "I read evil visitors on my doorstep today," she said glumly, and continued stirring. "But you're too pitiful to be evil. I must have made a mistake. —Ah! Now I see."

Elgar tried to see something in the murky liquid too, but it was as blank to him as his future appeared right now.

"I'm supposed to *protect* you from evil," Marge said. "That's it. You came my way so's I could keep you from harm."

She pushed her chair back from the table, angrily accepting God's will or Belial's or whoever's. "All right. Though I know you'll repay me with suffering."

"Oh, don't say that," Elgar pleaded. "How can you be sure?"

"Men," she repeated with tragic emphasis, her fingers curling toward the gun once more.

"One way you might help me," he suggested feebly. "Since you're supposed to anyway, I mean. You might, if it doesn't inconvenience you awfully, put that gun away. Just a suggestion, of course."

"You the first fool this thing ever fooled," she said. "It's old and rusty as me. Never even been loaded. See?"

Aiming just to the left of his ear, she pulled the trigger.

After the explosion, Elgar turned, shuddering, and observed a black smoking hole in Betty Grable's left knee. Though nothing could tarnish that immortal pin-up smile.

Marge rose sheepishly and put the gun in a drawer.

"Tell me about the other tenants," he said after a long, long exhale. "What's this DuBois guy like?"

Marge elevated her nose and sniffed haughtily. "Oh, Professor DuBois don't bother with the rest of us. He's a college president."

"Really?"

"Sure. The college is across town somewhere, he says. —Course I never heard tell before of no college selling degrees for fifty dollars.

But it's supposed to be legal and proper. I guess I'm too ignorant to understand these things."

Elgar caught himself wondering if the man would sell him a degree. After eight expulsions, the complete Ivy League circuit in four years, even Mothaw had given up. But then, he had given up trying to please her. Didn't he tell Borden so every day? The hell with college.

"What about the Cumbersons?" he asked. "The couple upstairs."

"Don't ask," Marge said ominously, beginning to stir her cup of oil again.

"Why not?"

"'Cause they been here twenty-five years and nobody's ever seen them, that's why."

"That's impossible," he said.

"It would be if they was *alive*," she said.

There was silence in the room except for the dainty tinkle of Marge's spoon in the cup and the rippling of hundreds of tiny, ghostly rodents, dancing behind her varicolored wallpapers and up and down Elgar's spine.

"Mr. Cumberson was already retired from the railroad when they moved here," she said. "That was twenty-five years ago. They were both over seventy *then*."

"And nobody's seen them since?"

"Nobody."

"Well, who pays their rent?" he wanted to know.

"Every Thursday a pension check comes for Mr. Cumberson. I never seen nobody take it out of the mailbox. But every Friday, it's gone."

Elgar was indignant. "You've been here fourteen years yourself!" he exclaimed. "You must at least have heard noises. In all those years, didn't you ever get curious, just once, and go up there?"

"I sleep sound," Marge said, "'cause I got nothin' on my conscious, and I don't look into what don't concern me. Landlord, if you want to go up there, go ahead. All I can say to you is, *I* got the powers, and I don't go. 'Cause my powers tell me, 'Let well enough alone.'"

"What kind of powers?" he asked fearfully.

"Oh, nothin' special. Nothin' worth botherin' about. Except, see, any time you got a little something troubling you, tell Miss Marge, and maybe she can fix it. A person robbing you, or crossing you, or spoiling your luck, or some little thing like that."

"I'll remember," he promised. That was motherly kindness glowing at him from behind the rimless glasses. At least he hoped so.

"What are the first-floor tenants like?" he asked. "Copee, isn't that their name?"

"Oh, Fanny's a good girl. Just a little ambitious, that's all. She's a good mother to those two boys."

"What about her husband?"

"I don't believe in speaking evil, Landlord. Besides, I'm concentrating now. If you want, you can go downstairs and meet him yourself."

She had lit a black candle, and smoke seemed to be curling upward from the cup while she mumbled unintelligible phrases. As the atmosphere was getting distinctly creepy, Elgar decided to follow her suggestion.

But felt not at all the dashing lover as he knocked at fabulous Fanny's door. Stuffed with sausages and badly shaken. Not the most romantic of conditions.

Worse, he hardly recognized his wild non-Irish rose when she bloomed wanly in the doorway. Face scrubbed, hair skinned back severely, lashes batting more with fear, now, than coquetry. Until now he'd repressed the whole business about husband and children, little-mother role not suiting her, somehow. But from the glorious dragons rampant on scarlet fields she had changed to a mournful, motherly Muu Muu of limp, gray seersucker.

The first-floor apartment was a Dragon Lady's lair, though: red walls, lowering reddish lamps, gaudy Chinese-type furniture crouched to spring everywhere.

Finger to her lips, Fanny let him in and said, "Shhh. Charlie's studying his history."

From the deepest armchair a curl of smoke rose. Pipe, not incense.

"Who goes there, wife?" came a voice from that vicinity. "Friend or foe?"

"Ofay," she answered, giving Elgar the key to the pig Latin the Enemy was not supposed to understand.

"Then let him wait hat in hand," came the answer. "As I have waited all day long in his employment lines and his unemployment lines."

"Now wait a minute," called Elgar. "I don't know where you were today, but those weren't *my* lines you were in. I don't have any lines. As it happens, I don't have a hat, either."

The chair swiveled. A thick tome was lowered with awful deliberateness to reveal ruddy-brown, warpath features topped by angry, upstanding black hair.

"Who dares to contradict me in my own house? In my castle which he has invaded?"

"As it happens it's *my* house," Elgar replied. "I'm the new landlord."

"And as it happens this sector of it is my castle. Within which I am king. You are here only on my forbearance."

"I am here on my business," Elgar corrected. "Which is to request your wife to remove her commercial advertising sign from my residential window."

The king rose from his throne to menace Elgar. Unfortunately his height, about five-four, and his bandy legs did not go with the imposing attitude. Elgar judged he could easily take him in a fight if necessary. Which might prove to be the case.

"So," Charlie intoned, "you would deny this poor woman the livelihood which she must earn to pay your unconstitutional rentals. Oh, I know you, mister. I don't need to know your name. Whoever you are, you are the exploiter, the Enemy."

He was beginning a kind of rain dance, hopping around slowly on one foot. Hop, turn, and point a skinny finger at Elgar's nose.

"What is more," he accused, "you have probably been coveting my wife and plotting to seduce her behind my back. It is not enough to be an exploiter, you have to be a seducer too. Like others of your breed. Oh, I know your kind."

"Charlie, please," Fanny interrupted. "He's not so bad really."

"They're all bad, squaw. See to your papooses. Make sure they are asleep. Some things are about to happen which I do not intend for tender young ears."

—My howls while he scalps me? Elgar wondered.

Fanny, leaving the room, gave him an eloquent eye-roll and a shrug which seemed to pooh-pooh his fears.

Clearing his throat for courage, Elgar said, "What were you reading when I came in, Mr. Copee?"—expressing, he hoped, the proper amount of polite interest.

The title "Mister" must have helped. Charlie growled almost civilly, "*The History of the Choctaw Nation*. Are you familiar with it? You should be. Three times your people made my people false promises. Three times you robbed them of their lands and forced them to move. Three times, yet not a hand of my tribe was raised against you."

He had the effective trick of all successful politicians, Elgar noticed, repetition for emphasis. Three times was the rule. Especially effective when the phrase repeated was also "three times."

"Bravo, Mr. Copee!" he applauded. "Ever think of going into the speechwriting game? You've got a real knack for it. Washington could use you."

"Laugh while you can!" retorted Charlie. "Your laugh sounds hollow, white man. Your short hour is almost up. You cannot delay vengeance forever. Soon we will ride the plains and reclaim our lands."

"You don't look like much of a rider to me," Elgar said. "Too bent over. You got to get that old back straight as a ramrod."

Charlie unconsciously corrected his posture, Elgar assisting with a slap on the back.

"Better," Elgar approved. "More like it. Don't let the shoulders sag, now."

"So history repeats itself," Copee said with bulging eyes. "First you rob me of my land, and then you come onto my reservation and dictate to me."

"Only about the signs, Chief," Elgar said. "This is not a commercial reservation."

"Well, that's good. Because I've just decided to pay no more of your commercial rentals. You stole my ancestors' lands. By rights you owe me and my descendants three hundred rent-free years."

"Well, you can't have them, Chief," Elgar said, facing up to him, glaring, their noses almost touching in a dangerously intimate pow-wow. "So you just better get on that horse and ride West. Hit that long dusty trail into the sunset, if you don't intend to pay rent, or if your wife intends to operate a business here. Either or both. That's all I came to say. Thank you."

Copee said, "Our tribe is slow to anger. But you have taken advantage of our patience too long. This time you have gone too far."

Everybody around here was sensitive to advantage taken, Elgar noted. Must try to avoid giving that impression in future.

"Charlie! No!" shrieked Fanny, back in the room in enchanting *deshabille*. Elgar barely had time to notice the interesting new item she was wearing, or rather not wearing. He was too busy watching her crazy husband remove something from the cushions of his chair.

A tomahawk. Which he waved over his head as he resumed his rain dance.

"The tribal wrath is aroused!" he chanted. "The ancestors must be appeased! The tyrant must leave the reservation! This is war!"

With a cute little side-arm windup, he suddenly hurled the tomahawk. Just missing Elgar's head, it dug deeply into the wall, jarring loose a shower of plaster, and hung there trembling.

"I'll bill you for the plaster job," Elgar said evenly. But he was moving fast.

Fanny, holding the door open for him with one hand and keeping up a wisp of pink froth with the other, whispered, "You lucky. This ain't nothin.' *Last* month he was a Black Muslim. Next time, come around in the daytime, Landlord."

Wheezing and puffing, Elgar tore up the street, remembering with shame that nothing had been accomplished yet in the way of measuring windows for weatherstripping. And not one "Paid" entry in any rent book, either. Worse, he felt an attack of gas coming on, and wanted badly to slow down for a burp or two. But seemed to hear moccasined feet slipping and slushing behind him.

"Borden!" he screamed as he whizzed around the corner, "Borden, there will be no cute phone calls tonight, you understand? Cancel all your other patients and prepare to see me in person. Man to man, face to face, Borden. This is war!"

3

Lankily Lincolnesque, faintly skeptical, Borden spoke with pencil poised. "And in just what ways does this Negress remind you of your mother, Elgar?"

Even a crease in his goddamned pajama trousers. Over them a natty plaid flannel dressing gown. Though the consulting room was as seedy as ever, and floured with circa-1890 dust. On Elgar's fees, couldn't he at least afford a cleaning woman once a week?

"Every way," Elgar replied. "Very massive. Very dominating. Very dangerous."

"Yes, and very black, if I recall your description. Your mother is a large woman, yes? But she is also white, no?"

That comma yes, comma no at the end of key sentences. Suggestion of Vienna. When it was palpably clear Borden had never studied under Old Papa Whiskers in Vienna. If, indeed, under any of his disciples anywhere.

"Hey, Borden, how come I never see any of your diplomas hanging around here? Could it be you don't have any?"

"I see I am arousing your hostility, Elgar," Borden said, tossing a dark, damp, Gregory Peck lock back from his forehead. He did not quite make it. It hung there limply, like the little girl's who was sometimes horrid.

"—Else why at this particular moment in our relationship would you be questioning my professional credentials?"

"Had to come up sometime," Elgar answered. "For twenty-five bucks a session, I don't want to be taken apart by an amateur. Destruction at the hands of a professional, or nothing. It's my right. I demand it."

A note of personal indignation crept into Borden's voice, then was put down by his relentless control.

"And how many of these so-called professionals do you think would make themselves available to you at this hour? No, Elgar, they keep office hours. In nice, air-conditioned, downtown offices. Not in festering rat-holes in the Trejour Apartments, convenient to patients and to nothing else."

Elgar felt remorse. With weak, watery eyes, long, knobby limbs, and catarrh due to chronic sinusitis, Borden was a poor second to Gregory Peck. A poor second to everybody, really, including plump, professional shnooks in plushy downtown offices. And, sniffling over there behind the owl-rimmed specs, he *did* look a bit rumpled and sleepy.

"Your questions are of course legitimate. I will answer them at another time. But why do you question my background and my competence now? Why *now*, Elgar?"

The bastard's instincts were sharp as a coonhound's, even when he was full of sleep. Elgar, blank, felt his teeth clamp together. Blocking. Stubborn.

"I will tell you. You are trying to involve me in an argument, a sideline. Because you do not want to hear that this woman who upset you today is not the same person as your mother."

Elgar banged his fist into Borden's cruddy old black leather couch, raising a puff of elderly dust. Real doctors had Danish modern, imported, the best, didn't need ratty antiques as symbols. But real doctors had office hours and professional patience strictly limited to fifty minutes an hour. Elgar needed a *lifetime* of patience. His fist went through the cracked headrest, landed in a nightmare of sleazy sawdust.

"It's hopeless, Borden!" he screamed. "Every time I try to do something, it involves people! And people are all impossible!"

"You mean," Borden said, "they have motives and wishes of their own. They will not gratify your every need instantly, the way your parents did when you were a baby."

"Like hell they did," Elgar said. "Like hell. They did no such thing."

"Of course not, or you would not be here with me tonight," Borden answered smoothly. "But you wished they would. And you still wish it. A happy babyhood. It is the point in life at which you are arrested, Elgar."

"I tell you," Elgar howled, "it's not just me, Borden! People are all sick out there! It's a jungle."

"Nevertheless, everyone out there is not your mother or your father, Elgar. And most of them are probably not as sick as you."

The growl began deep in Elgar's throat. "Ohhh, you imitation Viennese quack," he raged. "Ohhh, you sniffling Hollywood understudy, will you never listen to me? I tell you, today I was chased by raving Indians with tomahawks and frothing Amazons with revolvers. And they weren't even real Indians and Amazons, they were crazy phonies! Now how can you sit there like a badly designed effigy of Lincoln and tell me that is normal?"

"It is certainly," Borden admitted, "very odd behavior. At least by our standards."

"By any standards in any sane world, Borden! But the world is crazy, that's what it is. Crazy full of maniacs!"

He sat up on the edge of the couch and leaned forward, palms up, straining to communicate.

"Borden, this morning I was so happy. The sun was shining, I had a purpose, I loved everybody."

"You did not," Borden interrupted. "You have never loved anybody, Elgar. Not even yourself."

Elgar decided not to get caught on the horns of *that* old dilemma. He let it pass.

"Well, I had that good feeling. You know. The Best of Show feeling."

Borden nodded. Taking Best of Show with his champion Great Dane had been the brightest event of Elgar's childhood. Though even on that day of shining accomplishment the only identification under his picture in the papers had been "Owner."

"I was actually singing. Out loud. I was going to do useful work in the world. Keep busy. Be a landlord."

Elgar felt his face screw up grotesquely and grow inflamed. Thank God he was no longer ashamed to cry in front of Borden.

"Now I see there's nothing for me to do but join a Trappist monastery! And even there I'd have to get along with the other crazy monks."

"You would, Elgar," Borden agreed sadly.

"So what's the use, Borden?" Elgar wailed, tears gushing down his twisting face.

"The use of what, Elgar?"

"The use of all this talking and analyzing. What's the use of getting well if I have to live in a sick world?"

"Maybe then it will not seem so sick to you."

"Oh no?" Elgar retorted. "You mean, when we're finished, imitation Indians out to scalp me in broad daylight will seem perfectly normal? In that case, Borden, I'm quitting right now."

"Your privilege," Borden said. "If you are not interested in being happier and functioning more effectively."

"You don't hear me, Borden!" Elgar screamed. "Man, you don't hear, see, or read me at all. Oh, you are so dumb, Borden. Dumb, deaf, and blind." He pounded the couch for three-time emphasis. "Why should I be interested in functioning? How in hell can I be happy? If everybody else is crazy?"

"Perhaps you can help them to be less so," Borden said.

"Help those crazy, man-eating cannibals? Why should I? So they can eat me alive? Get away from me with that sick, social-worker jazz, Borden. All I want is to enjoy my life. Fast cars and sweet music and fast, sweet women. I can afford them. Why can't I enjoy them?"

"Yes, why can't you?" Borden's mocking flute note echoed.

"That's all I want," Elgar said defiantly. "Is it so much to ask? Why the hell do you want to complicate things by having me *help* people, for God's sake?"

"Elgar," Borden said, "perhaps you imagine I put up with crazy, man-eating cannibals like you for the money and the things it buys. But I assure you, no amount of money could pay me to be eaten alive like this."

Elgar sank back on the uncomfortable couch. "You great, big, sentimental fraud. If I ever find out you've been lying to me I'll murder you, you hear? And then I'll go out and commit atrocities on sweet old ladies." His gusty sigh was followed by a sour belch. "What's the first step, Borden?"

"First," Borden said, "we learn to distinguish between this very interesting and unusual Negress and your mother. So you can deal with each in appropriate fashion. Your mother is white, yes?"

"Borden, as I have said many times before, you are a genius of the obvious. Of course my mother is white, you dimwit! But take a picture of her and print up the *negative*, and you've got Madam Margarita."

"Madam Margarita?"

"Alias Marge Perkins. Second floor rear. Fifty dollars a month, which I have not been paid."

Borden raised a long, knobby, significant finger. "Just a thought, Elgar. Does the second floor rear have any special associations for you? A particular part of the house in which you grew up, perhaps?"

"It was the bathroom," Elgar said. "Oh, Christ, Borden, you're way off base. And we've been at it two hours."

"I am not at my best under such conditions, Elgar," Borden admitted stiffly. "Especially when my sleep has been interrupted. I too am human."

"Well, rest up then, baby," Elgar said. "You'll need it tomorrow. See you then. Usual time, same station."

"See you, Elgar," Borden sighed. "Sleep well, now." With a feeble Gregory Peck grin and a limply Lincolnesque wave of benediction.

Always the second-rate, Elgar thought gloomily, kicking the leprous paint on the stairs as he descended to what he laughingly called home. The Trejour Apartments, which he shared with desperately hopeful sellers of Fuller Brushes and encyclopedias and seedy senior citizens on meager pensions and smearily made-up chorus girls who were not above taking turns onstreet between turns onstage. And his own, private, lukewarm-running psychiatrist. Operating on the margin, like everyone else in the building. Without benefit of license or A.M.A. membership.

He expanded on his theme as he descended to his non-air-conditioned Inferno. Shirts and socks and ties off bargain counters. Ill-fitting "irregular" underwear torturing his crotch, Reduced for Quick Sale lettuce wilting his salads. Elgar bought these things not because he had to, God knew. Because he was compelled to. Because he had been educated early to deserving nothing but bargains: second-run movies, second-hand cars, retread tires, low-octane gasoline. And low-octane girls with pimples, and sorority pins, and brothers who belonged to the American Legion. —Except Sally, who qualified because she was so U she made him feel the requisite amount of discomfort. And Lanie, a first-rater who was determined to live up, or down, to her second-class birth.

Part of the problem of course was that all of Elgar's girls had to be the kind who would not be after his money. They had to be too kooky and independent (Lanie) or too scornful of wealth (Rita) or too rich themselves (Sally) or just too damned dumb (the rest) to know or care he had it. Elgar had proposed to nearly all of them, and kept proposing, at regular intervals, to test whether he was loved for himself alone. A girl could prove this to Elgar only by rejecting him. So far, all those put to the test had passed.

Continuing his descent he noted that the depressing plastic treads from one of the Seven Branches were missing from half the stairs. The defunct miniature bulb over his door was still unreplaced after two weeks. Jesus! With only half a chance—with only half a houseful of half-sane tenants—Elgar could easily be a better landlord than the owner of the Trejour Apartments. A treasure, indeed. Fit to be buried. Quickly.

Finally fumbling the key into the slot in the pitch-black door and twisting it successfully, Elgar kicked his way into his torture chamber and was greeted by the reeking bag of garbage he'd meant to take out that morning. Reached for the light switch, missed, plunged his hand into an overflowing ash tray. Swore, finally got a light on, and stood there in the midst of unwashed laundry, unread papers, unwashed beer glasses, unmade sofa-bed. At these rents, maid service not included.

There he stood, a monument to the inevitable human condition: surrounded by his own filth. Elgar Enders, heir of the tasteless ages. Worth, at this very instant, a quarter of a million dollars. Worth, at the unpredictable and joyous instant his old man's heart stopped beating, a half-dozen millions. Currently the possessor of thirty dirty pairs of thirty-nine-cent F. W. Woolworth socks, and not a single clean pair, and unable to do better by himself. Couldn't do anything better right now than penance.

But couldn't stand the place right now, either. Not until he was close enough to unconsciousness to sleep anywhere, in the handiest cozy gutter, even in his own apartment if necessary. Achieving the desired comatosity would require several hours and quite a few drinks.

Might as well be consistent about the pattern, Elgar decided. Go across town, other side of the tracks, and visit his second-class-citizen girl friend.

4

Elgar thanked God, for the hundredth time, that Lanie was always up after midnight. What better time to paint those nightmarish canvases, brown and black limbs and organs writhing in white limbo; and practice modern dancing, tragic shudders and leaps and thuds that reverberated from her high ceilings; and play her records about gin and sin and the man that done me in; and entertain her friends, a motley bunch of nightcrawlers including Elgar; and smoke in great hissing gasps until she reached the marijuana nirvana where, eyes slanting in withdrawal, skin sallowed by candlelight, mouth smiling La Giocondawise, she seemed more than ever a Eurasian monster he'd picked up somewhere on the Ginza.

Way-out by night, she was completely "in" by day, anonymous and all business behind the counter of the D-R Luncheonette, across from the Trejour. Working in tandem with Lucy the short-order cook, she was typically American and terrifyingly efficient: crisp white uniform, severely bunned rusty hair, a quick-frozen smile. Together they were like a pair of connected machines—reaper and thresher, washer and dryer—tall Lanie calling "Order toast!" and Lucy, compact and contained as an ebony statuette, responding instantly with buttered brown slices of joy.

Lanie's schizzy schedule, he'd learned, was a brisk seven A.M. to three at the D-R; a hearty supper from three till four; a loudly snoring sleep from four till midnight; then up, and up, and up. At sometime between dawn and seven each morning she pulled together her various selves, Vampira and Cho-Cho San and Bessie Smith and the rest, packaged them all in crisp Betty Furness cellophane, and trundled them off to work in an old M.G. that looked and sounded like a shopping cart.

Imagining violent Jekyll-Hyde convulsions—hair disappearing, eyes brightening—Elgar always wanted to stick around to watch the

28

transformation. *Werewolf Woman Becomes Doris Day,* a thrilling Technicolor feature. But he was never permitted to see it.

"Out, lout," she'd say, with a firm toe or elbow in his sensitive windpipe or worse. "It is my private hour."

Nor was he ever allowed in her bedroom. His part-time evening excursions with Lanie never proceeded farther than her living room couch, and once, when he'd taken the wrong turn stumbling toward the john in the dark, she had sharply screamed, "Stop!"

But at least she'd wrung the tensions from him in many memorably athletic pre-dawn hours, and by daybreak Elgar was always reconciled to living through another twenty-four hours anyway. It was nights when he needed Lanie or somebody, and her topsy-turvy schedule had saved his life on several occasions, nights when otherwise he would have carried out his ace in the hole, Plan S. —Though lifesaving was the furthest thing from the laconic intentions of Lanie, who often said she couldn't care enough to lift a finger to save a kitten drowning in a toilet. A description that aptly fitted Elgar, alone in the depths of certain damp nights in his cell in the Trejour. She didn't have to lift a finger, though; all that was necessary was that she be there.

And there she was, always. Dependable as the sun overhead each day were the lights burning every night in Lanie's loft over the laundry. The schedule never varied, though the program changed.

Tonight, he could tell from the street, it was her records, an unearthly musicale of Mississippi Delta howls and laments. Stretched out on the floor, the better to absorb the vibrations of Soul through every pore, Lanie ignored the jeroboam of gin he had brought for them. While one long, red, elevated, Danskinned leg beat time in the air to washboard thumpings and wailings about drinking muddy water, Elgar went to rummage in the kitchen for ice and to retrieve two glasses from the swamp of her sink.

When he returned the machine was clanking a new record into place. Through the soup of scratches on an ancient record came an angelic little voice he had heard somewhere before, probably in a high-church choir. But now it was crooning:

> *I'm a hard-workin' woman and you know I don't mind tryin'.*
> *I'm a hard-workin' woman and you know I don't mind tryin'.*

> *But if I catch you wrong, Papa,*
> *I know you don't mind dyin'. . . .*

"Shhhh," Lanie said, deigning to accept a drink but not to converse during the razzmatazz trumpet bridge between the sacred verses. "It's a collector's item."

Elgar coughed, spluttered, sprayed the air with gin as the voice went on, sweet, girlish and suddenly familiar:

> *I was out all night, my revolver in my hand.*
> *Out all night, my revolver in my hand,*
> *Lookin' for that woman who ran off with my man. . . .*

"An early Marge Perkins," Lanie said reverently. "Cost me a month's tips, and worth it. *Nobody* has Marge Perkins records any more."

Belatedly she took note of Elgar's predicament: choking to death before her eyes.

"What's the matter? Ginsy too strong for baby? Oh, oh, Mommy fix. Right away." She whacked him on the back with the massive strength that occasionally made him wish Lanie were not such a great, big, healthy girl.

"There. Now drink the rest of your gin, all the way down to the bottom. Atta boy, Elgar. Get all the vitamins so you can grow up big and strong."

> *Well, you used to be my true love, now you're my used-to-be.*
> *Used to be my true love, now you want to be free.*
> *But I'll bury you, Papa, before you bury me.*

"Isn't she wonderful?" Lanie exclaimed with delicious little shudders of appreciation all over and under the leotards. "So real. So alive."

"So dangerous, you mean," Elgar said with shudders of his own, violent ones in the vicinity of his stomach.

"She knows what love is all about, Elgar," Lanie said, pouting. "Which is more than you can say."

"The time is coming, Miss Elaine K. for Know-it-all Lacey, when you will wish you had shown some respect for me."

"Respect isn't the issue, Elgar," Lanie said gravely. She was beautiful when serious, the hazel flecks in her eyes lighting up to match her freckles. Shadows in the room softening the long horsy planes of her face. "I was simply stating a fact about you, the fact that you cannot love, a fact you know very well. I wish you could learn to keep your tender ego out of our discussions."

She stretched, swinging the heavy curtain of dark red hair that hung to well below her shoulder blades. She reminded Elgar of a bay mare he had once owned: coarse red mane, long graceful legs, large dark eyes like wet leaves. And good strong teeth: she had bitten him more than once.

"As a matter of fact," she said, "I don't know what love is all about either. Oh, I have lots of ideas, but no experience."

"It's a grim struggle to the death," Elgar said, "if I can believe your minstrels."

"Yes, but that's only part of it, Elgar. Why are you smiling that strange, smug way?"

"I was merely anticipating your reaction," he told her, "before telling you that today I enjoyed a command performance by your collector's item."

Lanie was up in an instant, neighing excitedly. "Marge Perkins? In person? I don't believe it! Where, Elgar? *Where?*"

"Well, perhaps enjoyment is not the precise word. I was, after all, a captive audience. And unfamiliar with the lady's reputation."

"She's only the Sepia Nightingale, Elgar. The Queen of Blues. The Tragic Voice of the Twenties and Thirties. She started out in New Orleans. When she came to Harlem, the lines stretched for five blocks outside of Small's Paradise. The cover charge went to ten dollars, and *still* they stretched. She had rooms full of orchids. Cars a block long. Proposals from European royalty. She only made a few records. And then she disappeared. Elgar, *where is she?*"

"If you will take your claws from my throat, and behave like a proper hostess, for once, and show some hospitality, for once, and get me another drink, maybe I will tell you. But only then," he cautioned, "and only maybe."

"Oh, oh," she said, withdrawing. "Great White Father wants the service due his whiteness. Yassuh, Marse Elgar," she said with a low bow as she picked up the glasses. Repeating the bow with her back turned on her way to the kitchen. "Yassuh, boss. Right away."

There it was. Every evening had to be spoiled at least once by her intruding the race thing like a two-edged sword between them.

"Lanie, please cut that out," he growled. "I've asked you before, now I'm telling you. It's unnecessary, especially with me. And it's ridiculous. Why, you have *freckles,* for God's sake!"

"On you it's freckles, boss," she said, returning with the drinks on a tray and elaborately offering one to him. "On me, it's melanin. Dat ole debbil pigment."

Raising the glass to her lips she looked at him solemnly, large brown eyes level below coarse auburn fringe. "Here's to pigment and its mysteries. For instance, its mysterious relationship to music. One more drink, and maybe I'll understand why it takes melanin to produce melody."

"I suppose you have never heard of English madrigals?" Elgar inquired coldly, refraining from joining in the toast. "Scottish bagpipes? Irish jigs and reels? Forget about those. I have an extensive musical education, I can refute you all night long. What about German music? Are you going to try to convince me *Beethoven* was a Negro?"

She did not answer; her eyes were hopeless black holes in a long, ironically chalky face.

"Anyway," he added angrily, "I'll believe it about all three B's before I'll believe it about you. Not that it matters, Lanie, you know it couldn't matter to me, but once and for all, are you colored, or not?"

"People see in me what they want to see," she answered.

"No fair!" Elgar shrieked, with the same frustration he'd suffered in the hide-and-seek games years ago when he was It and his brother Schubert, discovered behind the old oak tree, simply streaked across the lawn to another hiding place.

Lanie took a long, satisfied inventory of the way the red knit fabric clung to her long, satisfactory curves before looking up at him lazily and saying, "Actually I'm Greek and Creek. If you must know. A Greek father and a Creek Indian mother. How's that for a combination?"

"But that changes everything. Hooray!" he whooped. And started down on his knees to propose to her, as he already had, vainly, to all of his other girls.

"It changes nothing, Elgar," she said coldly, withdrawing from his touch as from contact with a crocodile, untwining herself from a black leather butterfly chair and rising. "I just said that to see how you'd react. Of course I'm colored. My grandmother is as black as that chair."

Still on his knees, he looked up at her in horror. "Lanie!" he pleaded. "Tell me the truth! My God. I don't know what to believe now."

"No, Elgar," she said, stepping over him neatly as she would a turd on her living room floor. "Why should I? As you said, it doesn't matter to you."

"Lanie, come back here!" he howled. One part of him hating, the other admiring the clean, athletic, independent stride, the muscles dancing under receding red jersey.

"Oh, for Christ's sake, Elgar," she said as she returned with a clinking glass. "I only went for more ice."

"Tell me the truth, Lanie," he said, still on his knees, hollow-voiced and desperate.

"Some other time, Elgar. When it's not so important."

"I think I get the point," he said, rising shamefacedly, feeling embarrassment tint his face to match her tights.

"Do you, Elgar?" she asked sweetly.

"Do you mind if I have another drink?"

"It's your gin," she said. "Help yourself."

If she had called him "boss" that time, he would have slapped her. And, what with the payload of rage he always carried around inside him, Elgar feared any slapping might get out of control.

"But Lanie," he began, waving his hand with frustration. Then he thought better of it. He paused a long time while considering the next question. "Do you like me, Lanie?"

"Of course I do, Elgar. You're a sweet guy."

"I am not!" he howled. "I've just proved it."

"Oh, that." She shrugged. "Everybody has that."

In the same tone in which she might say, "Everybody has germs." He had a sudden glimpse of the abyss at the bottom of which she and his tenants lived. He pulled back from it in horror.

"The sweet guys try to kid themselves into believing they don't have those feelings. They're ashamed of them. That's the only difference, Elgar."

"Yeah," he said, gulping his drink and quickly replenishing it because a moment ago he'd been about to ask her the touchy and terribly urgent question again.

—Yes, but why should it be so touchy? his reasonable mind questioned.

Because he made it so terribly urgent, came the instant, reasonable response.

Elgar sprawled disgustedly in the butterfly chair while Lanie coiled lazily on the India-print couch, regarding him with large, calm eyes. How could she be so casual five minutes after he'd been hacking away at her most sensitive spot? Repeated jabs and blows toughened, he supposed.

"I'm getting less sweet though, Lanie," he announced. "Come taste me and see. Every day in every way I'm getting more and more sour."

She laughed and declined his invitation. "Oh, not you, Elgar. I don't believe it. Why?"

"I am the proprietor of a madhouse, that's why. An apartment house over on the corner of Poplar and Jackson. Your precious torch singer is one of my crazy tenants."

Lanie whinnied with joy. "You've bought a house with Marge Perkins in it? Oh, Elgar, you're so lucky. You don't know how lucky you are."

As if Marge Perkins were a valuable antique or something. Well, maybe an antique, at that. But non-negotiable on today's market.

"Lanie," he said, "you're an athletic woman, you'd have done fine at track meets. Especially if they'd had an event called Jumping to Conclusions. Oh, in that you'd have taken all the medals. Actually I am the unluckiest of men. I think I was born under the Dog Star."

Her big mobile mouth drooped in a pout. "Oh, Elgar, really. Look at you. You've got everything. Looks, money, everything. Still, you're always complaining."

He raised a warning finger. "Didn't you hear me? You should listen more closely when I speak to you. I said my tenants were crazy. I meant it. One of them held a gun on me today. Another one chased me out of the house with a tomahawk."

She hooted. She whooped. She writhed, kicked, and wriggled in indecent spasms of laughter. So much enjoyment, all at Elgar's expense. He suffered keenly. But when she noticed his agonized expression hers too became serious.

"Oh, Elgar. Poor Elgar. Are *all* of your tenants colored?"

He nodded sadly.

"Have you collected any rents from them yet?"

He shook his head.

"None at all? Oh, poor baby." She got up, came over, took his face in suddenly gentle hands. Her eyes were melting. "Poor Elgar. You *do* need help."

He looked up at her, baffled.

"They'll run rings around you, Elgar. They'll destroy you. They'll drive you mad."

"I doubt it," he said, "not."

"Ever wonder how underdogs survive, Elgar? Through cunning. Craftiness and cunning. It's passed along from generation to generation. By word of mouth, by example, and by heredity. Only the clever ones survive. By now every underdog in this country has it. The necessary talent and know-how for beating the enemy."

"Who's the enemy?" he asked.

"Society, you poor bastard. You." Lanie seemed to have one brightening thought in all this gloom. "At least you have Marge living there. Society's been good to her. She ought to be on your side."

"She," he said, "is the one who met me at the door today with a revolver. And held it on me while I ate my breakfast." He patted his stomach delicately. "I still have heartburn."

"Hmmm," Lanie said thoughtfully. "She must have had a little hard luck lately. Is she still pretty?"

Elgar shuddered. "She's a great, big, hideous wreck. A monster. She practices witchcraft. And looks it."

"But the voice, Elgar?" Lanie asked urgently. "Is the voice still there?"

"Clear as a bell. I recognized it the minute I heard your record." He pondered for a moment. "It's weird, hearing such a sweet young voice come from such a horny old rhinoceros."

Lanie, lost in nostalgia, missed the heavy-handed pun. "She was always tall," she said. "But she used to be elegant. Slim and graceful. Well." She jumped up suddenly and shook herself like a young mare impatient to be rid of flies. "Let's get going."

"Where?" he asked, amazed. It was after three A.M.

"To your house, of course, idiot. I have to look the situation over. And I want to meet Marge Perkins."

She tweaked his ear painfully as she went by. "Oh, you're lucky you've got me, Elgar. You don't know how lucky you are. I can save you from a real mess, believe me. Back in three."

She was moving, in high gear, from her night-time languor to her daytime personality—brisk, efficient, overpowering—and Elgar was being towed along, in spite of vivid visions of tenants wielding deadly weapons with deadly seriousness on being aroused at this hour, and his being unable to blame them.

A managing woman, that was Lanie. A lady Chairman of the Board who had missed her calling.

He'd first seen her in action on the morning after one of his Great Debacles, a night spent barcrawling to postpone Plan S, and had known immediately that she was one of those rare ones who Always Knew What to Do. One crisp look at him and she'd called out, "A Bromo!" before he spoke a word, following it up with "Black and a cannibal!"

It sounded ghastly, and it was—black coffee and a raw-beef, raw-egg-yolk sandwich—but her hangover cure worked. From then on he ate breakfast at the D-R's counter every morning, and always let Lanie order for him, sensing his wishes from the way he looked. She never failed to distinguish Elgar's French-toast mornings from his soft-boiled-egg ones.

He was often grateful for her competence, but sometimes he wanted to shake it out of her. Managing women like his mother drew Elgar irresistibly—yet also threatened, like Mothaw, to set him dangling like a pretty golden charm from their bracelets. Large important women lent splendor and significance to conquest, and so he liked them—but he much preferred Lanie's night personality, languid and permissive, to her awesome daytime self. Much.

In three minutes exactly she was back, terrifyingly transformed.

"I don't know how I'm going to play it, Elgar. Probably by ear. I may decide to let them think I'm your wife. A heartless Jewish bitch. Do I look the part?"

She did: not the least terrifying thing about Lanie was her ability to look any way she wished.

She had coiled the thick russet hair close to her head, and put on a tunic, a lead-colored thing brocaded in silver, heavy and opulent, flaring over black stretch pants like a coat of mail. She looked medieval and noble, like Joan of Arc in full battle regalia. And also a little like Joan of

Arc's horse. Stowed in her leather saddle bag, in a cellophane envelope, was the next presto-chango outfit: a starched white uniform and sensible white, ripple-soled shoes.

"Lanie," Elgar said as they got into her struggle-buggy, "I've often wondered why you wait tables for a living. You're smart, you're good-looking, you could do anything you wanted. Sometimes I wonder if you're like me."

"Like you how?" she asked in a tone that rejected all possibility of comparison.

"Doing penance for your crimes. The ones you haven't committed."

She laughed—a little nervously, he thought.

"Lanie, I want to shake your hand," he said earnestly, grabbing it. "I think you live with the horrors as much as I do. But you rate congratulations. On you, they don't show."

She laughed again, nasal and cynical. "Look closer, my friend." Then she pulled her hand away from his and twisted the ignition key, bore down hard on the accelerator. The M.G.'s old horses snorted, coughed, nearly expired, then suddenly roared into life, shattering the night.

"Get smart, Elgar," she shouted over the wind shrieking past his ear. "Get tough. That's what you have to do. Encase that soft slob heart of yours in solid steel. Never believe any of their stories. No matter what they tell you, say to yourself, 'They're lying. I know they're lying.' Get up in the morning and say, 'I'm tougher. I'll get them before they get me.'"

"Who?" he shouted back.

"Your tenants, of course. Who else, idiot? Pay attention to me!"

"I wish *you'd* pay attention to your driving," he complained, for she was attacking the streets like obstacle courses, skimming curbs and corners, narrowly missing parked cars and poles. Finally they skidded to a stop in front of his house, a ten-minute drive in three.

He sat there, stupefied, for another minute.

"Come on, Elgar," she said, sensing his reluctance, seizing his hand and pulling hard. "I wonder how long it would have taken you to come back here if I hadn't decided to drag you?"

"Only a hundred years. Or thereabouts," he said as he was led inside.

But after Lanie's direct, "Miss Perkins, you're my absolute idol, I have every one of your records, I was playing them tonight, and I told

Elgar, I said, 'Elgar, I don't care what time of night it is, I have to meet her right away!'" Marge melted like a huge slab of Hershey exposed to intense warmth.

"Well just come right on in, honey. You hungry? There's some Creole rice on the stove."

"Oh, your famous perlo. I read about it in somebody's book, Langston Hughes, wasn't it? I'd love some. So would Elgar. Wouldn't you, Elgar?"

She was matching Marge's sugariness, granule for granule. It was sickening. Elgar thought he might want to throw up instead.

"Naturally he wants some, he's always hungry," Marge said, dipping up a rosy bowlful.

"Here, let me do that," Lanie said, taking the spoon from Marge's hand. "Don't you work now. We came to hear you sing."

"Awww," Marge said, clasping her hands behind her back. She hung her head and shifted shyly from foot to foot like an embarrassed child. In a rosy-flowered cotton playdress, size 52. "Awww, it's been twenty years since I sang for anybody."

"Oh, please," Lanie coaxed. "Come on. 'C. C. Rider.' Nobody can do it like you."

"Awww," Marge said again. It was unbelievable, the resemblance to an elephantine toddler asked to recite a Bible verse in Sunday school. "Aw, no, I can't be playing the piano this time of night." She winked and added, "Landlord wouldn't like it."

"Oh, you *do* have a piano!" Lanie shrieked in delight, bounding coltlike into the next room. She was being unbelievable too; unbelievable and unbearable. Elgar could not tell who was sincere and who was putting on an act around here. Probably a little bit of both apiece.

He followed them morosely into a dim front parlor furnished in early Lumpy-Gloomy, with more crazy scrapbook pages for walls and stiff lace doilies blooming on every flat surface. Squatting evilly in the center was the only item in the world darker and more massive than Marge herself: a square black Victorian piano.

"Hardly ever touch it any more," Marge protested as she was led to the stool. "Besides, it's out of tune."

Finally she said firmly, "No, child, I won't play. I'll just sing." And did so, sitting erect, hands folded in her lap, with odd, childlike dignity.

Elgar, never musical, fought down the urge to headlong flight that had seized him the moment he started to climb his stairs. He hung around bravely until she got to the line that went,

Gonna buy me a shotgun, long as I am tall . . .

Then he found himself edging rapidly toward the door, unnoticed by the rapt pair. What the hell. It was their party anyway, let them enjoy it. He sneaked out into the hall to light a cigarette with shaking hands.

A strong whoosh of wind instantly snuffed out the match for him. A soft flannel bundle like someone's bag of laundry landed in Elgar's sensitive middle, knocking his breath away. Thinking that a pillow fight was in progress, instantly angry and ready to retaliate, Elgar gripped the object firmly. But when he raised it from the floor it developed appendages that clawed and kicked and a hard little cannonball that butted him violently in the chest.

The second match he struck revealed the lively bundle under his left arm to be Walter Gee Copee. Dressed in flannel pajamas, feet, drop seat, and all. Eyes screwed tight, and bawling.

"Well now," Elgar said, lifting the boy to face him, "well now, what have I got here? Feels too solid to be a ghost. Too wiggly to be laundry. Can it be a sleepwalker?"

Walter Gee pummeled all of the accessible surfaces a dozen more times with hard little fists, then flung his arms around Elgar's neck, sobbing convulsively.

The spasms shaking the tense little body invaded Elgar's frame and frightened him. Until now his own suffering had kept him distant from that of others. What, he wondered wildly, were the symptoms of appendicitis? Epilepsy? Other seizures with possible brain damage?

All he could manage was a series of gruff there, there, theres accompanied by awkward pat, pat, pats. He was aware of his inadequacy. Yet somehow did not want to call Lanie or Marge, did not want to share this problem with anybody.

"My pop-pop crazy," Walter babbled. "Say he gone kill my mama. 'Bang bang,' he say. 'Bang bang.' My mama run away. My bubba, he run too. I all alone. I scared. It's dark down there."

This disjointed message delivered, Walter's shoulders gradually stilled. An incredibly tiny hand found its way into Elgar's. And held on with incredible strength.

"Well now," Elgar said, swinging the boy down, supporting the hard little rump briefly in the palm of his hand before releasing Walter Gee's weight to the floor, but letting the hand hang onto his for security (whose?), "well now, I know about the dark. If you're afraid of it, the only thing to do is go to sleep. Then when you wake up, it's light again. Ho. Only thing to do. So. Back to bed we go, ho. Ho. Ho. Ho."

Wondering, as he heard himself produce this glib patter, how the kid could possibly believe it, since he had never been able to believe it himself. Case in point: tonight, running to Lanie rather than face a dark room.

"Hold tight to my hand, ho. Off to yum-yum land, ho. Where is your room, Walter Gee? Show me where."

After a swipe of flannel sleeve across sniffles, Walter led the way to a door that opened into the first-floor hall. Inside were a pair of narrow bunkbeds, the top one empty, the bottom one very slept-in. Elgar, smoothing its disorder, was relieved that a trip through Sitting Bull's council chamber would not be necessary.

"I don't like my pop-pop," Walter Gee announced as covers were tucked in tightly under his chin. It felt safer that way, Elgar knew from experience.

"Well now, fella," Elgar said, "those are mighty strong words. You should think twice before you say them. *I* always do."

The next words were very soft and dreamlike: almost, but not quite, soft enough for Elgar to have imagined them.

"You be my pop-pop, Landlord."

Fortunately no reply was required. A soft, contented snore rose from the pillow. A small hand still clung to his large, dumbfounded one. Elgar, gently disengaging and slipping outside, could not help feeling large and strong in comparison.

He paused thoughtfully at the foot of the stairs and checked himself over routinely. Chest, arms, gut. Yep, solid. Firmer even than on that fine morning, seemingly ages ago, when he had set out to buy sundry items of hardware.

Unearthly voices drifted down to him: two witches, heads together over the rice cauldron, cooking up an infernal stew.

"Elgar needs help around here, Miss Perkins. Really he does. He needs someone like you on his side."

"Honey, don't worry, I'll look out for him. I have to. It's in the cards."

"You may even have to collect his rents for him. Oh, I know it's a lot to ask, Miss Perkins. Especially of a person who's a great star like you. But do try to let him think he's done it himself."

Elgar turned his back on the stairs. Obviously he was the last person they wanted to see at the moment. Well, the feelings at the moment were mutual. His empty apartment suddenly appealed, because there he could be alone in front of the mirror, to check the breadth of the shoulders, the girth of the biceps, the hard, steely glint in the clear blue eyes, and learn, maybe, what it was that the boy had seen in him. Then fall asleep, hugging the knowledge to himself like a comforting old toy that had been lost for years and was suddenly found again.

Girlish giggles rained down on Elgar; giggles at his expense, no doubt. The place sounded like a witches' dormitory at midnight.

Elgar restrained a last strong urge to charge upstairs, enraged sacred white bull, with the news of who was going to be the boss around here. News of whose house it was, after all.

No, he told himself as he strode outside, he would maintain manly silence. Hereafter he would be contained, and a gentleman. Firm. And when things began to happen around here, as they surely would starting tomorrow, he would stand aside nobly and let them think they had done it themselves.

5

A liquid, cooling breeze kissed Elgar awake from his sound sleep in tumbled, soiled sheets. The first morning of September. End of summer's slumming. Away with languors and odors. Up then, and singing, even though the singing be hopelessly off key.

Elgar obeyed, leaping into the shower with several appalling bars of:

> *H,*
> *A,*
> *Double r-a,*
> *G-i-n spells Harrigan.*

—Or does it? he wondered as he toweled briskly.

> *Proud of all the Scottish blood that's in me,*
> *Divil nor man can say a word agin me.*

To a tune strangely resembling "For He's a Jolly Good Fellow." Mothaw tried to make me musical. Lord, how she tried. An effort of a massiveness equaled only by her monumental failure.

Out again, scrubbed and shining, to select a tie. Wrinkling the fine, sensitive, aristocratic nose against yon paper bag with aromatic contents, waiting patiently by the door. Remembering to give thanks for small favors, such as one remaining clean set of underwear.

He put on his brightest blue tie, to stabilize his sea-change eyes. His eyes, like everything about Elgar, were fluid, desperately in need of anchors. He preferred them sky-blue for happiness, though wore green ties on mean days, gray ones on hopelessly bleak days.

On the dresser beside the tie clip (stainless steel, fifty-nine cents, Mothaw's gold gift—one long lost) lay the four rent books, unopened and uninscribed except for the four hopeful names on their covers.

This was the day he meant to write in each of them, *Received of for one month's rent payable in advance the sum of,* and his signature. (And show good cause, Mr. Copee, why it should not be written in your blood.) On second thought, a green tie might be the best choice.

Rent books and trusty Waterman tucked in breast pocket, Elgar swung out into the street and across to the air-conditioned igloo where he breakfasted. The D-R's chilly interior featured a white formica counter, booths and stools with white plastic cushions, all surfaces frosty-painted and disinfected. And Lanie, capably poised behind the counter in uniform like a tall Supervisor of Nurses.

Might as well let her know immediately that the patient had recovered. "Scramble two light," he said. "Extra cream in the coffee."

Her eyelids, with lavender circles above and below, parted wanly. That must have been some all-night songfest and gabfest. "Don't you want toast, Elgar?"

"No. Watching the old waistline," he said, and patted his iron middle.

Not one to give up easily, Lanie slammed a large orange juice down in front of him. "What was the big fat idea, running out on me last night?"

Sipping, he said, "Oh, you seemed to be having fun. I'm no music lover. Besides, I had to get up early this morning."

"Projects?"

"*The* project. On Poplar Street."

"Oh. In that case you'd better have some brandy in the coffee," Lanie prescribed gravely, and reached under the counter for the giant battered mail-pouch she called a handbag. Inside he knew was a cunning little flask, dark-blue glass and filigree silver.

He held up a warning hand. "No, thanks. Fortification will not be necessary."

"Whatever you say, Elgar." As she drew his coffee, steam from the urn flushed her cheeks prettily. "What's holding up those scrambled eggs light, Lucy? Are you laying them, or what?" With a distracted pushing back of her steamed and discouraged hair, forgetting that she had never given the order. Her partner looked hurt, but instantly put butter on the grill and began joyous beatings in a bowl.

"I tried to win Marge over to your side, Elgar. I used every argument I know. But I can't promise you she'll do anything for you. She's had a rough time lately. *All* of your tenants have had rough times."

"Don't you think," he said, "there may be another possibility, one you have not yet considered, Lanie? That I, myself, may be equal to the problems involved?"

"I think," she said, "you were a damned fool to get involved."

Those words, precisely, were Levin's on the phone two hours later.

"Yes, I said a damned fool. That was what I said, Elgar. Check. What was the matter with those municipal bonds I told you about last week? What, Elgar, did you find so repulsive about Allied Preferred? And if you were determined, really determined, to get into real estate I could have gotten you mortgages. Six per cent, guaranteed."

It's hopeless, Levin, Elgar thought. I could shout at you all day, still you'd never understand my needs. Aloud he said, "Levin, a mortgage can't talk to you."

"It can't throw a spear at you, either. Check? Or did I misunderstand you when you said that was what happened this morning?"

"No," Elgar said. "No, you did not misunderstand me. No, Levin, your hearing checks out one hundred per cent accurate. Perfect." He hung up and left the glass cubicle, fiendish fishbowl making private agonies public, to sit on the curb, supporting heavy head in hopeless hands.

Fanny, more tempting than ever in tight pink lace, had met him at the door, hair soft and sweet, voice crooning to match, promising reason. She had, she said, a job. And would get paid the following Thursday. The Cumbersons, she continued, would get their pension check at the end of the week, on Thursday or Friday. It was only necessary to catch the old man before he went out drinking on Friday night. And he was not to believe any of Professor DuBois' stories—that man had loads of money, especially on Sundays. His habit being to take up collections in churches all over town to further the work of higher learning, he would hit at least ten churches between the eleven A.M. tolling for services and the dismissal of Bible classes at three, clearing fifty dollars easy. As for Miss Marge, she would be good for her rent next Wednesday. Not tomorrow but a week from tomorrow, every other Wednesday, that was when the lady *she* worked for got paid.

"So all you have to do, Landlord, is come back Friday, Sunday, next Wednesday and next Thursday."

"But this is Tuesday!" he'd howled. "What the hell am I suppose to do *today?*"

Her rather grotesque suggestion elicited a reply in kind from Elgar. Soon their conversation was blazing merrily in the vestibule, a ball of fire tossed in spirited fashion between fishmonger and fishwife.

Unfortunately the vestibule was not soundproof. Though to judge by her expert use of language, Fanny could take care of herself nicely on any waterfront in the world, Copee came to his wife's rescue.

The vanishing American had vanished today, but this provided small reassurance. Copee was, Elgar gathered, only part Indian, and today he had reverted to pressing the cause of his other ancestors, and sporting their garb, a majestic swathing of brightly printed cotton. Apparently the vengeful African was his favorite role. He moved easily in bare feet and batik toga, and his awkwardness with a tomahawk was no cause for complacency, judging by the expertise with which he hefted a six-foot spear.

But just in case, backing him up with a baseball bat was his and Fanny's older darling, Willie Lee, a lean little warrior with mean little eyes that suggested there was nothing whatever left to teach him in school.

They stood arrayed against him, Fanny with sloe eyes blazing, her husband menacing in his gorgeous robes, and their redskinned, evil-eyed son—an exotic tribe who did not look exactly like Negroes, or Asians, or Indians, but like a blend of all three. A new breed, stranger than any of its components, and more sinister.

"Uhuru!" cried Charlie with a deft, sudden gesture that confirmed Elgar's suspicions that he was no stranger to spear-craft. "Out of my house, on the double, invader! Uhuru!"

"Freedom!" piped little Willie. "That means, 'Freedom now!' Mister, you better go."

"Howdy," said Elgar wearily. "I was just leaving." He turned and descended the steps just as the shaft swooped overhead with rocketlike grace.

Now, trying to forget the unfortunate incident, he became absorbed in the morose progress of a frail white candy wrapper down the gutter. Caught up in the whirls and eddies of last night's rain, it bobbed, backtracked, struggled weakly, drifted sadly sidewise, finally sank down the corner sewer, reminding Elgar all too forcefully of his likely future progress. If present currents were any indication.

For a bit of cheering contrast he thought of his older brothers: Moe, a thriving banker, and Shu, now happily managing three of the Seven Branches. Each had progressed easily and logically from the standard schools to junior exec jobs to management, acquiring on the way the standard one skinny wife and three fat children. Could either of them, with their perfect sense of order and sequence, ever possibly get into such a hopeless situation? And, if the impossible occurred, could either fail to become extricated, smoothly and with a handsome profit?

No, he knew, was the answer. To both.

There remained his father, Julius Pride Enders. Old Iron-fists himself, the King of Merchant Princes, with his standard solutions to the problems of Holding Your Own and Getting Your Return and Giving the Peasantry What They Want While Keeping Them in Their Place (Down). Applied to limited questions, Fathaw's answers were remarkably successful, though. No doubt, if Elgar phoned him, he would have a good suggestion or two for Holding Your Own Under the Present Shaky Conditions. But at the thought of calling Fathaw and asking, "What do you do when the peasantry hurls spears at you?" Elgar's stomach refused to stay in its place, became an angry jack-in-the-box demanding its own Freedom Now.

Elgar had demonstrated his own imperfect sense of sequence by taking up a series of undistinguished occupations—forester, stable hand, horse-farm manager, construction worker, building contractor, bum— while postponing plans to study architecture, plans to study law, plans to go into real estate, plans, plans, plans. The current abortive attempt at real estate would be viewed by now as an unfunny family joke. The latest illustration of his disappointing failure to jell as solidly as citizens Moe and Shu. Who every day in every way, mental and physical, in their small boxes of offices and their large, boxlike, eighteenth-century houses, were growing squarer and squarer. While Elgar, still suffering from a constitutional inability to shape himself along cubical lines, knew of his future only what he had always known: he could not stand to be like them.

This knowledge, however, was a frail stalk to depend on for support in one's upward climb from the gutter. For, if he was not like his brothers, who or what was he?

Elgar's reflection on glass panes, as he fled back into the phone booth, was a silvery, ghostly blur.

The minute he heard Fathaw clear his throat at the other end, Elgar knew it had been a serious mistake to call. That harrumph, the backfiring of a twelve-inch cannon, announced a heavy forthcoming barrage.

"What's the difficulty this time, Elgar? Haven't Neeby and Levin been following my instructions?"

Neeby was the Trusts and Investments man at Moe's bank, and his instructions were to turn certain regular sums over to Levin, who had *his* instructions on how much to invest and how much (a trickle) to release to Elgar. Steel-eyed Levin watched fish-eyed Neeby, and Neeby watched Levin, and Fathaw watched them both, and they both watched Elgar. Oh, it was a pretty, pretty net in which they had him dancing like a deranged butterfly, balancing his doom against his father's.

"Are you still seeing that crackpot talking doctor, Elgar?" Fathaw's respect reached out to encompass all solid things like land, figures, prime ribs of beef and machinery, but withdrew contemptuously from anything so slippery and limitless as talk.

"Yes," Elgar squeaked. "Yes, Fathaw. He's helping me."

"Well, why in hell do you need help? You're crazy. I mean you're not *that* crazy. All you need is a good hard job. A stiff upper lip. Some good fresh air in your lungs. Why don't you get away from it all? I mean camp out in the woods, rough it, don't waste money on one of those expensive resort vacations. Go up in Canada with your brothers and bag some deer."

The standard answers, with the standard reference to curbing expenses which always occurred in the first thirty seconds of Elgar's conversations with his millionaire father. Also the standard suggestion about hunting, which Elgar always ignored, out of a conviction he was bound to fail, being essentially on the side of the deer.

"Why must you always assume there is a difficulty, Fathaw? I called to ask what you know about real estate."

"What do you mean, 'what I know?' I know everything about it, of course. Know real estate like the back of my hand. That tract along the Upper County line. Built a shopping center up there recently. Now developing a town around it. Endersville. What's Levin suggesting? Mortgages?"

"Why must you assume I act only on Levin's suggestions? No, an apartment house, Fathaw. My own idea."

"Tricky business, apartments. More nuisance than profit. Anyone who would rent a place to live is a gypsy. A vagrant. Miserable, dirty little people. No sense of responsibility. Wear and tear on property. Precious little return on your money. Bad business, Elgar, for anybody except old men and widows. And you know I don't consider anyone old till he's passed seventy-five. My time is money, you know. Real estate's a large subject. Don't be vague. What's your problem?"

"The fact that you're not even past sixty-five," Elgar whispered into the phone, his clenched fist poised to drive through the nearest pane of glass, the one that held his own vague reflection.

"What?" the old man bellowed. "Speak up, will you?"

"The fact that as yet I've derived no income from this property. Have you any thoughts on how to collect rent from tenants?"

"Put it in the hands of a constable! Give them thirty days! Let him evict them!"

Put your problems but not your money into someone else's hands. Another standard answer which had worked well for Fathaw all his life.

"I don't want to do that, Fathaw. I want to handle it myself." Even as he uttered this plea he knew it sounded ridiculous. As when once he had pleaded, "Let go of the bike. I want to ride it by myself. Even if I fall flat on my face." Which, of course, he had done. His stomach went into such acrobatics at that point, Elgar had to put his head between his knees.

"Elgar," said the stern voice at the other end, "where exactly is this property of yours?"

"Right in the center of town here. Corner of Jackson and Poplar Streets."

"Elgar. Isn't that a *colored* neighborhood?"

"It seems to be," Elgar admitted. "Yes, Fathaw, that's what it seems. Of course," he added, "as you know, Fathaw, all things are not what they appear to be. My tenants refer to themselves as Creoles and Choctaw Indians. And sometimes, I believe, Nigerians and Senegalese."

"Elgar, you are even more of a fool than I thought!" roared his father. "Nigerians, indeed! Your mother and I are simply at our wits' end about you, Elgar. She worries about you constantly, about your bad habits, your foolish ventures, your undesirable companions. Frets night and day because you never visit us and never call. While your brothers are such loyal sons. What a contrast. I never know what to tell her about *you*. I never even know where you are. This nonsense of yours must stop, sir, do you understand? It must stop right now! I am going to put your mother on the phone in one minute. But first I want to know where you are, Elgar. I mean where you are right now. We're coming down there to get you."

"I am in Hell, Fathaw," Elgar said simply, and hung up. And, retracting his hand at the last instant, slammed the receiver through the nearest pane instead. Showers of glass sprayed his face, miraculously missing the dangerous-glinting green eyes.

Hurrying numbly through dim streets to keep his scheduled appointment with Borden, he was only vaguely aware of moisture tickling various upper frontal areas. Hence when the good doctor received him with cracks in his professional composure, with his mouth, in fact, wide open, Elgar was surprised.

Until he reached up and touched his forehead. His fingers came away bloody. Touched his cheek. Also bloody. His upper lip yielded another harvest of gore. Apparently the scattering fragments of glass had made him as monstrous as his father's vision of him.

"Just following my father's advice, Borden," Elgar said. "He told me to acquire a stiff upper lip. And it does seem to be getting numb, now that I notice."

Borden stared. "Elgar, I know you love to be dramatic, and I have my rules, but this seems to be an emergency. If you want to see a doctor about those cuts, I can reschedule your appointment."

"Funny, I thought you were supposed to be a doctor, Borden. You great big phony. Upset at the sight of a little blood."

Borden said smoothly, "It is not so upsetting as all that, Elgar. All the same I am willing to delay your hour for fifteen minutes if you want to go downstairs and wash up."

"No, let's get right down to business," Elgar said. "I can stand it if you can."

Borden replied, "You should know by now that I can stand anything, Elgar. Come in."

"However," he added, opening a cabinet to reveal a businesslike assortment of swabs and syringes, "there is no reason why I have to spend the next hour contemplating physical horrors in addition to psychic ones. No. Tilt the face up to me, Elgar. Turn it toward the light. Yes."

Borden's fingers were wonderfully deft and confidence-inspiring as he dabbed lightly with antiseptic, peered closely, grunted, bent with tweezers, and removed several splinters of glass from Elgar's scalp, finished by making rapid passes in the air with a roll of bandage.

Afterward Elgar went over to the mirror and checked. His head was neatly swathed and tied like the kid's in "Spirit of '76."—Yep, he thought, puckering his chin thoughtfully, yep. A professional job.

"Are you quite finished admiring yourself?" Borden inquired. "Then perhaps you will want to lie down over here and describe this latest hair-raising episode. Or should I say, 'scalp-raising?' You say it resulted from a conversation with your father?"

Elgar stretched out and studied the dismal patterns on Borden's mildewed ceiling. "You know I can't talk to my father, Borden. It's impossible. He always tried to make me feel like nothing."

"Apparently he succeeds," Borden observed. "Since, following your conversations with him, you always attempt to destroy yourself."

"Aaaaaah!" was Elgar's only comment. That and a pummeling of the couch.

"Yes. It is better to destroy my couch, Elgar. Though even better if you take out your aggressions on *appropriate* objects. Have you noticed, Elgar, that you have no trouble reacting with anger to any person except your father?"

"Oh, have I ever noticed," Elgar declared passionately, unconsciously echoing Borden's speech pattern. "Oh, brother, have I ever. Yes. Yes yes yes yes. When I talk to him I don't feel anything but weak. That and stomach pains."

"Which are, as we know, your way of feeling anxiety, Elgar. Stomach pains are anxiety, nothing more. There is nothing physically wrong with your stomach, as you know from having swallowed quantities of barium. As well as a number of even nastier concoctions in your various attempts at suicide, with remarkably limited results. Yes. Your stomach is actually an organ of fantastic recuperative powers, deserving of study by science, Elgar. Now tell me. How does your father achieve his annihilation of you?"

"He hasn't yet," Elgar said quickly. "I'm still here. Don't you see me here, Borden?"

"Of course," Borden reassured him. "I mean your psychic annihilation. How does he make you feel like nothing?"

"By knowing it all!" Elgar howled. "By having a formula for everything! By being so successful, he *is* everything!"

"And yet you know that statement is untrue, Elgar. Your father is not everything. This room, for instance, this desk, this chair, they are not a part of your father or his holdings."

"You don't know Upper County, where I come from," Elgar said grimly. "Up there, they would be. There's nothing in the whole county he doesn't own."

"I see," Borden said. After a pause to formulate his thoughts he announced, "Elgar, I think we have found the key to your identity crisis."

"Turn it!" Elgar cried. "Open this box I'm in. Tell me who I am." Adding bleakly, "Unless I'm nothing."

"No, Elgar, you are not a nothing," Borden said.

Hope shining through hopelessness, Elgar looked at him.

"You are an anti-everything, Elgar. Engaged in a vast crusade that dissipates all your psychic energies."

Elgar bared his fangs to growl at Borden's jargon.

"Wait, Elgar. Let me put it this way. You come from a powerful family with a totalitarian father who insisted that everything be done his way. Who even insisted that his children *grow* his way, as if you could make a birch sapling become a sycamore. As well as a mother who imposed her musical and other standards upon you, even sending you to a girls' ballet class. Yes. Your mother is another totalitarian figure. With her loud and constant insistence that your father is never wrong."

"It gets louder the wronger he is," Elgar said, and clutched his stomach. "Ouch!"

"Yes, it even hurts you to admit he can be wrong. Growth, Elgar. Painful. Yes. So you spent your childhood being something other than a sycamore, being a birch, perhaps, trying to grow big and strong enough to stand independent of all that Establishment—your father's estate, his enterprises, his millions, and all the powerful people who support him, including your mother and your obedient brothers. You wished to be a person, not a Representative of something you disliked. You were, we might say, a birch, but no Bircher, Elgar. But, to continue this rather appalling image, you are still only a slim sapling, and every time you spring up in your own form, your father slaps you down. With the force of a giant woodsman. A Paul Bunyan."

"That's right," Elgar said, nodding, reacting to his own fate more calmly than he would to an unfavorable weather prediction. "Yep. That's how it is."

"Is that all you can say? And in that tone of meek submissiveness? Elgar, what would you say should be the normal reaction to a person who carries out this systematic total destruction of another person?"

Elgar at least knew his lessons well. "Rage," he said, almost feeling it. "White hot, scalding rage!"

"But when your father attacks you, you feel—?"

"Nothing. Absolute, pure, numb zero. Less."

"And the rage only comes later?"

"Much later."

"And turned, always, on yourself. Yes. To the point of self-destruction. Which is why, Elgar, we have agreed that contact with your father is dangerous for you at present. At your present stage of maturity, even to telephone him is an act of self-destruction."

Borden paused before dropping the awful question into the silence. It shook the room with the force of a boulder.

"Then why, Elgar, did you phone your father today?"

"I didn't say I phoned him, Borden," Elgar replied stubbornly, fighting back his unreasonable fear of being caught. "How do you know? Maybe he phoned me."

Borden simply stared back at him quietly, that calm, empty stare which at times drove Elgar to fits of frustration. And, at other times, to fits of honesty.

"Yes, Borden, I called him," he admitted finally. "You sad imitation of Basil Rathbone imitating Sherlock Holmes, you know he couldn't have called me. He doesn't know where I live, hasn't been able to find me since I holed up here in the Trejour. So yes, Borden, I admit it. I walked into that sidewalk phone booth, that elegant glass coffin designed by Mies or somebody like him so all the world could watch my death throes, and put the coins in the box, and dialed my father's number myself. Why did I do that, Borden?

"—Because the tenants at my apartment house are driving me out of my mind. I haven't collected a cent in rents from them. I've collected nothing but abuse. I thought maybe the great Empire Builder would have a suggestion to help me clear up my minor problems with a small empire consisting of only four measly apartments. But he was no help at all, Borden. So I smashed my way out of the booth again." Christ, he was crying.

"You wanted him to be helpless," Borden suggested. "You wanted your father to meet with a defeat. It is what you have always wanted, Elgar. At the cost of your own life, if necessary."

Tears really flowing now. Stop bawling, he thought, you'll ruin the bandage, lying prone like this. Shut up or sit up, you slob.

"Elgar," Borden said softly, "I think it is too high a price to pay."

Funny, how Borden was really getting to look like Lincoln. Like the Old Emancipator himself.

"To summarize," Borden said with an elevated bony finger, "you feel a strong desire to kill your father. You can't stand this idea, so you try to destroy yourself instead. But you are getting better, Elgar. Today you only sliced yourself up a little. Also, I think you no longer need your father or his advice. I think perhaps you can arrive at your own solutions, now that you have made a beginning."

"Please, Borden, tell me. Where in the crazy mixed-up mess of my life do you see a sign of a beginning?"

"Buying this apartment building. Taking on new responsibility. I think it is a healthy project for you, Elgar. I think you can use it to work out many of your problems."

Borden glanced at his watch. It usually angered Elgar that he should never fail to notice the end of what must surely be the most fascinating hour of his day. However, today Elgar's rage, usually his trusty ally in every situation but one, had deserted him.

"Your hour is up for today, Elgar. I suggest you go back to your property and attempt to collect your rents. If you meet with resistance, take out your aggressions on your tenants. That will be good for you. And it will be appropriate."

Smiling bravely if wanly, the bandaged old warrior saluted his commander-in-chief, tottered out of command headquarters, and made for the front lines once more. To faintly fluting strains of "Yankee Doodle."

An hour later he was back in his barracks, staring distrustfully at a small, gaily printed white card. It had been far too easy. His instincts smelled a trap. Yet there it was in his hand, frisky and friendly as an innocent lamb.

This time Marge had come to the door to announce that she was the duly elected president of the newly formed Corner Poplar Street Tenants' Association, and therefore authorized to speak for everyone in the house. The C.P.S.T.A. had held its first meeting today, she said. In addition to the election of officers, they had aired their grievances and come to an important decision.

"*What* goddamned grievances?" he'd asked in disbelief.

"We'll get to those later, Landlord. But I can tell you one complaint was about foulmouthed language on the premises. Yours. So just be quiet and read this. Here."

The card she handed him said:

> *Does your blood feel tired, does your back feel bent?*
> *Help us raise the roof while we raise the rent!*
> *There'll be Fountains of Youth * and lots of eats*
> *At the corner of Jackson and Poplar Streets!*

FRIDAY EVENING,   *(ALCOHOLIC CONTENT)
SEPTEMBER 4TH   ADMISSION TWO DOLLARS

8:30 P.M. *'til ???*

"We used to have these lots in the old days," Marge explained proudly. "The rent comes due every week in Harlem."

"Well," Elgar said, smiling all over himself, even under the bandage. Pleased and shaken. "Well. What do you know? A party. Well. Am I invited?"

"Well of course, Landlord," Marge said, with indignant hands on her wall-to-wall hips. "You're the reason for the party. There wouldn't be any party except for you."

"Yeehoo!" he howled, ripping off the bandage like an imaginary ten-gallon hat and doing three rapid *battements élevés* between the top step and the sidewalk. "Whee! Yoohee!"

"There will be no rowdy conduct allowed," Marge said severely. "And you got to pay your way in the door, just like everybody else. After all, this *is* a rent party, Landlord."

6

Sally's brisk, broad-A accent on the phone informed Elgar that she was busy Friday evening. And every other evening that week.

"I have to make festoons for the Worthy Causes Ball, Elgar. All week long. I'm head of the Decorating Committee. We have to turn the hall into a pahk. An English country gahden."

"Why not come festooning with me instead? I promise you more festive festooning than you'll have with that bunch of do-gooding spinsters. I'm a worthy cause too, remember? With more than one ball."

"Yes, I know, Elgar, but there are others just as worthy."

"In that case have a merry time balling with them all, Sally dear. Also, until I call you again, a merry Christmas, New Year's, Easter, Halloween, and Thanksgiving."

Screw the stuck-up broad, Elgar thought. Matter of fact, it was probably what she needed. It had been a long time since she'd had a lesson from the master. And aging debutantes suffered from early menopause, in his experience. Oh well. Call Rita instead. She would be thrilled.

She was. "A rent party, Elgar? How wonderful! I can't believe it. I thought they ended back in the Thirties."

Everything ended back in the Thirties, as far as Rita was concerned. Including her happy young life, four years after she was born, a bouncing, rosy-cheeked peasant babe meant for digging potatoes but doomed to middle-class comforts like frozen French fries. Rita loved bread lines, tin-roofed shacks, crokersack dresses, chain-gang songs, wildcat strikes, company stores, and other manifestations of authentic misery. She spent all her current days mourning their disappearance, because it meant social workers were no longer really needed. Rita, holder of a meaningless master's degree from The Bryn Mawr School of Social Work, craved to be needed. Now.

"Be good," he promised her, "and maybe you'll get to take part in a genuine race riot."

"Oh, Elgar, how exciting! I can hardly wait. I'll be ready at eight on the dot."

Knotting his brightest blue tie, Elgar noticed that his eyes matched it gaily. He reparted his thick yellow hair carefully and combed it over the remaining scalp scabs. Never let Copee think he had made his mark with that badly thrown tomahawk.

Kicking the bag of garbage affectionately as he went out, Elgar decided to take Lanie's advice and make his tenants respect him. Drive up looking like the big property owner who could throw his weight around, in the big gray Lincoln instead of the roaring white Jag or his favorite, the little putt-putt Morris. Though the Lincoln's opulence was sure to offend Rita's social conscience.

"Really, Elgar. Such conspicuous waste. Those fenders alone would feed four Koreans for a year."

But she forgot about starving Koreans and jumped in quickly enough when he began pulling away from the curb in front of her parents' conspicuously wasteful, phony-Tudor mansion in the Jewish suburbs. According to Rita, they were a pair of poor, bewildered ex-radicals of the Thirties who kept acquiring wealth in spite of themselves. The more they ground their teeth in torment at the inequities of a society that permitted some to be rich and others poor, the more money perversely flowed toward them.

With Rita in her best peasant dirndl and Village sandals all a-twitter on his arm, he followed the cheerful buzz of voices and climbed the familiar stairs to Marge's kitchen. Found, in a steamy and fragrant atmosphere emanating from many simmering pots and pans, dozens of authentic dusky poor in attendance. Rita brightened instantly, as if they had come on purpose to cheer her up, though they seemed more absorbed in cheering themselves with the contents of many bottles.

At the door a tall, dapper character of the color and coolness of refrigerated lemon squash barred their way, extending a pearl-gray Homburg upside down in an immaculate, white-gloved hand.

"*Bienvenue,*" he said. "Meaning in translation, 'Welcome.' Assuming of course you have the necessary requisites for yourself and your fair companion. To wit, four silver coins or certificates. I mean dollars. Begging both youah pardons for my crass request."

In the background Marge, up to her elbows in steam, jiggled like a merry mountain. "Lord, Jessie, I believe this joint has got the classiest doorman in town."

His companion, a tall pared-down woman who was turning spitting pieces of chicken in a frying pan, giggled too. "Ain't he somethin'? I liked him even better when he was a Reverend, though. You should have heard him in the pulpit. I mean he read us some poetry. Especially at collection time."

"A thousand thanks, kind sir," the elegant doorman said when Elgar produced a five. He waved the hat. "Do me the generous favor of placing your contribution in this humble receptacle."

"Not until I see my change," said Elgar, who distrusted all dapper manifestations, especially those belonging to his own sex.

"Ah, yes, change," the doorman said. "I have something much better heah for you than ordinary legal tender. This extraordinary little certificate. Instantly translatable at yon bar into the liquid delights of your choosing."

"Who says so?" Elgar demanded, staring belligerently at a torn slip of paper on which was scrawled in faint pencil:

Good for 2 Drinks (Xcept Scotch)

The doorman executed a graceful, sweeping bow. "None other than P. Eldridge DuBois, suh. The first. At youah everlasting service."

"Oh, so that's who you are," Elgar said. "Just one question, DuBois. I've been wondering ever since I saw it on the bell downstairs. What's the 'P.' stand for?"

" 'Professor,' " was the answer. "Formerly, in the days of a deep religious vocation now lost in antiquity, 'Preacher.' But always and forever, suh, since my birth thirty years ago in the upper reaches of downtown New Orleans, 'Proud.' "

"Isn't he beautiful?" Rita whispered in Elgar's ear. "Striped blazer and flannels and everything. I don't believe him. He's not real."

"Chère Madame," DuBois said with another courtly bow, eyeing Rita's rough muslin blouse, her dirndl of nasty-green monkscloth, her

intricately leather-thonged feet and ankles, "or perhaps I should say, *Chère Mademoiselle,* I assure you, I am just as real as you."

Having paid this apparition, they were welcomed into the bosom of the celebration. Marge, directing activities from the range where she was stirring a gory mess of barbecue, introduced her companions: the bony woman waving a spatula and an evilly scarred young man with a bottle opener, both poised dangerously at the ready. Elgar cringed until she said, "Jessie, Jimmy, this is Landlord. Jessie, give Landlord a piece of chicken. Jimmy, give Landlord what he wants to drink."

Thus reinforced and reassured, Elgar wandered downstairs, for the party was overflowing into every apartment, and he was drawn down to the Copees' by the sound of throbbing drums. Being essentially nonmusical, with a tin ear that only the least subtle, most overpowering noises could penetrate, Elgar loved loud drumming. He had an extensive collection of percussive records which he kept at Lanie's, and often, after four or more gins, he liked to take off his shoes and leap about her apartment. He felt his performance made up in enthusiasm whatever it lacked in skill.

But Lanie always protested. "It's so painful to watch, Elgar. I never thought a person could suffer from total lack of rhythm."

As he walked into Fanny's and Charlie's apartment, the first person he spied was his erstwhile dance critic demonstrating her own very adequate sense of rhythm. For a partner, it seemed, she had bagged herself an authentic Nigerian warrior, complete with fez and flowing robes.

"Who's he?" he shouted to her over the *Drums of Passion.* "Is he Olatunji?" For he had heard that his favorite recording artist was playing a night club date in town.

"No," Lanie shouted back as she executed a belly contraction worthy of Little Egypt. "He's my garbage man."

Their right arms shot independently into the air. They kicked independently and wheeled, stiff-kneed, in opposite directions. Elgar, deeply stirred by all this ethnic frenzy, was about to take off his shoes and join them when the competition poured in.

Five girls in long, tightly wrapped cotton dresses and turbans, with scores of bangle bracelets. Four barefoot youths in golden earrings and colorful cotton tunics. And their bandy-legged leader, the Little King himself, most gorgeously robed of all, hefting his spear.

"Down the tyrants!" cried Charlie. "Up the volume! Freedom Now!"

At this signal the masqueraders paired off and began to leap athletically over and around Fanny's heavy Chinese furniture. Only one lamp was lit, providing a dim reddish glow and causing several bruised shins announced by strictly Anglo-Saxon curse words. To even up the partner situation, Lanie relinquished her male dervish and began dancing with one of the women. Whom he recognized, in spite of her wire and copper bangles and intricately wound Fruit of the Loom sarong, as Lucy, the glum genius of the griddle.

While the other dancers, alternating sexes, formed a single line that heaved serpentlike around the apartment, Lanie and Lucy took off into a stratosphere of their own, performing in perfect unison, like a woman and her reflection in a mirror. As the snake dance surged toward Elgar, he began to feel like a tender morsel meant for forthcoming stew. —Must go upstairs and get Rita, bring her down here, he thought. Not that she was a plumper and juicier morsel than he. Simply that Rita dearly loved all authentic ethnic scenes.

Va VOOM, went the drums. Va VOOM, va VOOM. With background screeches and chatter of fantastic jungle creatures.

"Salaam!" cried the dancers. "Aleikum Salaam!"

"Doom!" cried their leader. "Doom to our enemies! Doom!"

Elgar plucked at Lanie's sleeve as she drifted by, drowning in her partner's eyes. "Lanie, are any of these people real Africans?"

"Don't be silly, Elgar," she answered. "Real Africans have real things to do."

Disappointed, he decided not to drag Rita downstairs after all. If there was anything she hated it was non-authentic ethnic scenes.

The record finally ended, and what had been an impressive spectacle degenerated immediately into a sloppy masquerade. Deprived of the musical background they had leaned on, the dancers lost their grace, became awkward, overweight Americans flopping breathlessly into overstuffed chairs.

Copee alone was full of energy, perhaps because he had sat the last one out on his deep leather throne. Brandishing his spear, he took possession of the center of the floor and announced that he was calling a meeting of the African Solidarity Society to order.

"First we will have our historical inspiration, and then our business meeting. Tonight for inspiration we will consider the long line of the Lions of Judah. Ethiopia stretching forth her mighty hand over the continents, over the centuries. The proud history of Ethiopia is *your* history, members! You were not meant to be slaves. You were meant to be kings!

"That concludes our historical inspiration. Now we will go on to our business meeting. To discuss plans for the revolution to overthrow all warlords, landlords, and overlords. Also plans for the cake raffle next Saturday."

Copee took a quick look around the room. "All non-members must clear the room now. Our business meeting is private."

"I'll go," Elgar said gratefully. He rose quickly, preferring Marge's barbecue sauce to whatever Copee and his clan were about to cook up. Hers, at least, was intended for spare ribs. Theirs might be meant for him.

Copee nodded and turned his unnaturally bright little eyes on Lanie. "I said our business meeting is private, Miss."

Lanie held her ground.

"You," he told her with, for him, amazing patience, "must also make your departure before we begin our secret deliberations."

"I thought this was a public party," she said. "What society is this, anyway? And how can it be secret, if all your meetings are this noisy?"

Then, with a yawn, she stood up. "Oh, well. I really don't care to join. I never was much of a joiner, anyway. Especially of exclusive societies. Exclusive society has always bored me. Besides, they are playing my favorite kind of music upstairs. It is not, I regret to say, African. It is one hundred per cent American."

Elgar followed Lanie, in black leotards and moving like a gorgeous, impatient panther, as she bounded up the stairs. Marge's bittersweet music was indeed pouring out of her apartment. Its sadness, drawn from a well of fourteen years' collected tears, was incongruous set to tinkling ragtime piano. Particularly since the lyrics she was singing were:

Flat foot floogie with the floy, floy.

As he came in, voices were raised in greeting. "Hey, here comes Landlord!" "Jimmy, get Landlord a drink!" "Jessie, give Landlord some of those shrimps and a piece of pie!"

Knotty hands shook his, offering fat cigars. Soft hands, ample bosoms, pressing fore and aft, guided him to a comfortable chair. More people tumbled in. Dozens of strangers, all arriving at Elgar's party to wish him well. DuBois, slim and handsome, grinned goldenly by the door as he raked in the shekels. All around the piano, flat feet were shuffling with the joy, joy.

The mood was so infectious, Elgar decided to give in to it and forsake the sounds of distant drumming for awhile. He looked around. Nearly everyone in the room was in motion, but there was one shadowy corner of stillness. He studied its dim contours until they took shape as the most ancient couple he had ever seen. His neck a scrawny column rising from a high collar. Her dress a skinny column hobbled down to her ankles. Holding hands and smiling vaguely at each other, like a pair in an old tintype. Barely there.

Elgar asked the debonair doorman, "DuBois, who are those old people?"

DuBois glanced at them quickly and said, "I have never seen them before. But from their appearance I would surmise they are my unseen neighbors, the ghostly couple rumored to be resident on the third floor. Mr. and Mrs. Cumberson."

Mr. and Mrs. Cumberson were swaying to the music, but not in the proper rhythm. It was as if they heard an old pianola somewhere playing hymns instead of ragtime. Around each of their heads, which were fringed with white wool innocent of any heat treatments, a gentle nimbus of light seemed to be floating. Even the angels had come down for Elgar's party.

Echoing Elgar's thoughts, DuBois said, "You are favored this evening by a very generous attendance. The Cumbersons do not lead an active social life. Normally I myself am unavailable for this sort of occasion. But I decided at the last minute to come, although I had business elsewhere."

"What sort of business?" Elgar inquired.

"A convocation of my faculty. At the Church of the Hopeless Redeemed."

"Why may I ask is a college faculty, if it's legitimate, meeting in a church?"

"Who says it's legitimate?" DuBois replied. "Excuse my frankness. Churches are where the money flows. Churches and bars. Frequenters of bars," he added, tamping tobacco into a long, elegant meerschaum, "are of course deplorably lacking in the finer values. But, oh—" puff, puff "—how those good church people believe in higher education! Oh, how they love to give!"

"Speaking of money," Elgar said, coughing as DuBois emitted a thick cloud of smoke, "you owe me a month's back rent."

"I have already made my contribution to this evening," DuBois said stiffly. "At great cost, I might add, to my dearest personal principles. A DuBois is not brought up to mingle easily with the commonality. But I came in your honor, because I heard you were a gentleman. Please, sir, I beg of you, do not prove me wrong." He bowed. "I trust, when the evening's receipts are counted, you will find yourself satisfied."

"Trust," Elgar declared, "is something I'm pretty short on right now. With me, even God pays cash."

DuBois giggled, showing about thirty-five exquisitely porcelain-capped teeth. "Oh, I say, that *was* jolly! What a magnificent sense of humor. If you have a moment I would like to invite you to my nearby quarters. Second floor front, but quiet and peaceful. Hung with dark velvet curtains to shut out the vulgar world. We will share a bit of brandy like gentlemen. Of the ancient Napoleon variety, imported from France. Also I'd like you to feel the draft that comes in under my front windows. I think weatherstripping against the wintry blasts will soon be in order."

A good opportunity to evade this ever-painful issue suddenly presented itself to Elgar. "Door!" he shouted. "Somebody just sneaked in."

DuBois' reaction was instantaneous and effective. Screeching, "Come back here, you low-down cheapskate!" he tackled the fugitive neatly, brought down his man, and deftly extracted two dollars from his wallet. Then he got up, brushed himself off and resumed his post at the door, draped against it with all the casual elegance of a men's fashion drawing.

He is a con man, Elgar thought with odd frustration. The kind of character Lanie warned me about. But, dammit, I can't help liking the guy.

That was obviously going to be his biggest problem. With the exception of Copee, whom he had no trouble disliking, Elgar could not help liking all of these people and feeling at home with them. Particularly since they kept making it difficult for him to be unfriendly by shoving drinks and delicious viands at him along with expressions of cheer and good will. Must discourage this generosity hereafter, he resolved. It was undermining his position. Whoops, here came another piece of fried chicken and another mountain of potato salad.

"Eat up, Landlord. We cooked too much food. This is free."

From beneath the piano, where she had crawled to be as close as possible to the music, Lanie sent him a scowl. It seemed to say, "Stop smiling so broadly, Elgar. They'll never respect you at this rate. Stop it, idiot. Look mean. Like me."

Elgar looked away guiltily, though he had been glad to see her at the party, and sorry it had been time for another girl's number to come up in the strict rotation plan that kept him from being in short supply. Apparently Marge had invited Lanie anyway, and she had brought her co-worker Lucy along. Someday when his head was less ginsoaked he would have to figure out the strange connection between them that was evident when they danced. Also the even more sinister connection between Lucy and Copee's Congolese Commandoes. He wondered what the Pan-African Ku Klux Klan was plotting down below. Destruction, of course. But of what, and of whom? Copee had mentioned landlords, among other things.

—Oh well, Elgar thought recklessly, let them plot away, as long as the piano played on to drown out their unpleasantness. As long as Elgar's left hand was full of succulent chicken, and his right clutched a tumbler of gin, and a sweetly shimmering young fanny was swaying directly in front of him.

Elgar put his drink down and let his hand creep forward, within a dangerous inch of a pinch. Halting it there, he looked around furtively for Rita.

There she was in the far corner, untying yards of strangling leather straps and blissfully kicking her sandals away. Insisting shrilly that ragtime and blues were really direct descendants of Ukrainian folk music. And proving it with a barefoot folk-dance demonstration that, even to Elgar's inexperienced eyes, looked all wrong. But her audience, consisting mainly of the Cumbersons with their sweet, distant smiles, was tolerant, and she clogged merrily on.

Elgar, so used to a self-imposed Spartan existence, paused to consider his sudden embarrassment of riches. The shrimps which had suddenly materialized on his plate. His drink, miraculously refilled. The apparitions of many graceful women swaying in time to the music, all around him. And his own Three Graces—Sally, Yankee as white frame churches; Rita, stern and tragic as a synagogue (though laughing, now, with a wild abandon that could only mean her social conscience was temporarily appeased); Lanie, tall and tar-brushed and touchy as a wild filly of the veldt. He frowned. He was getting to be a goddamned one-man brotherhood movement, though his feelings toward none of them were exactly brotherly. He wondered which one would be awarded the apple of his eye. He would prefer it to be none of these overly complicated females, but, resigned to complications, he hoped it would be settled soon.

Then the graceful green fanny shimmering nearest his twitching hand suddenly turned around, and Eve appeared. Almost as casually dressed as in the garden, in a leaf-green satin *pareu* cut down to here and slit up to there, revealing blinding vistas of golden-brown. Eve, better known as—he had been right all along—Fanny.

She swayed toward him. Every one of her hundred little movements as she approached was temptation, springing from the innocence before the Fall. Thrilling him with an extra *frisson* of danger because he had eaten of the fruit and knew she had a homicidal husband downstairs.

Fanny came up to him and offered him a taste of her Apple Jack.

Lanie leaped by, engaged in a downright disgraceful dance with the scarfaced bartender, and cast a spiteful look at Elgar over her twitching shoulder.

"Watch out for that one, Elgar," she *sotto voc'd* as she wriggled past him. "I'm warning you. As a friend. Oh, I'm not jealous. Believe me. Certainly not of that fat beatnik you brought tonight. But this one is more than you can handle, boy. I warn you. She'll drive you into an early grave."

"Will you never believe that I can take care of myself?" he shouted. Defiantly, he gulped the entire contents of Fanny's glass. And goggled as all of one firm brown thigh, *all,* slithered out of the slit in the garment.

"My compliments to your designer, my dear," he murmured. "Get him to run me up a little something sometime. Along very basic, simple lines. Just an extra large fig leaf or so. Come here, dear. Sit down."

Marge, benign bulk, handed Elgar another tender leg of fried chicken. He seized it, drained his glass, drew Fanny onto his lap. What the hell. Warmth, friendliness, solicitude, good food, good music, comfort. Plus delightful tickles by willing and talented masseuse hands. What the hell. This was Paradise. Oh, if only Fathaw could see him now.

It seemed that for one night Elgar had been granted, as Marge would say, the Powers. From kissing Fanny, a first gentle exploration, so easy and uncomplicated, her little teeth nibbling his poor, thin, bloodless lips, he raised his head and waited for its contents—gin, wine, Apple Jack, and delirium—to stop spinning and settle into place. And, looking across the room through fog, encountered his nightmarish past in the shape of two trolls. He blinked, but the apparition of his parents would not go away.

"Oh Elgar," Mothaw burbled, coming toward him and extending jouncy arms clanking with slave chains, "you bad, bad boy. Staying away from me so long. You *mauvais* thing."

"This is the saddest day of my life, son," declared Fathaw. "That you would sink so low. Cavorting with low types. Swilling cheap spirits. Indulging in poor investments."

Mothaw took up the refrain again. "Elgar dear," she trilled, "you know how sensitive I am, musically speaking. Please ask them to perform something more soothing. Some nice, sad spirituals perhaps. If they continue this savage screeching and pounding I will be forced to *partir.*"

"We're leaving anyway, Mothaw, and taking him with us," Fathaw announced. "Back to Doctor Ludwig and the Green House. And this time he'll be in Wildflower Fields."

"Oh no," Mothaw protested. "Not my baby. Not the locked ward."

"Why not?" Elgar's father shot back to her. "Less expensive. Save us money. Do him more good. After all, Mothaw, your baby is thirty-four years old."

The leash on Elgar's temper snapped at that moment, probably at the reference to the Green House. He had almost succeeded in blotting out all memory of the year of his life he had spent in the world's most expensive nut-hatch, where the cost to his father, two grand a month, had been his only satisfaction. Covering a hundred acres, this well-padded loony bin had been equipped with a split-level swimming pool, a forty-piece orchestra, a stable of horses, golf and tennis pros, and suites for each patient with names like the Dahlia Garden, the Rose Arbor, the Honeysuckle Bower, and the Primrose Patch. Elgar had occupied the Orchid Garden, where visions of the dreadful clash between his blood and the purple bathroom tiles were the only thing that kept him from slashing his wrists.

But he had found other, if less effective, methods, and one day mad Doctor Ludwig had fixed him sorrowfully with his one good eye while the glass one made its escape to the wall, to announce that they were going to resort to shock. "So sorry, Elgar. But you haff been impossible to reach. You haff not helped us at all."

Fortunately the Green House had no locks, except on Wildflower Fields. The thought of angry electrical impulses exploring the tender pink corridors of his skull had set Elgar running. Straight to the arms of Borden, whom he'd heard about from another patient. ("This guy's not exactly legit, Elgar. He's better than the legits. He's one of the few remaining human beings on this earth.") Straight to the bowels of the Trejour, where no trolls would be able to find him.

"Elgar deah," Mothaw complained, "it is very rude of you to receive us in this fashion. Kindly ask that kitchen girl to remove herself from your lap."

"Whaddya mean, 'kitchen girl?'" demanded Fanny, clutching Elgar more tightly. "You think you're better than I am, or something?"

Mothaw, lifting eyeglasses that hung by a platinum chain, scrutinized Fanny's extensive exposure of thigh. "Elgar! Please dismiss this naked black hussy at once!"

"I can't dismiss her, Mothaw. I can't dismiss anybody. Haven't you heard? These people are free. Since 1865."

"Hear, hear!" cried Marge in the background. "Listen to Landlord. Tell 'em, Landlord!"

"She thinks just 'cause hers is white it's a gardenia," Fanny declared. "Well, I got news for her."

"Someday, Mothaw," Elgar said, with sudden unaccountable courage, "you must tell me the truth about where I came from."

Mothaw giggled. "Oh, really, Elgar. At this late date. Tee hee."

"Yes, really, Mothaw," he said earnestly. "Tell me the truth. I know you could never have given birth to me. How could you? You are not a woman. What you are is obvious. You are an effeminate man."

"Tell 'er, Landlord," Fanny encouraged. "Tell her about it. Like it *is*, Landlord."

Marge's living room was coming to life with the buzz of enthusiasm that always attends the start of a good fight. Even old Mrs. Cumberson opened her glazed eyes and nudged her nodding husband with her cane. "Wake up, Kincaid," she said. "I believe that young man's about to preach us a fine sermon."

Elgar gently eased Fanny from his lap and stood up bravely. Funny, he had always thought himself smaller than his father, a pale dot eclipsed in the shadow of His Monolithic Magnificence. Actually he was at least a head taller. He took a step forward, and the old man stepped backward.

Elgar cleared his throat bravely. "As for you, Fathaw—" he began, shaking his fist impressively. It was a good beginning. But as he stood there, staring at the familiar face which had turned dark red as a piece of calves' liver, he felt all feeling drain out of him. Where his rage had been was a large, empty circle. A zero.

Clutching his cramping stomach, Elgar turned to his mother and said lamely, "Parricide is a terrible crime, Mothaw, one I do not wish to commit. If you wish to prevent it, kindly get him out of my sight. And after this, keep him away from me."

A harrumph came from his father's throat. Elgar would never know what horrendously rumbling platitudes it was meant to announce. They were silenced forever by a long howl that began downstairs and continued uninterrupted to Marge's living room.

"Uhoooooooooorrrrruuuuuuuuu!"

Copee, at the head of his mummers, bounced into the room, pointing his spear at Elgar's father. "There he is! I have recognized The Enemy from his pictures in the press! Mark him well, members! He is the king of the exploiters. A leading exponent of tyranny. A builder of segregated housing and a cheater of the poor in his crumby chain stores. An opponent of unions, integration, emergent nations, the U.N., and civil rights!"

"Boooo!" went up the Society's rallying cry, and a dozen African throats gave out with a hearty Bronx cheer.

Copee clapped his hands. "Members of the Society! The Enemy's presence in our midst cannot be tolerated! We must eject him. A little ejection music, please."

Though it neatly wrapped up his immediate problem, Copee's speech made Elgar uneasy. God knew his father's presence in the same room was difficult to tolerate. But if this were going to remain a glorious, various world, Elgar had a feeling that all its presences would have to be tolerated somehow. Whereas, if Copee's ideas ever really caught on, nothing would remain but a few ejected fragments spinning dejectedly in space.

But Elgar was too late to stem the tide. One warrior improvised a gong from Marge's biggest pot lid. The others seized canisters and turned them into effective drums. The snake dance began to curl and writhe in a circle around Elgar's parents, turning them into small objects of pity, exorcising their powerful Furies from his soul.

"Charming!" cried Mothaw, who was inspecting the scene attentively through her eyeglasses. "Elgar, who are these quaint barbaric performers? How clever of you to hire them. I want them for my next soiree."

But she was being inexorably pushed, like her husband, toward the door.

There Fathaw at last found his majestic, rumbling voice. "Ruffians! Have a care for my hat, you are crushing it. Stand back there, I say."

At that point, Elgar was almost rooting for his father. But Copee's voice was still the loudest in the room.

"Down with you!" he chanted, bounding up and down. "Down with you and all other tyrants like you! Down the stairs!"

The Society moved, a single howling organism, in the direction he had indicated, sweeping two dozen million dollars before them. Charlie brought up the rear, screaming, "Warlords! Overlords! Landlords! Slumlords!" and other filthy words.

Elgar waved a feeble last goodbye to his parents, and slid from his chair. His head landed in a rough, scratchy nest of fabric. Opening his eyes, he found that it was Rita's lap.

"Elgar," she whispered tenderly, "I was proud of you tonight. I am afraid I have always underestimated you. I thought you were a decadent product of overrefinement. But now I see there is a deep conflict between effete culture and honest folk culture in your soul. Someday we must have a long, long talk to resolve all this."

The sound of war-cries rose from the street, Copee's the most audible and hideous, screaming, "Down with tyrants! Freedom Now!" until it was drowned out by the bellowing of approaching sirens. Elgar had a feeling the tyrants were the only ones who would enjoy freedom that night. The Society and its leader would have to spend another gloomy night plotting their doom in jail.

"Elgar," Rita said with gentle solicitude, "I believe you are suffering from cultural shock. Let me take you home."

"Shit on that," Elgar said. "I'm staying. No condition to drive, anyway. I entrust to you these car keys, dear Rita. Think fondly of me as your culture hero, and take yourself home."

He tried, heroically, to stand up, but fell forward instead on his hands and knees. "As our great leader, Booker T. Washington, once said, 'Those who cannot walk must first crawl.' Forward, then, on all fours if necessary."

So it was in appropriate beastly fashion that he followed the green beacon of Fanny's behind as it shimmered tantalizingly through the door.

7

"I was just checking to see if the babies was asleep," Fanny said, tiptoeing out of the little bedroom. "They was."

In an evening of surprises, her next act was the most startling of all. Unfastening two buttons, she stepped out of her green sheathing and stood there, blinding him. A bare brown flower extending welcoming petals of arms.

"Fanny, please," Elgar croaked. "Allow me to go through at least a parody of the preliminaries. To whisper a few sweet nothings, make a few false promises, fall for a few illusions."

Fanny shrugged. "What for?"

He had no good answer for her stunning simplicity. Only the foolish truth. "Because, Fanny dear, I am a product of a different culture. More formal than yours. Less free. Full of foolish little lies and comforting nonsense about courtship."

"You mean you're queer?" She shrugged, bent for her dress, and carelessly put it on again. "It's O.K., Landlord. I sure had you figured wrong, though."

Let it pass, he would correct her impression presently. With royal interest. Elgar might be a mass of anxieties, but fears about his ability to rise to any interesting sexual challenge were not among them. Except when sodden with drink, of course. And sometimes even then. With Lanie, for instance. Ah, memories.

Saronged again, Fanny removed several skewers, shook long black hair down her back, and padded across the floor toward him like a barefoot, beautiful Polynesian. Lacking only a hibiscus in her teeth.

"What a shame, Landlord. I know for a fact old Charlie is stuck in the hoosegow all night long. We could have us a wild old time tonight, even if you only liked women a little bit. You think maybe it would help if I tickled you? Here, like this?"

Her hands, behaving with a knowing lack of decorum, contradicted her air of innocence.

"Oh ho ho ho," Elgar said. "Oh hee hee hee. Oh, ha ha, Fanny. Stop."

Fanny continued to look at him with the same grave expression, though a glint of mischief appeared somewhere far, far back in her opaque black eyes. "Does that do anything for you, Landlord?"

"No," he said.

"Oh, hell," she sighed, folding her hands in her lap.

"I mean yes," he said hastily. "Yes, of course it does. It damn near drives me crazy, as a matter of fact. But—" he pleaded, taking her hand "—I want to talk to you first, Fanny."

"Oh, Jeeesus. Always talk, talk, talk. Sometimes I wonder if some people ever stop talking to eat, let alone do other things. Old Charlie, he's the same way. Every night a different lecture. African history, Indian history, world history, race history, till my head is ready to split apart. I say to him, 'Charlie, if I wanted an education I wouldn't've quit school. And I sure wouldn't have married you.'"

One question had been nagging Elgar ever since meeting this oddly assorted pair: raving beauty and raving maniac. Now, softly, he asked it. "What did you want when you married him, Fanny?"

"I wanted everything!" she said with a grandiose gesture, spreading her arms wide to embrace the whole world. She pulled all of it in to her lovingly, hugged herself, and added, "I still want everything. I married Charlie because he talked so grand. After he won his revolution, he was gonna take over the whole South. He would have it for his kingdom, and I would be the queen."

She threw her head back, elevating her chin, and extended one arm in a regal gesture that made it clear she was holding an invisible scepter. And imagining, no doubt, a sequinned throne flanked by a court of chorus girls draped in imitation ermine.

Oh, Elgar thought angrily, if only Hollywood could be made accountable for all its crimes. But all he said was, "Do you still think he'll make you a queen, Fanny?"

Fanny said ominously, "I believe *anything* can happen if a person puts his mind to it." Then she shrugged. "Oh, I don't know. Charlie says all revolutions takes a long time. But it's *already* been a long time. Him and his damn promises. And every year it gets postponed, he gets meaner and nastier, like a bitter old bottle of medicine. I was fifteen when I married him. I'm getting pretty old for a queen now. Willie Lee's nine. I must be twenty-four."

Elgar had been right about her idea of a queen: it was someone in the first flush of adolescence, riding on a fancy float, like Miss Wisconsin Cheese or Miss America. He felt the texture of her arm, an interesting combination of soft and firm, and corrected, "Twenty-five, you mean. That's pretty good muscle tone for an old lady."

Fanny glared at him. "I said twenty-*four*. Don't make it worse than it is, Landlord." She did some quick addition on her fingers and looked up at him triumphantly. "Yes, twenty-four, like I said. We got married on my fifteenth birthday, and Willie Lee was born right after the wedding."

Elgar felt a gaudy blush warm his cheeks. "Sorry. I didn't mean to get so personal."

Fanny leaped to her feet, blazing with incensed middle-class pride. "What's so damn personal about it? I don't have nothing to be ashamed of. My children are both legitimate." Her eyes narrowing with anger, her voice climbing rapidly to fishwife range, she screamed, "I can show you both the birth certificates if you don't believe me!"

Points of pride in this part of the world were apparently the same as those in the part Elgar came from, yet slightly different, too. Everything was just a little bit skewed, so that getting acquainted was like walking into a familiar house and suddenly discovering slanting floors. Elgar was more than ever convinced of his precarious footing and the need to proceed with caution over perilous abysses.

"Fanny, dear. Please calm down. I believe you. And it doesn't matter if I don't. Oh, God. All I mean is, they're fine, fine boys. You ought to be proud."

To his relief, she smiled. Proving that maternal pride, at least, was universal. That and parental willingness to talk about progeny at the slightest sign of encouragement.

"Willie Lee takes after his father," she said. "Always out looking for some action, kicking balls and batting them and throwing them around. I said to Charlie once, 'I'm sure glad Willie Lee's gone in for athletics. If he weren't an athlete, that boy might grow up and kill somebody, the way he loves to bang things.' But the little one, he's different. Dreamy. I guess he takes after me."

So far, Elgar's glimpses of the older boy had consisted mainly of the dust he raised on his way out of the house to play baseball—but he, too, had a feeling that no one need waste time worrying about Willie Lee's future. With a slight difference in emphasis, he might indeed be headed for the electric chair, but at the rate he was going, Willie Lee was more likely to wind up pulling down a couple hundred grand a year as a major-league outfielder. The small, soft, younger one, however, so precariously sensitive, so frightened of the dark, did give Elgar cause for concern. And more: he reflected, like a small mirror with nervous tremors rippling its dark surface, a picture of himself at the same age.

"Fanny," he asked suddenly, "what happened Monday night?"

"Monday night?" she echoed, bewildered. Apparently harsh events did not scar Fanny's memory any more than they touched her flawless skin.

"Yes, Monday night. I was here late, and I found Walter Gee in the hall upstairs, scared to death. He said Charlie had tried to kill you."

"Oh, *that* night." Fanny's upper lip curled in scorn. "We just had the usual old monkeyshines around here, Landlord. I wasn't scared or nothin'. Old Charlie has to grow a few more inches before he can scare *me*. He was tryin' to teach me some more of his damn dumb history. All about how the Egyptians was black kings, and so forth, and went out and conquered white kings, and so on, and blah blah blah. And I said, 'Listen, man, if I wanted history lessons, I wouldn't be here, I'd be back in school.' And he said if I was going to stay low-class and ignorant, he'd have to leave me, on account of his big future. He said he couldn't have any uneducated woman dragging him down when he became a big-shot race leader.

"I said, 'Well, I hope you dream about your big future in bed tonight, and I hope it keeps you good and warm. Me, I'm spending the night with a girl friend.' And I did, too. But Copee, he didn't believe me. He thought I had a date with a man. That was when he grabbed the gun. And I grabbed Willie Lee, 'cause he was still up, and I high-tailed it right out of here. I thought Walter Gee was sleeping through it all."

"No, he was awake, and he heard you, and he was frightened. He got up crying and screaming. I had to put him back to bed."

Fanny smiled to herself, an enchanting Mona Lisa effect. "That's my baby. Don't know why that baby loves me so. He's always hangin' around the house. Always under my feet, everyplace I go. Five times a day I say to him, 'Shoo, run away, go play.' Then I turn around and look, and there he is right up under my nose again. Beggin' for a hug and a squeeze and a story."

"Do you give them to him?" Elgar asked, as urgently as if it were his own child whose happiness was at stake.

"Sure I do, Landlord. I just about spoil him rotten, I guess. I figure *I* have to spoil him double, 'cause his father ain't got too much use for him. Charlie, he says he wants his sons to be warriors. But Walter Gee, he ain't studyin' about no war. All he wants is talk. Like you. And fairy stories and lovin'. And that goddamn green Wop ice cream."

Fanny grimaced at an unpleasant memory. "You know, Landlord, after that first day you was here, Walter Gee threw up all night long. I got so sick of carrying mops and pails, I didn't know what to do. Every time I'd clean it up, he'd go 'whoopsee,' and there it would be for me to clean up again.

"I got so tired, I was thinkin', 'Just let that Landlord show his face around here again. I bet I'll make him scrub some baby vomit. Believe me. I'll teach him to give money to little babies to get sick on.'"

Seeing his tragic face, she burst into hysterical laughter. "Don't look so sad, Landlord. I wouldn't make you scrub. Not really. You're too grand."

It was not a word that Elgar had ever expected to hear applied to himself. "Oh, Fanny, you're kidding me. Me grand?"

"Yes, you," she said. Her face held that adoration only Oriental women were supposed to feel for men. But then, it was a kind of Oriental face. "You're grand, Landlord. Like a king. Walking around all straight-backed and stiff-legged and smiling nice and kind. Talking to yourself about important things. With eyes that crinkle up and change color any way you want them to. And hair like a real gold crown. You're pretty, Landlord. You're almost pretty as me."

From Fanny, with her innocence that could not comprehend dishonest flattery, that was probably the highest compliment. She was such a child, he could not help wanting to treat her gently and with patience. Whoa boy, he told himself. Take it slow. But it was difficult to disentangle himself from those adoring eyes, those soft arms snaking around his neck, those restlessly exploring fingers that were taking possession of his royal person.

"No, Fanny sweetheart. Stop that. Oh, ho. Oh, hee hee hee. Fanny, listen. Postponement of satisfaction only heightens eventual bliss. I promise you that eventually. Certainly. But at the moment I am sodden with drink, and besides, I am a Puritan. Which means, I want to get to know you first, Fanny."

"Really?" asked Fanny.

"Truly," Elgar said. "I have a code, a strange one, I admit, but a code nevertheless, to which I cling. Violation of the body unthinkable without prior knowledge of the person."

"Oh, Landlord," Fanny said, kissing the top of his poor scarred head, favored target of tomahawks and spears, "you're sweet."

Then she bounded obediently from the couch. "O.K. Here I am. What do you want to know?"

He paused to consider. "Well. One thing I was wondering. Are you part Indian too, like your husband?"

"Yes. Just like him." When she giggled, Fanny's amazing chameleon features resembled a Siamese girl-doll's. "I mean, he don't know no more about his background than I do about mine. We're both all mixed up, probably. Isn't everybody?"

"Sure," Elgar agreed.

"Well, for all I know his people came from Timbuktu, and so did mine. But as far as I know, we're both colored." She laughed, recalling a recent episode painful to Elgar. "He really can strut some with a tomahawk though, can't he? I mean he comes on with that stuff like a real Indian. Well, maybe he is an Indian. Who knows? He say he gonna ride the plains and reclaim the lost Indian lands. He say he's the last of the angry vanishing Americans."

"Thank God for that," Elgar murmured fervently.

"The rest of the time," Fanny said, unconscious of implicit contradictions, "he say he an unrecognized African prince, ruler of a mighty tribe. And being a king, naturally, he's too great to take a job."

"And you with four mouths to feed. You have problems, Fanny."

Back turned, she stretched voluptuously until the ends of her hair touched the sweet high curve of her hips. "Oh, I don't worry. What for?"

"Thank God for that too," he said. Fanny, he suddenly realized, was what he had been wanting all along. A simple female, not perverse and touchy like Lanie, not complicated like Rita and Sally. Just a basic primeval She. Most girls in his experience were temptingly round and smooth on the surface, but full of intricate labyrinths and pitfalls within. Fanny, now, was a delightful relief: simplicity itself. Refreshing and reassuring. In spite of minor external complications such as one belligerent husband and two bright-eyed, curious sons.

The primeval She's dainty fingers reached around to the back and scratched a basic itch. She yawned and said, "I always figure somebody or other will come along sooner or later to help pay for the rent and the groceries."

Much later it would occur to him that, instead of happily planning a future without complications, he should have paused to listen to this small point in the conversation. But instead he said innocently, "Well, at least you have a job now, Fanny. You haven't told me how you like it, though."

"Oh, I quit that no-good, lousy job yesterday. They had a nerve. Wanting me to do dead bodies."

"Do *what* to dead bodies?" he asked in horror.

"Do their hair, of course," Fanny explained. "Style it for their layouts. I said to the lady who ran the beauty shop, 'Listen, I don't do no shampooing or tinting. I'm a stylist.' And she said she understood. She said, 'Yes, that's what we're hiring you to be. A stylist.' And the money was good, so I took the job. But I forgot to make sure I would by styling *live* women's hair."

"Well, I suppose that might make a difference," Elgar said.

Fanny shuddered. "You damn right, Landlord. Nobody wants to work with dead heads. That lady had three funeral parlors in town giving her all their business, and none of her girls wanted to do the work, and she didn't want to do it herself, but the money was too good to give up, four times as much as for live heads, so she hired me.

"—Well, I tried, Landlord. Really I tried. I went down in the cellar of that funeral home, and I saw this old woman laid out stiff there on a table, and I had my doubts, but I said to her, 'Look, if you'll be good and behave yourself, maybe we can get along.' Well, she didn't say nothin'.

But just about then, a little piece of paper started rattlin' on another of them tables, way across the room.

"I put down the curling irons and I said, 'Listen, lady, if you want me to style your hair for you, you better stop that right now.' But she didn't stop it. That paper went right on rattlin'. So I said to her, 'O.K., you had your chance. But you messed up, so goodbye.' And I high-tailed it right out of there."

Elgar's laughter ruined the effect of the solemn speech he had been planning. "But, Fanny, after all, it is a living. There are worse jobs. And with no other money coming in. Surely you don't want to go on relief."

"Why not?" She had a way of leaving him at a loss for answers with the striking simplicity of hers. "There can't be nothin' worse than doin' dead bodies for a living."

"Well, maybe not," he admitted. "But why not work in a regular beauty shop, Fanny, one that caters to more, uh, lively patrons?"

"Oh, I can't stand those places either, Landlord. They mostly bad as any undertaker's, all musty and dirty and gloomy. And they always want you to sweep and clean and scrub and do things like that, not just style hair. I always tell them, 'I don't like doing them things for my own children. I sure ain't gonna do 'em for you.'

"Besides," Fanny added with a show of temperament, "I'm an artist. I need inspiration for my work. I can't work in some grim old place where the paint's all peelin' off the walls and the rickety old three-legged chairs are all fallin' down and the windows ain't been washed in twenty years. I said to the woman who owned one of them places, 'You call this a beauty shop? It looks more like an Ugly Shop to me.'

"I hate them places," she added with feeling. "Anybody can see they've got no idea what beauty is. Now, if I had my own shop, I'd do it up right, Landlord."

Looking around the apartment, he had to admit that Fanny did have an urge to cleanliness and a flair, however exotic, for design. With black enamel and red lampshades and a few tin gongs and paper scrolls, she had transformed the place into a kind of Chinese temple. The kind that might be located in Beverly Hills.

Fanny's eyes, focused intently on an inward picture, looked right at Elgar without seeing him. "First of all, I wouldn't call it a beauty shop.

I'd call it a Beauty Saloon. And when I got through with it, it would look like a saloon. Believe me."

Elgar succeeded in hiding his delighted chuckle up his sleeve as she went on, "I'd have the walls hung with real oil paintings, and I'd have wall-to-wall carpets, and fountains, and sunken marble pools. And steam rooms, and massage rooms, and a forty-foot dressing table with a mirror framed with light bulbs, just like a movie star's. And all my chairs would be upholstered in fur. I wouldn't wear no tacky old uniforms, neither. I'd be the lady in charge, the *stylist*. I'd wear custom-made lounging pajamas, all different colors. Silk. It would cost a woman ten dollars just to have me *look* at her." Fanny's eyes began to see Elgar again. "And if she was real ugly, it would cost her fifteen. I can't stand to look at ugly things. Copee, for instance. He gets uglier every day. But you, Landlord, you're a *pretty* man."

Gently bringing her back to reality, or so he thought, he said, "I understand your high principles. Believe me I do, Fanny. But meanwhile you have to eat. With your husband out of work so much, don't you think you could compromise a little? Insist on working in a clean place, you have a right to that. But couldn't you put off the sunken marble tubs for a while?"

"Oh no," she explained with a bright, serene smile. "I don't have to. I've got other ways to make money. One thing I can do, I can always sue somebody."

Elgar's mouth was open, but no sound emerged.

Fanny went on in her sweet childlike prattle, "One time, years ago, I found out I was allergic to hair dye, Landlord. I got all blonded up, came home, and broke out in hives and a fever. So I sued the beauty shop and collected five hundred dollars. Now, every time I need money, I just go right out and get my hair tinted again."

Elgar finally found his voice. "For God's sake, Fanny. How many times do you think you can get away with a thing like that?"

"How many Ugly Shops do you think there are in this city?" she answered with calm rhetoric. Adding, with feeling, "I tell you, I hate them places. And that's not all I can do for a living. I can always fall down."

"*Fall down?*"

Fanny demonstrated, collapsing suddenly in a pathetic heap, so convincing he sprang to her aid. She sat up, unhurt and smiling.

"Like that. In a big department store or in front of a big old office building, any place where they got lots of insurance. Then I say there was ice on the sidewalk or oil on the floor. I have this slick little lawyer who always wins. He always tells me to show my legs, and then he says, 'Look at my poor client, her life is ruined. Look at this poor shattered woman. Look, look, look at her, gentlemen.' "

"Shattered how?" he wondered, struck by her buoyant health.

"Oh, all over, but mainly in my back. I always complains of low back pain. That's the best kind of pain there is, 'cause you can never prove a person don't have it. And there's all kinds of back doctors, nature practice men and such, who don't mind witnessing in court. They get up on the stand, and they say—"

"I know," Elgar interrupted. "Look at this poor shattered woman. Look at her legs and think of her back. Better yet, think of her *on* her back. —Fanny, what does your husband think of all this?"

"Oh, he likes it fine," she answered innocently. "He says it's a good way to get back at the exploiters. He says they been owin' it to us for three hundred years, anyway, so he's all for it. 'Specially when the checks come in. One time I got fifty dollars a week for fifty-two weeks. That was my most successful fall."

"Quite an achievement," Elgar said softly. "You frighten me, Fanny. I'm scared you might decide to sue *me* sometime. Though of course I know you wouldn't. Ha ha."

"Well, actually," she admitted, "I been thinking about it, Landlord. Unless you plan to put some storm windows in here this winter. The draft in this place gets mighty chilly sometimes on my low back."

"What the hell is this?" he roared. "What's going on? Ever since you people had that goddamned tenants' meeting, everybody's dropping hints about weatherstripping and storm windows. It's a conspiracy!"

"Now, now," Fanny soothed, "don't get excited, Landlord."

But that, as the sarong began to slip once more from its moorings, was precisely what was happening. It took quite some doing to warm Elgar's blood from the temperature to which it had been chilled by Fanny's description of her cute little hobby. ("Mr. Copee, what is your wife's occupation?" "Litigation, your honor. She's a professional.") But then, Fanny was quite some little bonfire.

As she ambled toward him with tantalizing slowness, she had a sudden thought, and did an abrupt about-face. "Wait! I forgot. I wanted to ask you something."

He groaned with frustration. A moment later Fanny emerged from the closet, bearing a six-foot length of elderly white-fox fur. Giving it one twirl around her neck, she minced across the floor toward him with the other end swinging pertly at her ankles.

"Is this the right way to drag a fur?"

It was a great opener for a comedy act, but Fanny's expression was dead serious. "What do you mean, 'drag a fur?'" he asked.

"*Drag* it. Like the rich ladies do. I hear tell they drag their furs on the ground all the time." She frowned and looked down at the foxtail tickling her ankles. "I guess I should let it trail more. But this white stuff gets so dirty. It's not practical like mink is."

"Oh, Fanny. Oh, funny, funny Fanny. Oh, you impossible child. Come here."

"Why are you laughing?" She ran to him, dropped to her knees before the couch, and looked up at him urgently, the long black lashes moist and trembling. "Don't laugh at me, Landlord. I'm serious. I want you to teach me how to be grand."

"How to be grand?" he asked.

"Yes, 'cause you know all about it. About how the society people do at dinner parties, and all. About opening night at the opera, and what you wear. How to curl up your fingers when you drink a social tea. All that stuff. *You* know. How to be grand."

"How to be grand," he repeated. "Well." Not the subject on which he was the world's foremost authority. It was a problem.

Then he had an inspiration, remembering the sack of Basic Supplies he had brought to the party. He had not realized that his tenants would provide a well-stocked bar which, occasional explosions of laughter from upstairs reminded him, was still holding out. Reaching for his coat, he felt around in its inside pockets and found the Basic Supplies still there.

"How To Be Grand. Lesson One. Get two glasses, two olives, and some ice."

Padding swiftly and silently on bare feet, foxtails whirling about her brown thighs, Fanny obeyed.

"Lesson Two. Watch me as I put ice in this vase. Pretending it's a Swedish crystal cocktail shaker, of course. Lesson Three. Pour gin over ice. Lesson Four. Add this much vermouth. Pay attention, this is very important. Only this much vermouth, and no more. One drop too much and you lose all your grandeur instantly. Quickest way I know to go straight from upper to lower class."

He handed her a spoon. "Now stir, Fanny. Gently, gently. Good. Now put an olive in each glass. Excellent. Now pour. Quickly, before the ice begins to melt. Superb. And now we drink. Ho. To grandeur."

Fanny, scrutinizing the contents of her glass with some disappointment, said, "It don't look like nothin', Landlord."

"It's called a Martini. I assure you, it's the only thing grand people ever drink."

"Oh, shuh. I don't believe you, Landlord. This tasteses nasty."

"I swear to you on my honor," Elgar said, hand on his heart. "These days, all the grand people drink nothing but Martinis. And these days, most of the grand people do nothing but drink. So you see, if you're going to be grand, you'll have to learn to like them."

Screwing up her face bravely, Fanny emptied her glass. "Ugh. In that case, Landlord, pour me another one out of that little old cocktail vase."

Two minutes later, she said, "That one didn't taste so bad. And it feels good after. Now I know why grand people are happy, Landlord. I feel happy now. Am I grand, Landlord?"

"Absolutely. That is one of the first symptoms of grandeur," Elgar pronounced. "Congratulations. But don't let it go to your head. Look out, Fanny. Don't drag me down on top of you until I've set my glass down. Fanny dear, if you are going to keep assuming such intimate positions, your knees gripping my waist, et cetera, don't you think you ought to learn to call me 'Elgar?' "

"Elgar. What a funny name. Where'd you ever get such a funny old crazy name, Landlord?"

"From my funny old crazy mother. She's mad as a hatter. You saw her tonight, you know how batty she is. With her own special form of madness. She's completely tone-deaf, all of us are, but she thinks she's the world's greatest appreciator of music. You think *my* name's peculiar, you should meet my brothers. Mozart and Schubert."

"Ha ha ha," Fanny squealed as she toppled him backward on the couch. "That's silly, Landlord. I don't believe you."

"It's not at all silly, Fanny. My namesake was quite famous in his day. Mothaw was disappointed because he turned out to be a minor composer. My brothers are named for major composers. I am merely a major disappointment. For many reasons. Fanny, stop that. Stop tickling me there. Ohhahaha. How can I talk to you if you keep kissing me? Umpfff? Umpfff. I told Mothaw she should be grateful for small favors, such as having only male children. Imagine a girl named Scriabin, how neurotic *she* would be. Oh, Fanny, you're taking off all your clothes again. And *my* clothes, too. Oh, but you're beautiful. Lovely little Fanny."

"Don't you fret, Landlord. You and me, we're gonna make our own sweet music tonight. Hold me tight, Landlord."

"Yes, Fanny. I know my name's silly, but do you think you could learn to call me 'Elgar' anyway, instead of 'Landlord'? What an interesting little mole here, under your left blossom. Oh, Fanny darling, don't do that. I mean, don't stop doing that. Oh, I don't care what you call me, Fanny. Call me anything, but continue. Please."

"You're grand, Landlord. Just look at that. So big and beautiful. Pointing right at me. Grand."

"Your hands, Fanny. Your mouth. Your hands. Your warm, sweet, moving everything. Oh, Fanny, I think I love you."

"I love you too, Landlord. Really I do. Grandly."

8

" "Well, Borden, I've found the solution," Elgar announced. "If you can't beat 'em, join 'em. Yep. That's what I've done."

Elgar moved jauntily around Borden's consulting room, whistling, his new blue cashmere muffler, a cool twenty dollars, cash, and no markdown, either, proclaiming his new happiness like a banner at his throat. He felt much too alive to sit down, let alone lie down on the couch. Instead he did a tentative step of the latest dance Fanny was teaching him, the pachanga. She had tried to teach him dozens of dances with nutty names: the slop, the frug, the hully-gully, the mashed potatoes, the merengue, the lemon merengue—but the way Elgar performed them, they all ended up looking like a lopsided, skipping two-step. What the hell, there was a new dance invented every week, and no civilized adult could be expected to keep up with them all. Fanny, thank God, was something else. He skipped and limped contentedly. Skip, limp, shake the hips. Skip, limp—

Until he noticed that Borden, behind the desk, was giving him the old skeptical fish-eyed stare. —Whoa there, boy, he told himself. Borden always said his stares were empty of meaning, and that when Elgar started assigning negative values to them, it meant subconscious trouble was afoot. As usual. Elgar sighed and went over to the couch.

But he still felt exuberant and sure of himself. "Borden, you see before you a new man. All because of a dream I had one night."

Borden shifted his posture, made his lanky frame perpendicular to the desk, alert and attentive. He was crazy about dreams. Elgar, being generous, tried to give him at least three a week.

"I dreamed I went away on a vacation to the Caribbean, Borden. For three months I lay on the beach and soaked up sun. When I came back, I was black as the ace of spades."

"Interesting," Borden said.

"You're damn right," Elgar said, "and I haven't even gotten to the most interesting part. This dream has a capper, Borden, a climax worthy of O. Henry. Listen. When I came back, all the other white people were as dark as I was. And that's not all, Borden."

"*Very* interesting," said Borden, scribbling furiously on his note pad. "Continue, please."

"Now get this. I asked them how come, and they said, 'They gave us our choice.'"

Elgar rolled on the couch, chortling, clapping his hands and his feet to applaud the cleverness of his own subconscious. "Now isn't that great, Borden? Isn't that just the greatest little old punch line you ever heard?"

"Splendid, Elgar. One of your best literary efforts. But I am surprised that you are able to appreciate its humor. Considering your earlier mood of disenchantment with darker-skinned people, based on their negative reactions toward you in the tenant-landlord relationship."

"Oh, but that's all changed, Borden," Elgar said. "Ever since the rent party they threw for me. That, and the dream I had the night after. It startled me so much I woke up, and while I was lying there, I got to thinking." He tapped his forehead. "Sometimes the power of this little old organ up here really astonishes me, Borden. I said to myself, 'Skin, what is it? Just an extra suit of underwear. And who in hell's business is it what color underwear I wear?' And then I said, 'Why can't I change my skin the same way I change my T-shirt?'"

He tapped his forehead again. "The mind is a powerful little old organ, Borden, it can make you into anything you want to be. I said to myself, 'Maybe I was born with a white appearance by accident. Maybe, judging by how much I feel at home with these people, I'm really deep dark brown inside.' And the minute I had that thought, Borden, I felt that way. It was such a strong feeling, it scared me. I even *tasted* myself. I was dark and sweet, like maple syrup. *My* flavor, Borden. *Me!*

"'—Ho,' I said to myself, 'Elgar, at last you know who you are. You have found your identity at last, Elgar. You are a Negro!'—And ever since then, Borden, I say to myself every morning, 'Elgar, think black.' And it works, Borden! Yeehoo!"

"Elgar," Borden said, "I follow you. Believe me, I do. I follow every word, right up until the point where you say, 'It works.' And there I am stopped by the evidence of my own eyes. Even to these admittedly myopic lenses, Elgar, your appearance continues to be strikingly Caucasian. Blond and fair. I might even use that unfortunate word, 'Nordic,' to describe you."

Elgar was not to be daunted today. "Appearance, what's that, Borden? Merely a trick of refracted light. Blink, and it disappears."

He snapped his fingers, then pressed his hand successively to his forehead and his heart. "What counts is what you think in here, Borden. And what you feel in *here.*"

"I see. At the feeling level, this transformation has been a success."

"Not merely a success, Borden. A triumph. And after all, why not? Nobody wants to be what he started out to be. The grass is always greener, and its growth is annoying under your feet, et cetera, et cetera. Maxims from the earliest dawn of civilization, Borden, not merely applicable to modern times. My tenants, I have observed, do not wish to be Negro Americans. They wish to be Creoles, Indians, and Africans. They are bored with the designations they were born with, so they change them at will. Why shouldn't I?"

"But the designation 'white' carries with it the privileges of superior caste, Elgar," Borden said softly. "In trading it for a lower caste, and giving up those privileges, are you not taking another step in your long pursuit of unhappiness?"

"All I can say to that, Borden, is: look at me. Do I look like an unhappy man?—No," Elgar answered his own question. "Of course not. I am a bouncing, bubbling symbol of joy! How can you say I haven't found the right answer this time, Borden?"

Borden said, "I don't think there is any one right answer, Elgar. I simply question, as I do with every patient, whether every change is synonymous with progress. Your outburst against your parents at the rent party was, as we know, real progress for you. It represented real movement, growth, liberation. But I question—" he raised a finger "—but I do not criticize, you understand, I merely question—whether your current outlook is a step in the same direction. I am not sure. Perhaps I haven't heard enough about it yet."

"Well, what have you got those great big hairy ears for? Pull the plugs out of them and listen for a change, Borden."

And Borden did, attentively, while Elgar described the past four months with Fanny. Heavenly hours in the Chinese-modern living room, with the plaster Buddha lamp casting his benign glow of blessing on the happy couple. Whose passions blazed hotly enough to make a brilliant light all their own. Fanny's amazing inventiveness, in love as in dancing, releasing all of Elgar's chilly Nordic inhibitions.

"Now you on top. Now me. Now everybody every which way. Tickle my whosis with your whatsit. How about there, Landlord? Are you ticklish there too?"

"Oh, Fanny, you dirty, dirty girl."

"Well then, I'll race you into the shower, Landlord."

His one disappointment was that she had never learned to call him "Elgar." To make up for it, he had all sorts of names for her. Including Kittycat, Taffybabe, Honeypot, Sugartit, Angelcakes, Babyface, Purrypuss, and Loveypie.

—All this playful intimacy made spectacularly easy, during the first month, by Copee's serving a term of thirty days for inciting to riot, disturbing the peace, and attacking the Established Order. ("I knew somebody like you had to come along soon, or I would've died, Landlord. That little dried-up Copee hates so much, he's got no energy left for loving any more.")

Then came another salutary diminution in Elgar's estimate of his father's powers. He had expected the authorities to build Copee a private reservation under the county jail, but at the end of the thirty days he was released. From then on, Fanny's inventiveness and Elgar's legitimate reasons for being on the premises had served them well.

Elgar might be unstopping a toilet on the second floor, or applying a coat of paint to the porch trim, or adjusting a valve in the basement water heater. He never knew when a team of golden dragons would appear, cavorting on glowing fields of ruby satin and brown skin. Fanny, winking at him and beckoning.

"Now?"

"Now."

Thus did the spice of anticipation flavor the routine of otherwise humdrum days. Thus they continued to steal their love at odd moments—sometimes *very* odd moments, as for instance the day when a team of three roofers, tramping heavily up and down on the sidewalk, finally wearied of waiting for someone to admit them, placed their ladder, began to ascend, and were treated to a fascinating view through Fanny's window. But thus far they had escaped observation by the wrathful eyes they most wished to avoid. Elgar's scalp was in the best of possible conditions, uncreased by spears or tomahawks, and massaged daily by loving, professional hands.

"It's almost a miracle, Borden," Elgar said. "Almost four months we've been at it now—like wild animals, unbelievable—and still he hasn't caught us, hasn't come anywhere near it. Sometimes I almost suspect him of deliberately staying away."

Borden paused before asking, "Why do you imagine he would want to do that, Elgar?"

Elgar answered innocently, "Well, for one thing, I'm supporting his family. Do you think that could be it, Borden?"

Borden did his best, but could not suppress a small, dry chuckle before answering, "Perhaps."

"May be," Elgar said, and reflected that Copee, chronically unable to hold a job—or, rather, so volatile that no job could hold him—had probably never known such security. In addition to a few odd presents for Fanny, Ming and mink and such, Elgar was the source of free rent, gourmet groceries, and the kindest, most loving treatment his wife had ever provided.

Fanny even reported, wide-eyed, a recent softening in Charlie's attitudes—not sweetness, perhaps, but a reduction in tartness—a willingness to read the evening paper all the way through once without throwing it on the floor and stamping it to shreds, that boded ill for the future of the revolution, but well for Elgar.

"It's wonderful, Borden. Fanny is a wonderful, wonderful girl. By now we're so close, it's fantastic. I can't tell where my body ends and hers begins. Just the other day I got a terrible shock. Fanny's skin is always smooth, and suddenly it seemed to have turned rough and scaly as a dragon's. I didn't know till I opened my eyes that I was kissing my own arm."

"If I may interrupt, Elgar," Borden said, "here we see the reason why you have up to now avoided a deep attachment with one woman. Your identity is so weak, you are always in danger of losing it completely in another's. Your almost frantic round-robin of simultaneous attachments in the past has served a very real need, protection against the fear of losing your identity, which is so easy for you to do. Which you have, in fact, now done. You love a Negro, therefore you *are* a Negro."

"Oh hell, Borden," Elgar said uncomfortably, trying to squirm away from this truth, "it's not just Fanny. It's all of them. Now that I hang around the place all the time, I naturally get hungry. Well, Marge cooks for me. Fantastic meals. Roasts with gravy, hot home-made rolls, mashed potatoes, two other vegetables. And every night before I leave, DuBois and I have a brandy."

"May I ask how much all this service is costing you, Elgar?" Borden inquired softly.

"Less than I pay you, you bastard!" Elgar shot back. "A hell of a lot less. I just don't nag them about the rent any more. It's worth it. I'm happier than I've ever been in my life, Borden. I feel better around these people than I ever did with my family. I'm at home with them. I tell you, I've become a colored man, at least inside."

He added, with a happy chuckle, "And I've got a chemist working on something for the outside, too. Not this phony fast-tan stuff, something permanent. He thinks he'll have the formula in a few more weeks."

"So then you will complete the transformation," Borden said. His voice was dangerously calm. "Elgar, I congratulate you. What better way could you find to destroy your father, with his narrow prejudices and rigid standards?"

"Lay off me, Borden!" Elgar screamed. "I warn you, this time you're going too far. I've found a good life for myself, and I mean to keep it. What the hell? Fine meals, good friends, and a loving woman who doesn't offer any strings or complications. You ask me to turn my back on this, Borden? What the hell. I've found Paradise!"

"Then all I can do is congratulate you again, and ask, Elgar, 'Are you ready for Paradise?'"

"Who cares?" Elgar crowed, kicking his feet in the air. "Ready or not, here I come. Whoopee!"

"You see, Elgar," Borden said with a disturbingly benign smile, "I do not wish to be a wet blanket. The arrangement you describe has many features of happiness. But it is my business to be suspicious. It is what you pay me to be, after all. And I cannot help suspecting this new mood of exuberance and its tendency to extremes. It reminds me too much of the behavior of a mother bird who tries to distract the hunter from her nest. A performance, Elgar, a flashy and nervous performance, in a very high key. Suggesting the possibility of future lows."

"You gloomy bastard," Elgar said in a surly monotone, "now you're trying to say I'm manic-depressive. You know that's not true. I'm obsessive-compulsive. All the best doctors have always said so."

"Actually, Elgar," Borden said mildly, "you have all the classic symptoms of *all* the classic neuroses. That is why I treat you as a highly individual case."

"Oh, you low-down skunk," Elgar moaned, pounding the couch. "Oh, you snake, you worm, you shellfish, I would call you a lower order of animal, but the one you belong to hasn't been named yet. Why do I come here to be made miserable, when outside of here I'm so happy?"

Borden's insinuating voice reached him from a great distance. "Is there, then, no flaw in this rosy picture, Elgar?"

Elgar felt around inside himself, through the syrupy masses of bubbling happiness now congealing around a bitter core of honesty, and managed to bring up the core.

"Well, yes, one flaw, Borden. One. The kids. Fanny's kids."

"Oh, yes. I remember you had formed the beginnings of a paternal attachment for the younger one, Walter."

"Yeah, I used to play with him sometimes, tell him cowboy stories and things. I even bought him a bike and taught him to ride it."

There was pride in Elgar's voice as he added, "That was three months ago. Now you should see that kid go. His feet barely reach the pedals, but he's the fastest cowboy on the block!"

His elation subsided as he continued, "But now he runs away when he sees me coming. And his older brother's the same way. 'Course Willie Lee's always on his way out anyhow, to play baseball or football or something. But he used to let me pitch to him once in a while, and field his flies. —Time was, they both thought I was the greatest thing God ever invented. Now they run away from me as if I were the Great White Leper or something."

"What do you think is the cause of this unexplained change, Elgar?"

"I think," Elgar admitted, "they suspect what's going on. Oh, they haven't seen us or anything, we've been extra careful about that, but still, kids *know* things. Especially wise older kids like Willie Lee, and he probably told his little brother. The dirty-mouthed little monster. He eats up all his father's crazy Indian and African lore, and he probably said they should make a pact to have a tribal vendetta when they grow up. Sacrifice my blood to the ancestors, probably. Feed my bones to the buffalo."

"And how do you feel about the boys' turning against you?" Borden inquired.

Elgar shrugged. "I guess it's natural. I know they've never had it so good—warm clothes, good meals, new toys and everything—but that doesn't make them love me."

"Did it make you love your parents?" Borden interjected.

"No," Elgar said. "After all, I'm humping their mother pretty regularly. I guess resentment is a natural juvenile reaction."

After a pause he added, "It makes me sad, though, when I think about the train I have for Walter Gee for Christmas. Best goddamn train you ever saw, reverses and chugs and whistles and even steams. I wish he'd at least let me show him what it can do."

"Well," Borden said, "one thing every adult must learn is that every pleasure must be paid for with some pain. Every gain followed by a loss, Elgar."

"Why?" Elgar screamed childishly. "Why, Borden? Why?"

Borden, sitting limply at the limits of his knowledge and skill, simply shrugged. Limply.

And said, "See you the same time tomorrow, Elgar."

"Like hell," Elgar said. "Tomorrow is Christmas, you bastard. See you the same time day *after* tomorrow."

9

"An integrated milkshake, please, Lanie," Elgar requested as soon as he made contact with his favorite stool at the D-R.

"Black and white shake!" quick-witted Lanie translated instantly, and turned to look at him with narrowed, suspicious eyes. "Why are you so happy, Elgar? You got the Christmas spirit or something?"

"Is there a law against it around here?"

Elgar noted, after a brief survey, that the management of the D-R had taken the smallest possible notice of the approaching holiday. A single funereal wreath of laurel was the only seasonal touch relieving the glacial atmosphere. Stately and puzzling, it hung on the wall behind the counter, between *Sizzling Cheese Steak 50* and *Double Dipt Malted 45*.

"There's a law against it around *me*," Lanie said. "I hate, loathe, and despise Christmas. It's a time when single people have to take cover or get out of town. The only ones who enjoy it are people with families."

"Then why don't you get yourself a family?"

"Oh, they threw me out long ago."

"I don't mean the family you were born with, Lanie. I mean get a new family, one that suits you. Like I've done."

"And where do you find ready-made families lying around, just waiting to adopt you, Elgar?"

"Oh, all over. Usually in houses. It helps if you own the houses they live in."

"I was afraid of that," Lanie said, and sighed. "Elgar, how much money did your tenants turn over to you after the rent party?"

"Oh, a lot. Fifty bucks, give or take a dollar or two."

"A lot, huh? And how much back rent do they owe you now?"

"What's the difference?" Elgar screamed. "Six, seven hundred dollars, what difference does it make? I don't need it. I'm filthy rich anyway. The main thing is, I've found some people who love me."

Lanie's voice was richly cynical. "Oh, sure. Everybody loves the goose that lays the golden eggs. But they also hate the goose, because it can lay golden eggs and they can't, and they have to go on taking its eggs, and feeling guilty because it's such a nice goose. It's very, very complicated, this sort of thing."

After a loud sucking-up of the bottom inch of his milkshake, Elgar said, "You're too smart to be a waitress. Too pretty, too. Marry me, Lanie."

"Oh, that's *far* too complicated," she replied.

Elgar did not feel the usual relief; for once, he had not wanted to be turned down. "I love you, Lanie. What could be simpler than that?"

"Nothing could be less simple," she said. "You've got to love yourself first. And what do you do all day? You need an occupation if you want a wife."

"I don't have to do anything," he reminded her. "I can still afford to take you away from all this."

"Maybe I don't want to leave all this," she said in a dangerously flat voice.

"Never mind about that. Listen, Lanie, I don't care about skin colors any more. I don't believe anyone else really does, either. Oh, when life is rough, people look around for a scapegoat, and the most obvious one is the handiest, but when life is good, I don't think anybody has time to hate anybody else. You know what else I believe, Lanie? In the near future, we will change our skins as easily as we now change clothes. Today a red skin—" he snapped his fingers "—tomorrow, a blue one. It will all be done with pills."

With moist eyes Lanie reached out to correct something off-balance in his appearance. "Oh, Elgar, you fool, why don't you straighten your tie? Here, let me do it. There."

He pulled away from her ministrations. "Well, I don't care if you turn me down. I have some other people to love me now."

"That's what I mean when I call you an idiot, Elgar. Stop wanting love so much. What good is it, anyway, if you have to buy it? And what do you do with yourself all day long while you're basking in all this high-priced love? Unstop their drains, scrub their woodwork, carry out their ashes?"

"The expression is 'haul their ashes,' I believe," Elgar said with a twinkle. "Sure I do those things. I'm their landlord."

"Like hell you are. You're their big, fat patsy. Their Great White Father. Their Santa Claus."

Elgar was suddenly painfully conscious of the suitcase at his feet and of its contents, the red and white costume in which he planned to appear tonight before Fanny's kids. Also the rucksack beside it, full of toy trains and sugar plums and such. He could still hear Fanny saying excitedly, "This will be their first white Christmas, Landlord. I mean, their first with a white Santa Claus."

And it was going to be their best Christmas, too, he had made sure of that. Inside the sack were a professional bat and ball and a stupendous Erector set to end all Erector sets for Willie Lee. And for Walter Gee there was the wondrous train, a wooden bird that climbed a pole and sang, "Cuckoo, cuckoo," a tin acrobat that did back-flips and somersaults in perpetual motion, and the last set of wooden blocks in town, the result of combing a dozen stores, because Elgar hated plastic. All this plus giant, old-fashioned candy canes, and chocolate coins with beautiful gold wrappers, and popcorn balls wrapped in colored cellophane, and long, lovely licorice braids, the kind that made good toy whips.

Running from store to store, stuffing his sack like a madman, Elgar had contrasted his plans for Fanny's boys with his own bleak Christmases past. Mothaw would wrap Moe's and Shu's hand-me-down shirts and sweaters for him in fancy papers, and in another package would be the set of antique lead soldiers Elgar received every year and was allowed to play with only on Christmas Day, after which they were locked up in a closet for another three hundred and sixty-four days.

Elgar had hated those annual Christmas-present soldiers. Their chipped paint, their scarred faces, their broken bayonets had depressed him. He had felt cheated of a time which for all children, even the poorest, was an orgy of tearing up gaudy wrapping papers and stuffing yourself with junk to the point of glorious sickness. Moe and Shu had, of course, taken their practical presents and their lectures like "little men." But because Elgar was not a little man but a child, a child who knew they were not poor, but rich, he traced a large part of his current rage to those early Christmases.

He planned to make up for them all tonight, to roll on the floor with the boys and the trains and the toys, to stuff himself silly on dates and nuts and popcorn and raisins and eggnog. Basking all the while in Fanny's benign, permissive smiles. He much preferred her enthusiasm to Lanie's grim discouragement. He suddenly felt relief that this sour-tempered, sharp-eyed Amazon had refused to share his future. She would certainly spoil all his fun. And fun, for the first time in his life, was what Elgar was having.

To avoid looking Lanie in the eye, he studied her tightly secured cap, like a white paper bird with fluted wings, stabbed through the heart with two monstrous stilettoes. —When you live in a delightful soap bubble, he thought, beware of Greeks and Creeks wearing hatpins, and jolted himself right out of there.

Elgar's Yule ebullience took a sudden drop, never to rise again, when Fanny's husband answered the door. For over three months Copee had been a convenient Absence rather than a threatening Presence, and so the very sight of him was quite a shock, even though his dark-blue business suit, white collar, and calm tie were less menacing than some of his former costumes. His attitudes, however, were unchanged.

"Take those things right back where you got them from," he ordered Elgar on sight. "I don't need your charity. I have a job. I can support my family."

Elgar inquired, mildly, what sort of job. Thinking: javelin thrower? labor agitator? bar-room bouncer? ethnic dancer? human cannonball?

"I don't see why it concerns you, but I am professor of history at Dr. DuBois' college."

Elgar leaned hard against the wall to steady the house, which was beginning to tilt severely. "How can you be? That college of DuBois' is a big fake, and he's a big phony himself. He told me so."

"Not true," Copee said. "The college is real. The charter is real, and so are the degrees. The capital improvements program has been delayed, that's all. Meanwhile, classes are held at various churches throughout the city."

"Well, what do you teach them? The history of hate? Three hundred years of reasons for being angry?"

"It is enough, for now, that I teach them *some*thing" Copee declared. "Education will make all things possible. As we rise out of ignorance, we will confound our exploiters."

He gestured toward his well-filled bookcases. "I never finished high school, but I am an educated man. There is an answer to everything in those books of mine."

"Well, answer me this," Elgar requested. "Is it fun being angry all the time? Why not try being pleasant for a change?"

Copee's eyes, deepened by suffering, were like burnt-out holes in his face as he replied, "You have no right to expect me to be pleasant, mister. After three hundred years of using us to make your fortunes and keep your lives running smoothly and pleasantly, you should not expect us to love you. The best there can be between us is respect."

Elgar looked at this tense, intense little man and wondered, briefly, whether he might turn out after all to be the kind of leader who would guide his people to a new Promised Land. And also wondered, observing Copee's glazed-over eyes, whether he had become more or less sane.

He certainly seemed sure of himself as he continued, "I teach the truth. The simple truth, and nothing more. It is not my fault if you don't like to hear it."

"Which truth?" Elgar wanted to know. "The one about riding the plains and reclaiming the lost Indian lands? Or the one about reserving the entire South for a new kingdom, with you the king? I don't call those truths. I call them myths, dangerous myths, and I don't like them. Also, I don't like the way you treated my parents at the party. I know they're pretty terrible people in many ways, but they weren't doing anybody any harm that night."

"They were harming *you,* and, to a lesser extent, me as well. I am a more honest man than you. I do not show hospitality and kindness to my enemy. I have the honesty and the courage to throw him out of my house."

Five feet four inches of pure menace, Copee moved closer to Elgar. "You have no right to criticize me, no right to tell me not to go to extremes. You could go on any beach and become blacker than I am, but still you would not understand why my entire life has been a choked-back scream. Why, now that I've found an audience, I can't stop screaming until I've won every battle. Why, it is all I can do—" he extended trembling, twisting hands "—why it takes every ounce of my artificial Western civilization to avoid strangling you with these hands."

Elgar recognized rage when he saw it, and also recognized Copee's right to be angry. Nevertheless he had a right to an opinion too, and he expressed it.

"I don't think skin color should be that important. As you said, it's just an adaptation to the sun. I don't see why more people don't understand that. And I do know how you feel. I've felt that way many times myself."

"No," Copee said, "you have never come anywhere near feeling like this. Just remember this—when you get up in the morning, you merely put on your clothes. When a colored man gets up in the morning, he puts on his armor."

"Look at you—the finest flower of Western civilization," Copee went on, pacing around Elgar in a small half-circle. "Spoiled, babied, and pampered all your life. Which makes you soft in the body, slow in the reflexes, and lazy in the head. While I am hard as a rock and fast as an antelope. I hope I never have to fight you. Because if that became necessary, I would probably kill you."

"Why should you want to fight me?" Elgar asked innocently.

Copee leaned close to Elgar's ear and said in an intense whisper, "I don't want to. But I will if you don't keep your goddamned white hands off my wife!"

Then, proving that he meant what he said about wishing to avoid conflict, Copee stalked out of the house.

The moment her husband was gone, Fanny popped out of the closet in a pink cotton pinafore, clutching her white-fox stole as if it were a live, warm, comforting pet.

"Is he gone now?" she asked.

Elgar nodded.

"Well, that's a relief. What a tight call. Whoee, Landlord. You're lucky you didn't come around a couple hours ago. You'd of got chopped up into hamburger. We'd of had meat loaf for the next six Saturdays."

"What happened, Fanny?"

"Oh," Fanny said calmly, "I just told Copee I was pregnant again. Right after he came home and told me about his job, I told him *my* news. He said somebody else must be the father, because he's only been with me a couple times in the last two months. He figured it was you, on account of the way you're always hangin' around."

Fanny batted her eyes and shrugged. "I told him I had nothin' to do with you hangin' around the place, that you was the Landlord and had a right to be here any time you wanted."

"So what did he say then?"

"He said he wasn't gonna bring up no white man's bastard so it could grow up and exploit *him*. He said if the baby turned out light-skinned he'd have to leave, 'cause if he stayed he'd kill me and it both. And maybe you too, Landlord. He said he wanted to leave me right now, but he'd wait till it was born, to give me a chance to prove him wrong."

"Oh, Fanny," Elgar blubbered, "I never meant to get you in trouble." He tried to embrace her, but got white-fox hairs up his nose instead and sneezed violently.

"Gazoon tight," Fanny said. "Don't worry, Landlord. I ain't in no trouble. I already fixed his ass. I mean I fixed it *good*. I called my little old lawyer, and he said any child I'm carrying is legally Charlie's. And whatnot, and furthermore, and whereas, I can slap him with desertion papers and non-support orders, and garnishee his salary, and attach his car and everything else he owns. And after that I can sue for divorce and collect alimony. I could have his ass tied up so tight in lawsuits, he wouldn't be able to sit down for twenty years. I told him so. Copee, he decided to stay a happily married man. At least for a while."

"Lord help me if I ever cross you, Fanny," Elgar said fervently.

"Oh, my lawyer told me what to do about *you*, too," Fanny said with an inscrutable little smile.

They sat in tense silence, Fanny on the sofa with crossed legs, swinging one gilded slipper, and Elgar cowering in the corner, until finally he burst out with, "Don't you think it's his, Fanny? After all, you told me you and he were getting along better lately. It must be his. Don't you think so?"

Elgar had many fears, and his fear of getting a woman with child was one of the strongest. It was not a deterrent to action, of course; merely a cause for regret and worry afterward. But until now he had fathered no unblessed events, and the cumulative effect of a lack of consequences had served to make him ever freer and bolder over the years. He reflected ironically that amoral Fanny's main effect on him would probably be to make him more conventionally moral in future.

Fanny's only answer was an indirect one. As casually as if she were announcing plans to go shopping, she said, "Well, I think I'll go downtown and fall down tonight. A *pregnant* fall really ought to pay off."

The horror started deep inside Elgar, as if his navel had just been plugged into an electrical current. It spread in rapid tingling circles until his fingers shook and the hair rose up on his head. A pregnant fall—with, just possibly, *his* child inside her.

Taking out his checkbook, Elgar said, "How much would it pay off, Fanny? Tell me. I'll pay you *not* to fall."

Mischief brightened Fanny's eyes. "Well, you write the check, and we'll see, Landlord."

Wondering how he could possibly have ever loved with this creature with an adding machine instead of a heart, Elgar wrote out a check for five hundred dollars.

She took it from him and smiled. "O.K. That'll do for this month, Landlord. Seeing's how you went out and bought all those nice toys and things for the kids. Go on, drop them under the tree now. Copee won't know the difference. He'll think I bought 'em myself."

Halfway to the door, Elgar paused and growled, "What do you mean, 'that'll do for this month?'"

"Well, this won't last me forever," Fanny replied serenely. "Sooner or later I'll need some more money. And there's only two ways I can get it—from you, or from falling down."

He groaned, because he had never been in a worse bind, and went out to get his S. Claus sack of goodies and gumdrops. When he returned, Fanny had lit the Christmas tree lights. Oh, festive. Oh, merry. Oh, jolly. Oh, joyous Noel. Oh, hell.

Worst of all, he realized that his misery was all his own fault. He had overlooked the one glaring flaw in his glowing Christmas plans. His little adopted family already had a father.

"Only sad thing is, Willie Lee and Walter Gee won't get a personal visit from Santa Claus, because you can't hang around here much longer, Landlord. But I guess a person can't have everything."

"Keep trying. At the rate you're going, you'll make it yet, Fanny."

Staring at the pretty winking stars on the tree, Fanny said, "I have funny thoughts sometimes when I look at colored lights for a long time. You ever have funny thoughts, Landlord?"

"Yes," he said, "but I can't think of a single funny thing right now."

"Well, I can. Funny thoughts like, 'I wonder do Miss Marge's roots and herbs and powders really work?' " She dipped into the treasure trove of her brassiere and produced a wizened yellow tuber.

"Miss Marge gave me this the first day you came here, Landlord. She said it was a real powerful root, would attract love and money and success, all in one. Only one trouble with it, she said. When I got all those good things, I'd have to pay for 'em with bad things."

Elgar, unpleasantly reminded of his latest discussion with Borden, uttered a noncommittal "Ummm."

Fanny continued to chatter. "I can't have you any more. That's one good thing I've lost, Landlord. I'm going to have this baby, and not know whose it is till I see it, and that's another bad thing. But I got this check you gave me, and that's a good thing. I expect Miss Marge knows what she's doing when she whomps up these lucky charms."

"Give it to me a minute," Elgar said so softly she obeyed him without question.

Elgar knelt, placed the root on the floor, stood up, and jumped on it repeatedly, shouting in rhythm with his jumps, "I don't believe in magic, I don't believe in magic, all you people are crazy, sick superstitious crazy, I'm the only sane person around here, and I hope the roof caves in on all of you."

When the root was completely crushed into fine powder, he stopped.

Fanny said with wide eyes, "Oh, you shouldn't have done that, Landlord. Anyone who smashes a lucky root turns bad luck on himself. And you jumped on it seven times. That's seven months of bad luck you got coming, Landlord."

10

"Where I come from, voodoo is no joke, Mr. Enders," DuBois said as he handed Elgar a large snifter of brandy. "In New Orleans, it's still a very serious business. And I myself have seen too many strange things happen to ever laugh about it."

"You mean to say you believe in roots and powders and all that magic stuff?"

By way of answer, DuBois got up and went over to his tweed jacket, which was neatly draped over the back of a small, black, female-shaped chair upholstered in raspberry velvet. The entire apartment looked like a stage-set for a Victorian play—flocked wallpaper, velvet curtains, gilt mirrors and sconces. Like a set-up waiting for a photographer to shoot it and slam it into the center spread of a decorating magazine.

But DuBois was at home in it. He fumbled in the pockets of the jacket, withdrew a little leather envelope, held it up and said, "Do you know what this contains? A dried toadstool, a hair of a tomcat, a hair of a dog, one of my own hairs, and one of Miss Perkins'. All liberally sprinkled with a powder of ground roots and dried herbs. Now you or I could combine those ingredients and get no special results. But when Miss Perkins does it, they bring good luck—because she has great Powers."

He shrugged and tucked the pouch into his pants pocket. "You ask if I believe in magic. Well, let's just say I always try to keep this somewhere on my person, if possible."

"Actually I dropped in to ask you about something else, DuBois. What's this story Copee's been giving me about going to work for you?"

"It's true," DuBois said. "He is the new head of our History Department. He has no degree, of course, but his knowledge and his scholarship are amazing. Besides, we can always grant him a degree or two if necessary."

"But that college of yours is a fake!" Elgar cried. "You told me so yourself."

"It is no more of a fake than I am. No more, and no less," DuBois said mysteriously.

Then he explained. "I ran out of churches to collect offerings from. I'd been to all of them at least once, and to some three and four times. I decided that if I was going to keep this racket going a few more years, I'd have to start having some *real* classes, or nobody would believe me. So—so far we have art, music, English, history, and business courses. Naturally I'm holding the classes in the churches. That way, the congregations will be more sympathetic when we start collecting for our Building Fund."

"And when you get your Building Fund together, will you build a building?"

DuBois shrugged. "I don't know." He seemed to be considering the question for the first time. Then, charmingly, he grinned. "Probably I will. When I get older, running a real college will probably be a lot easier than promoting a phony one."

"I suppose colleges have been founded for screwier reasons," Elgar said. "But offhand, I can't think of a single example. Congratulations, DuBois."

"I don't feel like someone who should be congratulated," DuBois said. "It scares me, the thought of going legit. In a few years I'll probably have a big paunch, and smoke fat cigars, and vote Republican. I may even have ulcers, and have to go on a special milk diet. Instead of staying lean and agile and sharp-eyed, the way an outlaw has to be."

"How does a person become an outlaw, DuBois?" Elgar inquired mildly. The way he might ask for a recipe for apple pie.

"One is born to the calling," DuBois answered. "Many are called, but few choose. You see, society decides which of its segments are going to be outside its borders. Society says, 'These are the legitimate channels to my rewards. They are closed to you forever.' So then the outlawed segments must seek rewards through illegitimate channels. In other words, once my Great White Father declared me illegitimate, I had to be a bastard."

"Is Uncle Sam your Great White Father?"

"Exactly. The white society is my father and, in a figurative sense, every Negro's father. Our mother being Africa." DuBois chuckled.

"In my case the paternity is not only figurative but real, a generation or two removed."

"And if your Great White Father were to acknowledge you after all these years, kill the fatted calf, welcome you home, and say, 'This is my beige-skinned son, who was lost and is found again,' what then?" Elgar asked.

"Why, then I suppose I'd have to take my legitimate place in his family. Get a job, pay taxes, carry out my trash once a week like any other citizen. What a bore." DuBois sighed. "In a sense that is what has begun to happen anyway, through my contacts with you."

"Me?" Elgar exclaimed. "Oh no, DuBois. Don't hang it on me. I'm in no condition to be anybody's father." The notion of fatherhood had far too many alarming associations at present.

"You were born to that condition, by virtue of being rich and white and powerful. The natural-born representative of society's power to confer and revoke rewards. And you have seduced me toward legitimacy by virtue of being decent. Although," DuBois added reflectively, "also somewhat of a fool."

"Why do you call me a fool?" Elgar asked, hurt and bewildered.

"Because there's no reason for you to be decent!" DuBois shrieked, turning a suddenly distorted face toward him. "A landlord is supposed to be brutal, stingy, insulting, and arrogant. Like the police, like the magistrates, like all the authority-figures of white society. That's what we're used to. That's what we understand. We're accustomed to our enemies, we know how to deal with them. A landlord who tries to be a friend only confuses us."

DuBois got up and moved restlessly around the room. "I must confess, in my talks with you, I have been led to be somewhat ashamed of my conniving and scheming activities. Activities which I once considered my natural birthright, my only channels to success. Now, by your efforts to be a decent landlord, your willingness to see me as a fellow human, you have made me uncomfortable with conniving and scheming."

"Well, gee, DuBois," Elgar said. "I had no idea I was having any effect on anybody. Gee, that's good to hear. Thanks a lot."

"I am not complimenting you," his tall, dapper tenant said with a crooked, painful smile. "I only wish it were otherwise."

"Me too," Elgar said after a pause for thought. "Now I won't be able to buy a degree from you, and that hurts. On the legit side of the tracks, where I come from, a degree is an important thing to have."

DuBois grinned. "Well, hurry hurry hurry. We're having a special on degrees this week, while we're still illegitimate. Get your B.A. and your M.A. at the same time. Only forty-nine ninety-five for both. Further discounts if weatherstripping is applied to the prexy's windows before winter gets really bitter."

"Never mind," Elgar told him. "I don't want a phony degree to impress phonies. I left that part of the legit world a long time ago. I don't care what my mother and her friends think of me. All I care about is what I think. And how I feel." What he felt at the moment was a touch of rage, so he added, "And you'll goddamn well wait till I'm good and ready to put weatherstripping on the windows. You don't need it anyway, with those curtains."

While DuBois chuckled, applauding this burst of meanness, Elgar walked over to the bay window at one end of DuBois' large rectangular room and touched the heavy maroon velvet hangings. "Amazing the way you don't hear any traffic sounds through these things, even though you face the street," he said. "You can't even tell whether it's day or night in here."

He seized a tasseled gold cord and pulled. The curtains swished back slowly, and he perceived the location—Poplar Street; the time of day—twilight; and the traffic conditions—peculiar. Cars only had one lane in which to travel in either direction, because a van was backed up to Elgar's house, and two men were struggling to load something onto it, something white and heavy which he recognized as—it couldn't be, but it was—a stove.

"Someone's moving out, DuBois!" he cried. "Without giving me any notice. Who can it be?"

"I imagine it's the Cumbersons," DuBois replied calmly. "Another brandy?"

"Hell, no, man, this is no time to sit back and sip brandy. Look, they're taking my sink, too. And my refrigerator! My God!"

"I think you *had* better have another," DuBois said. "Don't be angry. They're very old, remember. Their heads are even fuzzier on the inside than on the outside. They've lived here for so long they probably think the kitchen fixtures belong to them. —In a way they're right, you know. Think of all the rent they've paid out over the years. It ought to have brought them *something* solid to hold onto in their old age."

"There's only one flaw in that beautiful argument, DuBois," Elgar said. "None of that money was paid to me."

"None?" DuBois echoed with a startled movement.

"None," Elgar lied, because some deep cunning instinct told him to.

For the first time, DuBois seemed to falter. "You mean you never got the money orders they sent you?"

Elgar pounced on this. "How do you know what they sent me? And how did you know they were moving out today?"

"I'll answer your questions in order," DuBois said.

"First, you must realize that the Cumbersons have never left the nineteenth century. They have no idea of what's been going on for the past sixty-odd years. Mr. Cumberson, for instance, has never understood why he gets a pension check every week. He thinks there's been some awful mistake, that he's been taking money that isn't his, and that any day now the government officials will be around to drag him and his wife away if they can't pay it all back. Which, of course, they can't. So he and Mrs. Cumberson have been in hiding all these years up there on the third floor."

"Good Lord," Elgar said, moved to pity at the fate of all ignorant people, tunneling through the world like moles, missing all the bright lights and candy canes and carousel rides. Perhaps there was logic in Copee's one-sided craziness; perhaps education was the only important thing. Perhaps.

"Yes, they're in hiding up there, so every week I cash their check for them and divide it into so much for rent and so much for them to live on. Plus a small commission for myself."

"DuBois," Elgar said sincerely, "you are the lowest form of rodent life I have ever seen. Much lower than a common sewer rat."

"Do you think so? I don't," DuBois said as he lit a cigarette in a long jade holder. "First of all, I only take five dollars of each check myself. Which I justify by saying that it will go toward the education of future generations. For the Cumbersons, there is no future. Only a vague, cloudy past.

"—Now to answer your second question, as to why they may be moving. There was a government-inspector sort of person on the premises yesterday. He wanted to look at all of the apartments, including the Cumbersons'. I told him to come back after the holidays. He agreed, and left, but they heard and saw him. They were probably frightened. Probably thought he was coming for them."

"Good Lord," Elgar said again, sympathizing out of the depths of his own irrational fears. He looked down at the street again, just in time to see Mr. Cumberson help his frail wife up onto the running board and into the cab of the van, shut the door behind her, and climb aboard the back to ride with their furniture, all with old-fashioned gallantry and grace.

"Damn it," Elgar said, "damn it, DuBois, I shouldn't have dawdled so long with you. I should've gone down there and stopped them while I had a chance."

He wasn't sure whether he was thinking of reclaiming his appliances or of reclaiming the Cumbersons for the future. But it was too late for either. The moving van had turned the corner, taking the oldest fixtures in the house along with it.

"No," DuBois said. "It's too late. Better let them go."

"What will happen to them now, DuBois?"

"Oh, they'll find another apartment, or they'll go to the old folks' home. Either way they'll let me know their new address, so I can go on cashing checks for them. Otherwise they'd have to trust somebody else. Somebody who would probably be more unscrupulous than I am."

"I don't know why I should care," Elgar said. "I should worry more about what's going to happen to me. If I go on running this madhouse I'll end up in a real one. But—DuBois, go out there and chase that van. Take a cab; I'll pay for it. Find out where they're going. Don't say anything about the kitchen fixtures. Just look after them. I can't now. I have to see that dragon you elected president of your benevolent and protective association. I want to hear what *she* has to say about this."

Running out of DuBois' apartment into the hall, he bumped into the person he sought. Literally, unavoidably bumped into her, because they were on a collision course, and Marge's width was the same as the corridor's.

After they had both stopped seeing red and blue pinwheels, Elgar said, "All right, Madam President, *I* have a gripe this time. Some of my tenants have just moved out without giving notice. And they've taken all my kitchen fixtures with them. Now, in your capacity as duly elected president of the Corner Poplar Street Tenants' Association, what have you got to say? More important, what are you going to *do?*"

Marge shrugged helplessly, then said, "Maybe first you might go upstairs and see if it's really happened."

"Oh no," he said, remembering her fear of the seldom-seen nonagenarians. "Not just me. *We.* We're going up there together. Right now."

This time Elgar provided the motive power—a firm grip on her right hand, caught behind her back in a hammerlock—to propel a reluctant Marge up a flight of stairs.

"Remind me never to trust sweet old ladies again," he said as they stared at the wreck of the Cumbersons' kitchen, with linoleum curling up around the edges of hideous blackened squares where sink, stove, and refrigerator had sat for twenty-five years.

"—In fact," he continued as he inspected the rest of the apartment and found that nothing had been left behind except dust bunnies which stirred at his every step, "—in fact, remind me never to trust *any* of my tenants again."

"But," he continued as he tossed approximately nine hundred wire coat-hangers out of a closet, "being a landlord means trusting people with your property. That's what it means. So if I can't trust my tenants, and I can't be around all the time to keep an eye on them, there's only one thing left for me to do. Throw you all out."

"Isn't that what you were planning on doing anyway, Landlord?" Marge inquired coldly.

Elgar, continuing his debate with himself, ignored her. He was in the grip of an exciting new idea. "—Unless," he said suddenly. "Unless. Maybe. Yes," and began to prowl about the place with sudden purpose.

"This is the best apartment in the house, Landlord," Marge declared, adding fuel to the flame of his imagination. "Big as Fanny's and Charlie's, but up high, so you don't hear so many street noises."

"—'Course," she went on, "that City Hall inspector who was here yesterday said it needed improvements. He was real mean-looking and serious when he said it, too. I 'spect he was what scared the Cumbersons away."

For the second time in the same day Elgar let this piece of information float past him without grabbing it. He was too deep in other plans.

"If you ripped up that rotten linoleum, what would be under it, I wonder?" he addressed an imaginary companion. He knelt, grabbed a piece, tugged, and found that the kitchen had a fine hardwood floor, marred only by the darkened areas that had been devoted to major appliances. Suppose he did not replace them? It was a good-sized room, it would make an excellent study or den.

Like one inspired, he continued to prowl rapidly. Stripped of its dividing partition, the living-dining arrangement would be a handsome hunk of living room. The bedroom was also of decent, man-sized proportions. He opened another door and discovered more good fortune: there were, at least, a few plumbing fixtures the Cumbersons had neglected to take along.

It only remained to ask himself several questions. Such as: Would he save enough money (cost of new kitchen fitments plus present rent at the Trejour plus incalculable amount of losses his presence on the premises would discourage) to make the move worthwhile? And: Was he ready to get along in the big world out here without having Borden always handy in the same building? The answer to the first question was "Yes"; to the second, "Maybe yes, maybe no."

The ayes carried. When the time comes, Elgar told himself, you make yourself ready, ready or not.

"Marge," he announced, "I don't want any more tenants."

"Well, you ain't gonna put *me* out. I've been here fourteen years. This is my home, and I've got rights."

Her indignant stance amused Elgar. "Squatters' rights?" he asked.

"No," she corrected him, "civil rights. I knew there was gonna be some discrimination around here after that City Hall man came snooping around. I never heard of such nerve!"

The conversation was again venturing dangerously close to deep waters full of sharp reefs and treacherous shoals. Elgar was aghast at how often these issues came up, coloring everyone's attitudes. Maybe that was what being "colored" really meant.

"What's a city inspector got to do with discrimination?" he wanted to know.

"Well, that's all these government people want to do! Put colored people out on the streets, so they can build high-priced houses for white people. And after I been livin' here for fourteen years!"

"You can stop worrying, Marge," he reassured her. "I won't let anybody put you out."

Her voice was ragged with scorn. "*You!* Why, you're behind it all! I knew it the first time I laid eyes on you. I told Fanny, and I told the other tenants, 'That sneaky little Landlord plans to put us all out so he can live here someday himself.' Now you know that's the truth, and you can't deny it. Can you?"

He couldn't. So instead he said, "Listen, Marge, I didn't say anything about putting you out. I said I didn't want any *more* tenants. I didn't say anything about getting rid of the ones I have."

"You mean you're gonna leave this apartment unrented?"

"No. I'm going to fix it up and live here myself."

Marge was indignant. As if DuBois were right, and dealing with a landlord who insisted on being friendly was a problem beyond her powers. "You're gonna move right in here with us?"

"Why not?"

Like a giant infant, Marge sucked on her index finger while she puzzled that one out. Finally she was forced to admit, "Well, I don't know why not. It might be a good idea."

"Sure it's a good idea," Elgar said. "For a new tenant, I'd have to put in a whole new kitchen. For myself, I won't need a kitchen, because you'll go on fixing my meals for me."

"Well, I don't know," she said. "How much are you gonna pay me, Landlord?"

Elgar had been busily planning where the flight of back stairs should be built from Marge's kitchen to his. With this preoccupation, it took several seconds for her remark to reach him.

When it did, he shrieked. "Pay you? *Pay* you? Why, you monstrous old cow, you owe me six months' back rent. Work that off first, and then we'll talk about payment."

"I don't work for nothin'," Marge said firmly. "Why should I? First, I got to put up with your bad language and name-callin'. Second, I got to close my eyes to your disgraceful carryings-on, if you know what I mean. Third—"

"That's enough!" he shouted. "Yes, I know exactly what you mean. You mean to blackmail me. All right. Twenty-five a week."

"Twenty-five?" she repeated incredulously. "For a *live-in* job?"

"But Marge," he exploded, "you live here already!"

"No matter. It's a live-in job. At your beck and call night and day."

"Thirty," he said, though he knew he was a victim of blackmail and black arts combined. "And forget about the back rent."

"I already forgot about it," Marge said. "What about the *front* rent? What about that?"

"Forget about that too," he mumbled.

"Well," she said, "all right. I'll keep house for you. If I don't have to cook."

"Well, of course you have to cook! Why do you think I'm hiring you—for your gorgeous, breathtaking looks? Haven't you *been* cooking for me all along?"

"That was different," Marge explained calmly. "That was for pleasure. This is a *job*."

"Ooh," he said, feeling the old gorge rising and the temperature shooting up to the boiling point. "Ooh, Marge, if I pay you thirty-five, I promise you, you will earn every penny of it. I will reduce you to a shadow, I promise you. When I am through with you, your rear end will resemble a pair of grapes, and the rest of you will have the silhouette of an ebony toothpick.

"The first night I move in, there will be a seven-course banquet for twelve. —No, make that nine courses. From soup and fish to nuts. The next day, I will have a cocktail party for about forty guests. All types of mixed drinks, and a lavish buffet. —And following that, a series of elegant little intimate dinners.

"—What is more," he said, following her around the room, his fiendish imagination working double time, "what is more, I plan to expand my wardrobe, from twelve suits to forty-five. I am going to purchase a hundred shirts, too, and they must all be ironed and starched at all times. —As for this apartment, if I find so much as a speck of dirt in it anywhere, you will swab it with water-color brushes.

"In addition," he said with devilish glee, "I plan to tie a string to your left tit, and run it through the ceiling, and keep the other end at my bedside. When I want you, I will tug the string, and if you do not come promptly, I will give it a twist. Like this!"

Marge took two nimble steps backward to get out of his reach.

"Oh," Elgar gasped, "oh, you'll be sorry you ever tried to haggle with me, you old garbage scow. You'll regret organizing the tenants against me, too. Because now I'll be right here to keep an eye on all of you."

Marge said coldly, "You don't know who you're talking to, mister. What you plan on paying me by the week, I used to get by the hour. So let's have one thing understood right now. I won't stand for anything less than complete respect."

"Yes, ma'am," Elgar responded automatically, as he would to any large dignified lady-presence.

She was satisfied. "Fine. I assume my salary starts right now."

"How can it?" he exclaimed. "There's nothing for you to do yet."

"That's not my fault, is it?" Marge executed a mammoth mock curtsey. "Will that be all now, Landlord?"

"Aah!" he raged, left standing amid the rubble of the bombed-out disaster area that was to be his home. "Of course it's all. Get out of here!"

11

Reading from left to right, the row of bells in the vestibule now said:

1–*Copee*
2–*M. Perkins*
3–*P. Eldridge DuBois*
4–LANDLORD

The blue and turquoise rug was down in the living room of Apartment 4; the turquoise and Nile-green chairs added notes of color that made a beautiful chord with the long blue sofa; and the elegant walnut bookshelves had been built into the former kitchen, together with the stairway for Marge to use in bringing up Elgar's meals. Everything was ready, including his title on the mailbox, a friendly little gesture which Elgar appreciated even though it would probably throw the mailman into a nervous breakdown.

All of his tenants greeted Elgar politely, morning and afternoon, and were most gracious about making their complaints and requests. If the number and frequency of these seemed to have increased, and if the politeness seemed a bit frozen, perhaps these were simply the unforeseen consequences of moving onto the premises. Elgar told himself he had no reason to be uneasy. Still, he was.

During the months it had taken to renovate his apartment, Elgar had tried to ignore the negative possibilities of his new situation. Instead he had concentrated on the joys of selecting a shade of paint for the walls (a happy Heaven-blue, to anchor his eyes at their best point in the slippery spectrum); ripping up the torn linoleum and sanding the floors beneath; rewiring the apartment to carry air conditioning; and visiting furniture showrooms with swatches and paint samples in hand.

All these, Borden kept assuring him, were healthy, normal activities. Elgar agreed, perhaps a shade too fervently, that he was enjoying them. But in the back of his mind a small kernel of doubt had taken root and begun to grow.

Borden had suggested, "When you're troubled and don't know why, sit down and make a list of all the possible reasons." So, at the end of his first week in his apartment, Elgar tried this.

Things to Worry About turned out to be a fairly lengthy compendium:

"1. Plumbing smallwares and electrical fitments in this house are in a deplorable condition. I note a shabbiness at many metal knees and elbows, and yesterday Marge showed me a real horror in her apartment: a fluorescent light fixture which had sprouted two sockets and one light bulb, like some monstrous, self-reproducing desert cactus. It frightened me. So did the underside view of Fanny's sink, where various leaks had been dammed up with friction tape and newspapers. I am not a master plumber or electrician.

"2. I am no longer in love with Fanny, especially now that her stomach enters a room before her feet do. In all honesty, I cannot imagine what I ever saw in this shrill, demanding, shrewish creature. I feel, however, that this attitude is ungallant of me under the circumstances, so I bend over backwards to be nice to her. But more gallantry on my part simply results in more demands on hers. ('I want wall-to-wall carpets, Landlord. I like to go barefoot at home.') I am not a saint. Nor am I a director of the Chase Manhattan Bank. Not yet, anyway.

"3. I am going out of my mind with suspense over whether Fanny's unborn little stranger will be a little familiar. I am not ready to be a father, particularly of a kid with the problems this one is bound to have. Living with two hundred million white Americans, including me.

"4. No word, since the party, from Mothaw and Fathaw. Though from them, no news is good news, this makes me uneasy. I am not a Favorite Son. I am not even prodigal, though I have spent more money on myself in the past few months than I ever allowed myself to spend in all my past life. If Fathaw knew how much money has gone into this apartment, he would have purple apoplexy, probably fatal. This too makes me anxious, as I want him to die, but do not want to be the cause of his death.

"5. Lanie is never at home when I call. Someone who sounds like Lanie always says that she is out.

"6. Now that I have moved into my house, I feel less at home in it than before. I wonder constantly, 'How do I behave with these people? What is my role?' It is all terribly confused. I thought my living here would make us one big happy family, but instead we have regrouped into new formations, with everybody but me knowing where the lines are drawn. Are we friends or enemies? Am I proprietor or servant? And what is the nature of the gulf that has opened up between me and my tenants? Is it a moat filled with ravenous alligators, or a mere mirage? If the former, how can I build a bridge across it? I am not an engineer."

Elgar rolled over on his back on the bed (custom-cut foam rubber, $399.95) and tried to see a solution to his problems on the ceiling. It was blank. But the room was full of distracting noises; the neighborhood was a factor Elgar had overlooked in planning his little penthouse snuggery. His tender pink ears were assaulted each night by the lurch and screech of the nightly auto accident and the scufflings and swearings of dedicated violence, sounds he had never thought could come from the throats of humankind. The night at the corner of Poplar and Jackson was darker than anywhere else.

In the daytime the sounds were equally wild, consisting mainly of the screams of mothers calling home their doomed, damned children, and in addition there were the odors: of grease, of smoke, of heavy cooking, and of unnameable things, things he dared not speculate on, that ought to be buried or burned. It was a hot, heavy July, the year since he had first seen the house nearing completion, the term nearly at the full for some horrendous beast to be born in these streets. And Fanny looking as if she bore a watermelon around her equator.

Elgar groaned and twisted on his expensive bed, picturing Fanny, pear-shaped and sullen, giving him contemptuous backward glances as she waddled away with her monthly blackmail money. And her husband, once so comfortingly absent, suddenly turning up everywhere, in the halls, in the vestibule, even in the cellar, and impaling Elgar with piercing looks. Looks that said: "Watch out. Your days are numbered. Today I appear before you unarmed, but do not be deceived. In my apartment I am honing the edges of my best tomahawk to razor-sharpness. Against the natal day, which will also be your fatal day."

Even DuBois, that model of civility, seemed to have deserted him. When Elgar knocked on the door behind which he had once shared so many brandies, so much camaraderie, he heard supercilious giggles followed by ominous silence. DuBois had once called him a fool. Were he and his friends laughing in there, amid the cozy glow of all that Victorian-bordello decor, at the fate of the poor foolish landlord? Probably, Elgar told himself glumly. Also probably toasting his soul with imported cognac to speed it on its journey to Hell.

Snubbed, exploited, and under sentence of death, he lay there feeling very sorry for himself. Very much in danger of blubbering all over his handsome new, blue $79.95 bedspread.

"This has got to stop," Elgar said aloud, and sat up. He did not need Borden to tell him that he was nurturing the seedling of a beautiful paranoia which needed only a slight shower of encouragement to burst into full bloom. There must be a simple explanation of his predicament, a logical reason why someone so well-meaning should suddenly find himself in the middle of so much menace.

Marge, he thought, leaping up suddenly. Marge would give him the answer if anyone could. She was the duly elected representative of the tenants; she would know what was on their minds. And, though she fed him, thrice daily, in a surly silence that made him suspect the food of being poisoned, she had promised Lanie that she would be on his side.

Though Elgar's stomach quivered in protest, he would have to trust the person who had met him with a deadly weapon when he first crossed his threshold.

He ran down his back stairs, rapped on Marge's kitchen door, opened it without waiting for an answer, and found her in a Kaffeeklätsch with his erstwhile love.

"You aren't really my friends, are you?" he half bawled. "You don't really like me living here, do you?"

"Not if you're gonna keep walking into people's private apartments when they're having a private discussion," Marge answered somberly.

Fanny, never shy, chimed in, "Yeah, you act like this here is a jail and you're the warden, Landlord. Everywhere we go, here *you* come. Always snoopin' around. Well, we're not in jail, Landlord, we're free people in a free country."

Elgar had, after all, learned a good bit of elementary psychology from his sessions with Borden and Doctor Ludwig. He immediately began to wonder why they were both so defensive. A quick glance at the table provided some strong clues. Marge had laid out a pattern of strangely designed cards—not a standard deck—in front of a flickering black candle. And propped against the candle was a blue-eyed, blond, plastic boy-doll, stuck with numerous needles and pins.

"When times get desperate," Marge said as she aimed a long bodkin at the cherub's heart, "desperate measures has got to be taken."

She stabbed, and Elgar gasped as a sharp pain clutched at his chest.

"I hate to do it," Marge said, "but what must be, must be."

"But why?" Elgar cried. "What have I done?"

"Don't waste time blabbing with miscellaneous visitors, Miss Marge," Fanny said. "Let's get on with business."

"Right," Marge said. "Stick with me, honey, and we'll get things straightened out fast." She thoughtfully aimed another pin at the doll's viscera.

"Men," she declared, "are not to be trusted. They're skittish as bunny rabbits and baby deer. They're here today and here tomorrow. They come and they go."

"You said a mouthful, Miss Marge," Fanny agreed.

"They come and they go," Marge intoned, "they sail and they light, just like birds flying North and flying South. And a man is just as silly as those damnfool birds. A bird is led by its beak, and a man is ruled by the compass needle in his pants. When the needle points North, North is where he flies. When it swings around to South, he turns around and follows. Just like a crazy loon."

"Tell me some more, Miss Marge," Fanny urged. "Read me the rules."

"The rules is this. A man is ruled by his compass needle, and a woman is the magnet. Plunk her down someplace with a baby in her lap, and she'll settle, because she's got a metal magnet inside her that attracts the man, but that magnet is also attracted to the earth. It's a powerful magnet, and it's what holds a woman down. Women has got the power of gravity, plus all the burden of gravity dragging on them."

"Oh, Jesus," Fanny exclaimed with sudden religious fervor. "It's the truth, Jesus, you know it. Talk that talk, Miss Marge."

"We would be better off," Marge said, "if all the men on this earth would just up and *disappear!*"

Then, almost simultaneously—shook! ffft!—she plunged the bodkin home and blew out the candle. Elgar's heart flickered and sank with it. He felt himself all over to make sure he was still there. He continued these reassuring pattings of himself in the dangerous darkness while Marge moved about the room, intoning a chant with lyrics like those of a football cheer or of the rock-and-roll songs he had heard on certain very bad mornings when the clock-radio dial had been set at the wrong place on the drunken night before. Marge's chant went something like:

> *Boola boola baba,*
> *Ya ya ya,*
> *Baba baba boola,*
> *Ya ya ya.*

Then silence, thicker and more threatening than any silence Elgar had ever experienced, worse even than a sleepless night at the Trejour. Silence like a huge, furry animal breathing over him and Fanny as they sat huddled in that close, black little room. Something was moving in that awful stillness, something with rank breath and rakelike claws that planned to punish them for their guilty love. Elgar hugged himself tightly. His squeezing arms reaffirmed the solidity of his body but failed to dispel the notion that there was a monstrous new Presence in the room which intended to strangle him. Beside him he could hear Fanny's birdlike breathing as well as the rhythmic *Tsk! Tsk!* of her chewing gum. But there were no other reassuring sounds.

Then—fffsht!—there was a blaze of light across the room, and a sharp, nostril-searing odor. Marge, lighting a sulphur match and holding it to the stove.

"You *still* ain't had that pilot light fixed, Landlord," she remarked crossly.

Before he could make an excuse she interrupted, "Hush! Never mind. Fanny, honey, hand me that doll baby."

Fanny obliged, then screamed as the effigy was tossed into a giant pot to join God only knew what ingredients. Marge turned from the stove and advanced toward them, monolithic and grim as a carved stone fetish in the blue light of the gas burner.

"Ya ya ya," she intoned. "Fanny, light the candle again."

Fanny inquired amiably, "You got a match, Landlord?"

Elgar's hands were cold as he plunged them deep into his pockets and found a crumpled matchbook with one light left in it. Its message was strangely reassuring:

> *D-R Luncheonette*
> *Open 24 Hours*
> *4 Tasty Snax*

Another, if not a saner, world existed outside of this room, Elgar kept reminding himself while Fanny relit the lopsided black candle and Marge, at the other end of the kitchen table, occupied herself with a knife and a plump young frying chicken. She was struggling to remove the plastic wrapper and the label:

> *Super-Rite Markets*
> *$1.39*

"This chicken," she grumbled, "should be alive. But in this world, we got to do the best we can with what we can get."

In spite of his fright Elgar was moved to appreciate this sturdy practicality. Then Marge plunged her hand into the chicken and drew out heart, liver, and gizzards in a plastic bag.

This was too much, even for her. "Shoot," she muttered in disgust. "I was supposed to *cut the heart out*. Oh, well. What's a woman gonna do? Even the potions come in plastic bottles these days. —Fanny, honey, hold out your hands."

Fanny obediently extended her graceful, childlike hands. As he watched the dainty fingertips which he had once covered with fervent kisses being smeared with chicken blood, Elgar found himself retreating in horror, his teeth clicking uncontrollably and his hair curling upwards from the nape of his neck to the crown of his head.

Fanny's head swiveled in his direction. "Landlord, where do you think you're going? Come back here!"

Marge joined in. "Yeah, we need you. Stick around and help us make the spell work right."

"You used to have plenty of time for me when I didn't have no problems," Fanny accused. "Now I'm all helpless and in trouble on account of you, it's the least you can do to stay awhile and be sociable."

She had pushed Elgar's most sensitive button, the one that operated his guilt mechanism. Feeling like an apprentice embalmer assisting at his own funeral, he approached the table again as, from beneath it, Marge pulled the most repulsive object he had ever seen. A dried, leathery, grinning, seven-foot snake.

"Sit down there and take hold of one end, Landlord," she said.

But Elgar was retreating again. "Get yourself another boy, Marge. I wouldn't touch that thing with a ten-foot pole. I couldn't."

"Sit down!" Marge roared and, under the same compulsion to obey as when he had first entered her kitchen—a room, he now realized, reeking with occult influences against which no mere mortal could stand a chance—he sat.

They made a strange triptych there in the candlelight—Elgar holding the tail of the snake, Marge supporting its head, Fanny, in the middle, with her bloodied fingers clutching its belly—while in the background strange shadows leaped and fell in chiaroscuro patterns on Marge's fancywork walls.

"Now pray, child. Pray *hard*," Marge urged.

Elgar felt a sudden lifting, as if a shell had exploded silently nearby and was raising him out of his chair, at the same time creating a violent concussion in his head. A shudder like an electric shock went through his fingertips. Fanny screamed as, in their hands, the snake moved. Just one small, twitching movement, but Elgar would always swear it had been real.

Then, her chair toppling backward, Fanny fainted. Lay there like a crumpled Pocahontas doll, her long black braids spread on the floor, her dress drawn up immodestly about her crazily placed thighs. In her first honest-to-goodness fall.

Elgar, bending over Fanny, felt for and found the reassuring thuds of her heart.

"Leave her be, Landlord," Marge said sternly, turning on the lights. She retrieved the doll from the pot and restored it to its place of honor on the table.

Elgar straightened and apologized, "I'm sorry I walked in here, Marge."

"I'm sorry you ever showed up around here in the first place," was her grim reply. "My Powers told me you were the evil on my doorstep, that very first day. I should never have doubted my Powers. They're never wrong."

In her hand a pin was poised, aimed at the midsection of the doll. Its features, melted and twisted by the hot water, bore a crude but amazing resemblance to Elgar's.

He spoke very rapidly and sincerely. "Marge, I assure you, you were mistaken. I have never had anything but the best of good intentions. The warmest of good wishes, I assure you, for the welfare and well-being of my tenants."

"Hah!" Marge's laugh was short and cruel. "If that's so, just answer me this, Landlord. When you bought this house, weren't you planning to put us all out in the street, along with the trash and the garbage? Now is that true, or not?" She moved the pin a fraction of an inch closer to the doll.

"Well, yes, it's true in a way," he admitted, remembering his dream of a private world enclosed by three-story glass walls and shimmering green curtains. "But only in a way. Marge, don't do that. Please. I beg you."

But she chose that moment to drive the pin home. As it pierced the effigy's middle, Elgar's stomach contracted violently, bending him double.

"I've changed my mind, though," he croaked as he staggered toward the door. "Can't you people see anything? I've changed."

12

Somehow Elgar managed to drag himself down the stairs, out on the streaming, teeming street, and downtown, to the clammy caresses of the D-R's air conditioning. Leaning pitiably over the counter, because he still could not straighten up, he met Lanie's smirk with a leer.

"Go ahead, be smug," he told her. "It's all right. You have my gracious permission. In fact I will write 'You told me so' a thousand times on this napkin if it will make you more charitable in your affections, Lanie."

Lanie seemed unaffected by this outpouring. Encouraged by her calm presence, he went on, "I am desperately in need of affection, Lanie. You were right. I was wrong. My tenants hate me, one and all. They are hatching sinister plots against me, making *gris-gris* with kitchen grease and household gods, paring the vegetables for a cannibal stew. Planning to destroy me with tintinnabulations of double-boiler lids."

"I told you so," was Lanie's infuriating reply. "Lucy, fix a lemonade for this poor, shattered man."

"Orangeade," he corrected. "But I've been so good to them."

Tides of laughter cascaded from Lanie. "Oh, Elgar, you slay me. That's the funniest, saddest remark I've ever heard." And in the depths of her crinkled eyes there were tears. For him.

"I wish you'd let me in on the joke," he said in hurt bewilderment. "I've never been in more need of a laugh, Lanie."

"Look," she said with the maddening patience of an aunt instructing a five-year-old. "Being good to people doesn't necessarily make them love you. If you overdo it, it can even make them hate you, Elgar."

"All right," he admitted. "Maybe I've been a fool. Maybe I've gone about this landlord business in the clumsiest possible way. But I don't see why it should've earned me so much enmity."

121

"That's not your concern, Elgar," Lanie said brusquely. "Let them love you, hate you, ignore you, what's the difference? All you should want from your tenants is respect. And payment of rent when due. Asking for anything more," she added with a glint of danger in her eyes, "is asking for trouble."

"But I want more," Elgar protested. "I want more out of life than a bunch of entries in a bunch of rent books. I want friendship. I want closeness. I want love, Lanie."

"Elgar," Lanie said, "there's no reason why you can't have these things. You've just been looking for them in all the wrong places. *Honestly,*" she went on with an impatient gesture, "I just don't understand you. Anyone as handsome as you are has no business crawling through the world on his belly, begging for handouts. Elgar, have you any idea of what a beautiful man you are?"

"No," he admitted. "Only sometimes, when I see myself in a mirror. And then only when I'm feeling exceptionally good." He patted his belly gingerly. "I haven't been feeling so good lately."

"Well, then, look," Lanie said. She stepped aside to reveal a mirror. A sexy, blond devil, a cross between Alan Ladd and Apollo, smiled back at him out of clear blue eyes.

"Hello, old buddy," Elgar greeted himself. "You do look pretty sturdy there. Hmmm. I'd give you at least a fifty-fifty chance to survive."

"Your chances will be better than that," Lanie said, "if you'll take my advice, Elgar. Remember what I told you a long time ago. Don't get so emotionally involved with your tenants. Treat them all as what they are. Strictly business relationships."

"It's too late for that, Lanie," Elgar said miserably.

Lanie looked cross. "Is it Fanny? That slinky little fox. I'll bet you're still in love with her."

"Of course not, Lanie," he said sincerely. "I've never loved anyone but you." But he backed away from the counter hastily, lest he not be believed. That was a mean-looking paring knife in Lanie's right hand.

"Don't try to fool me, Elgar," she said. "I know all about your little back-stairs romance. Marge filled me in on all the details. And now there's going to be a sordid little sequel, isn't there?"

She had put down the knife; her laughter was murderous enough. "Honestly, Elgar, you kill me. Big-hearted, liberal, enlightened Landlord.

With nothing but the noblest of motives. And a house full of squalling mulatto brats."

Keep cool, he told himself. Don't show your anger. That way lies loss of control.

Managing a twinkle he inquired, "Lanie, what did you have for dinner last night? You don't eat this awful D-R food, do you?"

"Beef tips in wine and asparagus," she replied, swabbing the counter energetically. "No, of course not, Elgar. Don't change the subject on me."

"I was wondering," he said slyly, "if maybe you'd had fat-back and greens."

Lanie straightened. The angry color spreading on her cheeks made her radiant. "I don't believe I've ever heard of those foods," she said with all the offended purity of a propositioned Miss America contestant.

Elgar chuckled triumphantly. "You're white, Lanie. You know it. Why don't you come clean and admit it to me?"

"Why don't you learn to leave people alone, Elgar?" she countered, wringing the cloth in agitated fashion. "You keep pushing at them, trying to get inside their skins, because you think it's warm and safe and cozy in there. Well, it can't be done, Elgar, whether their skins are the same color as yours or not, so why don't you learn to live in your own skin instead?"

Score one for me, Elgar thought. At least he had gotten past her smugness to an honest reaction. Aloud he said, "Lanie, I know it hasn't occurred to you, but there might be two reasons why I try to get under your skin. One might be to annoy you, just as you think. But the other might be my clumsy way of showing that I like you. Is that so wrong?"

As she was silent except for a neigh of scorn, he switched the subject. "By the way, I just came from visiting your heroine, your idol. The great chanteuse, the one you persuaded to be my friend. You know what she was doing, Lanie? Sticking pins in an effigy of me."

Lanie made no effort to suppress her witch's cackle; more and more, he suspected her of joining Marge secretly at midnight meetings where incantations were spoken over foul vapors.

"I tried to talk to her, Elgar, yes. But there are some barriers between people that can't be overturned overnight, no matter how much persuasion you use."

"Such as?"

"The ones you like to pretend don't exist, Elgar."

He had a flash of inspired memory. "They call us ofays. 'Ofay,' that means 'enemy,' that's what Fanny taught me."

"Apparently you didn't learn your lesson very well," Lanie said, full of bridling sensitivity at the mention of Fanny. "Or else you're a good Christian, Elgar, the kind who believes in loving his enemies. I could never understand people wanting to be martyrs, myself."

"I come down here," Elgar complained, "looking for a little sympathy, a little solace, and all I get is a lot of wisecracks. What gives you the right to be so smug, anyway? Haven't you even made one tiny human mistake in all your life?"

Lanie's eyes clouded over; if he hadn't known her better, he would have thought her about to cry. "One," she admitted. "But that was the only one I was allowed."

Elgar did not pretend to understand. "Well, I don't want to be a martyr," he said gruffly. "I don't want to be anybody's enemy, either, Lanie. I only wanted to be a friendly landlord. And look where it's got me." Deep in bitterness he dismounted from the stool again. "Not a friend in the world."

"You miserable cheapskate," Lanie muttered as he started to walk away. "With all the money you have, you never even leave me a tip."

He whirled, shrieking from the depths of his torment, "What do you people expect me to do, anyway? Kill myself because I was born white, good-looking, and rich?"

"No," Lanie said through closed teeth. "Just don't expect so goddamn much sympathy."

"You're my friend, Lanie," he exclaimed, hurt and shocked. "Or at least you used to be. Do you want me to treat *you* as a strictly business relationship?" He fished a quarter out of his pocket and offered it to her.

"If you did," Lanie said grimly, "you'd owe me a hell of a lot more than that. Keep your lousy two bits, Elgar. I hear Fanny's planning to slap a paternity suit on you. You'll need it by the time she finishes bleeding you for everything you've got."

She was practically screaming at him; the thin surface of her poise had cracked to reveal jealousy blazing from her eyes and steaming from her nostrils. Elgar sighed. Now he knew why Lanie had been avoiding him. It would take a diplomat, an acrobat, a veritable dervish with words to convince her that Fanny had only been a temporary fascination. If a potentially fatal one.

To hell with it, he thought, and left. Feeling indeed like Job, with woman trouble, the oldest trouble of all, in addition to stomach trouble and tenant trouble. —Had one of the early Christian martyrs ever been a landlord, he wondered?

A loud and passionate debate was going on in Marge's apartment as Elgar climbed the stairs. He paused once more on the landing outside her door, but this time something warned him to hesitate before barging in. Instead he flattened himself against the wall and listened.

". . . time, I tell you, for the dispossessed to rise up and inherit the earth! We no longer ask for what is ours. We *take*. And give no quarter." That was Copee, rasping away like a buzz-saw.

"He wants more than a quarter, Charlie," Fanny's voice intervened reasonably; she had evidently made a full recovery from her occult fit. "He wants four hundred and fifty dollars, cash, which is what we owe him in back rent. Plus seventy-five for this month. And a hundred and thirty from *you*, DuBois."

Elgar could hardly believe his luck. He had always wondered what went on at his tenants' meetings. Now it seemed he had stumbled on a secret session of the Corner Poplar Street Tenants' Association, called in response to his recent reopening of the issue of back rents owed him. —Though he doubted, as he continued to listen, whether his mild, half-apologetic tour of the premises could have aroused so much ire.

DuBois, of course, was courtly and controlled. "I have always been willing to fulfill my share of all contractual obligations, providing the other party is willing to fulfill his. But it says in my lease that the lessor will provide sufficient control of climatic conditions to ensure the lessee's reasonable comfort. After a frigid winter spent without the benefits of insulation, I am forced to suffer through a humid summer, because my wiring is of insufficient magnitude to support an air conditioner."

"He's got *four* air conditioners up in his place," Marge observed. "It's so cold I wear a shawl when I go there."

"How does it look up there now?" Fanny wanted to know. "I'll bet he's fixed it up grand."

"Child, it even *smells* like money," Marge assured her. "Everything fresh and new."

"Huh!" Fanny exclaimed. "I asked him a whole year ago, and I still ain't got no new linoleum under my sink. It's all worn away. I'll bet *he's* got wall-to-wall rugs!"

Elgar was thunderstruck. It had never occurred to him that his innocent comforts would generate a spirit of envy and mutiny among his tenants.

"Also," DuBois said, "my bathtub faucet drips constantly, interfering with my slumbers. An irregular dripping, which is exquisite and endless torture. One might accommodate oneself to a *regular* dripping. But lying awake, waiting for the next drop, not knowing when it will fall—"

"*You* don't know what torture is," Fanny interrupted excitedly. "You don't live on the ground floor. Ever since the lock fell off our door last winter, I lie awake nights, thinkin' about all the burglars and prowlers and rapers in the neighborhood—"

"Surely, my dear," said DuBois in acerbic tones, "you don't expect to inspire lust. Not in *your* condition."

"I look better than you!" she shrieked. "You're just jealous of me 'cause Landlord likes me better!"

"Silence, wife," Copee interjected. "You are destroying our unity."

"I tell you," Fanny went on, unperturbed, "I can't sleep nights, for fear of somebody bustin' in here and kidnaping my babies."

"It might be a blessing," sighed DuBois. "To enter the vestibule, just once, without tripping over scooters and velocipedes and other miniature modes of transportation. What a relief."

"You hate children too!" Fanny screamed. "Just like you hate women. Because you know you'll never have any, that's why!"

"Silence!" Copee cried.

"Him and his damn phony college," Fanny muttered. "Lording it over everybody else. Lousy, fancy faggot. Who does he think he is?"

"Are we going to make it true, what they say about us?" Copee pleaded. "That colored people can't stick together? Or are we going to organize against the oppressor, move forward in solidarity, assume the leadership of the world revolution?"

"You and your damn revolution," Fanny said. "I'm sick of you, too, Charlie. Why can't you pay some attention to *little* things for a change? Like getting a lock put on the door to protect your wife and children?"

"Because," Copee said quietly, "the lock should have been put on nine months ago."

"Ohhh!" Fanny wailed. "You're right, Charlie. We all got along better before he came. And now we got nothing but trouble. Either I'm gonna have to sue him for neglect and paternity, or divorce you on grounds of extreme cruelty and aggravation. I don't even know which."

"Woman," Charlie thundered, "you have no decisions to make any more. You are going to be a wife to me for a change, and obey me. And that means joining me in taking a stand against this white invader."

"The trouble is," Marge put in, "he don't act like a white man."

"For God's sake, woman, think like a black woman! Has he pulled a veil over your eyes? All day long you cook for him, serve him, tend him, scrub his slops. He has reduced you to this servile situation, and yet you say he doesn't act like a white man. What else, in God's name, does he act like?"

"I do get tired sometimes," she admitted. "Middle of the night, zing goes the buzzer. 'Marge, cook me up a snack.' So I shuffle downstairs, like a servant is supposed to shuffle, like I seen Hattie McDaniel do it one time in the movies, and I make hamburgers. I take them up to him, and he says, 'Cook them some more, Marge. I like them real dried up.' So off I shuffle again and refry them hamburgers till they taste like cardboard. Me. Famous recording artist. Former star of stage, night clubs and radio. Shuffling around in old house-slippers at three o'clock in the morning."

"So. He subjects you to this humiliation, and yet you say he does not act like a white man."

"No," Marge answered, "he acts more like a child. Like some little child who's scared of the dark. I get the feeling he rings for me at night because he's lonesome. Not hungry, really. Like a child asking his mother for a glass of water because he wants company."

"I have no patience with such sentiments!" shouted Copee. "The misguided tenderness of black women has held us back for centuries. Whole armies of them, weeping over Miss Ann's headaches while their children were starving in the back cabins."

"He don't have headaches," Marge said. "*Stomach* aches are what he has. And I don't have no children, neither."

"If I may be permitted to clarify matters," put in DuBois, "I think Miss Perkins was voicing a complaint."

"That's right!" burst from Marge. "Sometimes I get tired of his foolishness, and I won't do a thing he asks me. I treat him real mean, sometimes, and he don't even notice the difference. This Landlord is a problem. And he's always *there!*—Except sometimes it's like he ain't really there at all."

Elgar shivered at this confirmation of his worst fears.

"Miss Perkins," DuBois said, "has put her sensitive finger on the core of the problem. This Landlord refuses to act like a white man."

"Explain yourself," Copee growled.

"Gladly. We have had neglectful landlords before. The bathtub faucet in my apartment has been dripping for three years. Only recently has it begun to irritate me excessively."

"Get to the point, get to the point!" barked Copee.

"The point, my dear sir, is that it is extremely difficult to deal with *this* Landlord. He refuses to be an abstraction, which would make it easy to hate him. He insists on making his presence known and felt. And he is *ever* present. It is not his policy that disturbs us, but his proximity."

"Your fault for making him want to live here, DuBois!" Copee accused. "You practically *seduced* him, with your wit and your brandy and your clever conversation. Oh, I saw how you left your door open every time he came, so he would hear your music. Very clever. I heard you, giggling up there late at night together. Very cozy. I have known for some time that there was a rotten apple in this house, and it's you!"

"Yeah," Fanny said, "and he's jealous of me 'cause Landlord likes me better."

"Order!" Copee cried, banging on something.

"Insulting me," DuBois said, "will not change the facts. It is difficult to live on an intimate footing with one's enemy, and continue to hate him. Our instincts tell us to feel one way, our experiences another. It is a situation that makes us all uneasy."

"It makes me sick," Copee said, "to see how you are flattered by his friendliness. You are so eager for the crumbs of his favors, you don't see what is going on. He is putting you to sleep only to exploit you all the more. And this latest piece of news proves it!"

What piece of news, Elgar wondered. Moving closer to hear more distinctly, he touched the door with his shoulder. It swung open, and he was exposed to his accusers.

The weight of Fanny's scorn was overwhelming, perhaps because she was now so enormous. "There he is again," she complained. "Can't even have us a meeting in private without him listening at the keyhole. Put him out of here. Out, out, out!"

"No, let him come in," her husband said. "He might as well hear our decision now as later."

He raised his voice to address Elgar as if he were declaiming to a deaf man. "Because of intolerable conditions, we have decided to withhold the rent from you. Our rent strike will begin immediately and will continue until conditions are relieved."

Two things occurred to Elgar: first, that he had been paid no rent in months anyway; and, second, that his tenants had agreed on no such thing.

"What gives you the right to do that?" he asked.

"History," Copee replied. "A long history of oppression and dispossession, which is now repeating itself."

Elgar turned to Marge. "How come he's running things, Marge? I thought you were the president of this outfit."

"Hey, that's right," Marge said, and lumbered to her feet. "Copee, how come you took over this meeting?"

"Don't let him trick you," Charlie said, holding her at bay with a bony finger. "He is trying to divide us. We must not lose our unity."

Simple curiosity gave Elgar the courage to ask, "What's all this history you keep talking about? And what's it got to do with me? You'll have to explain. I never finished college."

The little man's eyes darted angrily around the room, rested for an instant on his wife's bulging belly, then returned to Elgar.

"My grandfather," he explained unnecessarily, "was a Choctaw Indian. He told me how his people were dispossessed from their lands like cattle and herded like sheep onto reservations. How they died like flies in transit. He made me promise that when I grew up, I would revenge this injustice. Ride the plains and reclaim the lost Indian lands."

A complicated bit of zoology. Also a tall order for a small Negro boy. "Wow," Elgar said. "No wonder you're confused."

"And are you any less confused? Do you know, even as well as I do, who you are?"

Whoops. Copee had obviously been making a close study of his landlord's weaknesses.

"Of course not!" he answered himself with ringing scorn. "If you knew where you belonged, you would not have moved in here with us. You lack a sense of your own history. So let me tell you who you are, historically speaking."

Elgar looked at Copee hopefully.

"You are the colonel who massacred my Indian forebears when they refused to be shipped out to the reservation. And you are that other colonel, that Southern one, who raped my great-grandmother and fathered an infant whom he proceeded to enslave. My grandfather on the other side."

Elgar was disappointed. He did not think he was either of these unpleasant characters. It simply did not seem likely, considering his sloppy performance at military school: forever marching off on the wrong foot and putting his sword-belt on backwards. But he had no stronger evidence to offer. All he had was a deep conviction, growing stronger every year, that he did not belong to his family. Probably a witch had snatched Moe's and Shu's real brother from his cradle and deposited Elgar there instead. Running off with a fiendish cackle, which he could hear even now.

No, that was Fanny, enjoying his discomfort.

Elgar stared at his assembled tenants, the "family" he had hoped to belong to at last, and realized how fantastic that illusion had been. He had hurled himself blindly at the first mirage that looked like a loving family, only to find that he was an unwanted foreign body, an irritant which they desperately wanted to expel.

And for reasons he certainly could not deal with. In spite of their highly vocal complaints, his tenants' dissatisfaction did not spring from tangible things like leaky plumbing and worn linoleum. The sophisticated DuBois had hinted at the deeper reasons—old hostilities, deeply buried suspicions, murky race-memories of injustice and treachery—things dark and formless and slippery as the invisible insides of a drain.

"Ingrates!" he shouted suddenly, not knowing why. "After all I've done for you."

That statement was definitely a mistake. Elgar's tenants closed ranks against him with an almost audible *click*. Four pairs of hardened eyes looked at him out of rigid masks: beige, gold, russet, and brown, suddenly become a solid wall of black.

Elgar had never really seen color before. Not clearly: not as an erector of barriers, a builder of fences, a definer of roles. Now he did, and he felt very pale.

"You're right," he admitted. "I'm very confused."

Fanny cackled again.

Elgar had meant to go on, however vainly and clumsily, to explain his unfortunate statement. *What I meant was: "All I meant to do for you."* *Or, more accurately: "All the love I wanted to give you, and get back."* But it was too late. At the sound of that cackle, he turned on his heel and left Marge's kitchen. Marched upstairs, locked his apartment door with the inside chain (he must have known all along that there was danger on the premises, else why had he installed it?), and lay down to await his disappearance.

But, though he turned the air conditioner up to Super Kool and pulled the blanket over his head, it did not come.

What came instead, flickering faintly at first, nearly drowned in a flood of self-pity, but lighting up, finally, like a dependable flame, was rage. Red-hot, flaming rage.

They wanted him to act like a white man, did they? Well, Elgar was not sure how a white man was supposed to act, but he would damned well find out, and take steps not to disappoint them.

13

The constable, a tall, burly man in a damp shirt with frayed short sleeves, was clearly someone who knew how a white man should act. Elgar resolved to take a few lessons from him.

"You should've come in here months ago," he said, looking incredulously at Elgar's rent books. "It's unbelievable. I've never seen such arrears."

Elgar bowed, modestly acknowledging the compliment.

"Take my advice," the constable said, scratching lank brown hair salted with dandruff, "you won't give these people another inch. They'll take a mile every time. They're like children, you know. Only one way to deal with 'em." He banged his fist on the table for emphasis. "Treat 'em rough, and make 'em respect you."

Elgar nodded, his admiration for the constable increasing. Obviously he was a man who got up each morning in such a frenzy of racial rage that he ripped the sleeves from his shirts before putting them on.

"Way I look at it," the constable continued, "these people shouldn't be here in the first place. They'd be better off back where they came from. After all, it's a white man's country."

"I have a tenant who disagrees," Elgar said. "He thinks it belongs to the Indians."

The constable grunted his lack of comprehension. "Well, how do you want me to handle this? Do you want me to crack down on all of them? Or just some of them?"

Elgar hesitated, thinking of Walter Gee and Willie Lee and their anticipated sibling. Or possible half-sibling. "Well," he said, "there's a young mother with two children on the first floor. You might be a little more lenient with her."

"Young, did you say?"

Elgar nodded.

The constable gave an unsavory chuckle. "Boy, I knew there had to be something like that going on, or you wouldn't have stood for this kind of treatment. Can't say I exactly blame you." He clapped Elgar familiarly on the back and winked grossly. "I like to play around myself now and then. But I always keep business and pleasure separate. Take my advice, you'll do the same. It's good policy."

Elgar, stiffening at this assumption, said stonily, "Treat them all the same."

"No special favors?"

"No special favors."

"Well, suppose I have to get rough? Do you want me to padlock the apartments if I have to?"

"Give 'em hell," Elgar said.

Practicing his new attitude, he swaggered back to his house, his jaw jutting at a mean angle, his eyes flashing like emeralds. He wished for a chew of tobacco to tuck into his cheek or a sprig of straw to protrude from his mouth at a rude angle. Lacking these props, he would condition himself according to the best approved methods, which he had read about in one of his favorite self-help books, *Make Yourself Dynamic*. The author, Baxter A. Bold, M.D., had said, "Repeat the desired result to oneself at bedtime, on arising, and in rhythm with one's daily activities."

Harden the heart, Elgar said, as he stepped on a crack in the pavement with his left foot. And, as his right foot hit the next crack, *Toughen the hide.* Left, right, left, right, *Harden the heart, toughen the hide.* This worked splendidly for a block and a half, until he missed one of the cracks and had to go back for it. Oh-oh. Old, compulsive habits returning. Necessary consequence of cultivating the proper attitude. No gain not followed by a loss, Borden had said.

Elgar swaggered and leered his way home. *Harden the heart.* They'd be better off back where they came from. A stretch of empty stores with broken windows. *Toughen the hide.* Copee thinks the country belongs to the Indians. Well, I, for one, am ready to give it back. At least that small sector I own. *Harden the heart.* A strange, dim window cluttered with inflammatory tracts. Enough to keep Copee hopped up for a year. The Higher Enlightenment, Inc., Knowledge Is Power. Black Men, Demand

Your Rights. Judas Was a White Man. Keep moving, this is dangerous territory. *Toughen the hide.* Develop resistance to spears and tomahawks.

Reaching his own block Elgar noticed that every building on the opposite side of the street bore a jaundice-colored poster, as if all the households over there had been struck by some contagious disease. Details of lettering, however, were not visible in the deepening twilight.

Curiosity overcame his indifference, and he paused to speak to the news vendor on the corner, Old Mose, whose face was ashen from standing out of doors in all weather. "Good evening."

Though Elgar was his worst customer, usually Mose had a cheerful word for him and a broad, gap-toothed smile. But tonight he replied glumly, "What's good about it?"

"Well, I don't know," Elgar said, squinting up at the sky. "It's clearing up nicely. A bit humid, maybe. But the rain's over. That's good, isn't it?"

When the old man stubbornly refused to smile, he added hastily, "I mean, at least it's not *bad.*"

"Bad enough," the old man said. "The buzzards are circling. A sign of the end."

Elgar looked up at the sky again, expecting to see portents of doom. Then, following the old man's finger, he corrected the angle of his gaze and saw that an industrious poster crew was now busy putting *his* side of the block under quarantine.

"When the Blighters come," Mose said, "the bulldozers ain't far behind."

Elgar did not understand a word of this. It occurred to him that he should stroll down to the corner more often. Oh, not for a paper, but for a talk with Mose. Otherwise he would continue to be the last one in the neighborhood to know what was going on.

"I been on this corner fifty years, man and boy," Old Man Mose said. "Guess I ought to be glad I'm not a property owner like you. Yep, that's one thing to be thankful for. I can always pick up my stand and move on, sell my papers somewhere else. But just the same, I'll sure hate to see this neighborhood go."

Elgar's defiance reared up. "What makes you so sure it's going anywhere, Mose?"

"I tell you, I been on this corner fifty years—"

"—Man and boy," Elgar supplied.

"—man and boy, and I can tell what's happening long before it happens. I tell you, they've made up their minds to take this neighborhood, and it's got to go. Whoosh!" Old Man Mose imitated an explosion with his hands. "I just hope they take their time about it, that's all. Say, another two, three years. That way, I may die before it happens."

"Nonsense, Mose," Elgar said with false heartiness. "You're good for another quarter century."

"I hope not," said Mose. "At my age, a man hates to change. I'm sort of attached to this corner. O Lord. That's a *real* bad sign."

Elgar, following the direction of Mose's eyes, saw yet another crew of poster-hangers turn the corner smartly, their materials under their arms. They conferred briefly on the corner, then scattered in several directions down the block.

"The Dislocators," Mose said gloomily. "First the Inspectors, and then the Blighters, and now the Dislocators. All in a matter of weeks. I stand on this corner all day long, seven days a week, and I tell you, this time the buzzards ain't fooling around. They're in a hurry this time. O Lord."

Clutching his middle suddenly, Mose began to rock back and forth. Elgar was alarmed until he leaned over and heard the prayer the old man was mumbling.

"O Lord, please send me a dying pain. You know I'm too old to move on, Lord. Please take me soon."

Elgar tucked the paper under his arm and headed home. Among other things he was a lousy predictor of weather. A sudden pelting of rain made him quicken his steps. At his door he stopped, staring upward, while streams of rain trickled down his face, giving him the appearance of a man crying copious tears. For the first time since he had persuaded Marge and Fanny to remove their advertisements, the front of his house was disfigured by two garish pieces of printing.

One poster announced, in red letters on a white ground:

A PUBLIC MEETING
ON URBAN RENEWAL

to be held on a forthcoming Thursday.

The other, in black letters six inches high on jaundice-yellow cardboard, declared his property to be:

UNFIT FOR
HUMAN HABITATION

by authority of the Housing Code Commission.

In Elgar's mailbox, a smaller version of the second eyesore gave the reason for this decision. In a blank space under the heading, *Violations,* someone had written in rough pencil:

> *No kitchen facilities in Apartment 4.*

The notice was signed,

> *Compliance requested within 30 days or condemnation proceedings will be initiated.*

> > *Respectfully yours,*
> > *V. S. Phosdicker, Executive Director*
> > *The Housing Code Commission*

The nerve of those nit-picking City Hall nitwits. After all the real estate taxes Elgar had paid. No kitchen facilities, indeed. The most fat-headed of judges could not fail to see the logic of Elgar's case. With Marge only one flight below, who needed kitchen facilities? First there would be the fist fight, and then there would be the court fight, and Elgar would emerge triumphant from both.

But Phosdicker loomed as a larger adversary than Elgar had imagined. He was obviously in on the secret that had always eluded Elgar, the secret of acquiring power; he was practically a one-man interlocking directorate of the city's housing agencies. For, in the Landlord mailbox, in addition to a fistful of junk—one ad for a muscle-building course (You Too Can Be Fit for Massive Retaliation); one charity appeal (the Foundation for Obscure Diseases); a real estate offer (Own Your Own Hideaway Island in the Gulf of Mexico); and a fat envelope of folders from a travel agent (Bermuda Beckons, See Sunny Spain, You'll Love Life on the Riviera)—was another jaundice-colored envelope stamped with the official seal of the city.

Elgar stuffed the ads in his pocket for future reference—someday he might need a hideaway island or an obscure disease. Someday, too, he would undertake a research project to ferret out the identities of those ubiquitous agents, the compilers of commercial mailing lists. He spent a blissful ten minutes dreaming up this project, picturing the sneaky, trench-coated agents he would hire, the miniature cameras he would attach to mailboxes, the lobby he would start in Congress to have all third-class envelopes impregnated with fingertip-sensitive chemicals, until he could put off opening the official-looking envelope no longer. Its cheap, soft paper tore as easily as the skin of a rotten fruit. Plucking out its contents, Elgar read:

OWNER
Premises
709 Poplar Street:
 Your property has been scheduled to be acquired and condemned for demolition as part of the first step in clearing land for Urban Renewal Project #23-71b, under the provisions of Section 336 (d) 5, Municipal Planning Code, and Title I, U.S. Housing Act of 1964. . . .

There followed a number of mysterious initials, presumably referring to government agencies which lent the weight of their authority to this outrage, and the hopelessly unambiguous statement:

 This is your notice to vacate the premises within 120 days. Kindly address all inquiries to this office.

 Respectfully yours,
 V. S. Phosdicker, Commissioner
 The Blight Control Bureau

This, then, was the way doom announced itself. A form letter, one of thousands, not even addressed to him by name. Authority, as usual, did not take the trouble to recognize Elgar before it annihilated him. He would not mind going before a firing squad if they were going to execute him *personally.* But all the rage inside him boiled up at the idea of being designated, merely, "Owner," which was as ignominious as "Prisoner Number 00000."
 He called his lawyer, Nimmo, an eminently successful shyster who never stopped smiling because he had never lost a case.

"No dice, Elgar," was the lawyer's succinct verdict. "An apartment's an apartment, whether it's owner-occupied or not. And under the city's housing code, an apartment has to have kitchen facilities. You have to vacate or comply. But under the circumstances, I'd advise you to do neither."

"What kind of advice do you call that?" Elgar demanded. "Am I paying you all those retainers just to tell me to sit back and do nothing? Did you need two years of law school for that?"

"Three years, Elgar," Nimmo corrected amiably; it was impossible to get his goat. "The city's going to acquire your property anyway. Why waste energy fighting windmills?"

"Because I want to fight," was Elgar's obstinate answer. "Because I am angry. Anger is a normal human emotion, Nimmo, one that demands release, though I wouldn't expect you to understand that. After all, you were recommended to me by Levin."

"Forget about it, Elgar," Nimmo said smoothly. "You're in the heart of an Urban Renewal area. I don't know why the city bothered to slap you with a violation at this point. But that's their confusion, not yours."

Elgar was never too emotional to recognize a truth. I make everybody's confusion mine, he realized. Copee's. Phosdicker's. Marge's. The whole goddamn world's. Enough, this has gone far enough.

Nimmo's smile came through the phone and practically irradiated the room as he said, "Sit tight, Elgar. Don't fight City Hall. Just hold out for the highest price. And stay cool."

Elgar made up his mind to follow his lawyer's excellent advice. That way, Nimmo's way, led to serenity, success, and the presentation of thirty-two pearls of assurance to the world. Pondering the mysterious relationship between dentistry and destiny, he craved a front like Nimmo's, an impregnable front of gleaming, healthy enamel.

What were Nimmo's words? *Stay cool.* With a great exhausted sigh of relief Elgar sank into the chair nearest the air conditioner (18,000 B.T.U.; $400.00) and felt his head of steam evaporate into a giddy lightness. He was free. Free! Phosdicker was not The Enemy, but an angel sent straight from Heaven to release him from bondage. Elgar could forget about his tenants. He no longer need even retain the services of the constable. Phosdicker, sterling fellow, had taken the whole matter out of his hands. Hail, Phosdicker, conquering hero! Friend, brother, and fellow white man, hail!

His left hand crept slowly, irresistibly toward the pile of travel folders. You'll Love Life on the Riviera. Hail, happy playland, far from this teeming city and its quarrelsome inhabitants. Far from vengeful husbands, complaining ex-mistresses, dripping faucets, parthenogenetic light fixtures, and housekeepers who indulged in cabalistic practices. Elgar closed his eyes and saw a smiling vista of azure skies, golden beaches, and delectable bodies completely exposed except for a few discreet triangles. Corks popping from bottles of sparkling wine. Restful background babble of incomprehensible tongues. Phosdicker, his genial host, inviting him to advance and partake of these delights.

From that moment on, Elgar's body continued to inhabit his apartment, but his being was elsewhere: on those golden beaches, under those smiling skies. He clung to his favorite chair by the air conditioner, poring over his travel folders, and getting accustomed to wearing his first bikini. The effect in the mirror was, he found, disconcerting. But someday soon, aperitif in hand, he would stroll across an unfamiliar terrace magnificently unconscious that he was nearly naked.

Meanwhile he practiced, and posed, and planned, and took great pains to avoid his tenants. The locks and washers went unreplaced, and the trash cans piled up like fantastic towers in the basement, and Fanny's linoleum crumbled, presumably, from tatters to shreds. When Elgar buzzed for his meals, he retreated into his bedroom, locked the door, and came out only after he had heard Marge leave. He picked over the food, excellently prepared though it was, and left most of it untouched, because he suspected her of slowly poisoning him. He had proof: he was becoming daily weaker and paler, like a creature that lived underground.

For the most part, Elgar's tenants seemed to cooperate by avoiding him. But one morning, in the hall, he bumped into DuBois, and was as startled as if he had seen an apparition. His elegant tenant lifted his hat politely, said "Good morning," and passed on. That was all. But Elgar, staring at the graceful retreating back, could see DuBois grinning sardonically as he moved on down the hall. The grin was broad and mocking, with overtones of death, like a skull's. Elgar had developed X-ray vision.

Indeed, all five of his senses had become heightened since he had gone into seclusion. His skin was now pale and translucent, and the nerve fibers beneath were exposed and throbbing, like the newly visible blue veins. His ears, delicate and vibrating as sea anemones, were sensitive to every creak in the house, every muttered conversation, every moan. Late at night he heard Marge chanting obscene spells below, while somewhere beneath her, Copee muttered, "Hate, hate, hate," and Fanny performed a shrill descant, "Money, money, money." The sound of DuBois' leaking faucet, an irregular but constant dripping, kept Elgar awake.

Still, by living like a burglar in his own house, scuttling spiderlike down the stairs on his few necessary errands, he managed to avoid embarrassing confrontations. Generally, for example, though it still lacked a lock, Fanny's door was sufficiently closed to allow him to slip past without being seen.

But one afternoon, as he was leaving the house for his appointment with Borden, it was wide open. Through it he could see Walter Gee dancing about to the music of the radio; performing barefoot, with solemn grace and shaming expertness, one of those intricate dances Fanny had tried to teach Elgar. The Watusi perhaps, or the hully-gully, or the woolly-bully. Whatever it was, Walter Gee did it wonderfully, his head bobbing, his arms flinging upward in rhythmic alternation, his small rump wagging in a perfect frenzy of identification with the music. Elgar stopped and watched, sure that the child's total absorption would prevent his being noticed.

But Walter Gee looked up and saw Elgar. He stopped dancing, and his face, which had been poker-straight, became as animated as his body had been. "Landlord!" he crowed. A baby once more, he held out his arms and took a tottering step forward.

And Elgar fled the house as if he had met a grisly ghost instead of the most gorgeous expression of joy he had ever seen.

14

The way to Borden's led through the slums, past the open doors of noisy bars and churches, past alleys choked with rubbish and lots piled high with the corpses of automobiles, to ragged streets where neat little houses sat side by side with junk shops of every description. Blight, indeed; everywhere Elgar looked he saw confirmation of Phosdicker's supreme rightness. But, passing the junk-shop windows, he looked in vain for his own reflection.

Instead he was greeted by Venuses with permanently stopped clocks in their bellies, smirking porcelain Cupids, convoluted Chinese screens, rusty iron blunderbusses, ivory backscratchers, boot-scrapers, opera glasses, and beaded chatelaines. And at this very moment the country was full of dedicated little people, hard at work producing paintings on velvet, cathedrals built of toothpicks, hand-tooled leather footstools, original creations in rhinestone jewelry. A whole beehive of industry; it made Elgar dizzy.

For he had been born with the curse of good taste and, worse than cruelty or dishonesty, he hated junk. Yet the income from its sale provided the lining for his pockets: he was, by virtue of his inheritance, a veritable Prince of Rubbish. It was not an attractive identity, even for someone as badly in need of one as Elgar.

Then he stopped in front of one window and stood there, transfixed. He saw something he instantly craved.

This antique dealer, either more imaginative or less affluent than the others, had chosen to display a single item in his window rather than crowd it with hundreds of tasteless objects. Of dully gleaming bronze, rounded to accommodate a sturdy, medium-sized masculine figure, with dozens of clever little rivets and hinges and openings at crucial

intervals, it was splendid in its solitude. The most splendid suit of armor
Elgar had ever seen.

He knocked at the door until the dealer came to an upstairs window
and shouted down, "I'm closed. Come back tomorrow."

But Elgar, intent on the object of his desire, refused to go away.
When the dealer's head disappeared, he resumed his clamor at the
door.

Finally the dealer's face reappeared at the window, wearing an irritated
expression. "What do you want?"

"The suit of armor in the window!" Elgar yelled. "How much?"

"Not for sale."

"*How much?*"

"That's an authentic suit of knight's armor from the Middle Ages.
Five hundred dollars."

"Sold."

When the dealer opened the door, Elgar was waiting with check in
hand. "Don't bother to wrap it. I'll wear it," he said.

It took some doing to convince the proprietor that he had no wish
to haggle over the price. ("I won't take less than four-fifty for it. It's the
only one of its kind in the city." "I'm not asking you to take less than
four-fifty. Here's my check for five hundred.") It also took some doing
to strap and harness Elgar into that triumph of medieval metalworking.

But soon, as the sun sank lower over the dangerous city, he was
clanking happily along. Encased in hammered bronze from the crown
of his head to his toes. Peering out at the menacing world through the
slits of a steel visor. Progress was both noisy and difficult—he seemed to
have gained five hundred pounds—and comments as he moved along
the street were both suspicious and derogatory.

"Is there a man inside there, Mommy?"

"Of course not, darling. It's a robot."

"Wonder what he's advertising?"

"Must be a new restaurant. Or a body shop."

"Tsk. The lengths some people will go to for publicity."

But Elgar did not mind. They could not touch him now. He clanked
serenely on. *Encase that soft slob heart of yours in solid steel,* Lanie had
said. Well, however belatedly, he had taken her advice. *Harden the
heart. Toughen the hide.* By artificial means if necessary. Now he could

cope with Copee's anger, with the poisoned darts of Marge's black arts, with the combined enmity of all the other residents of 709 Poplar Street. As well as with Walter Gee's love, which was worse. It was a bit cumbersome, dragging all this protection around with him, but it was safe. When speed of transportation was required, he could always get himself a tank. He wondered what kind of a trade-in the Army would give him on a Lincoln, a Jag, and a Morris.

Elgar tipped his visor to the Trejour's doorman, racetrack tipster Eddie, former retailer of *Books of Knowledge*. Eddie was normally unshockable, but his mouth was open, his eyes frozen as Elgar, sounding like a Jamaican steel band gone berserk, charged through the lobby toward the elevator. When the elevator operator, laconic hipster Henry, refused him entry by pointing hysterically to the posted sign about weight limitations, Elgar jangled up four flights of stairs. And set up a fearsome howling and clanking outside Borden's door.

Borden was not fooled by the armor. He knew—who knew better?— that a mass of contradictions named Elgar Enders was inside. Consisting of an outer layer of bluster and bravado, and a tender, vulnerable pink core. Wailing, in there, like an infant deprived of its favorite toy.

"Come in, Elgar," he said. "Divest yourself of that ungainly costume, and make us both more comfortable."

"I'd rather not, Borden. I plan to wear this all the time. It protects me from danger. And, believe me, I lead a dangerous life. Constantly under attack from all directions."

"So do we all, Elgar," Borden answered. "We are bombarded by gamma rays, air pollution, germs, the elements and the hostilities of our fellow man. Why should you have special protection? Come out from that fortress, Elgar, and rejoin the human race."

Elgar still refused. "Need to grow a new skin, Borden. The old one's much too thin. I assure you, I mean to come out of here eventually. But only after I've toughened my hide."

"Elgar," Borden argued, "it is true that no one can harm the person who wears armor. But no one can help him, either. If you were a sardine, I would know how to get at you. But you are my patient, and I cannot reach you inside that elaborate tin can."

"All right," Elgar growled, his voice booming and hollow inside the cavern of bronze. "Come and help me with the buckles, Borden."

And soon, dressed in shirt and trousers but feeling extremely naked, he was on the couch, warily exposing the outer layer only.

"Well, it's all over, Borden," he declared with a jauntiness even he felt to be false. "House, tenants, complaints, problems, the whole shooting match, off my hands." Which he dusted. "The city is taking over my property for Urban Renewal. Tomorrow is the community meeting. The day after tomorrow, a plane takes off for the Riviera, and I mean to be on it. Hallelujah." That sounded feeble, so he repeated it. "Hallelujah, I said."

Borden observed dryly, "I hate to think of you boarding a plane in that suit of armor, Elgar. The overweight charges alone should be appalling. If they let you on board."

Really, Borden was terribly dimwitted at times. It was difficult to believe he had ever gotten through college, let alone medical school. Elgar sighed and explained patiently, "I only need the suit before I get on the plane, Borden. To help me make my getaway. I have to achieve some distance from my tenants. Distance—" he paused, searched, then found the right word "—and anonymity."

Borden's usual iron control melted, and he laughed. "I can hardly imagine a less anonymous costume, Elgar. It is like a battleship on a city street. Yes. A battleship. Announcing your presence for miles around."

Elgar said resentfully, "For Heaven's sake, Borden, if you can't offer some constructive help, don't criticize. I have to do *something*. Have to correct my original mistake with my tenants. Getting involved. I know better now. A landlord is supposed to provide light and heat, remove trash, and make repairs on the premises. He's not supposed to get involved in his tenants' lives."

"Who says so?" Borden inquired sharply.

Elgar wasn't sure at first; then he remembered. "Lanie."

"And what makes Lanie the final authority on landlord-tenant relationships? Why shouldn't you get involved? Since, it seems, you are already." Borden paused, like a man aiming a hypodermic needle, before plunging the point home. "Perhaps it fulfills some of your basic needs, Elgar."

"One need, Borden. Only one. My need to suffer."

"What about your need for an occupation, Elgar?" The sly devil had spotted the one fly-speck in Elgar's balm of bliss.

Elgar ranted blindly, "Who says I need an occupation? That's a lot of malarkey, Borden. I don't have to fall for that crumby propaganda. I can afford not to work, so why should I? From now on, I mean to have fun."

"Elgar," Borden said, "it is true that you have the opportunity to be a playboy, if that is what you really want. But you should think twice about what it means. 'Play, boy.' Excellent advice for boys. Yes. But a man must work."

"Where do you get off, Borden?" Elgar howled. "I thought you were supposed to be on my side. Now you sound like my old man!" He was sitting up now, and shouting. "Here I get a chance to get rid of my problems, turn loose a houseful of maniacs that are nothing but a chain around my neck, and enjoy myself for the first time in my life, and you throw cold water on it! You joyless, gloom-spreading bastard. People like you are what make the world such a miserable place. If you have to be miserable, Borden, why do you have to spoil the fun for the rest of us?"

Borden waited till this tirade was over, then said gently, "Now, Elgar, perhaps you will tell me how you *really* feel about being deprived of your property."

Elgar sighed, lay back, searched his bosom, and found to his surprise that it burned with outrage. "Ah, what difference does it make how I feel about it?" he said in a different, tired voice. "The city has the right of eminent domain—something they inherited from some goddamn king, can you imagine that, Borden, and they call this a democracy?—so they can step right in and take me over any time they feel like it. I'd feel better about it if I thought they knew what they were doing. But they don't, Borden, they're more confused than I am. In the same day they slapped me with a Notice to Vacate and a Notice to Comply. Signed by the same man, a numbskull named Phosdicker. Some bureaucrat who's so big his left hand doesn't know what his right is doing. Did you ever hear of such stupidity, Borden? A man has no rights any more. Private property has no meaning. And this is the type of mentality that rules our lives. Creeping bureaucracy. A blind, sprawling monster with no brain."

Borden chuckled softly, and asked, "Now who sounds like your old man?"

As Elgar had no answer beyond a sucking-in of his breath and a glazed, horrified stare, Borden went on, "So now we see that you do not really like the idea of giving up your property, Elgar. Having recognized this, what do you intend to do about it?"

"Nothing!" Elgar shouted. "I'm trying to tell you, Borden, the city is doing me a favor. Good riddance, I say. Good riddance to a pile of troubles!"

Borden stared at him.

Elgar's fists unclenched. His hands, his whole body went limp with honesty. "What can I do about it, Borden? I might stand a chance against the Authorities if I were a different kind of guy. But there are two kinds of people in this world. Heroes and victims. You know which I am."

Bitterly, he added, "Oh, Mothaw knew what was up when she named me. She didn't name me George, for leadership, or Vincent, for talent, or Henry, for tycoonery. No, she had to name me for a failure. A guy who only wrote one tune, a tune everybody hates, and then kept writing it, 'Pomp and Circumstance' backwards, 'Pomp and Circumstance' sideways, 'Pomp and Circumstance' upside down, until he must have hated it himself. Christ. I hear it all the time. It's my theme song, Borden. The dirge of a victim."

"To some," Borden said, "it is an anthem of triumph, Elgar. Usually played on glorious occasions, which have, I admit, been notably lacking in your life. Your not, for instance, having graduated from any school."

"That's what I mean," Elgar cried. "I'm a failure. A victim. Not the kind of guy who can take on the Authorities in a fight, and win."

"Actually," Borden said, "there is only one Authority you have to fight to rid yourself of that conviction. And we know who *that* is."

Elgar placed both hands on his stomach to restrain it from jumping out of place.

"Also," Borden said, "heroes have to begin as victims. At least that is my understanding, Elgar. Their heroism consists of overcoming their original condition. Perhaps you are fortunate. You have been given unusual opportunities for becoming a hero."

"Arrgh," was Elgar's only response to that cheery bit of optimism. He rolled over on his stomach, to quiet it, and said, "You seem determined not to understand me, Borden. I don't want to put up a fight. I'm happy to give up the house. Delighted. Overjoyed." As if to spite him, moisture fell from his eyes to water the dusty black leather. He ignored it and went on, "That Urban Renewal notice was my Emancipation Proclamation! I'm a free man! Cut loose from all my problems. And day after tomorrow I'm off for Paradise. Yeehoo!"

"So," Borden said thoughtfully, "you will now seek Paradise on foreign shores. I take it your dream of a domestic Paradise has ended in a rude awakening, Elgar."

Elgar was down, suddenly, to the inner layer of himself, the core of suffering. "Worse than that, Borden," he said miserably. "It's turned into a hideous nightmare."

"And you are now a fallen angel. Expelled from the regions of pure bliss by a jealous and wrathful God. With great powers of vengeance in His almighty right arm."

"Do we have to go into all this theology, Borden?" Elgar inquired. "I never had a very good attendance at any Sunday school. Mothaw was a Theosophist, and Fathaw wouldn't knuckle under to any formal religion. He's so important he speaks to God directly, on a private line. On the fourth button of his office phone, I believe."

"Elgar," Borden said, "you know we never discuss religion. I simply employ religious imagery as a useful tool, in the hope of tricking you into new insights. Do you not recognize this all-powerful figure I have described?"

"My father," Elgar said, and belched. "Who else? There just couldn't be two people on earth like him."

"On earth, Elgar? Or sitting on a marble throne, floating high in the clouds? From which he judges, condemns, and refuses to hear appeals?"

It was true; the distance Elgar had put between himself and his father had simply made the old man more awesome. From his remote office in Upper County, he was still pulling the strings that made Elgar's life resemble the nervous, jerky antics of a marionette. This realization caused renewed discomfort in Elgar's digestive tract, so he quickly repressed it. "Borden, let's abandon this line of approach. It's not helping me in my present predicament. Let's talk about my tenants. I want to become indifferent to them. I want to forget all about them."

"And how do you expect me to help you with that, Elgar?"

"Put me to sleep. Hypnotize me. Condition me. Make me," Elgar pleaded, with a desperate glance at Borden's face, "a white man."

Borden's eyes were kind, but all other emotions were withheld from them. Except for a faint gleam of amusement, which made Elgar furious. "You illiterate slob," he accused. "I suppose you never heard of Pavlov."

"He did some interesting things with dogs, as I recall. But you are human, Elgar, not canine. Or, hopefully, human is what you are becoming. There are, at least, certain encouraging signs." He counted them on his fingers. "You are involved with your tenants. You find it difficult to abandon them. This means you feel, and to feel is to be human." Borden looked at him in genuine puzzlement. "Why, Elgar, do you wish to give up your humanity?"

"Because, you oaf," Elgar screamed, "I'm suffering!"

"That part of your suffering which stems from the human condition," Borden said gravely, "I am not in a position to relieve, Elgar. But perhaps I can help you with that needless part of it which is caused by your father."

"Oh, God," Elgar groaned, "here we go again. Why do you have to keep dragging *him* into it, Borden?" He sat up and held his head in his hands.

"Your father," Borden said relentlessly, "makes it impossible for you to tolerate much happiness, Elgar. Because he has been incorporated in your personality as an overdeveloped conscience. Yes. Surrounded by affection and comfort, you get nervous. You begin to conjure up the harshly critical image of your father, accusing you of monstrous crimes. And it is easy for you to see this image wherever you look. Whenever someone who formerly smiled at you greets you with a frown."

Elgar got up from the couch indignantly. "Let's change places, Borden. You lie down here and talk. I'll sit over there and listen. Because if you think I am upset over mere facial expressions, you are the one who is crazy, not me. I tell you, Borden, things have been happening which are far more sinister."

"I do not deny that there may be negative factors in your environment, Elgar," Borden said, lighting his malodorous pipe with infuriating calm.

"There is *murder* in my environment, Borden!" Elgar screeched. "Not 'negative factors.' Murder. Intent to murder by spearcraft and witchcraft."

"—But," Borden continued, "I cannot control those factors, so I must concentrate on your father. I am convinced that he is the real agent who has expelled you from Paradise." He jabbed the pipe-stem in Elgar's direction for emphasis, and said sternly, "And will *continue* to expel you from any future Paradise, either here or abroad, until our work is finished."

"Disgusting," Elgar growled, "the way you guys manage to complicate the simplest issues. Theology. Mythology. Psychology. Whew. I'm sick of the whole complicated mess. —I tell you, Borden, my tenants have murder in their hearts, and I'll be glad to get away from them. What's more, I'll be glad to get away from you. You creep," he added, and wished he had thought of a stronger word. For a dark, terrifying suspicion had taken root in his mind, threatening, for the first time, the deepest level of his trust in Borden. Borden did not want Elgar to give up the house. He most emphatically did not want him to board that plane. And he insisted on bringing the discussion back to Elgar's father. Why?

Elgar did not like the answer which kept insinuating itself, but it was persistent. *Because, you sap, he wants to keep you dependent on him. Because he doesn't want to give up that lovely, easy twenty-five bucks an hour. One hundred and twenty-five smackeroonies a week.*

Oh, it was horrible, seeing smears of clay on Borden's shoes. Suspecting calculating greed in his eyes as he said, "As you wish, Elgar. You can, of course, board that plane this week. —But I fear, no matter where you travel, you will take your father with you."

With a polite bow of his head. Pretending to respect his patient's freedom. Part of the pose of professional objectivity.

But was it any more than a pose? Was Borden, with his accent and his catarrh and his shabby office, really a qualified professional? Or was he what Elgar had always suspected, a phony, seedy, money-grubbing quack?

"Then I'll buy two tickets," Elgar said grimly, and left.

15

At the community meeting, which was held in the basement of a church, a series of wonders was unveiled.

On a screen at the front of the room, a row of shabby houses appeared. Ragged children played on their steps; trash and litter disfigured their sidewalks. At the flick of a slide projector, this sordid scene was replaced by a group of handsome dwellings rising above landscaped grounds. Through these grounds, graceful people strolled at their leisure, shaded by trees that normally would take twenty years to grow, but had sprung up in seconds through the magic of modern visual aids.

Elgar, on the front row beside his lawyer, observed these phenomena in the same relaxed frame of mind with which he would watch any good entertainment, because he was fully reconciled to losing his house. He had reviewed his investment: several thousand dollars, several hundred hours of labor. There were nails he had driven, leaks he had patched, certain cracks he had caulked against the cold and the damp. And other improvements of a more personal nature, justifying some slight sentimental attachment. But none of it added up to anything really worth fighting for.

A map was projected on the screen, and Elgar recognized several neighborhood landmarks: the church in which they were assembled, the railroad tracks a block away, the abandoned Schneemyer Department Store warehouse, and Motley Square, a seedy little triangle of a park popular with consumers of cheap wine. As he watched, fascinated, the church, the warehouse, and the railroad tracks disappeared, swallowed up by the expanding park, and the park was ringed by a pretty little circle of buildings, popping out one by one, like pimples, on the face of the map.

Elgar was so enchanted by this display that he began to applaud. He was glad that such an excellent show had managed to draw a full house including all of his tenants and several hundred others from the neighborhood. Nevertheless, he was the only one applauding. When he realized this, he sat on his hands.

When Phosdicker rose to address the group, he proved to be a likeable old fellow, open-faced and sincere, with a sorrowful delivery that implied a deep concern for his audience. You felt he had gained every one of his numerous gray hairs as the result of worrying about the individual fate of everyone present. And his half-dozen young assistants had such indistinguishably clean-cut good looks, such unabashed eagerness to please as they scurried about to supply their leader with supporting documents, that Elgar could not help liking them too. They resembled nothing so much as a litter of cute, fuzzy blond puppies.

Striving considerately to keep his syllable count well down, Phosdicker launched into his Law of Irreversible Tendencies, a formula for determining whether a case of neighborhood blight was curable or terminal. His accents were grave, but the dear old man could not keep an eager twinkle out of his eye; it was his theory, his pet, and he loved it dearly. Elgar understood, and pardoned him.

There were, it seemed, certain symptoms which infallibly made for a grave diagnosis, including unlidded trashcans, broken windows, abandoned cars, and ailanthus trees. The latter were particularly crucial; the Authorities had found, Phosdicker declared sadly, that no neighborhood could be saved once it had exceeded the fatal ratio of one ailanthus tree per dwelling unit.

Poplar Street, it seemed, suffered from a plague of three ailanthus trees per each of its dwelling units. Elgar stared, aghast, as Phosdicker, with the kindly manner of a good gray doctor reluctantly showing his patient a hopeless X-ray, displayed a photograph of the ominous sproutings in Elgar's side alley.

"What's wrong with trees?" Marge challenged from her chair directly behind Elgar. "I *like* trees."

Elgar turned, stared disapprovingly, and placed a finger to his lips for order.

Children, Phosdicker went on, sweeping the large miniature population of his audience with a sorrowful glance, were another symptom of Irreversible Blight. Not that the Authorities had anything against children in principle. After all, heh heh, they had once been children themselves.

Elgar gave a discreet, sympathetic little chuckle.

No, it was simply, Phosdicker said, fixing a grateful look on Elgar, that no neighborhood could healthfully support an infant population in excess of one child per ten square feet of dwelling space. Beyond that sanitary and civilized ratio loomed the horrors of overcrowding, contagion, substandard schools, illiteracy, and juvenile delinquency.

Fanny, on the other side of the room, sprang up indignantly.

"Well, how come I ain't been put in jail," she wanted to know, "if it's against the law to have children? I mean, of course," she qualified with a chilly look at certain other mothers around the room, "*legitimate* children."

Before she resumed her seat, DuBois rose languidly at the end of Elgar's row.

"If I may be permitted to make a suggestion," he said. "This problem might be somewhat alleviated, if the Authorities saw fit to encourage other forms of human association than the single one to which they give their sanction. I refer of course to those forms of love commonly practiced among the ancients. In the Golden Age of Greece, for example. The Age of Pericles."

"Er, yes," Phosdicker said, looking completely bewildered. "Thank you."

Elgar had been living with his tenants for so long that he no longer noticed much of their strangeness. Now, seeing them from Phosdicker's point of view, he was embarrassed. The poor old guy had been thrown hopelessly off his track by DuBois' and Fanny's comments. Also, he had lost his audience. The polite silence which had attended the first part of the meeting had given way to ominous buzzings and considerable scrapings of the folding chairs which had been loaned for the occasion by a neighborhood funeral parlor.

Phosdicker declared valiantly that he would try to answer every question. "I believe the lady in the second row spoke first," he said, addressing Marge. "Let me say, madam, that I share your tastes. I, too, like trees. I agree with the poet who said that a tree is, ah, a superior form of poem. That is why our plan includes the devotion of three full blocks to a public park, which will be planted by the city with stately oaks and elms. Also provided with a refreshing lake ornamented with

graceful swans. As well as winding paths, rustic seats, and bosky dells."
Phosdicker wiped some perspiration from his forehead. "Pardon me if
I wax poetic. But it will be a lovely spot."

The afternoon was full of surprises. Elgar had come expecting to
be enraged by the proceedings, and instead found himself thoroughly
entertained. He had planned to hate Phosdicker on sight, but instead
was beguiled. The old man was so upright, so courteous, so *lovable,*
somehow, with his tousled gray thatch and baggy gray suit and wobbly
bifocals behind which his nearsighted blue eyes beamed with the best
of intentions. Besides, he had a charming faculty of expression.

"Charming," Elgar said. But no one heard him; Fanny was on her
feet again.

"Well, if we got so many children, how come nobody thought of
building a park for us while we still lived here?"

"I'll tell you why," Marge answered her. "It's 'cause we got no civil
rights."

Oh, this was unfair. Elgar deplored this sort of willful distortion.

In the pandemonium of shouts and floor-stompings which followed,
Phosdicker and his staff scurried to marshal their forces. As they scrambled
about, tumbling over one another in their haste and zeal, easels were
knocked over, papers were scattered, and blueprints were spilled to
the floor. But eventually order was restored, and an impressive array of
charts, maps, graphs, and drawings materialized at the front of the room.
Behind these protective ramparts, the Authorities held an impromptu
conference. Finally Phosdicker emerged, pointer in hand, and cleared
his throat impressively.

"I wish to correct the unfortunate impression that a, hmmm, racial
bias has anything to do with the subject under discussion. Blight, ladies
and gentlemen, is purely a function of economics. Strictly a matter of
dollars and cents."

Elgar nodded. That ought to clear things up, he thought. That ought
to show them.

Phosdicker pointed to a vertical bar graph. "When the median annual
income in a neighborhood falls below this level, that neighborhood is
in danger. That is what has happened here, my friends. Poplar Street is
poor, and therefore Poplar Street is sick. There is only one way to restore
a neighborhood to health. And that is to raise the median annual income

to this level or beyond. In a word, my friends, there is only one color that concerns us here. Green."

There should have been a storm of applause at the close of that fine bit of rhetoric, but there was only an ugly silence. In that silence, Marge's voice boomed out, close to Elgar's ear.

"What's wrong with trees?"

Really, her obtuseness was annoying. But Phosdicker refused to be provoked; his self-control was admirable. He ignored her and said, "Now to answer that lady over there. And that gentleman, also, if I understand the nature of his question. I do not wish to be misconstrued as a person who dislikes children. How could I? I have four children myself. And ten grandchildren."

Then this fine old bureaucrat was a splendid old patriarch as well. Ten grandchildren. For a moment Elgar thought Phosdicker was going to whip out a wallet and produce their pictures in evidence: ten blond, tubby, nearsighted children tumbling and frolicking on unblighted lawns.

But he merely said, "No, the plight of our little ones is my chief concern. As it must be the concern of every serious-minded citizen."

Walter Gee, meanwhile, had grown restless. He slipped away from his mother and knelt in the aisle, aiming an imaginary gun at Phosdicker.

"Rat tat tat," he said. "Zap zap bazoom. You're dead."

For an instant, a flicker of dislike leaped up behind Phosdicker's glasses. Dislike and fear, as if it were a copperhead he saw crawling toward him, and not a small, copper-colored boy. The expression was quickly wiped away, but Elgar wished he had not seen it.

Phosdicker quickly recomposed his features; courteous concern, as before, was all they expressed as he continued, "A large and overcrowded child population, as I say, is one symptom of a sick neighborhood. But there are many others. Broken windows, marginal or failing business enterprises, absentee landlords—"

Elgar was not sure whether it was in defense of himself or of Walter Gee that he found himself suddenly on his feet. "What old absentee landlords?" he shouted. "I'm right here, Phosdicker. You see me here, don't you?"

"Yes, sir," the old bureaucrat said. "Oh, yes sir, I do see you. Most certainly."

Elgar had more to say. But as he became conscious of Nimmo tugging violently at his sleeve, he subsided in shame. He had not, after all, intended to be guilty of bad behavior at this meeting. His tenants had already provided enough of that.

"Well, O.K.," he said lamely. "I just wanted to have my presence recognized. For the record, so to speak. Now it has been. Thank you."

He sat down, blushing and trembling with self-consciousness, glad that Nimmo had saved him from making even more of a spectacle of himself. He flashed him a grateful smile, which his lawyer returned brilliantly.

"Attaboy, Elgar," Nimmo whispered. "Remember what I told you. Stay cool."

Elgar nodded apologetically. He had not meant to slip from his vantage point of detachment to one of hot involvement with the proceedings. He was not sure how it had happened, but he was determined to exercise stricter self-control after this.

"In summary . . ." Phosdicker was hurrying to wind up his speech, as if he feared further interruptions. "To restore a sick neighborhood to health, we must give it an economic transfusion. And how do we propose to do this for Poplar Street, my friends?" Phosdicker, beaming (he really *was* a good man, you felt it; he really believed in the good he was doing), answered his own question. "By making it a place where prosperous people, successful people, self-respecting people, *property-maintaining* people will want to live."

With difficulty Elgar restrained himself from rising again to deliver a census of his household. One famous recording artist, one professor of history, and one college president were not to be sneezed at, after all. But he was resolved to hear Phosdicker out politely.

"Are there any questions so far?"

There were none; Phosdicker emitted a happy sigh. "I will now turn the meeting over to Mr. Henry Moss, of the building firm of Pachysandra and Moss, Inc., who will explain how his firm plans to develop this neighborhood."

At that moment there was a loud disturbance at the back of the room. Elgar turned to see what late arrival could be causing the commotion.

It was an old woman, one of the rag-picking crones of the neighborhood, grandmother to some forty of its distressingly numerous children. Old Lady Coggins, she was called.

In a hoarse, chilling voice that carried to every corner of the room, she croaked, "Old Man Mose done kicked the bucket! Old Man Mose is dead!"

A chorus of grief responded to this announcement.

"Lord have mercy," one woman cried.

"Mercy," others echoed. "Mercy."

Testimonials arose. "Many's the time he loaned me money."

"Did my errands."

"Watched my car."

"He always had something pleasant to say."

"He was a good man."

"God rest his soul."

"Amen."

Somehow the stage had moved from the front of the room to the back, and Old Lady Coggins occupied its center. "You killed him, you devils!" she shrieked, pointing a terrible finger at the blanching Authorities. "You killed that good, sweet, kind old man. And we *all* might's well die. For all you care!"

Shrieks, moans, sobs filled the air. The assemblage was taking on the lively character of a Baptist funeral. Understandable, since they were in a Baptist church. But Elgar felt it was all terribly excessive. After all, old men died natural deaths every day.

He determined once more to set a good example by giving these kind gentlemen, who had obviously gone to great pains to prepare an edifying program, the polite hearing they deserved.

Eyes front again, therefore, to where the next speaker stood, a sickly smile on his face, waiting for the hubbub to die down. As Elgar recognized that crocodile smile, that squat, toadlike figure, that, that piece of Blight on the human landscape, he felt his eyes turn a blazing green.

Moss was the real estate agent who had originally sold him the house.

"Zap zap," Walter Gee cried from the aisle. "You're dead."

Elgar no longer wished that Fanny knew how to control the exuberant behavior of her brood. That behavior, he now felt, was based on unerring instincts, and he was sorry to see Fanny snatch Walter Gee from the aisle and deliver a sharp swat to his tail.

When the noise of mourning subsided, Moss began in a high, froglike voice, "Er ah, I feel in all due modesty that I should not have been called on to appear at this meeting."

Right you are, Elgar thought. That was your first mistake.

"But Mr. Phosdicker insisted that I come. So here I am. Against my will, ha ha."

Moss paused, waiting for laughter. There was none, so he continued squeakily, "Mr. Phosdicker and his staff really deserve all of the credit on this fine, ah, occasion. Mr. Phosdicker and his staff have worked very hard. They have developed a fine, ah, plan. A splendid plan."

The creature was actually attempting a show of humility, when his jaunty, cocky manner made it clear that humility was something he had never felt. What he did feel, apparently, was the need to give Phosdicker's boots a copious licking. The boots were beginning to gleam. Also, as Elgar could tell by the twitching of his nostrils and the ebbing of his self-control, a faintly rotten odor was beginning to emanate from the proceedings.

Make one more false move, Moss, he muttered. Just one.

And of course Moss made it, with a vague wave of his pudgy, doll-like hand at one of the maps. "As I say, the city has developed a fine plan here. Fine, ah, schools, fine streets, fine recreation facilities. We are merely proposing to develop the housing areas. We hope our houses will attract a type of buyer who will be a real asset to the community. Er ah, I won't go into details, but we plan to have five models, starting at twenty-nine thousand, nine hundred ninety-nine dollars. The Monterey, the Eldorado—"

Elgar leaped to his feet so suddenly that Nimmo did not have a chance to restrain him. "You say your houses will start at thirty thousand?"

"Twenty-nine thousand, nine nine nine," Moss purred, clicking off the figures like a comptometer.

"Well, where are my people going to live?"

"Your people, sir?" the agent asked, with a bewildered look at Elgar which did not include recognition.

Elgar suddenly realized that he was on his feet. He looked wildly around the room for the support of familiar faces. Nimmo, on the front row, whatever he felt, was smiling; he would smile in the same genial way at a massacre or a thermonuclear explosion. I do not know who you are, Nimmo, Elgar thought. Nor do I know who Phosdicker is, and I fail to recognize any of his assistants. But these other people, these dispossessed people, I know *them*. They have caused me to laugh, to suffer, to lust, to tremble, to shed tears. They are therefore a part of me. Me. Myself. Mine.

"Yes," he said, "my people. Where are they going to live? Seventy-five a month is the top they can afford."

"They will be relocated elsewhere," Phosdicker put in smoothly. "We have an excellent Relocation Service. I was going to explain that last."

Moss, meanwhile, had collected himself, taken in Elgar's well-nurtured good looks, the good fit of his suit (the last one Mothaw had bought him), the subtle stripe of his shirt, and added them up to mean one thing: a Buyer. Licking his lips hungrily, he said, "But we will be happy to accommodate *you,* sir. I would suggest the Catalina. Thirty-foot living room, walnut-paneled den, master bedroom with a dressing room, dining room with terrace—"

Elgar decided to ignore this Moss/Mouse person, who was beneath contempt, and direct his remarks to Phosdicker, who was not.

"Suppose they don't want to be relocated?" he asked in a hard voice.

This apparently had not occurred to Phosdicker; he knotted his brows in puzzlement. He was clearly a kindly old man. Elgar hated to destroy the pretty symmetry of his theories. But Walter Gee was wailing, and he had to make Phosdicker hear that sound.

"I believe you mean well, but I think you have overlooked a few things here, Phosdicker. There are such things as loyalty to a neighborhood, such things as habits and ways of life, that don't like to be uprooted. Even an ailanthus tree has roots, Phosdicker, and it doesn't like to be torn up. Now I understand how you have to think, in terms of statistics and symptoms and so on. I know you have to see things on a grand scale, I appreciate your problems, and, as I say, I believe you mean well, but you have overlooked one thing. These are people you are dealing with. Not statistics. Not even trees, Phosdicker. Human beings."

Fanny led the stamping, screaming applause. While it thundered about his ears, Phosdicker looked pained. Finally the noise died down and he tried, with hurt dignity, to solve what he saw as the only problem.

"Sir," he said, "I am sure the city will offer you a fair price for your property."

"Christ. Is that all you think I want?" And, Christ, he thought, what a low opinion white people really have of themselves. It would have been easier if he could hate Phosdicker. But the old gent was obviously so well-meaning, so noble in his confusion, that it was difficult. Nevertheless, Elgar tried. Putting the discussion on Phosdicker's terms helped.

"All right, Phosdicker, have it your way. I am merely outraged because I am a property owner and a taxpayer. The money to acquire and clear this land is coming out of public funds, right?"

Nimmo suddenly came to life. "Right," he said happily, delighted that his client had brought the discussion around to his province; now he could earn his fees. "Sections 336 to 339, Municipal Code; Sections—"

Elgar gave Nimmo a nod of thanks, cutting him off. "Well," he said, "those public funds come out of my pocket. So have it your way, Phosdicker." He pointed a finger at Moss. "What I really resent is seeing them used to line the pockets of that cheap, lying, chiseling—"

Phosdicker rebuked him gravely for failing to play by gentleman's rules. "Now you are hitting below the belt, sir. That accusation is without foundation, and grossly unfair."

Elgar had no doubt that it was, but it was the only way he could make a dent on Phosdicker. The old bureaucrat really could not see why Elgar's tenants should mind being shoved around to make way for his lofty theories. He was not a cruel man or a crooked one. No, their humanity was, quite simply, beyond his understanding.

"I resent your accusation, sir," Phosdicker said huffily.

Rightly he resented it: Phosdicker was as honest as the day was long. He was an old-fashioned, dedicated civil servant; a fine, upright, honorable old man, Elgar thought. God help us all. A monster.

"Mr. Moss here," Phosdicker explained stiffly, "was good enough to come here today to explain his firm's proposal."

Ah, yes. Mr. Moss was good enough. Then why is Walter Gee *not* good enough? Explain that, if you please.

"—But whether his proposal will be carried out is still an undecided question. I, sir, have no stake in the decision. And no influence, either."

Elgar's mind was turning over as rapidly as his Jaguar's motor. "You mean there's a chance he won't get to build his Eldorados after all?"

"Yes," the old bureaucrat admitted. "To date his proposal has been the only one received by the Authorities. Alternate proposals may still be submitted. But as yet none have been received, so I see no reason to assume—"

Elgar was raging inside, but his surface was as frosty as Nimmo could wish. Oh, gladly he would smash Phosdicker's glasses from his nose if he thought it would make him see Walter Gee even as clearly as he saw his own grandchildren. But he knew that would be futile; the old man was blind, blind alike to the evil beneath Moss' warty skin and the humanity beneath Walter Gee's. However, the possibility of another way of fighting had begun to dawn, and, with it, the possibility of victory, because he did not share Phosdicker's particular terrible confusion.

"Nor do I, Phosdicker," he said, flashing a smile that was at least as brilliant as Nimmo's. "I see no reason to assume anything at this point, do you?"

"No, sir," Phosdicker said in bewilderment.

The center of power at the meeting had shifted several times, and in the last two minutes, Elgar had grown accustomed to the novel sensation caused by its settling on his shoulders. Like a new, well-tailored coat, it lent him a certain grace, and gave his movements a new sureness. With great efficiency he gathered together the materials Phosdicker and his crew had brought; with enormous and elaborate courtesy, he brought the meeting to an end.

"No reason, for instance, to assume that we cannot part friends."

"Why, of course not, sir," the old gentleman said, extending a cordial hand. "What is your name?"

"Owner" had been his only designation on the most glorious day of his life until now, the day of the dog show twenty-four years ago. It was time a new day dawned.

In the background, "Pomp and Circumstance" played majestically as he heard himself say, loudly and clearly, "Elgar Enders."

16

"Landlord," Marge asked, "you really gonna keep us from gettin' put out in the street?"

"Sure he is," Fanny told her. "You heard him at the meeting, didn't you? Told those white folks what for, he did. Told 'em *right*."

"Well, how you gonna stop it from happening, Landlord?"

"Never mind. He can do anything. Can't you, Landlord?"

"Yeth," crowed Walter Gee, jumping up and down in agreement with his mother. "Landlord can do anything. He's Superman!"

"One can certainly tell," said DuBois, "when a person is accustomed to dealing with the Authorities. It was most gratifying to observe how they quieted down when he spoke, and became respectful."

"*Yeah,*" Fanny said appreciatively. She stood up and struck a pose that was an impressive imitation of grandeur, aided by her imposing new contours. "'No reason to assume *any*thing, Mister Phosdicker.' I really dug that bit, Landlord. I said to myself, 'Aw, *git* it, Landlord. Show 'em who's boss. Bring it right down front.'"

Walter Gee chortled, applauding his mother's brilliant performance, then scrambled up into Elgar's lap, while Marge handed Elgar a fat white envelope. "Here, Landlord. On behalf of the Tenants' Association."

Elgar ripped the envelope open and stared in disbelief at its contents. One hundred and ninety dollars. Cash.

"After you left I took that meeting over and ran things *right*, Landlord. From now on, everybody pays their rent nice and regular. And on time."

Elgar did not need to ask how the decision to pay up had been reached by the Tenants' Association. When Marge chose to throw her considerable weight behind an argument, it was as good as won.

Marge blew her nose. Her glasses looked suspiciously misty. "I'm so happy I could cry. After all these weeks and months of wondering and worrying, knowing we'd have to leave, not knowing when. Everybody nervous, everybody suspicious of everybody else."

"Including me, apparently."

"Well, sure, Landlord. We figured you just bought the house so's you could sell it back to the city and make a fast profit."

The reason why his tenants had mistrusted him was, after all, concrete. They had thought he was part of the machinery of dispossession. Naturally. It was always Elgar's fate to be mistaken for somebody else.

"'Course," Marge went on, "you had us confused for a while. No landlord ever acted like you before. Friendly. Almost human. Whoever heard of a *human* landlord?"

"Yeah," Fanny chimed in. "We was used to havin' to fight with the landlord for heat, hot water, repairs, everything. And then here you come, movin' right in with us. Makin' all the repairs yourself. —'Course," she added, "your repairs are pretty pitiful, Landlord. My sink is leaking again. And the linoleum underneath is getting awful raggedy."

Elgar stifled his urge to cry out against these complaints. Would his tenants never be satisfied?

"Like I said, Landlord," Marge said, "you had us so confused, we didn't know whether we was comin' or goin'. 'Cause we found out we liked you in spite of ourselves."

"But then," Fanny said, "we heard about the Urban Renewal plans, and Charlie, he said, 'See? He's a white man. It's like I been tellin' you all along. You can't trust 'em. White men is all the same.'"

"*Landlords* is all the same, is what I said," Marge contributed stoically. "They can't help bein' evil. They born that way."

Such was the fate of Elgar's individuality: forever drowning in the swamp of other people's categories. Reality being dangerous to his tenants, they had more reason than most to divide it into two simple compartments: good and evil, for-me and against-me. Black and white. But now there was hope that they were beginning, cautiously, to take off their blinders and recognize *him*. If this happened, the rest of the world might fall in line.

"Marge," he asked, "how long have you known about the Urban Renewal business?"

"Oh, a long time, Landlord. Months and months. How could we help but know? Them faggoty City Hall men been all over this block for months. Pokin' their noses in our business. Askin' questions. Besides, it's been in all the papers."

Papers. He never read the papers, preferring not to know about all those huge tidal-wave events that made him feel like a helpless piece of flotsam. Wars, riots, recessions, revolutions: they were all part of the giant plot to swallow up Elgar and make him disappear.

He waved the jaundice-yellow notice. "I swear to you, Marge, this notice I got two weeks ago was the first I ever heard about Urban Renewal in this neighborhood. That real estate agent never even hinted anything about it when I bought the house. The dirty little rat. I had no idea."

Marge's lip curled scornfully. "You expect me to believe that, Landlord? I wasn't born yesterday."

"Well, maybe that's your trouble, Marge," Elgar said grimly. "Maybe you've lived too long." He patted Walter Gee's head. "This boy here, he knows enough to trust me on instinct. But you, when you look at me, you don't see *me* at all. You see some kind of a fuzzy photomontage of all the other people who ever did you wrong. Landlords. White people. Men. Now I admit I belong to all those categories, Marge, but I am something else besides. I am *me*. And that cancels out all the other things. Now, will you please look at *me* for a change, Marge? And listen?"

His voice was harsh, and choked with rasping sobs. Startled by its stridency, Marge did fix her eyes on his face.

He went on in a more reasonable tone, hoping to appeal to her common sense, "Marge, do you really think I would've spent so much time and money fixing up this apartment if I'd known I would have to give it up?"

Like all dragons Marge had a heart of pure candy. Melting, now, like her eyes. "I'm sorry, Landlord. You ain't a white man, not really. At least not *all* white. I always knew that."

"And I," said DuBois, shaking Elgar's hand, "always knew you were not one of the common brutal sort. —Not," he added with a faraway glitter in his eyes, "that I object to a bit of brutality now and then."

"Now I can have this baby in peace, knowing I'll have a place to bring it home to. Thank you, Landlord."

Fanny kissed the top of Elgar's head while DuBois continued shaking his hand. Walter Gee bounced up and down on Elgar's stomach as if it were a trampoline. But the stomach bounced back; today it was tough enough to take it. Marge, beaming moistly, passed coffee and sandwiches. What a party. All his tenants surrounding him with approving smiles and encouraging babble. All but one.

"Where's your husband, Fanny?"

"Oh. *Him.*" Her pouting lower lip extended like a small shelf. "He's down in the basement, all by his mean, miserable little self. I told him to come straight up here and apologize for what he said about you at the tenants' meeting. He said no. Said this was just another one of your tricks. Said he has to see *proof* a white man can be decent before he changes his mind."

So. Another pair of blinders to remove. By force, if necessary. "I'll go down and talk to him."

"Won't do no good. He's stubborn as a mule. You just have to wait and let him see for himself. When he finds out we don't have to leave this house and go on no reservation, he'll change his ways."

"Yes," DuBois remarked. "That should put the quietus on Little Big Noise for a while. At least let us hope so."

"But how you gonna stop 'em from dislocating us, Landlord?"

"If you do not have faith in the Landlord's powers, Miss Perkins," DuBois chided gently, "perhaps you might have faith in your own. You might make some sort of charm that would help him prevail against the Authorities. A sort of super-efficacious witches' brew, or stew."

"Yes, why don't you?" Elgar chimed in. "I'd be glad to get you any ingredients you need." —Including, he thought eagerly, hairs from the head or other anatomical areas of one V. S. Phosdicker.

"I just wanta know how he's gonna stop 'em," Marge said worriedly, ignoring the suggestion. "What's he gonna *do?* When those government people get going, they mighty determined."

Elgar waved his hand grandly. "I have a plan."

"Hooray!" Fanny cheered. "Landlord has a plan. Let's leave him alone so he can think about it. Get off his lap, Walter Gee. Come on, everybody. Come on."

And, tiptoeing with amazing quietness, considering her size, she led the parade of tenants out of his living room.

Elgar bent and picked up the official letter. He pictured Phosdicker at his desk somewhere in the basement of City Hall. At this very moment, he was probably signing hundreds of these little disease-colored missives. "Blight," he was saying happily, with a wiggle of his nose. "I can smell blight a mile away."

"Begin to tremble, Phosdicker," Elgar muttered. "For this time, you are up against a worthy adversary."

"Kindly address all inquiries to this office," he read again. No, it would not be in a spirit of kindliness that he would address future inquiries to that office, but in a spirit of hostility and out-and-out mutiny. After he had surrounded the house with sandbags, equipped the roof with mortars, and mounted machine guns in every window.

Then he calmed down, and his fantasy collapsed. Bluster would not accomplish his aims. Neither would open warfare. No, he had to have a plan to present to the city. A plan that mastered *their* Master Plan.

Elgar sat for ten minutes with the tips of his fingers together. Then for twenty minutes with fingers intertwined and thumbs against his nose. Then tried leaning back, hands behind his head, feet up on the desk, bare toes wiggling with excitement.

Elgar had always had a sensitive eye and a love for forms and their arrangement in space. Plus a built-in taste barometer and a disregard of convention—or, rather, a basic innocence of convention—that allowed him to be highly original. But his previous plans—his unrealized design, for instance, for his own residence—were mere charming toys compared to this sweeping vision of an entire community. His imagination roamed the entire field of his vision, probed details, filled in blank spaces, stepped back, checked, and found the entire picture pleasing. It would work, he knew it in his bones; it would work, it would be beautiful, and it would *pay.* In his feeble, easily discouraged gropings in the directions of real estate and architecture, Elgar had absorbed more knowledge than he knew. His ideas on design, costs, construction, and materials were sound. Any architect could put them down. He even had an architect in mind. He was only stopped at one point, to which he kept returning. Money.

Levin, on the other side of a high, altarlike desk, regarded him sorrowfully.

"Even if you sell all of your holdings, Elgar, which I do not advise, which in any case your father will not permit—"

"Leave my father out of this, Levin. You and I will get along fine if we play fair with each other. But bringing up my father is dirty pool. *Very* dirty pool."

"—Even, as I say, if you convert all of your holdings to cash, which is not advisable, Elgar, you will not have the money required for a project of this scope. Check?"

"The government will lend me the money, Levin, that's the beauty of this thing. I looked it up, it's all in the U.S. Housing Act. Section 221 (d) 3, Levin, you should keep up with the times."

"But you have to have *private* money before you can get any of that public money. And no institution will lend it to you, Elgar. How could they? Institutions have to have some consideration for their investors, after all. And with your lack of experience, your record of recklessness with your assets, your habit of making emotional rather than rational decisions—oh, it is impossible, I tell you, Elgar. Impossible. Check? Now please go away."

Elgar took a deep breath, swallowing all the expletives he felt like showering on Levin so that, instead of causing the stockbroker pain, they merely created painful air bubbles in Elgar's stomach. Swearing at Levin would accomplish nothing; it was as futile as his idea of mounting artillery on the roof. In his own way, Levin was as helpless as Elgar. He was merely another Authority-Figure. And all Authority-Figures were doomed to rigid performance of their roles—to stubborn conservatism, to nay-saying instead of yea-saying, to Right Thinking which led to conclusions that Elgar knew in his heart were inevitably wrong, wrong, wrong.

Elgar had always been a loser in his battle against Authority, but lately, secretly, he had begun to cherish a different picture of himself, as a sort of David in modern dress: modest, self-effacing, a bit of a clown, perhaps, a bit of a dreamer, but carrying a mighty slingshot in his hip pocket. Now that he could no longer anticipate a successful encounter with that giant, the city, there was no point in ranting and raging. There was, in fact, nothing left for him to do.

Except sadly fold his pile of the architect's preliminary drawings (those cleverly staggered buildings, those cunning little apartments, those absolutely elegant copper drains), and pick up his royal-blue beret

(French wool, $8.95, the first cheerful purchase he had made in months), and walk out of Levin's office with quiet dignity.

Only one course of action was left to him. Borden had told him what it was. But did he dare to take it?

Even though he had felt the mantle of power settle on his shoulders at the meeting, even though he had felt the laurels of the hero, along with Fanny's kisses, on his brow that morning, Elgar's quivering stomach, his wobbly knees, answered "No."

Not that. Anything but that.

No.

But Walter Gee had said, "Landlord can do anything." And Fanny had kissed him.

He braced himself with a double gin and tonic, then went to the phone and dialed.

"Fathaw? How are you? It's me, Fathaw. Elgar."

"Speak up, boy. What's on your mind? I'm a busy man, you know. Don't waste my time."

"I know you're busy, Fathaw, that's why I almost never call, but the fact is, right now I need your help with something. If it's not too much trouble, that is. I hate to trouble you." Sickening, the way the cringing whine had crept into his voice. Anticipating defeat. Practically guaranteeing it.

"Gotten a girl in trouble, I suppose. Smashed up one of your cars again. Or running up gambling debts. Well, whatever it is, Elgar, I assure you, this time I am not going to bail you out of your troubles. You have made your bed; now you can lie in it, and I hope it's damned uncomfortable."

Elgar broke in at this point. "No, it's none of those things, Fathaw." But his voice was not angry; it was thin, weak, despairing.

"Well, what is it, then?" Julius Pride Enders thundered. "I don't have all day, Elgar. There are four visitors in my waiting room, officials, heads of corporations, important men. I can't keep them waiting."

"Well, the fact is, I do need money, Fathaw. Quite a lot of money, in fact."

There was considerable spluttering and choking at the other end of the line. Elgar both hoped and feared it might be fatal. He stood by respectfully, holding the receiver at arm's length, until the static cleared and became somewhat intelligible. Then, cautiously, he brought the phone closer to his ear.

". . . adequately provided for. More than adequately. That is the trouble with you, Elgar, you have had it entirely too easy. I was telling your mother the other day, if I'd had a tenth of your advantages when I started out, I'd have been fortunate. But I had nothing. I am a self-made man. Product of the School of Hard Knocks. And I did it all the hard way. Now, if you'd had to do the same, it would've been better for your character. I have been far too generous with you. But it is never too late to start building character. Hereafter I will correct my errors. You will get no further help from me for your foolish, frivolous—"

Don't cry, Elgar admonished himself sternly. Whatever you do, don't cry. "But it's a worthwhile project I have in mind, Fathaw. If you'd just let me explain—"

"How can it be worthwhile if you're connected with it? Don't try to pull the wool over my eyes, Elgar. That may be all right for your degenerate friends, bums and loafers like yourself, you may be able to impress them, but I know better. Oh, yes, 'Face facts' is what I always say, and it has been painful for me, Elgar, but I have faced the facts about you. I had great hopes for you once, but you have turned out to be utterly worthless, a bum, a loafer. . . ."

The words beat on like hammers, pulverizing Elgar into shreds. And from shreds to pale atoms, invisible, immaterial, floating away on the air.

"Why, at your age I was a millionaire. *Seven times* a millionaire. And I didn't get there by loafing and gambling. I got there by working day and night, seven days a week, no rest, no vacations. All so I could have something to pass on to your brothers and you, you ungrateful little—"

Elgar, who had never gambled in his life, gripped the phone with both hands and said hoarsely, "What am I supposed to be grateful for, Fathaw? The tough meat you fed me? The blue milk I drank? The unheated bedroom I slept in?"

"Are you being sarcastic? I was trying to build some character into you. But I failed. Yes, I can face facts, Elgar, painful though they are. I failed."

"Yes, you are right. You failed!" Elgar screamed into the phone. Damp trickles down his cheeks. He mopped them with his shirt sleeve. "You are always right, Fathaw. I hope it makes you happy."

"Elgar, I suspect you of trying to be sarcastic with me. I do not have to take that from you. One more word of sarcasm, let me tell you, and—"

"But I was not being sarcastic, Fathaw!" Elgar cried, beyond all hope of self-control. His intestines tied in a million tender knots. "I was being completely sincere. I was agreeing with you. You know how you like to have people agree with you, Fathaw; well, that was what I was doing. I was saying, 'Yes, Fathaw, you are right. You failed.' And I was going to go on to tell you exactly *how* you failed. Not only as a character-builder, but as a father, as a human being, as a man—"

"Enough!" came the roar. "I have had enough of this pointless babble, Elgar, and enough of these time-consuming conversations. I do not wish to hear from you again. Do you understand me, Elgar? Do not bother me any more. I wish to forget all about you. As far as I am concerned, you do not exist. Is that clear, Elgar? *You don't exist.*"

"Yes, Fathaw. Clear."

Perfectly clear.

Click.

17

Things back to their norm of misery. Fanny bucking her eyes at him as of old, and switching down the hall in high disdain. Marge serving meals like a lead automaton, eyes downcast, a sigh with every step. DuBois keeping his door closed night and day. No light emerging from beneath, but plenty of music: "Danse Macabre," "Valse Triste," and the "Marche Funèbre."

But this time there was no mystery about his tenants' behavior, Elgar having crept downstairs early for mail inspection and seen every box stuffed with a jaundice-yellow Notice to Vacate. And Walter Gee running to hide his face in his mother's swollen apron as if he had seen an ogre. That will do, Walter Gee. You don't know what a real ogre is. Yesterday I spoke to a real one, and today—

Today I am pale as skim milk, and as liquid, without any outline. Ghastly, evanescent, an apparition without form or substance, I do not walk to my appointment with the good doctor Borden, I flow. Pondering my unreality as I go.

To the good doctor Borden, who deserves my sympathy, or such sympathy as a specter can muster from his spectral soul, because he is up against such staggering odds.

"Borden," Elgar sobbed, flinging himself on the couch, "everybody hates me. My tenants, and Lanie, and probably you, too."

The doctor was nervously alert, like a bird dog scenting game. "Tell me, why should I hate you, Elgar?"

"Because," Elgar confessed, "I've had such rotten thoughts about you. That last session, Borden, a nasty suspicion got into my mind, and I couldn't let it go. I got to wondering, 'Why doesn't Borden want me to give up the house? Why doesn't he want me to go abroad?' No matter how I tried, Borden, I couldn't put the answer out of my mind.

'Because he doesn't want to give up the money he gets from me. The easiest money he's ever earned.'"

"It is not so easy as all that, Elgar," Borden said with a sigh. "Also, I am not a mind reader. I had no idea that you were entertaining such thoughts. But you should not feel guilty about them. They occur with every patient."

"Really?"

"Really. All patients occasionally resent the fees we charge, and accuse us of greed. This usually occurs at a time of high resistances. You did not like what I was pointing out to you last time. Therefore you had these thoughts."

Elgar was silent.

"There is no way to answer them, Elgar, except to point out that I have ample income for my needs. Yes. Also a waiting list which would supply whatever you took away."

Elgar looked around Borden's dingy office. The only new addition in two years was Elgar's suit of armor, which blended splendidly with the general decrepitude. "Borden," he said, "if you're doing so well, how come this place looks like a museum of Salvation Army rejects?"

"Ah," Borden sighed, "my preference for these furnishings, that is *my* problem, Elgar. Yes. But you are paying me good money to deal with yours. As you realize. So let us return to your opening statement. You say everybody hates you. Well now, you have always been prone to exaggeration."

"I *never* exaggerate, Borden."

"Perhaps you do not exaggerate your thoughts. No. That is the one area in which you could not exaggerate, because they are more extreme than any description could paint them. But your thoughts are not reality, Elgar."

"Well, I thought my tenants all loved me, and now I think they hate me. They are trying to annihilate me, and they're succeeding. I'm barely here."

"Not your tenants, Elgar," Borden said calmly. "Someone else."

"Ouch!" Elgar cried as his stomach went into a complicated contortion.

"Your tenants may have caused you some discomfort of late, Elgar," Borden said. "But I suspect that the real culprit is your father. As usual."

This time, Elgar could not deny the accuracy of Borden's suspicion.

"I suspect," Borden continued, "that your present situation with your tenants is not as bad as you think it is. Also that it was not formerly as good as you imagined it to be. You see—" he said, spreading his hands "—your blissful vision of Paradise with your tenants was like a piece of pastry anyway. What we call in Europe a puff-paste. A meringue. Destined to collapse unless filled with something substantial. Easily punctured because supported only by hot air."

"But it *was* good, Borden," Elgar insisted. "Listen. For the first time in my life I found some people who really loved me and wanted me. Sort of a second family. So naturally I ran to this second family, eager to be adopted. So naturally I got despondent when they turned their backs on me."

"Interesting that you describe this situation from the point of view of a child, Elgar. But let us pass over that for a moment. Describe to me your former idyllic life at your apartment house. Give me every detail. As you envisioned it. As it seemed to be."

"Well," Elgar said, "for one thing, I've fixed myself up a really decent apartment. Beautiful things, arranged just the way I want them. Comfortable chairs. Thick rugs. A king-sized bed."

"How were the furnishings in your childhood home, Elgar?"

"Miserable, Borden. Cold and bare. My father thinks too many cushions around the posterior are bad for the character. So instead of upholstered furniture, he bought us library benches. Big, hard, ugly library benches from some cut-rate country auction. Can you imagine how uncomfortable they were to sit on, Borden?"

Borden stirred sympathetically in his creaky, unupholstered swivel chair. Careening crazily on a broken hinge, it almost spilled him to the floor.

Elgar waited politely until the doctor had recovered his balance before continuing, "My brothers and I had to sleep on Army cots, too. Part of our Spartan upbringing. And the heat was always turned off upstairs. So in winter we had to jump into bed and shiver for an hour before we fell asleep.

"—And the towels! My father would buy second-hand hotel towels and rip them in half for us. Each of us boys got a half-towel once a week. You could never get yourself dry on those towels, and you had to have a special way of folding them to hide the ragged edge.

—Now I have beautiful thick towels a yard wide, Borden. With my own monogram."

"If I may speculate, Elgar," Borden interrupted, "I would guess that there is still a moment of doubt when you step out of your shower and reach for one of those towels. A moment when you fear that your father is watching you."

"Borden," Elgar admitted grudgingly, clutching his stomach, "you know too much. You know so much, you bastard, you could blackmail me for the rest of my life. That's why you're worth every cent of blood-money I'm paying you."

Borden inclined his head, acknowledging the compliment, ignoring its customary abusive language. "But go on, Elgar. In addition to rugs, towels, and other physical comforts, what were the other elements of your happiness on Poplar Street?"

"Oh, you've already heard about it, Borden," Elgar said. But when pressed he again described the bliss that had begun with the love-feast of the rent party: his love affair with Fanny, Marge's motherly generosity, his comradely sessions with DuBois. "And now it's all gone, Borden! Where did it go?"

"Frightened away, I suspect, by your moving in. Moving in too close too soon. By settling yourself on the premises you have probably aroused some suspicion among your tenants. But nothing like the murderous hostility which you imagine, Elgar."

Elgar was far from convinced. "Oh, no?"

"No. You have a need to picture this hostility, because you feel you must suffer for your former pleasure. To your overdeveloped conscience, a punishment must be meted out for every reward. According to some strict system of bookkeeping set up by an arch balancer of the personal books. A sort of office manager of the psyche. Who is, as we know, your father."

"Ouch!" burst from Elgar, followed by another outcry. "But my father's got nothing to do with it!"

Borden said mildly, "You still deny, Elgar, that your father is the source of your difficulties? Perhaps we can find further evidence."

Elgar had all the evidence he needed, in his guts. "No," he confessed in a low, trembling voice. "I know he's my biggest problem. In a way. But only in a way. I didn't want to admit this to you, Borden. But I called my father yesterday."

To do him credit, Borden restrained himself from shouting a triumphant "Aha!" He simply said, "Continue."

Elgar's stomach relaxed a little. "Well," he said, "I found out why my tenants hated me. They thought I was part of the Urban Renewal scheme. Or, at least, that I stood to profit from it, and was going to sit back and let it happen. Well, at the community meeting, I got mad, and I don't know what happened, but for ten minutes, I felt like a hero. For a whole day I was a hero to my tenants, too."

"Yes?" Borden asked. "And then, Elgar?"

"And then I realized there was only one way I could change the city's plans. I could have an Urban Renewal proposal of my own, if only I had the money. So I called the old bastard and asked him."

"And what did he say, Elgar?"

"He said," Elgar said, "that as far as he's concerned, I don't exist." He sat up in panic and looked at his feet. They had not vanished, after all. Reassured, he lay down again. "And ever since then, my tenants have been treating me the same way. Like I'm not there, except that they notice a bad smell or something, and they wish it would go away."

"There may be some other explanation of your tenants' behavior, Elgar. Something that has nothing to do with you." Elgar started to interrupt. But Borden raised his hand for silence. "People are not merely the instruments of your pleasure or the agents of your pain, Elgar. That is the way the young child sees people, his parents, for instance, because he thinks that the world revolves around him. But really, people have other things on their minds, Elgar. They are not always thinking about you."

"But I want them to think about me!" burst from Elgar.

Borden was suddenly very still, very attentive. "Why?"

A small voice answered, "Because, unless they pay attention to me, I don't feel real."

Borden smiled triumphantly. "Now we are seeing something very important, Elgar. We are seeing that you have to imagine that people love you or hate you, because otherwise you don't exist. Any kind of strong feelings, even negative ones, are better than this vacuum, this nothingness in which you cease to be.

"—But you see, Elgar, a healthy person has a sense of himself which does not depend on the reflections of others. Even alone in a room without mirrors, such a person knows who he is."

Elgar from experience had very little faith in that idea. Alone in a room without mirrors, he would simply disappear. He had not even known what he looked like until Lanie showed him. There was simply not enough of him to survive the hatred of others or, worse, their ignoring him. He told Borden so.

"That is why you have to begin now to build an identity, Elgar," the doctor said, and closed his notebook.

The closing of that book, signifying the end of the hour, was like the closing of a door on hope. "But how?" Elgar howled.

"Start anywhere, Elgar. It does not have to be a very large or important beginning. That is where you have made your mistake, thinking you have to be as important and all-powerful as your father in order to exist at all. —As to the advisability of calling him, well, we have discussed that before. Perhaps, this time, you had to do it. Perhaps, now, you are strong enough to handle it. We shall see."

The great choking bubble of anguish in Elgar's throat finally broke and was released as speech. "I'm *not* strong enough, Borden, that's what I've been telling you! My father's almost destroyed me. I'm barely here. One more push from anybody, and I'll vanish."

"Then at least," Borden said, "you realize now that your father is more dangerous to you than anyone else. Perhaps, now, you will cease blaming your problems on your tenants and everyone else around you. That is tremendous progress, Elgar."

"But—"

"Now, Elgar, I am not going to indulge you any longer. This has been a very successful hour. You should be pleased. See you tomorrow."

Poplar Street presented a panorama that almost frightened Elgar back uptown. Unusually large crowds had formed on both sides of the street, and Elgar, feeling that both sidewalks were unsafe, proceeded cautiously up the middle, placing his feet firmly on the white line, swerving when necessary to dodge a large station wagon filled with hostile, dark faces and a rickety old Buick filled with grinning, friendly ones.

"Get the white man's boot off your faces before it's too late!"

Elgar looked across the street and found himself staring into the fanatical red eyes of the speaker. Copee, in the business suit that was his new uniform, had found himself a soapbox and an audience.

"You don't have to go back to Africa," he told them, "but you do have to go back to your holy African dignity! Back to your holy innocence, before the white man branded you with his stigma of inferiority! Back to the way you felt about yourselves before he abducted you from your homes and exploited the sweat of your beautiful black bodies and raped your beautiful black wives! Back to the time when you were kings and queens! You have forgotten who you are; you have lost yourselves in the white man's confusing world. Now, I beg you, hold up your heads again, be kings and queens again, be proud!"

The sweat pouring down Copee's forehead mingled with the tears from his eyes as he held out his hands and pleaded, "Be proud, my people—please, please, PLEASE be proud!"

All around Copee, dusky feet shuffled uncertainly in the dust, as if his listeners did remember having once trailed clouds of glory, but so vaguely that the memory was only the faintly disturbing shadow of a dream. Elgar's heart went out to them. He wanted to cry out, "I understand; I am one with you, if not of you. I too have forgotten who I am; I too am lost."

Across the street Copee's competition, a band of skilled performers on the bongo and conga drums, took up the pause with artful thumps and flutterings. The crowd turned their faces in that direction: a welcome diversion, better understood. One of the musicians took out a harmonica, wiped it across his mouth, and began to improvise a solo against the intricate drum rhythms. Several members of Copee's audience started to wander across the street. But they changed their minds and stayed with Copee when he found the rhythm they understood and loved best, the rhythm of the preacher:

"Who took you away from your rightful homes? Was it or was it not the white man?"

"It was, brother, that it was."

"Who set you to work in his blazing fields and his steaming kitchens? Was it or was it not the white man?"

"You are telling it truly."

"Who snatched your sons away from you and sent them to die in his wars? Was it or was it not the white man?"

"Lord, it's the ever-livin' truth!" An old woman, uttering these words, leaped straight into the air, tears pouring down a wrinkled face that was like a piece of tanned leather.

"And who is now so mean—so selfish—so hard in his heart that he is turning you out of your homes—tearing them down and putting you out in the street to die? Is it or is it not this same white man who kidnaped you, exploited you, robbed you, raped you, lynched you, and today doesn't want your children in his schools?"

"It is, yes it is! The same one!"

"The very same!"

"Amen, brother. Tell it again!"

"And I'll tell you just why the white man doesn't want your children in his schools. They might learn to read—and then they might find out just how evil he is! They might get to read this book I have here—by a *white man*—who confesses, himself, just how evil it is to be white! Now, friends, the writer of this very famous book talks about the evil of whiteness. He says that all evil things have always been white, from whales and sharks and bears to ghosts and men! Now just listen while I quote from this book from a famous white writer:

> *'What is it that in the Albino man so peculiarly repels and often shocks the eye, as that sometimes he is loathed by his own kith and kin? It is that whiteness which invests him, a thing expressed by the name he bears.'*

"Now, what more proof do you need, friends? Here we have a white man confessing that white people are loathsome and repulsive!"

"Hear, hear!"

"And they smell funny, too," the leathery-faced old lady declared, adding her own footnote to Melville. "White folks smell like wet dogs when they get up in the morning. I've lived with 'em, and I know."

"But there is more, my friends!" Copee cried. "Listen while I read to you:

> *'The Albino is as well made as other men—has no substantive deformity—and yet this mere aspect of all-pervading whiteness makes him more strangely hideous than the ugliest abortion. Why should this be so?'*

"—*I'll* tell you why it's so—because the white man *is* an abortion, a monster who was never meant to survive. Without the sweat of your bodies and mine—without the sacrifices we have made and the abuses we have suffered—he never *would* have survived!"

"Amen, amen."

"Preach it, brother, preach it loud and clear."

"Now let me tell you what this white man says about other white creatures. He says:

'Witness the white bear of the poles, and the white shark of the tropics; what but their smooth, flaky whiteness makes them the transcendent horrors they are?'

"Now my message to you is this: The white man who charges you high rents for slum apartments and high prices for cheap merchandise is a shark."

"Amen."

"The white man who has you in the grip of his cruel economic system and won't let you go is a grizzly bear! With a hard-frozen Polar bear heart!"

"Ain't it the truth?"

"The white man who comes down into your neighborhood and robs you and cheats you—but won't let you come into *his* neighborhood to live—is the lowest of God's creatures! Learn to know your enemy, brothers and sisters—learn to recognize him so you'll always know who he is!"

Copee pointed a skinny, accusing finger at Elgar. "And there he is, my friends! Right there in your midst."

Elgar froze in the middle of the street as fifty pairs of eyes turned on him with dark, enigmatic stares. For a terrible moment he positively craved the non-existence that always threatened him. He wanted fervently to disappear, but visible he remained, as Copee went on with his accusations,

"He may say he is a decent landlord—but all the while he is planning to dispossess us!

"He may pretend he is a man of good will—but we know better than to trust his good will after three hundred years of his lies!"

"Well said, brother, well said."

"He may even try to pretend he is our friend—but we know no white man can be a friend to us! The black man's only friend is the black man!"

"Tell it like it is!"

"He may even—now hear this, my friends—he may even try to camouflage his color by coming to live among us—but he can't get away with that, he remains a ghastly, unnatural white! An abortion of Nature, a mistake of God! He can't help his evil nature—he's a born monster! He'll trick you and cheat you the minute you turn your back. He'll dispossess you and dislocate you for the sake of a lousy dollar. Because the dollar is all he cares about—he doesn't care about you!—Look at him, my friends! Do you want to be like him? Is *this* what you want to integrate with?"

"No, no!"

"No! Give this abortion a wide circle, my friends. Have as little to do with him as possible. Turn your backs forever on the ghastly white man and his unnatural ways!"

At the beginning of Copee's oration, Elgar had felt the pleasant glow of being part of a group, a member of an interested audience. Then, when Copee singled him out as the object of hatred, and he felt all eyes turn on him, he had imagined he might be the victim of mob violence.

But when, instead of cries of "Lynch him!" and "String him up!" they simply turned their backs on him, drawing closer to Copee and excluding Elgar from the circle, he became *no one*. Because Copee had made of him a fantastic symbol that had nothing to do with his real self, Elgar was suddenly no one at all. All his other selves—lovable fellow, brave fighter, excellent horseman, good plumber, ardent lover, sincere friend—had simply vanished with the turning of those backs.

Elgar found himself running with the floating ease of a dream. Holes in the crowd opened up magically to let him through, then closed up behind him as if he had never been there. Touching no one, he traveled as swiftly as the wind; seen by no one, he was as colorless as water, as insubstantial as air.

But at least he still had the title, LANDLORD—there it was, on the bell—and the duties and responsibilities it implied.

In the gloom of his first-floor hall, which was no more brightly lit than the Trejour's because someone, probably Fanny, kept stealing his light bulbs, Elgar removed a bundle of papers from one pocket with a trembling hand. These were the requests he had jotted down:

Fanny wants inside bolt on her door.
Marge has no pilot light on stove.
DuBois needs washer on bathtub faucet.
Fanny needs new linoleum under sink.
Landlord's toilet is so noisy, you can hear it flush all over the house.

The bottom one, rumpled and much folded, with a year's creases, still was:

Measure windows for weatherstripping today.

—Need new light bulbs in hall, he thought, but instead of doing something about it, he jotted it down on a piece of scrap paper, bundled it in with the rest of his pile, and shoved them all into his pocket again, along with the Worry List. Pockets, he felt, were where problems belonged

Running up the steps to his own apartment, Elgar thought he saw a snake, thought he heard a hissing sound. From far off, he also heard tom-toms (or were they bongos?) and the unearthly howls and screeches of jungle beasts and birds.

Once inside his apartment, he seemed to hear voices. Fanny and her husband, equally bent on tearing him apart. Mothaw and Fathaw, arguing over which parent would have ultimate possession of his tattered soul.

"Neither of you! None of you!" he screamed on his way into the bathroom. "I belong to nobody but me!"

He peed, then stood in front of the toilet for a very long time, trying to remember what he had come in for. Finally, sighing, he flushed the toilet and walked out of the bathroom.

Fortunately the flushing really was loud, loud enough to drown the shrill voices in his ears. He returned to the bathroom and checked the medicine cabinet for the cache of sleeping pills he had hoarded against the possibility of a night like this. Yes, they were all there, three dozen golden beauties, ready to be mixed in a Plan S cocktail. If he couldn't silence the voices in one way, he would in another. Forever.

Mothaw was at his elbow as he bent over the toilet tank, exclaiming in bird-chirps, "Oh, no! Not my darling! Mustn't soil his beautiful, sensitive hands with nasty, messy plumbing repairs! Those hands will belong to a great violinist someday."

Elgar was shaking when he finished operating on the toilet, but he *did* finish, in spite of Mothaw's protests.

Next, he got out the yellow-pages phone book and looked up Saf-T Screen and Storm Sash, Incorporated. Fathaw stood behind him as he dialed, and when Elgar ordered custom storm windows and screens for the entire house, the paternal claws almost choked him. But again, not quite. Merely a soreness in the neck muscles that persisted while he was calling the gas company for Marge.

Gas. Now that was an idea, he thought after hanging up. Now he had *two* possibilities.

Elgar lay back on the monogrammed initials of his royal-blue bedspread (extravagant at $79.95; at home they'd had plain cotton blanket spreads) and considered his choices, meanwhile allowing himself to become a battlefield for his parents, the locus of the battle somewhere inside himself, while his mind coolly rose above it. Let them fight it out between themselves, he had nothing to do with it; he was not a person, merely the object of their passions. While they battled he would calmly consider his two alternatives. Call Lanie, or call Borden. No, that was not what he had had in mind. Neither of them could help him. He needed somebody right there on the premises. Now.

He did not know how long he slept, flat on his back and fully clothed, having a dream in which he implored his executioners, "Why do you hate me? I've been so good to you," while Lanie's magnified, distorted face was like a giant balloon as she laughed and laughed at him endlessly.

He was awakened by a new presence in the room, a mere shadow of a movement, an echo of a noise. His first thought was that he had swallowed the sleeping pills, and they had failed him.

Elgar's instantaneous rage changed to relief when he realized he had simply fallen asleep. Then he remembered that he could not use gas. His apartment had no stove. He had to go through with his original Plan S, after all.

He got up, went to the bathroom, took the supplies from the medicine chest, returned to the living room, and went over to the bar-chest under the Picasso drawing, a blobby matador and bull, cheap at eight hundred dollars, which none of his tenants but DuBois had appreciated.

This would be quite literally a cocktail to end all cocktails. A masterpiece. One part gin. One part wine, gentle Rhine water, loving mother's milk. And thirty-six pretty, fizzy little sleeping pills, cadged from Borden and other doctors one at a time and hoarded over the years. Off with their pretty plastic jackets, pop! and drop the precious powdered contents into the glass. Stir, and prepare for sweet dreams. Add a cherry for insouciance. S for slumber. And surcease. And suicide. And—

"Stop!"

"Who said that?" Elgar inquired mildly—having faced annihilation, nothing could frighten him. He began to explore the darkened room. By this time his hands were educated to recognizing the contours of small, soft bundles. Walter Gee again. Eyes sealed shut with sticky lashes. Tearstains in wobbly stripes down his face.

Elgar grabbed the child and shook him angrily. "You almost made me knock my drink over, shouting out like that in the dark. See what you almost made me do? It would take me another two years to save up that many pills."

This only made the boy scream louder and babble more incoherently.

Relenting, Elgar led the way to the large Nile-green chair, the one with the high back. He sat down in it and pulled the wailing boy onto his lap.

"Now what's the trouble this time, buddy-o? What's bothering you now? Be a big boy, Walter, and tell me."

"Mama she go hopital. Gone to bring home baby bubba. Pop-pop, he talk crazy. All night long. I alone in the dark. Don't like it in the dark. I come up here because you have lots of lights. How come you don't have the lights on, Landlord?"

"All you have to do is ask. Our aim is to please," Elgar said, and gently lifted the boy from his lap. He leaped energetically around the room, turning on the Japanese bubble lantern, the aluminum-cone twin-cobra, the floor torchère, the Tiffany prettylight, all of his delightful adult toys, until the apartment blazed like Macy's lamp department. "After all," he said with a grand gesture and a bow, "the first thing the Lord said was, 'Let there be light.'"

As the candlepower in the room increased, the boy's sobbing slowed down. By the time the reading lamp on the desk went on, he was talking volubly and clearly. About his father's plans to organize his members into troops and march on City Hall after he had killed Mama and the new baby. And about his mother's and Miss Marge's belief in magic.

"They say they talk to ghosts in the dark. They burn candles in the dark to make the spirits come. I don't like it. I scared of ghosts. The dark is full of ghosts. I come up here because it's light up here. Can I stay?"

"Well, sure. Glad to have you. You will never know how glad, Walter Gee."

"*Can I stay?*"

"Sure you can. Any old port in a storm, hey? Here, I'll tuck you in. Right to sleep you go. Ho. Leave all the lights on while you sleep. I'll crawl in with you a little later. O.K.?"

"O.K."

That was Walter Gee's last word for many, many hours. He dented the pillow like someone who meant business. He did, however, hang onto Elgar's thumb, since his own was busy being sucked, while he drifted off to cotton candyland.

Elgar sat on the edge of the bed and pondered. For all the limitations of his powers of self-expression, the kid obviously had intelligence. In fact, he was smart as a whip. Not merely shrewd in the way of cunning little animals, but bright, and alert, and alive. Already he had difficulty talking straight, however. In another year or so he wouldn't be able to think straight, either.

Walter Gee deserved a better chance than the atmosphere of violence and confusion in which he was being brought up. But how in hell was he going to get it?

As soon as he could disengage his thumb, Elgar got up, picked up the Plan S cocktail and poured it down the john, which now flushed quietly. After that he sat up, while the boy slept on, and drank beer, and pondered, and smoked cigarettes, and pondered some more, until the natural light in the room outshone the artificial. Working up, against a world that arranged to waste this small life and so many others, a rage to end all rages.

18

Thinking about Walter Gee, hoping he was still sleeping the lovely sleep of trust upstairs, Elgar arrived at the door of the Copees' apartment raging strongly enough to battle Goliath, let alone one undersized, intensely nationalistic tenant.

But it was like stepping off a curb that wasn't there; he met no resistance. The door swung back instantly at his touch, and once he was inside, a quavery voice from one corner of the darkened living room greeted him with, "Come in, brother. Peace." It sounded like an old man.

The curtains were drawn over tightly closed Venetian blinds, as in the happier days of his and Fanny's love-trysts. Stumbling nostalgically over her bronze Buddhas and ceramic lions, Elgar finally located the source of the greeting: an ancient specimen of humanity cowering on the floor in the corner.

Elgar squinted through the lurid shadows cast by Fanny's Woolworth dragon lamps. About three minutes passed before he realized that the pitiful little heap of russet skin and bones on the floor was Charlie Copee. Shaking all over, with tremors in his voice as he said tenderly,

"Peace, brother. Love and peace. I wish to apologize for all my angry words and actions. I have seen the light, and I am ashamed of what I have said and done. I want us to be brothers. I want to shake your hand."

When Elgar complied by stretching out his hand, Copee took it in both of his and hung on desperately.

"Brother," he said, "a terrible thing has happened. After a week of fasting for freedom, I woke up this morning, and found I had turned white overnight."

Elgar, never confident of his own hold on reality, checked and double-checked the evidence of his senses. Copee obviously had been fasting;

he had lost about twenty-five pounds. But just as obvious, even in the artificial sunset of the room, was the unchanged red-clay hue of his complexion.

A pair of skinny brown claws gripped Elgar's hand. "This morning," Copee whispered, "for the first time, I felt all of the black man's hatred turned against me. It shook me, brother. It really shook me. I never knew it was so strong."

"Maybe it isn't," Elgar said, feeling suddenly sturdy and hopeful and sane, "except in your mind."

"No." Copee began to shake like a bunch of dry leaves in a strong wind. "No, it is terrible. I know. It is like the hot breath of a hundred wolves. I have felt it, and I know. Now I want to ask you something, brother. Please tell me. How do you stand it?"

"Well, I don't know," Elgar said. He pondered. "For one thing, there's this phone number I call."

"Call it then, brother," Copee begged him. "Please call it now."

Amazing how all of Elgar's frothing, bubbling rage had diminished to a small, clear stream of pity. When Borden answered, he got his message across as quickly as possible.

"Borden, I know it's too much to hope for, you fraud, you don't even have a medical degree, but do you have any connections with a hospital?"

Surprisingly, Borden answered, "Yes, Elgar. Why?"

"I need the butterfly-net boys in a hurry. I have a prize specimen for them. One of my tenants."

"Is it Copee?"

"Borden, you never cease to amaze me," Elgar said. "With your psychic intuition, you don't need a degree. How did you know?"

"From your descriptions in previous sessions. You have variously referred to all of your tenants as crazy, Elgar. But I always felt that Copee was the only one who really merited that description. His generalized hostility, his elaborate constructions of systems to distort reality, his various disguises, et cetera."

Copee's little coal-like eyes were watching Elgar intently, with passionate hope, as if he had found a new religion and Elgar was the object of his faith.

"Borden," Elgar said, frightened, "I've really got my hands full here. It's peaceful right now, but I don't know for how long. Any minute it may get turbulent. Talk about identity crises. Wow. This guy takes turns being everybody."

"Why it is wise to settle for being oneself, Elgar. All right. You hold on while I call the rescue squad on the other line."

Copee reassured Elgar, "Do not be afraid, brother. I am not angry any more. How can I protest against my fate? It is absolutely fair and just. Turning white is my punishment for hating the whites so much. For preaching hatred in the classroom and on the street corner. For going on a seven-day hate fast. Now I have become what I hated so much. The ways of God are mysterious, brother, but they are always wise and fair."

There was something attractive about Copee's madness, something that drew Elgar closer. As if, in reversing all his angry attitudes, Copee had found a kind of luminous, holy peace.

This shone from his eyes as he said, "I must ask you to forgive me, brother. Because I have hated you the most, it is your forgiveness I need most."

Elgar was moved to greater pity than he had ever felt before. Also to vague stirrings of guilt, since Charlie had every reason to hate him. "Well, you have it, Charlie," he said. "Consider yourself absolved." Meanwhile wondering what was going to absolve *him*.

"Oh, thank you," Copee said fervently. "We have much to talk about, you and I. The plight of our lost brown brothers, doomed by history to walk in darkness. They are the burden we carry on our shoulders, brother. We must lift them up, or they will drag us down. To a terrible fate. I am talking about the war between the races, the war to end all wars. Armageddon. The destruction of the entire human species."

Elgar was almost hypnotized by the warmth in Copee's voice and the inspired light in his eyes. While sane by all the standard definitions, Charlie had been crazy; now, having flipped, he seemed to have attained the highest and holiest sanity.

Careful, boy, Elgar warned himself. Remember your own sanity is none too strong. Watch out. He'll soon have you believing black is white and down is up. Next he'll convince you you're Moses. Or Gandhi. Or Martin Luther King.

"We must not allow that to happen, brother. And it can happen, believe me. Their anger is so strong."

"Tell you what," Elgar said. "We'll form a committee."

"Excellent," Copee said. "Organization is the first step. We must hold a meeting immediately. To elect officers, adopt by-laws and write a constitution."

"I nominate you for president, buddy. Only fair thing. After all, it's your organization."

"I accept the nomination," Copee said solemnly. "My platform is peace."

"I'll vote for that," Elgar said. "I guess you can consider yourself elected, Charlie. Seeing as how I'm the entire membership."

"I appoint you my lieutenant. And I delegate to you the responsibility of recruitment."

Elgar was getting tired of this game. It reminded him of the way he'd felt, back at the Green House, when the other inmates had threatened to draw him into their powerful fantasies. One particularly persuasive nut, believing himself to be Supreme Commander of the Allied Forces, had singled out Elgar as a likely general. They'd spent many happy hours together plotting and mapping the campaigns of World War II, until Elgar had disagreed with his commander on the issue of troop deployment in Italy.

Shaken, stripped of his rank, and drummed out of the service by his irate superior, Elgar realized he had begun to take his generalship far too seriously. Had been saluting himself daily in the mirror, carrying a hand-whittled swagger stick, and clicking his heels smartly on entering the dining room. He must be constantly on his guard lest something like this happen again.

"Any questions, Lieutenant?" Copee asked gravely.

"Uh, where were we?" Elgar wondered. "Oh, yes. Recruitment. What are the ground rules, Chief? Is this organization restricted, or is it interracial and international?"

"Oh, yes," Copee said. "Completely unrestricted. We will call it—the Pan-Humanity-Solidarity Society."

"Solid," Elgar said. "I'd sort of hate to confine the movement to bearers of the white man's burden. After all, they've done a pretty sorry job up to now. Pan-Humanity-Solidarity. I like it, Chief. I like it."

Oh, God, he thought immediately, it's happening. You're beginning to take the game seriously. He's a nut, remember, a *nut*. It takes one to know one, that's why he's pounced on you.

If only Borden would get back on the phone. Borden, his one stable reference point in reality. The way sailors needed the North Star to guide them through black seas, Elgar needed Borden to help him find his way out of the gathering chaos.

Meanwhile those intense little eyes kept watching him. Fixing him with pinpoints of light that were sharp as bayonets. Charging him with responsibility, the last thing he wanted, responsibility for saving the world.

"What? Borden, is that you? Oh, thank God."

"Yes, Elgar," responded the familiar voice with the welcome hints of Vienna in its peculiar intonation. "The lepidopterists are on their way, with a police escort and sirens."

"Well, it's about time. If they take more than fifteen minutes, they'll have to cart away two specimens instead of one. I mean it. For Heaven's sake, Borden, don't hang up on me."

"No, Elgar. They should be there in ten minutes. Meanwhile let us talk."

"About the patient?"

"Yes. About you."

"Well," Elgar confessed, "last night I was pretty bad, Borden. Everything sort of piled up and got to be too much for me. I was ready to swallow the hemlock. Even had it all mixed in a glass. But things began to happen around here, and I got too busy to commit suicide."

"Too busy committing your tenant instead."

"Oh, ho ho ho. Very good. Oh, that's funny, Borden. I never knew you had a sense of humor. You poker-faced Prussian phony, you."

"There are a number of things you never knew about me, Elgar. For instance, I really am an emigré from Vienna. I got out of there during the war. Just in time." Borden sighed. "But enough of my life story. Yours is far more interesting. When will I hear the next thrilling installment?"

"Well, I don't know, Borden," Elgar said with a trace of peevishness. "Last night was when I really needed you. But you kicked me out of your office at the end of the hour, so I had to get out of the box I was in all by myself. Now maybe I'll be too busy to see *you* for a while. Turn the tables a bit. Ha. How would you like that, Borden?"

Borden, for some odd reason, seemed to like it fine. He even chuckled. "Good, Elgar. A sign of health. As long as you realize you must continue to pay me for your scheduled appointments, whether you keep them or not."

"Oh, you mercenary dog," responded Elgar. "Five minutes I've known you're Jewish, and already I want to say something anti-Semitic."

"Better you should say something anti-German, Elgar. They are the ones who left me with a number of sick relatives to support over there. And me, the only intact survivor of the family, forced to get out with all records of my training and experience destroyed."

Elgar was contrite. "Oh, I'm sorry, Borden. So sorry. Why didn't you tell me this before? Now I see why you stay at the Trejour. Now I see so many things. Forgive me for doubting your legitimacy, Borden. I was blind. Judging you on material evidence only. Just because you had lopsided chairs and a broken-down couch and no rugs. And I'm the one who hates materialism. Wow. —When I get straightened out I'm going to buy you some new furniture, Borden. Start thinking about the color scheme. Meanwhile you're welcome to the money whenever I cancel. I may have to miss a couple of hours in the next few days. I have a lot of people to look after here."

"An even better sign of health, Elgar."

"Why?"

"First it is necessary to stand on your own two feet. But the minute a man finds himself in that position, the next thing he should do is reach out his arms."

"You phony, you have arms of simian proportions. What were you doing with them last night, when I needed you?"

"I see you," Borden said smoothly, "for one hour at a time, preferably your regular, scheduled appointment hour. I do not give you extra time, Elgar, unless you are suffering a crisis. And these days, you are doing much too well to have crises."

"You smug s.o.b., you're wrong. Wrong, do you hear me? Last night I was schizzy as a see-saw, suicidal as a buzz-bomb. And you pronounced me healthy. You fraud. You fake. You sent me on home to die." Elgar was crying as he said this, because he did not want to believe his doctor could make mistakes. He wanted him godlike, infinite in his powers and patience, omniscient in his understanding. For he believed his sickness was so uniquely crippling that only a towering, Almighty personage, reaching down from a great height, could lift him out of it. If Borden were merely another man extending an equalitarian handshake across a room, he was weak, he was fallible, and Elgar was lost.

"Elgar," Borden said, "I may have made a mistake in judgment in sending you home yesterday. I frankly admit this possibility because I think you are ready to accept it. There are limits to my powers as there are to any man's. But something saved you from suicide last night. I have faith in that something which is larger and stronger than myself."

"It was a child, Borden. A five-year-old boy, afraid of the dark."

Borden was silent for a long time before he said, "Please convey my thanks to that child, whoever he may be, for whatever he did to render my mistake a minor one. That is the kind of fortunate occurrence that gives us faith to continue, Elgar."

"Yeah," Elgar said, "but what about my faith in you? What's going to happen to *that* now, Borden?"

"Hopefully it will continue, but it will grow more realistic, Elgar. As it is supplanted by faith in yourself. Yes. You must learn that there are limits to all things. Even love. Even mine for you. If I loved you and indulged you without limits, I would not be able to help you. You too must learn to love without losing yourself, Elgar."

Also hate without losing yourself, Elgar thought, his eyes on Copee. Who sat crosslegged, staring lovingly into space, in a beautiful trance.

Aloud he said, "Oh, for Christ's sake, stop apologizing, Borden. After all the times I've cried 'wolf' and gotten away with it, you were right to chase me out of there yesterday. Don't worry, I'll keep my appointment tomorrow. I may not be able to make it today, though. If my ears don't deceive me, I hear two sets of sirens outside.

"One is playing high C and the other is playing D sharp, and they are both stopping outside my door. Mothaw may have been right about my musical sensitivity. It is a terrible discord, Borden, excruciatingly painful to my ears. I must do something to stop it right away."

19

As Elgar hung up, there was a violent crash outside. He ran to the door and found two ambulances joined, bumper to bumper, in dangerous copulation. Two men in white coats were arguing with Fanny in white fox, and she was winning.

"Here I come with a new baby, and here you jackasses come, driving like the street belongs to you. Well, when I get through suing you, your pay will be tied up tighter'n a drum for forty years. Where you from?"

"We're from the State hospital," one said.

"Well then, I'll sue the State," replied indomitable Fanny. "It has plenty of money."

"We're here on an emergency, Miss," one of the white-coats said.

"What do you mean, 'Miss'? You see me carrying this baby and you still ain't got sense enough to call me 'Madam'? Right in front of my own house, too. I'm gonna sue you for slander. Public slander. You think you got an emergency, you ain't seen nothin' yet. Believe me. I got rights, you know."

"Yes, she has," Elgar put in. "Civil rights."

"Oh, hey there, Landlord," Fanny called, waving a blue bundle. "Look what I brung home."

"You the guy that called for a rescue wagon?" one of the white-coats asked. There were two of them, one white, one Negro, ready to carry Copee off to an integrated Heaven.

"Right this way," Elgar said to them. "Don't go in there yet, Fanny. I have to speak to you a minute."

"What's the matter?" she asked, resisting his attempts to keep her from going inside. "Where are Walter Gee and Willie Lee?"

"They're fine, Fanny, fine. Don't worry about them. It's your husband. He's not so well."

"That ain't nothin' new, Landlord. He ain't never been well, not as long as I've known him. What happened? Did he finally go all-the-way crazy?"

A plain "yes" was called for, but Elgar was unable to speak plainly. "Er, you see, Charlie needs help, Fanny, and I sent for these gentlemen because I thought they might be able to help him."

Fanny looked suspiciously from Elgar to the two white-coats and back again. "He never wanted no help from nobody before. He never even let nobody come close enough to help him. What's going on? Can't nobody talk sense around here? What kind of a hospital is this *State* hospital, anyway?"

Looking gravely at Fanny, the Negro attendant raised his right hand, pointed his index finger at his ear, and delicately rotated it in a small, graceful circle.

"Well, why didn't you say so in the first place?" Fanny demanded. "Listen, you guys better be careful if you going in there after Charlie. That husband of mine is a handful. He subject to throw spears and hatchets and things at you. He might even have brung up some of them little old hand grenades he was making in the cellar."

"What?" roared Elgar. "Hand grenades? In *my* cellar?"

"For the revolution. It was all set to start the day I went in the hospital."

"Get the strait jacket, Waldo," the white attendant said to his colleague. "And have a hypo ready."

"Oh, those precautions won't be necessary," Elgar assured him quickly. "The, er, client is quite calm and peaceful this morning. He has undergone a radical personality change."

"You better believe it," Fanny said. "Any time Copee gets peaceful, there's been some *big* changes made. What's been going on around here, Landlord?"

"I promise you there won't be any trouble, if you'll just let me handle this," Elgar told the orderlies. "He thinks he's the leader of an important political movement. And I'm second in command, so I have to obey his orders. He'll probably want to sign you up as members on sight. Just play along, will you?"

"Sure, buddy," Waldo said. "We love to play games. Don't we, Sidney?"

"Take us to our leader," Sidney sang out, loud and clear.

"First," Waldo said, "there are some papers for the lady to sign. Didn't you say the patient was your husband, Miss?"

"If I did," Fanny replied stonily, "you must not of believed me. Landlord, you gonna be my witness when I take these jackasses to court?"

"Now, now, Fanny," Elgar said. "Calm down."

"If you will just sign here, Miss," Waldo said, holding out a long piece of paper.

"Son of a bitch," Fanny said. "Here I am holding this baby, big as life, and you're practically calling him illegitimate. When you know I'm a legal married woman, or you wouldn't be asking me to sign my husband in the crazy house. I got a mind to call my little old lawyer right now."

"First sign the papers, Fanny," Elgar urged.

"This is disgusting. I ain't got no pen, and I got no hands free to hold one, neither. Landlord, hold Wesley Free for me a minute so I can sign the papers for these dumbasses. Be careful. He just woke up."

The blue bundle that had been so quiescent while Fanny held it was suddenly thrust into Elgar's startled arms. It instantly began squirming.

Elgar handled the baby like a large egg, slippery yet crushable. He shut his eyes tightly, lest he look down and see himself repeated in miniature. Dear God, he prayed, there are enough neurotic, mixed-up people in this world already. You know You don't want any blue-eyed, blond African Indians.

Fanny came over and parted the top edges of the blanket. "Ain't he cute, Landlord? Look. The spittin' image of his father."

Finally Elgar worked up enough courage to open his eyes and look down. The baby had Copee's spiky black hair, and his arrogantly curving beak, and his evil, squinchy little eyes, and his reddish-brown-mud complexion.

Fanny bent over the baby and tickled its chin. "You his, you ugly little thing, you," she said with obvious love and pride. "You all his. You one hundred per cent legitimate. Like all my children."

"Oh, thank you, Lord," Elgar breathed. "Your ways are mysterious. But they are always wise and fair." It was the most hideous baby he had ever seen, but he was deeply sincere when he smiled and said, "You have a beautiful son, Fanny."

The baby gave Elgar an evil look, belched, and tensed all of its muscles into one small ball of hatred. It felt like a clenched fist. Elgar, alarmed, bent and peered more closely. Wesley Free threw up all over him.

"Landlord," Fanny inquired, "what's all this mumble-jumble on this paper here? My lawyer said I should never sign anything without reading it first. Said a girl has to watch out for her legal rights."

"It's just giving them permission to take Charlie away, Fanny. For a little rest." Elgar, trying vainly to wipe his face on his sleeve while holding the squirming infant, wished he were going instead.

"Well, why should I give these jackasses permission to take Charlie? They ain't doctors. They ain't even *drivers*."

"There are doctors at the place where he's going, Miss," Sidney said.

"He means 'Ma'am,'" Waldo corrected quickly, seeing the sparks leap up in Fanny's eyes. "And we promise to drive very carefully."

"Oh." Reaching into Elgar's shirt pocket for a pen and using his shoulder for a desk, Fanny signed her name with a flourish. She waved the paper at the attendants. "In that case, there it is. Signed with a ink pen, nice and legal. Landlord, watch out for Wesley Free's head. Don't let it joggle."

"Yes, Fanny," Elgar said, and endeavored to obey, shifting one hand to cup Wesley Free's skull while the other supported his damp lower areas. He noticed how emergencies seemed to bring out Fanny's quality of command, her ability to take charge in all situations. He had not suspected her of possessing this managerial ability before. Now he had something new to discuss with Borden. Perhaps, unconsciously, he was always drawn to managing types, however they masqueraded as sweet, uncomplicated little wisps of femininity.

He was saved from further speculation by the apparition of Charlie in the doorway, wrapped in a blanket, with one arm extended in a regal salute.

"Peace, brothers," he croaked. "Let the meeting come to order."

"Charlie!" Fanny cried. "What are you doing out here with nothing on but a blanket? My best one hundred per cent virgin's wool blanket, too. Get in there and put some clothes on!"

She ran up to her husband and tried to supplant his missing modesty, pulling the edges of the blanket together as she shoved him gently toward the house.

Charlie refused to move. "I do not know you, woman," he said. "Kindly release me."

"You don't know me?" Fanny echoed in disbelief. "But you were gonna kill me a week ago. Don't you love me any more, Charlie?"

Charlie continued to gaze at her, unmoved, with kindly, curious eyes.

"Charlie, remember you wanted to kill me because you thought I was gonna bring home a white baby? Well, you don't have to. Look!" Snatching Wesley Free from Elgar's shaky embrace, she held him up to Copee. "He's the spittin' image of you, Charlie. You have another son."

"Another poor atom of brown humanity. Born to a life of misery," Copee intoned. He looked at Elgar significantly. "Unless we work to change the conditions of his life, brother. We must dedicate ourselves to an unsparing effort."

Elgar nodded, moved in spite of himself by Charlie's strangely sympathetic madness.

"You are mistaken, Madam," Charlie informed Fanny kindly. "That cannot be my child. First of all, I have never seen you before. Secondly, as you will see if you will only look at me, I have the misfortune to be a white man."

"Ohhh!" Fanny wailed, tears running down her cheeks, her face distorted into a caricature of woe. "This is awful. Ohhh!" She leaned against Elgar for support. "I liked him better when he was mean, Landlord," she sobbed. "At least then he *knew* me."

Wesley Free began to cry in sympathy. His mother thrust him back into Elgar's reluctant arms, retreated to the running board of the ambulance, and huddled there, trying to contain her sobs.

Elgar cleared his throat. "Chief," he said, "these are two of our most trusted members. They've come to take you to an important meeting."

Copee seemed to falter for a moment. He inspected the faces of the two attendants. "I suspect a plot," he said, and wiped his sweaty forehead with the blanket. Then he looked at Elgar. "But who can I trust, if not my faithful lieutenant?"

Elgar felt himself beginning to sweat too. "You can trust me all the way, Chief," he said. And privately he vowed, *I will never give you any reason not to. Never again.*

"Fine," Copee said. "I am needed at the front now. I know you will do a fine job of carrying on your responsibilities here at headquarters, Lieutenant."

Hastily shifting Wesley Free to the curve of his left arm, Elgar saluted. Copee returned the salute, then drew himself up in military fashion, tightened the blanket around his shoulders, and swaggered toward the ambulance. Waldo and Sidney respectfully brought up the rear.

At the running board Charlie paused and politely assisted Fanny to her feet. "There have been many innocent casualties in this terrible conflict," he said. "Look after this unfortunate woman, Lieutenant. See that she has what she needs for herself and her child. She is obviously very confused."

"I will," Elgar promised.

"Oh, Landlord!" Fanny wailed. She found the protection of Elgar's right arm while her youngest nestled in his left. Both of them bawling at top volume. "He went crazy with jealousy, Landlord," she confided between sobs. "Soon as it came time for me to have this baby, he started to rave. 'Cause he thought it was yours."

The ambulance pulled away from the front door and Elgar shepherded the survivors into the house.

Fanny seemed to recover quickly once they were inside. "Whoee, Landlord, I'm a mess," she said with a glance at the mirror. Reaching inside her pocketbook, she pulled out nine pennies. "Copee's gone to the crazy house, and this is all I've got left. With three children to support. How'm I gonna live?"

"Don't worry, Fanny," he said. "You heard me promise your husband I'd take care of things. I'll think of something."

"Well, fine," Fanny said, inspecting her hairdo in the mirror. "First time I saw you, I felt better about things around here. I said to myself, 'I know that cute li'l Landlord ain't gonna evict *me*. He's too nice for that.'" She patted a flyaway curl into place. "I sure need to go to the Ugly Shop soon, though. Can you let me have twenty dollars to start with, Landlord?"

Wesley Free was drooling contentedly on Elgar's pure silk tie. The combination of his complacency and his mother's was too much for Elgar. "Fanny," he said, "you are neglecting your responsibilities as a mother. Take this infant away from me. No, wait. First get something to clean me up with. I'm all over vomit, ugh."

"Baby vomit won't hurt you none, it's nothing but milk," Fanny said, dabbing at Elgar's front with wads of Kleenex. "There you are, Landlord. Keep your elbow under Wesley Free's head. Don't let it roll around in the air so much."

"Wesley Free," Elgar said, holding the infant away from him, regarding its scowling face with mixed tenderness and repugnance. "Walter Gee. Willie Lee. Fanny, will you please tell me where you get these names?"

"I like them better than old, dead musical composers' names," she said with telling effect. "They rhyme with each other real nice. They rhyme with Copee, too. And this one's middle name means something. Free he's gonna be. Right along with his mother."

"I take it," Elgar said sarcastically, "that you are already getting used to the idea of living without your husband, Fanny. That you may even be looking forward to a little freedom."

"Landlord, you know my life with Copee ain't been no Sunday school picnic. What you expect me to do? Run and jump off a bridge 'cause he's gone?" She gave a practical shrug. "That wouldn't help nobody. My babies need me. Copee, he's crazy, so he belongs in the crazy house till he gets better. Should I want him here at home to drive *me* crazy, too? Me and my three children, all crazy? How would you like *that,* Landlord?"

Elgar felt an odd frustration. She was right. Yet in the world he came from, people knew enough to pretend a decent interval of anguish in these situations. Conventional hypocrisy, he felt, had its comforts. Fanny's hard-headed realism had none.

Worse, with devastating flutterings of her eyelashes, she was beginning to unbutton her blouse as she undulated gracefully in his direction. Trouble and the successful completion of a pregnancy both agreed with Fanny. She was slimmer, of course, yet rounder in the right places. Utterly adorable, as always, and, as always, utterly unprincipled.

"Oh, no!" Elgar said, and pushed her away violently, rejecting her with a force equal to the strength of the temptation. "It's not going to be like that, Fanny."

"Take it easy, Landlord," Fanny said. "I wasn't getting undressed for you. It's just Wesley Free's lunchtime."

With a great air of dignity she took the infant from Elgar's arms, applied him to her bosom, and curled up in Copee's big leather chair. Turning a modest and disdainful back to Elgar.

He was not fooled by this touching display of maternity. A moment ago she had clearly offered herself to him. In silence punctuated only by the noisy smacks of Wesley Free's greedy feeding, he pondered his problem. Lighting a cigarette because he needed something to put in his mouth, too.

Process of elimination was one helpful technique, Elgar had found. In order to define what the situation was, he would first define what it was not.

"First of all, Fanny," he said, "you are not going to be my concubine."

"Why not?" she asked. "Don't you like me any more, Landlord?"

How explain to her that his torment and near-suicide the night before had opened vast, empty, echoing spaces inside him? Spaces that her middle son's trust and her husband's strangely benign sickness had rushed in to fill? He was simply no longer the same irresponsible creature he had been in the days of his delightful romps with Fanny. Then he had been happy to explore a thrilling new world of shooting galleries, Ferris wheels, and merry-go-rounds. Now, however reluctantly, he recognized that the carnival had struck its tents and gone home.

Feeling the wrinkles settle into his brow one by one, as if stitched by the sewing machine of Time, he said, "I like you much more, Fanny. Perhaps that's why. Besides, the boys are getting old enough to understand things. And I made a promise to their father."

Fanny returned to the mirror and tucked Wesley Free casually under her left arm while she combed her hair. "Well, could you let me have that twenty anyway, Landlord? I think I'll get a tint job at one of them Ugly Shops. Then I can sue and collect a thousand dollars."

"Fanny," Elgar accused, "people like you have no right to have children. How you dare bring them into the world is beyond me. You are vain, silly, greedy, self-centered, irresponsible—"

"What do you mean?" Fanny said. She penciled her eyebrows with little feathery strokes, accentuating the fetching tilt of her eyes. "I'm a good mother. I do the best I can."

Elgar, sighing, relented a little. "I guess I shouldn't blame you for your crazy, money-making schemes, Fanny. I guess children need good fathers, too."

Fanny said calmly, "Well, you'll do till Copee comes back home again, Landlord."

Elgar just happened to look up in time to catch her delivering a smug little slant-eyed wink, a private congratulatory message, to herself in the mirror. From across the room the baby seemed to sense Elgar's sudden flare-up of anger. He began to cry lustily.

Roaring to make himself heard above the caterwauling, Elgar shouted, "No, Fanny! I am not going to be anybody's Great White Father!"

Well, now he had defined what the situation would not be. What would it be, then? More to the point, was it really his problem? Did he have to concern himself with Fanny's future? Let her take her squalling brood and pack them off to the poorhouse. What did he care?

He was stopped by the memory of Walter Gee's hand in his as he fell asleep last night. And by the shining trust in Copee's eyes as he charged him,

"Carry on here at headquarters, Lieutenant!"

And then he had an idea. A crazy idea but, remembering the flash of executive ability which Fanny had shown out on the street, one that just might work.

"Listen, Fanny," he said eagerly, "you told me once you wanted to be grand."

Fanny shrugged, as if to say, accurately, that grandeur was not the most practical inspiration for her present situation.

"Well, Fanny, I'm going to make an honest woman of you. I'm going to make you as legitimate as your children."

Fanny was skeptical. "How you gonna do that, Landlord?"

"I," he said, "am going to give you a chance to have the beauty parlor of your dreams."

"Beauty Saloon, Landlord," she corrected. "My own Beauty Saloon."

"All right. Beauty Saloon it is," he said, keeping a straight face with an effort. "I want you to go out and find a location for it, and buy everything you need. Sunken bathtubs, gilded hair-dryers, baroque douche fountains, the works. Don't stint on expense, Fanny. I'll pay for it all."

Fending off an avalanche of hugs and kisses, he added hastily, "—With the understanding, of course, that this is only a loan."

Fanny drew back suspiciously. "What's the catch, Landlord?"

"Only one. You have to do it all in four weeks. One month from now, you must be open for business. And I mean *business,* Fanny. No more collapsing on sidewalks, no more lawsuits, no more low back pains. And no more hanky-panky with me."

"Just tell me one thing, Landlord. Why are you doing this?"

Elgar sighed. "Let's just say I feel it will be cheaper in the long run than having you as a mistress, Fanny."

Fanny was suddenly very brisk and businesslike. All her coquetry had vanished. "Let's see. I'll need to find a place. And I'll need booths, dryers, rugs, cabinets, chairs—" Her eyes narrowed as she considered the enormity of the undertaking. "You say I got four weeks to get my business together?"

Elgar nodded. "Four weeks."

A damp, wiggly little bundle was thrust once more into Elgar's arms. The beige blur moving rapidly past him was Fanny, on her way out to acquire a business.

"Hey!" he called, startled; in the excitement of his new idea, he had forgotten all about Wesley Free. "Hey, come back here a minute. What do you feed this? What?"

"Don't look at me," Fanny said. "I'm a career woman now."

"Well, what am I supposed to do? I'm a career *man*."

"Call the doctor. His phone number's on the table there. Get a formula. Byeeee!"

Fanny waved to him sweetly, then vanished. Leaving Elgar with an unexpected burden in his lap, a burden he had not bargained for.

Elgar, looking down at the infant, decided to talk tough to him. Man to man. He cleared his throat and said gruffly,

"Listen, you. We have clearly established that you are not my son. Right? That has been established beyond any reasonable doubt. Check? So don't go getting too familiar. And don't get too damned *comfortable.*"

Wesley Free snorted, stirred, opened cloudy blue-black eyes, and arched his faintly visible brows. Then he smiled, an idiotic, contemplative smile that conveyed his satisfaction with his present circumstances, nestled against Elgar's shirt front, and began to drool.

20

The most amazing thing about little children, Elgar decided as he looked down at Walter Gee, still snoring contentedly in Elgar's bed, was their fantastic adaptability. He plopped the baby down beside his brother and rang the buzzer for Marge.

It was not long before he heard a heavy tread on the stairs and she entered, bearing a coffee pot, a covered dish, and the morning mail on a tray imprinted with the gaudy trade-mark of a well-known beer. In surly silence she poured his first cup of coffee into a cracked mug decorated with the emblem of the U.S. Navy, and stood there scowling at him as he sipped it.

Ah, well. At least the coffee was deliciously brewed. Elgar had achieved the outlines of the elegant life, even if certain details remained to be filled in.

"You better eat that omelet before it gets cold," Marge admonished him in her customary grim manner. "It's a *cheese* omelet. Made with four eggs."

"How do I know it isn't poisoned?"

Marge gave him an astonished look. "You've owned this house for over a year now, Landlord. You mean you still don't know who your friends are around here?"

"I know you're not one of them. How can you be? You scowl at me like a dragon. You snap at me like a crocodile. You order me around like, like—" He had run out of reptiles, and finished lamely, "like a four-star general."

"Shoot, that don't mean nothin', Landlord," Marge said calmly. "That's just my way, especially when I got worries on my mind. After all this time, you ought to be used to it."

Evidently she was not going to change. That was her prerogative. But Elgar, for his part, was not going to fall for any more of this rough-exterior, heart-of-gold propaganda. "You'll have to eat that omelet yourself, Marge," he told her.

"I've cooked for fussier eaters than you," she retorted. "Including fourteen husbands."

"And I'll bet nobody ever thought to ask you before whatever became of all those husbands." Elgar tapped his forehead. "That's because I'm the first person you ever ran into who can think for himself."

"Well now, I'm going to tell you a thing or two, Landlord," Marge replied angrily. "You want to know what my husbands died of? The same thing that's killing me. Poverty." She gestured at the room around them. "Look at what you've been able to do to this place. Only a few months ago it smelled like poverty, like every other place in this neighborhood. Now it smells like brand-new dollar bills."

Her head sagged; the wrinkles in her face became more prominent. "Love can't last around poverty. Neither can a woman's looks. There's a saying, 'Love flies out when the wind flies in,' and it's true, Landlord. If you've never known anything different you can stand it somehow, I guess. But, my God, I used to have a six-room suite at the Theresa and all the champagne I could drink. Now to be kicked out of my home, miserable as it is, and have to go to—to—" Her neck developed taut cords as she tried to complete the sentence and failed.

Elgar drew back huffily. It was unfair that he should be charged with personal responsibility for all the inequities inflicted on humanity. Yet it kept happening, and was probably the reason why his friendly, familiar tenants kept turning into angry strangers.

His hurt showed in his voice as he said, "I thought I was giving you a pretty good deal, Marge. Not many women can earn their living without going out the front door."

"Millions can," Marge said somberly. "Ain't you never heard of house-wives?"

Elgar was crushed. Moreover, since he was unable to imagine a fifteenth man who might be willing to marry Marge, he could not think of a helpful answer.

"It don't matter, Landlord," Marge said briskly. "The job's all right, I guess. It's just—well, I had an idea once I'd have a different kind of life."

He asked daringly, "What kind of life would you like, Marge, if you had your choice?"

"I'd like to do what I do best. Sing." Then she looked down at the floured apron covering the vast expanse of herself and moved to hide it with her crossed arms. "Ah, but look at me. Just look. They'd laugh me right off a stage."

Marge sighed. "Poverty did this too, Landlord. The worse things are, the more you eat. Bread and potatoes and gravy, all the wrong things. In a way you were right, Landlord. I did feed two of my husbands to death. Hubert and Henry ate so much of my food, they had heart attacks."

Elgar was depressed by this piece of news. What she had to say next was even more depressing.

"The rest of my husbands all spent my money and robbed me, Landlord. When I got wise and wouldn't put up with it no more, they left me. Every last one of them. Finally I decided I was never going to trust another man again. But it was too late. I was forty-five years old and broke and all washed up. I gave up my career for love, and what did it get me? Nothing but memories."

"But what a rich and varied collection of memories, Marge. Fourteen husbands, after all. A whole treasure-chest of recollections to brighten your old age. I envy you."

"Then you're a fool for envying a fool," Marge said sharply. "I was nothing but a fool for any man that came along and handed me a lot of sweet talk. And look what I gave up for it. A future in show business."

"Maybe you could make a comeback," Elgar offered hopefully.

Marge shook her head. Her face bore a tragic expression, as if she had given up. Observing how her tiny features and rosebud mouth had almost vanished into the vast sponge of flesh that was her face, Elgar hardly blamed her. But he was not going to allow his defenses to be weakened.

"A minute ago you claimed to be my friend, Marge. Well, if that's so, how come I caught you sticking pins in that doll that looked like me?"

To his surprise, she threw back her head and laughed richly. "Is that all's worrying you? Land sakes, Landlord, you are one funny man. That doll wasn't supposed to be you. That was Fanny's baby."

"Fanny's baby?" he repeated in bewilderment.

"Well, you see, Landlord, we was trying to make sure it wouldn't be a white baby. The idea was to make sure, if it was white, it wouldn't be born alive. It would only live if it was colored. I hated to do it, but Fanny was so desperate, and that husband of hers was talking so crazy, I had to do something."

"Well, congratulations," Elgar said. He indicated the sleeping cherubim. "It seems your work was successful, Marge."

"Awww," Marge burbled. "Ain't they cute? Awww!" Cooing and gurgling, she went over to the bed to get a closer look at the children.

Elgar followed her. His renovation had included opening the entire apartment to the sunlight by eliminating the living-dining partition and putting a new, large window in the back wall. As the light spilled down on the sleeping children, gilding their skin to the luster of bronze, he was struck by a thought. The colossal importance of light in the world.

Like all great ideas, it was a simple one, and Elgar, in his simple way, felt a tremendous excitement. His own most miserable hours had been spent in the airless darkness of his cell in the Trejour; his happiest ones in places like the D-R where the kilowatts flooded every corner. Long ago, at home, his misery had been underscored by his father's use of twenty-watt bulbs in every lamp and his miserly insistence that they be turned off when not in use. The mansion in which he grew up had been a dim cave full of totems and trolls that were nonetheless terrifying when they turned out to be the clothes tree or the tea wagon. He wondered what kind of dragons lurked for Walter Gee in the shadows cast by his mother's red and green Chinese lampshades. What a child's eyes might see in the flickering light of Marge's black candles. Read in a decent light, he thought, perhaps even Copee's history books might lend themselves to more optimistic and charitable conclusions about the nature of man.

His enthusiasm sputtered and died. A day or two ago he'd had a ghost of a chance to bring light into lives stunted by darkness. Now he himself was a ghost, and that chance was forever past. With a sigh Elgar abandoned his speculations and returned to the sleeping children.

Walter Gee, still snoring loudly, had curved his body, unconsciously forming a wall to guard his baby brother against falling out of bed. Wesley Free lay on his back, his mouth firmly stoppered by his right thumb in consolation for the disappearance of his mother's warm nipple. Elgar felt a sudden overpowering tug of tenderness, followed by a surge of other strange new feelings which he tried to fend off by silently, sternly addressing the sleeping infant.

You are not my son, Wesley Free. True, you might have been. But you are not. Facts are facts. Face them. I admit my exuberant and ill-considered behavior with your mother may have helped to drive your father out of his mind. And that out of some confused idea of making it up to him, I offered to set her up in business, forgetting all about you. True, you are very small and helpless. Somebody has to be responsible for you. But not me. It's not going to be me.

"Face facts, Wesley Free," he said aloud, gently removing the pacifying thumb. "Your parents can't afford orthodontia."

Wesley Free replaced the thumb with a smack of satisfaction.

Elgar, unwilling to lose this contest of wills, removed it.

It was instantly replaced.

This time Elgar unstoppered the baby's mouth with a touch of roughness.

Wesley Free tensed his body and screwed up his face, his tiny stirrings causing Elgar more apprehension than the rumblings of a volcano. But then he seized Elgar's index finger in his miniscule fist and clung to it. And, instead of crying, opened his eyes and smiled.

Elgar smiled back, with equal, helpless idiocy, and the distance between what-might-have-been and what-was was suddenly, irrevocably closed.

"*All* babies have blue eyes, Landlord," Marge said as if she read his thoughts. "And his are very *dark* blue."

"I know," he growled, waving this unwelcome intelligence away as the tiny hand gripped his finger with a strength greater than all reasonable arguments. *You little devil, you are as clever a seducer as your mother,* he thought. *And you have great hands for reins.* His mind raced ahead to the first pony. The first car. It ought to be a Healey. Clothes from England, of course. And shoes from Italy; Italians the only ones who know how to handle leather, anything else ruins growing feet. He ought to go to Yale. Oh, God, do they have a quota system? What the hell, I'll buy him a college. I'll *build* him one.

Marge's soft voice reached him from a great distance. "Poor little things. They ain't got no father. Pretty soon they won't even have a home."

"What?" Elgar roared. "What did you say, Marge?"

"You heard me, Landlord." She glared at him. "It's hard enough on us grown-ups. But I don't see how you can stand to see these poor little children put out on the street."

Elgar was used to her baleful glare, having lived under it for months. But he could not stand the sad new crinkles of disappointment around her eyes. They spoke of hope abandoned, of bitterness picked up like an accustomed burden. Of *him.*

As Wesley Free sank back into sleep with a smug smile and his thumb triumphantly in place, Elgar charged toward the phone.

"Yes, Fathaw, I know what you told me the last time. You have told me quite enough for a while. Now, for a change, you are going to listen, because whether you like it or not, Fathaw, I exist. You almost succeeded in destroying me, but I survived. Which proves I am stronger than you are."

The effect was like the reversal of a telescope. The increasing volume of Elgar's voice shrank the awesome sounds at the other end of the line until they trailed off into weak monosyllables.

"As for you, Fathaw," Elgar shouted, "do you know what you are? You are what you try to make others seem. A nothing. A zero! A mere dummy propped up by your possessions. All your crumby activities and junky enterprises—managed by your advisers! All your opinions and attitudes—borrowed from dead old fogies! You yourself have done nothing, thought nothing, said nothing new in sixty years! You *are* nothing! And you always will be."

There was an unfamiliar sound at the other end of the line, strangely resembling a chuckle. But of course it was not. Elgar went on, "It is impossible to get something from nothing, Fathaw. That has been my mistake all these years, trying to get love from you, when you did not have it to give. I know better now. I no longer expect you to be a father to me. Actually *I* am more of a father than you are, though I am not really a father at all. I feel more like a mother, if anything. Yes, my feelings a moment ago were distinctly maternal. Along with everything else, Mothaw may have confused my sexual identity. The ballet class and all that. —But I ramble. The point is, I no longer expect love from you, Fathaw. But there is something you have that I *do* want, and I mean to get it."

The chuckle this time was unmistakable. Also the warmth, the first he had ever detected in his father's voice. "Good for you, Elgar. Stood up to me at last. Never knew you had it in you. Good for you, boy. What do you want?"

Elgar took a deep breath, then plunged. "Money."

There were no majestic rococo curses at the other end of the line, no roars, no splutterings. Only a brief, reasonable question in a polite, interested voice. "What for?"

The shock of this robbed Elgar of some of his combativeness. The old note of apology crept into his voice. "Well, I have a project in mind, but it's complicated, Fathaw. It may take a little time to explain."

"Take all the time you need, son. I have all the time in the world. Wouldn't admit this to everybody, but the truth is, I'm semi-retired these days. Younger men taking over more and more of my operations. Beginning to feel a bit useless, if you want to know. Now let's hear your idea."

And Elgar, a delicious lightheadedness coming over him as he remembered that his father's motto was "Time is money" and generosity with one commodity was likely to mean openhandedness with the other, went on to explain about the forthcoming Urban Renewal. About the plans of the bureaucracy, whose wrongheadedness his father heartily joined him in condemning. About the possibility of submitting an alternate proposal geared to the needs of the community; a proposal which, he was careful to point out, would be extremely profitable.

"I know I can do this thing, Fathaw, and I know I can make it pay. I can build a community of low-rental apartments, and I can make a profit renting them, and, what's more, I can do it with taste and style. I have an architect who has some fantastic ideas. Cinder-block construction, to save money. Plenty of play space for children. Lots of sliding glass doors, for light. Light, that's what the world needs, Fathaw. Light. And good, solid drains."

"But in addition to drains, the world is run on good, solid financing—"

"Well that's where *you* come in, Fathaw."

"Hmmm. Interesting. I might want to come down and take a look at your plans. I might have a few ideas, a few contacts—"

The old Empire Builder was scenting new fields for empire. Elgar knew when it was necessary to be firm. It was difficult, but he managed to say it. "No, this is *my* project, Fathaw. I want to do it by myself. All I want is a loan."

"A gift, boy. Why wait for me to die? I'll make over your share in the estate to you now."

"No, Fathaw!" Elgar screamed. "A loan. Out of my profits I'll pay you back. In less than ten years."

"Very well," the old man sighed. "A loan it is. Neeby will get his instructions. Any amount you need. Regular interest rates and all that. Ten years to repay. Will that do?"

Elgar was weak. "Yes, Fathaw. That will do very nicely."

"And Elgar—"

"Yes, Fathaw?"

"Don't blame you for being so hard on me. Made a lot of mistakes over the years. Marrying your mother was the first one. The woman's a damned fool, always has been. After that I did nothing right, trying to make up for her foolishness. Thought I was building character into you boys. But I failed. Truth is, your brothers have no character at all, they're a pair of unimaginative little yes-men. I detest them. You're the only one has any spirit, Elgar. And independence, too. I like that. But maybe you'll be easier on me when you're a father yourself. You'll find out it isn't so easy."

After hanging up, Elgar glanced over at his bed. It was hard to believe that its angelic occupants could be a source of serious problems. But Fathaw was right. The problems were not long in coming.

There was a clatter of feet in the hall. Then a cry, "Hey, Walter Gee! Catch this sidewinder!"

The unidentified flying object which followed made contact with Elgar's Tiffany lampshade and scattered glass in all directions.

Crying, "Look out! Here come the Rocket Men!" Walter Gee leaped up and dove beneath the bed. Wesley Free set up a wailing that sounded like a full-blast police siren. And Willie Lee, with a sheepish look on his face and a fielder's glove on his left hand, came slinking into Elgar's bedroom.

That Tiffanylight had cost Elgar eighty-nine fifty. And the infant's bellowing was throwing him into a panic.

"Marge," he said, "do something. See about feeding these children. Make them some junket or something. Junket and gruel, isn't that what babies eat? And give me some gruel too. My stomach feels tender."

Marge calmly located the zippered blue baby-bag Fanny had left behind, rummaged around in it, and came up with a bottle. "Here. Give this to the little one, Landlord."

Elgar shakily obeyed, inserting the bottle into what appeared to be the proper orifice: the source of those ear-rending sounds. But Wesley Free, after a half-minute of experimentation, rejected the nipple and howled all the louder.

"I think he misses his mother," Elgar said. "Oh, Marge. Help. What are we going to do?"

Four feet and two inches of battle-toughened manhood, Willie Lee strode purposefully across the room. "Gimme that," he said. He took the bottle from Elgar, inserted it with cool professionalism, and—miracle of miracles—Wesley Free was instantly silenced except for greedy sucking noises.

"You got to hold it up straight, Landlord. Otherwise he can't get none."

Elgar inquired, in awe, where Willie Lee had gained his impressive experience.

"Him," Willie Lee said, pointing to Walter Gee's head, which was just beginning to emerge from beneath the bed. "I used to give him all his bottles when he was little. Changed his diapers, too. Come out from under there, scaredy cat. Ain't no Rocket Men around here. Ain't nobody but me and Miss Marge and the Landlord."

Elgar suppressed the scolding that had been on the tip of his tongue. Oh, he had suffered severe damages. Certainly. That had been a rare and valuable lamp. But as he watched Willie Lee undertake the diaper-changing operation with one deft hand, he decided it would not do to order the boy out of his apartment just for pitching baseballs into it. His other talents were far too valuable.

"Well, I think you're doing real nice here, Landlord," Marge said cheerily. "I'll run make some lunch. You go on entertaining these children."

"Marge, don't leave me!" Elgar cried. But she was already gone.

"Is this your baby, Landlord?" Walter Gee wanted to know as Elgar, with absent-minded skill, picked up Wesley Free and burped him.

"No!" Elgar shouted defensively, realizing how natural the action had been. "Of course not!" Then he softened his voice and explained patiently, "No, it's your baby, Walter Gee. I mean your mother's baby. Your mother's and your father's. In other words, your baby brother."

"Oh," Walter Gee said with great lack of enthusiasm.

"Is that all you can say, Walter Gee? This is your new brother. His name is Wesley Free. Aren't you even glad to see him?"

"What for?" Walter Gee replied. "He can't play with me. He can't even talk to me. All he does is eat and sleep. What *good* is he?"

Elgar had to admit that Walter Gee did have a practical point. "Well," he said, "at least you can hold him for a while."

Walter Gee condescended to do this, but with considerable disdain. Willie Lee, meanwhile, was showing ominous signs of restlessness. "It's raining," he said, pacing around the room, staring glumly out the window. "Looks like it's gonna rain all day. Can't play baseball. Can't play nothing. What are we gonna do?"

"Games," Elgar said desperately. "We'll play games."

"What kind of games?" Walter Gee asked suspiciously.

"*Indoor* games," Elgar said. But when pressed he had to admit that this was the limit of his inspiration. He could not think of a single indoor game except Spin the Bottle, highly inappropriate in an all-male situation, and charades, too difficult to explain to a five-year-old.

"Well what *are* we gonna do?" Willie Lee asked peevishly.

Elgar's voice rose in a high-pitched whine reminiscent of Fathaw's lecturing tone. "What's the matter with you youngsters nowadays? Don't you have any initiative? No inner resources? No backbone? No reserves of imagination to invent productive uses for your leisure?"

The two boys stared at him, owl-eyed, blank, and faintly hostile.

"We'll tell stories," Elgar said helplessly.

"Rocket Men stories!" Walter Gee instantly amplified. "Death-ray rocket guns. Zap zap bazoom. Battle with the Mars monsters. Flights to the moom."

Walter Gee had suddenly learned to talk, but he was acquiring a strange vocabulary. "Moon, not moom," Elgar corrected.

"I got a couple good comic books downstairs. I'll get 'em," Willie Lee said, adding considerately, "They're easy to read, Landlord."

Soon he came staggering back under a four-foot stack of vivid periodicals from which Elgar, to defend himself against the accusation of functional illiteracy, undertook heroically to read aloud "The Adventures of the Venusian Pelepods" (a race of four-legged people, with giant foreheads and brains to match, who lived in caves); "The Battle of the Sirian Satellites" (waged with invisible, lethal rays issuing from the fingertips of a twelve-fingered band of stalwarts); "The Death of the Moon-Crater Creatures"; and Walter Gee's favorites, "The Rocket Men on the Moon (or Moom)," "The Rocket Men Fight the Crab People," "The Rocket Men Meet the Dinosaurs," "The Rocket Men and the Venusian Women. . . ."

"More!" cried Walter Gee, bouncing up and down on the bed while Elgar, suffering a graveled throat, paused to light a cigarette which certainly would not help, "More Rocket Men stories! More, more, more!"

Four hours and twenty Rocket Men stories ("At last we meet face to face, Rothgar, King of the Pygmy Humanoids. Tell me where you have hidden Wanda, Queen of the Asteroid Belt, or I will vaporize you with my Miniaturized Transistor Volt-Ray—") later, Elgar stumbled downstairs to find out what Marge was doing about lunch.

21

Instead of the businesslike clatter of pots and pans, the frivolous tinkle of honky-tonk piano issued from Marge's apartment. While from up front, DuBois' lair, came the crash of breaking glass followed by shrieks and high-pitched laughter. It sounded like the rent party was beginning all over again.

Barging into Marge's place first, Elgar bellowed, "What's going on, Marge? I thought you came down here to fix us some lunch. Now it's way past dinnertime."

Marge turned from her keyboard with a weary, languid air. "I decided to brush up on my music. See if maybe I can make a comeback after all."

"Excellent," Elgar said, "but meanwhile, where's my dinner?"

Marge pointed to a tray on the table. "There, Landlord. I was just about to bring it up to you."

Elgar stared at the meager contents of the tray. "You were going to bring me Melba toast and fruit salad? With that dab of white stuff on the side, which I presume is cottage cheese? I *loathe* cottage cheese."

"I'm on a diet," Marge explained. "I have to get my figure back. For my career."

"Well, I'm not on a diet!" Elgar exploded. "And neither are those brats upstairs. For God's sake, feed them, Marge. And get them to bed." He went on, with a few picturesque phrases, to tell Marge what he thought of her warming up her voice when she should have been warming up a good, nourishing meal.

Tears started in Marge's eyes. "Landlord, I thought we was friends now. I thought you had some respect for me. Now here you are talking to me like I'm some old slavey or something."

If there was anything Elgar could not stand, it was a woman's tears. Dating from the time when Mothaw had used hers so copiously to blackmail him into guilty good behavior.

While Marge sniffed and dabbed at her eyes, he wondered how much it would cost to manufacture and distribute a single, small, 45 R.P.M. recording. Probably no more than it was costing him to finance Fanny's Beauty Saloon. A small fortune, in other words. He shuddered. Oh, well. Call Levin in the morning. Sell a few more shares of Allied Preferred.

Picking up the tray meekly, he bowed and said, "Begging your pardon, Madame. You are, after all, a great star. A ravishing concert artiste. Far above culinary chores and other mundane concerns. I will serve the dinner, Marge. Go on, get your repertoire in order. Tomorrow, or as soon as it can be arranged, you will cut your first recording in twenty years."

Doctor Ludwig was right, he thought as he jiggled upstairs, carrying the precariously balanced tray. I must be mad. I am certainly behaving in a most irresponsible manner.

He counted off the indications of madness:

One, offering to finance Fanny's new beauty shop.

Which meant: Two, taking on the care of her kids.

Three, backing Marge in her chosen career.

Which added up to: Four, robbing himself of his one remaining solace, a decent housekeeper and cook.

Come and get me, Borden, he thought. Let them take me away, to anywhere but the Green House. I think I would feel at home in the padded cell next to Copee's.

Elgar could not rely solely on his thoughts, however. His stomach, the site where he felt most emotions, was the most reliable index of his condition. And in spite of everything a small glow of happiness had ignited down there and was spreading, as if he had downed a shot of good brandy.

Gently but efficiently, he wiped the tears from Walter Gee's face and the crumbs of dinner from his chin. He stacked the comic books in a neat pile beside the bed. He got Wesley Free comfortably installed for the night in a pulled-out bureau drawer, and told the older boys to get into their pajamas and play with the electric trains until the sandman arrived.

"Does the sandman have a rocket?" Walter Gee wanted to know.

"No, but he has a ray-gun, for boys who stay up too late and talk too much. And so do I."

Walter Gee collapsed into delighted giggles, and Elgar was at last free to eat his own dinner. He swallowed six slices of Melba toast in an effort to fill the void that had opened up in his midsection. Incredible, he thought, how much Melba toast tasted like cardboard. And cottage cheese like shaving cream.

Nostalgic visions swam before his eyes, visions of the voluptuous dinners Marge had cooked for him in pre-diet days. Ham hocks, for instance. Now there was a subject worthy of an ode. In its uncooked state a ham hock was homely and repulsive. But when cooked by Marge it became a transcendent mystery, rich, tender, dripping with aromatic essence, surrounded by beans which were pearls. Elgar's empty stomach growled. Maybe Marge would still have the makings of a snack lurking in a corner of her refrigerator. He picked up the tray of dinner dishes and carried it downstairs.

"Them as eats," Marge said sternly the moment he appeared, "has to wash dishes."

While Elgar silently rolled up his sleeves, she added apologetically, "I'm sorry, Landlord. But if I'm gonna play the piano again, dishwater is no good for my hands."

Elgar nodded and plunged his arms deep into thick suds while Marge pranced back to her piano. Anything for art. A cigarette dangled rakishly from one corner of his mouth; ashes fell negligently into the water. His face was pleasantly caressed by steam as he listened to the sounds floating in from the living room:

> Oh, some men like whisky and some like sherry wine,
> But my cornbread and cabbage drives 'em out of their minds.
> Whisky makes you frisky and wine is very nice,
> But they all go crazy for my black-eyed peas and rice.

There was a soothing self-forgetfulness in the chore of washing dishes, Elgar found; soon his hunger had evaporated. And he took a deep pleasure in making all neat and clean and tidy, creating a corner of perfect order in a chaotic world. When he dried the last cup and placed it on the shelf, Elgar was conscious of real regret. Also of the full restoration of his powers.

Now to take care of DuBois, he thought energetically. DuBois was giving a party up there; there could no longer be any doubt about it. The demoralizing shrieks and giggles emanating from his quarters could no longer be ignored. Nor was it possible to dismiss the recording of an art song, sung by a soprano with several cracks in her upper register, which was being played at top volume.

Elgar had little liking for classic female vocalists, and even less for people who giggled enthusiastically over their performances. At DuBois' door, he gave a rap of stern authority.

The creature who opened the door wore a ruffled white shirt, black tights, a red satin cummerbund, and, on the fringes of his large, melting eyes, a distinct decoration of mascara.

"Do come in," he entreated. "You're just in time for the performance. Freddy and Roger are going to do the can-can."

DuBois, presiding over the phonograph in the corner, replaced Florence Foster Jenkins' "Morning" with Offenbach's liveliest passage, and the room was suddenly aflutter with a storm of lace petticoats and bloomers, flapping above the hairiest, knottiest legs Elgar had ever seen.

His companion kept twittering away, like an amiable sparrow. "Aren't Freddy and Roger a scream? What a camp. Marvelous. My name's Monty, but you can call me Mona. Doesn't DuBois give the most divine parties? Why hasn't he invited you before?"

Elgar found himself clenching his fists and jutting out his jaw in an exaggerated demonstration of masculinity. "Because I'm his landlord," he said, "and I object to this sort of party."

"Oh, don't be an old party-pooping prune face," Monty/Mona coaxed. "Stick around. The fun's just beginning. Here comes Clarence, he's going to do the Dying Swan."

Elgar goggled as a gigantic (six-four), muscular ballerina wobbled into the room in a pink tutu, crossed his hands gracefully, and began to collapse toward the floor in a series of pathetic shudders. Before his forehead touched the handsome Oriental carpet Elgar had bounded to DuBois' side.

"I can't have this sort of thing on the premises, DuBois!" he shouted. "I have three boys to raise!"

DuBois, courteous even when drunk, looked at Elgar cross-eyed across the rim of his highball glass, bowed, and said, "Sherves you right for conshorting with women."

"Never mind *my* problems," Elgar said. "DuBois, do you think this sort of thing is suitable in a college president? One who hopes to guide the young, mold their characters, inspire them toward a future of good citizenship?"

—Strange, he observed, and sickening, how in times of stress his tone, his stance, his very locutions were reminiscent of Fathaw's.

"What goddamn college?" DuBois said. "Begging youah pardon for my gross profanity. We only collected ninety dollars for our Building Fund. I ask you, whoever heard of a college with an endowment of ninety dollars?" DuBois waved his arm, sloppily spilling half of his drink. "I shpent it all," he said, "on this party."

The can-can dancers, on for an encore, linked arms with the Dying Swan, and exited kicking to enthusiastic applause. Their last gesture, an insouciant bump and grind delivered with their backs to their audience, did something unspeakable to Elgar.

For the third time in one day, he felt a powerful urge to make a suicidal offer, and was unable to restrain himself.

"DuBois," he said hoarsely, "suppose somebody offered to endow your college? Do you think you could manage to reform?"

DuBois drew himself up with the dignity of a general, though he tilted slightly. "Shertainly," he said. "I have not fallen as low as you may think. I could always resume my habits of discretion. Shtrict discretion, I assure you, and impeccable behavior. My private character would of course continue to be my own affair. But my public character and deportment would be without blemish, if such a generous individual were to materialize on the philanthropic horizon. It has been singularly bare of late. The philanthropic horizon, I mean."

Elgar hastened to qualify his initial impression. "I don't mean an endowment as big as Harvard's, now. I was just thinking of a substantial contribution to your Building Fund. Say, twenty-five thousand dollars."

DuBois wiped the last of his Scotch from his lips and set the glass aside, as if taking a firm pledge. "For twenty-five thousand dollahs," he said fervently, "I would marry anyone you suggest. Even Miss Perkins."

The idea had its merits. But Elgar assured DuBois that such a drastic step would not be necessary; he had, for the nonce, only one small request, to which his tenant willingly acceded, turning up the volume and replacing the Offenbach with Judith Anderson howling out the agonies of *Medea*. This ear-splitting tragedy soon had the desired effect of clearing the room.

When the last mincing guest left the premises, Elgar sighed and mopped his brow. It wasn't easy, being a father.

Fortunately the children had slept through it all. Elgar checked and found their small forms spread-eagled luxuriously in his giant bed. He himself would sleep, if sleep were ever going to be granted him, on the narrow couch in his living room. If he had known what would be involved, Elgar told himself for the thousandth time, he never would have become a landlord.

The job had its rewards, however. An hour later, tired but content with the feeling of a day well spent, Elgar lounged on the couch in Fanny's apartment while she chattered about the events of her day and served him the Martinis she had learned to mix with wondrous skill. They were cozy and relaxed together, comparing notes with an impersonal casualness, like a typical modern couple. She having spent the day wheeling and dealing in the business world, while he was occupied with the house and the care of the children.

Fanny reported, "I found the perfect building for my Beauty Saloon, Landlord. It used to be a department store."

Elgar almost choked on his olive. "A department store? I know your dreams are on a grandiose scale, Fanny, but this is a bit too much."

Fanny tried working her old enchantment. She came over and tickled him under the chin. "Aw, don't make such an angry old face, Landlord. It was only a little bitty department store."

Elgar fended her off, holding her at arm's length. *"How* little bitty?"

Fanny shrugged prettily. "What you think, Landlord? You think I carry a ruler and a tape measure around with me all day?" She held her hands about a foot apart. "It's no wider than this. Just a cute little building."

"In a choice downtown location, I suppose. Where every square foot is solid gold. Fanny, how much is the rent on this cute little building?"

Fanny decided to approach this crucial question by degrees. "First let me tell you about it, Landlord. I don't have to do a thing to the place.

It's all interior decorated, with purple carpets wall-to-wall, and lots of mirrors, and great, big, sparkly chandeliers. And everywhere you look, they got these cute little Cupid-statues, and vases full of pretty little goldy flowers and leaves. I sure wish you could see it, Landlord."

He could, and it was hideous.

"The best thing is, the decorations won't cost me anything extra, Landlord. Everything goes with the place. It was all left behind by the department store."

"Which went out of business because of overwhelmingly high overhead. Yes, Fanny. I understand perfectly." Elgar groaned and struck his forehead with his fist. "What a fool I was, to think you might have a head for business. There's nothing in that head of yours but cotton fluff. Which passes for white-fox fur."

Fanny's voice became strident. "Listen, Landlord, you gonna be proud of me when I tell you what happened. The agent wanted four hundred a month for that building. But on the way out, there was this little crooked step, and I tripped on it and fell. Damn near broke my lower back. When I got finished telling the agent how much I could sue for and collect, he came down to *two* hundred."

"Fanny," Elgar said in genuine admiration, "my apologies. You are a brilliant businesswoman."

"Oh, it wasn't nothin', Landlord," was her modest reply as she refilled his glass. "After I signed the lease, I spent the afternoon looking at furniture. I found an artist to paint me a Muriel. And I ordered a cute little bar."

"Did you say 'bar,' Fanny? Are you equipping a beauty shop or a night club?"

"Beauty Saloon," Fanny corrected. "How many times I got to tell you it's a Beauty *Saloon,* Landlord? I plan on serving Martinis to my customers."

They clicked glasses, then, and drank to that. Also, in turn, to each other's good health and the health of Fanny's business, items calling for one Martini apiece.

After that, nestling closer to Elgar, Fanny murmured sleepily that she had instructed everyone to send the bills to him. And that his splendid generosity had moved her to gratitude.

"You always did look good to me, Landlord," was how she put it. "But after four of these little old Martinis, anybody would look good to me. Even my husband would look good right now."

This mention of Copee caused Elgar to make a drastic movement away from temptation. Spilling a wide-eyed, suddenly wide-awake Fanny to the floor.

"No, Fanny," he said. "Though our little former arrangement was very pleasant indeed, as I have told you before, there are many reasons why it cannot continue. I do not need to enumerate all of them. Three of them are presently sleeping in my quarters upstairs."

It was an admirable, lofty speech, worthy of Fathaw. But for some reason Elgar did not deliver it in the dignified, upright position which was appropriate. No, for some shameful reason, having to do with the spectacular effect of Martinis on his libido, he found himself down on all fours, crawling around on top of Fanny. His hands had developed a loathsome independence; when he willed them, for modesty's sake, to pull her skirt down, they began clutching at her little panties instead. His body too went into obscene convulsions of which Elgar did not approve. To a vulgar-minded observer, it would have been instantly clear what Elgar was trying to do with all those violent heaves and twitchings. But vulgar minds misjudge; this was precisely what, with every painful lurch and moan, he was trying *not* to do. Elgar fought valiantly, but he was losing, drowning; there was simply too much of Fanny to deal with at close quarters; too much thigh, too much scent, too much *skin*.

It was Fanny who, with quick thinking and a quick movement, saved them both at the critical moment. Rolling over, she removed her maddening softness and sweetness from his grasp. Elgar lay there panting and applauding. Bravo, Fanny.

Fanny stood up with a tight little smile of renunciation, so painful that her eyes were closed, and said tenderly,

"Good night now, Landlord."

And Elgar marched upstairs to his austere couch, where he slept the sleep of the righteous.

22

L evin was shaking his head sadly.

"Elgar," he said, "these items here, they are not investments. I do not know what to call them. Except, possibly, disasters."

A tear welled up in each of Levin's small, sharp eyes as he ran them over the bills for Marge's recording and Fanny's Beauty Saloon fixtures. A sob caught at his voice.

"Time and time again I have tried to teach you the principles of good financial management, Elgar. I am a patient man. But I am also human. And these, these outrages go beyond the limits of human patience. They are, *urrrlp*—"

Elgar turned his head politely while Levin coped with an attack of what seemed to be violent nausea. Finally the stockbroker, with a ghastly noise, succeeded in overcoming the object that was gagging him.

"Very well, Elgar. We will start all over again. Repeat after me: 'The first principle of sound investing is safety.'"

"'The first principle of sound investing is safety,'" Elgar recited dutifully.

"'The second principle of sound investing is reasonable assurance of return.'"

"'The second principle of—'" Elgar stopped short. "Hey, hold it, Levin. This is why you and I will never be soul-mates. Why, I might say, our marriage was not made in Heaven. You will never understand one fact which I have suspected for years, and now know to be true. There are forms of return on money that cannot be counted in dollars and cents. Profits, Levin, which cannot be totted up on your electronic calculators and multi-digital computing machines."

Levin raised his eyebrows. "Such as?"

"Satisfaction. Pleasure. The feeling of usefulness to others. You can't call those items 'income.' But they belong on the black side of the ledger, Levin."

"I see." Levin's brow was knotted painfully; he was trying very hard to understand. "At least, I think I see, though really, Elgar, you have an appalling tendency to babble at times. But I believe I detect a meaning beneath your incoherence. You are interested in philanthropy. Very well. That is a legitimate interest. But if you wish to contribute to a charity, Elgar, why not choose one that is tax-deductible?"

"I do not choose my charities, Levin," Elgar said haughtily. "They choose *me*."

Levin managed a brave little smile. "We will try again, Elgar. Because, although you are one of my most difficult accounts, and by no means the largest one, I am fond of you."

Elgar was touched. "Really, Levin? I hadn't known." He had not believed Levin capable of fondness for anything except money. And not even that, since the love of money had something fleshly and robust about it, like gluttony or carnality. Levin was completely ascetic, from his plain black shoes to the natural tonsure of his bald spot. No, it was not money he loved, but its spectral side-effects: interest, dividends, yields, growth percentages, capital gains. The spirituality of money so to speak.

Levin sniffled. "Really, Elgar. In spite of all the troubles you have caused me and continue to cause me. Now please repeat after me: 'The first principle of sound philanthropy is tax-deductibility.'"

"That's too hard to say," Elgar told him.

"Then I give up," Levin said, burying his face in his arms. "Go away, Elgar. What more can I do for you? I am only human. Check?"

Elgar took pity. "Look, Levin, I know our trains don't run on the same track, but that doesn't mean I don't appreciate all you've tried to do for me. Really. I don't want you to think me ungrateful, and I'm willing to cooperate as much as I can. That's why I know you'll be glad to see that note I have there, about a contribution to a college building fund. Twenty-five thousand dollars, every cent of it tax-deductible. Now, doesn't that make you feel better?"

Apparently it didn't. Levin raised his head, but his expression was, if anything, more somber.

"Several thousand accredited colleges in the United States, Elgar, all venerable institutions with fine faculties, fine programs, fine campuses, and you have to pick one that, as far as I can see, does not exist anywhere. Except, possibly, in someone's head." Levin's voice took on a pleading tone. "Now, please reconsider, Elgar. If you are interested in higher education, what is wrong with Yale? Or Princeton? Or a smaller college if you prefer. I have a number of fine small colleges listed here in this directory. Tufts, Oberlin, Grambling, Hood—"

"No, Levin," Elgar said stubbornly. "I'm sure they're all very fine schools. But I made a promise to somebody. My word of honor, Levin. You wouldn't want me to go back on my word of honor."

"I had such a nice little portfolio worked out for you," Levin said sadly. "A lovely little portfolio. Well-balanced, diversified, half growth stocks, half yield stocks. —Ah, well. Good afternoon, Elgar. I wish I could say it has been nice seeing you."

But Elgar was not ready to depart. "Don't dismiss me so quickly, Levin. Those were just the preliminaries. We haven't gotten to the main item on the agenda."

Levin bowed his priestly head in silent prayer. "And what is that, Elgar?"

"My plan to develop an Urban Renewal area."

The stockbroker's glazed, rigid expression was frightening. Elgar explained rapidly, "Now don't panic, Levin. I'm not going into this blindly. I've looked into the angles, the laws, the financing, the city's Master Plan, and I know my ideas are sound. What's more, I've convinced my father to lend me the working capital."

"Ah," Levin said with infinitely tender melancholy. "So that explains it. I should have known it was too good to be true. This note I have here from the man at Upper County Integrity Trust. What's-his-name."

"Neeby," Elgar supplied.

"Yes, Neeby. On the basis of this information from him I spent all of yesterday working on that portfolio for you, Elgar. Striving for a fine balance between solidity and liquidity. Therefore, both steels and oils were indicated. A bit of spice in the form of a few exotics, South American tin and copper, Ceylonese tea. As well as electronics, for expansion, because every portfolio needs yeast, Elgar. Oh, I can tell

you, I created a beautiful structure. Graceful, imaginative, even a bit
daring, some might say. But resting solidly on a firm base of bonds
and insurance."

Elgar was impressed. It was like hearing Frank Lloyd Wright describe
the creation of his finest building. Or Betty Crocker explaining her most
famous cake. "Gee, Levin," he said. "You did all that for me?"

"Yes, all for you, Elgar; unbidden, and without hope of reward. But
what thanks do I get? I spend a whole day slaving away in your interests,
and then you come to me, still determined to embark on this fantastic
scheme for which you have no background, no experience—"

Elgar was beginning to get angry. "I've convinced my father I know
what I'm doing. Why should it be so hard to convince you?"

"Perhaps," Levin said, regarding him with sad, beady eyes, "because
I know you better, Elgar. That regrettable purchase of real estate. These
latest indiscretions. What may come next, I shudder to imagine."

"The way you talk, Levin, you'd think I was going to embark on a
career of drunken revels and orgies. Or even worse things. Insurrections,
revolutions, overturning the social order."

"I think," Levin said mournfully, "that I would find those activities
preferable, Elgar."

"Levin, you're the original prophet of doom. Always expecting
the worst. I think you missed your calling. You should have been an
undertaker, you have such a gift for gloom."

"Perhaps, as you say, I am pessimistic," Levin replied. "So let me try
to be an optimist, just this once. If I were, I would assume that you plan
to turn your assets over to me, for sound and prudent management.
But that would be too much to hope for, Elgar. Check?"

Elgar nodded.

Levin sighed. "All right, Elgar. Tell me, again, what you are going
to do, and I will try to get used to it."

Out of respect for his solemn surroundings, Elgar permitted himself
only one *entrechat,* with only one click of his heels in the air, before
answering,

"I am going to become this city's biggest landlord."

"A plate of beans and franks, Lanie!" Elgar cried, rapping imperiously on
the D-R's counter with a sugar jar. "Nourishment for a hungry man!"

"My, you're getting masterful, Elgar," Lanie said admiringly. "I *like* masterful men."

Under her warm, bold look, he felt himself blushing all over. "Well, hurry it up," he grumbled to cover his embarrassment.

"I think you should have the liver and onions, Elgar," Lanie said solicitously. "Even if you don't need it, a little iron never hurt anybody."

"Beans and franks, I said!" He banged the salt and pepper shakers together. "And cole slaw. And coffee!"

"You don't have to be so noisy about it," she reproached him. "*That* isn't masterful, not really. Now, if you insisted on what you wanted in a *quiet* voice, that would impress me." Turning in Lucy's direction, she called, "One Number Nine, well done!"

Number Nine was liver and onions.

Elgar recalled Borden's comments about managing women. Female Authority-Figures more dangerous because more insidious. Danger and allure combined in one object, inspiring both desire for conquest and castration fears. Result: ambivalence. Anxiety. And fascination.

Lanie was a size 38-C, an admirably constructed Mothaw-figure. Elgar had been celibate a long, long time. Observing, as Lanie bent over, that her top two uniform buttons were unbuttoned, and that the third, crucial button was threatening to pop under the strain, Elgar felt his ego-defenses crumbling.

"I won't eat it," he complained. "I won't pay for it, either. What kind of a world is it, anyway, when a man can't get the meal he orders?"

"What interests me," Lanie said with another warm look, "is that you're here at all, Elgar. What happened? Has Marge's cooking finally gone sour?"

"No, it's stopped," he said. "But you must know that. You know everything, don't you?"

Lanie took a deep breath, with spectacular effect. The button hit the sugar jar, *pinged,* and ricocheted into Elgar's water glass. He grinned triumphantly.

"Bull's-eye," he said.

Anger brightened Lanie's eyes while confusion colored her cheeks. Altogether, a very fetching and vivid effect. "No, Elgar, I don't know everything," she said, clutching her lapels. "I never pretended to. But I *have* been talking to Marge a little. I think it's a wonderful thing you're doing, helping her make a comeback. In fact, I think everything you've been doing lately is wonderful. Only—"

"Say it."

"I'm afraid to. I don't want to seem like a know-it-all."

"That never stopped you before," he said, grinning insolently.

Lanie looked puzzled. "Elgar, you've changed somehow. I can't put my finger on it exactly. But you're different." Her hand dropped absently as she gazed at him. Elgar's grin broadened.

"I even wonder about what I was going to say to you," Lanie said, and turned her back angrily. "Maybe it doesn't really apply."

"Say it anyway."

She faced him again, breathing heavily, but reinforced by a safety pin. "All right. What do you expect to get out of it all?"

"Nothing," he said quickly. Too quickly.

"That's good," Lanie said. "I mean, you don't expect tribute of any kind, do you? Gratitude. Or affection. Things like that. You don't have fantastic expectations like that, do you, Elgar?"

"No," he said warily, wondering if it was the truth. Having indulged in a few pardonable fantasies about streets named after him, children ditto, and statues of himself in public squares.

"Because, if you do," she said, "you may be in for a disappointment."

"Why?"

"Because people are perverse. *All* people, but underdogs especially. I told you before, they tend to bite the hand that feeds them, because it's slapped them so many times."

"I know your theory. Some people are mad at society. Maybe they have every right to be. But that doesn't affect me. I'm not society. I'm *me,* Lanie."

He stared at her hard, getting the point across. She blinked first. "Elgar, there *is* something different about you."

"What were you saying, Lanie?"

"Only that in my experience, it's impossible for any colored person to really like any white person."

He was thinking about those hideous paintings of hers, the disembodied dark limbs locked in perpetual battles with each other and their surrounding white space. "Your experience," he repeated. "What exactly *is* your experience, Lanie?"

She sighed. "Well, I guess if I'm going to shoot my mouth off, I have to back up what I say." Dipping beneath the counter, she came up with a wallet and flipped through its card section to find a picture.

"*That* was my experience," she said, handing it to him. "Marriage. In a manner of speaking."

The guy in the photograph was rugged, broad-shouldered, and handsome. The prototype of every American girl's dream, except for one minor detail. He was black.

Elgar felt it was important to show no reaction at this point, in order to get the full story. He returned the wallet to Lanie without comment.

"He was the campus hero, Elgar. Out to prove he could get everything, captaincy of the football team, presidency of his class, honor society, valedictorian, everything. Including me. Naturally he won."

Her face, shadowed by bitterness, was not so pretty now. "Unfortunately," she said, "he carried the battle over into marriage. Everything I did had to be wrong, because I was white. Everything he did had to be right, because it disproved the doctrine of white supremacy. It wasn't a marriage, it was a re-enactment of the Civil War."

Elgar wondered why he felt so disappointed after this recital, then realized he had finally grown secure enough to consider proposing to Lanie, and had been secretly pleased with himself at the amount of heroism this indicated. Now, perversely, she had turned out to be white after all.

"Why the charade, Lanie?" he asked. "Why have you pretended to be colored all these years?"

Her eyes twinkled again. "I never pretended to be anything, Elgar. You just made certain assumptions, and I liked to tease you. You tease so easily. —Or you used to," she added quickly, noting his dangerous scowl.

"Actually I didn't care what you thought, or what anybody thought, for that matter. I wasn't sure where I belonged myself. Before my marriage I was white. Afterward I was identified with my husband, so I was colored. Then came the divorce, and there was no turning back, so I just stayed where I was, in limbo." She shrugged. "An uncomfortable place, but you get used to it after a while. My family and friends had disowned me. I didn't have any family except Lucy. —Tommy's sister. She sort of looks after me."

He followed her surreptitious glance at the short, dark, fierce girl who was grimly occupied at the other end of the counter. Cooking a meal he did not want.

"Well," he said, "at least Lucy likes you. That sort of knocks a hole in your theory, doesn't it?"

"No," Lanie said, and lowered her voice, "she just likes being able to boss me around. She got me this job, got me my apartment, tells me what to buy, what to wear. Makes all my decisions, really. I hate the way she manages me, but I've come to depend on it. I guess that's why I have to manage everybody else." She looked up at him, blinking suspiciously moist lashes. "I'm sorry."

Elgar reached for her hand. "I'm sorry too. Sorry you've had such a hard time. No wonder you like the blues."

"I know what they're all about, Elgar."

"But that doesn't mean the same sort of thing will happen to me, Lanie. My tenants and I are getting along fine."

"Oh, Elgar," she said, reaching for a handkerchief, "you remind me so much of myself, the way I used to be, you make me want to cry. So innocent. So vulnerable. Not enough sense to build fences between you and other people. Always stumbling into the fences *they've* built, because you can't see them. Just a great, big, lovable blob of protoplasm, open to everything and everybody. Without a skin."

She touched his cheek. "Grow a skin, Elgar. I'm warning you, skin is very important. It's your own personal fence against the world."

"Well, I'm not so sure," he said. "I'm not sure skin is such a good thing. For instance, it occurs to me that's why you and that guy never made it. You never got past your skins. —But that's presumptuous of me," he added, noting her trembling lashes, "and besides, I'm being rude. You hadn't finished. Do you have any other pieces of advice for me?"

"Just one, Elgar," she said, using the hanky. "Don't play Great White Father. I'm telling you, it's the world's most thankless job."

"Even," he asked, "when you're a father to kids?"

That one really rocked her. Her face looked stricken. "Oh," she said in a small voice, "oh, I don't know about kids. I only know about adults. They're the ones who surround themselves with barbed wire. Try to get close to them, you get cut to ribbons. But kids might be different, I guess. I don't know."

A plate of liver and onions had materialized in front of Elgar. "I detest liver," he said with calm loathing, and pushed it away. Masterfully.

Lanie quickly took the plate away. And stood there, holding it, with a troubled look on her face. "I guess you're right, Elgar. I don't know about everything. Maybe you *have* grown a skin. Maybe that's what's different about you."

"Maybe I have," he said. "It's been a long time since you made a detailed inspection."

She blushed, embarrassment throwing her slightly off balance. Elgar liked her better that way.

"Maybe I do have a warped viewpoint," she said. "Maybe I'm becoming a sour old maid." She blushed again. "In a manner of speaking, of course. Do you think I'm in danger of becoming a sour old maid, Elgar?"

"I would watch my step," he said gravely.

She sighed. The pin broke. She ignored it. Her face was soft and speculative. "I really don't know about kids. I never had any. I guess I never will."

"Don't be too sure," he said. "You're making progress, Lanie."

She gave him the warm look again, but it was less bold, more uncertain. "Uh—do you want your hot dogs grilled or boiled, Elgar?"

"Boiled," he said. "And not too well done."

"I'll cook them myself," she said, and switched spectacularly all the way to the grill, where she shoved her co-worker aside with her elbow. "Move, Lucy."

"Cole slaw on the side," Elgar ordered happily. "Double order of baked beans. I'll have my coffee now. —And turn down that goddamn air conditioning. It's freezing in here."

Lanie was whistling the blues while she worked. But it sounded like "Pomp and Circumstance" again. These days, everything sounded like "Pomp and Circumstance" to Elgar.

It was not, after all, such a bad tune.

23

Let there be light, the Lord said.

And there was light.

Sunlight, great golden gobs of it, spilling into every corner of the apartment, making a cheerful shambles of the electric trains on the rug, the remnants of breakfast on the coffee table, the scattered items of male apparel in assorted sizes, the charts, maps and documents heaped everywhere.

I am a man obsessed, Elgar thought happily, lighting a cigar as he studied the latest pretty renderings the architect had brought him.

"Hmmm," he said, "very interesting, McMenamee. I like these staggered rooflines. And these courtyards, very nice. But give me more light. More glass, man! Put in some skylights! Open up those rooms!"

"But, Mr. Enders," the architect protested, "those changes will increase the cost by as much as thirty per cent."

Elgar blew noxious smoke at the cringing architect. "Don't you dare add another penny to the cost, you thief! You chiseler! Get the cost down even lower. These have to be *low-rental* units, don't forget. And they have to pay back my investment in ten years! I am not in business for my health."

—Or am I? he wondered after the architect had left with a bow and a scrape and a promise to return with revisions as soon as possible. His eyes in the medicine-chest mirror were an unflinching, steely blue. His jaw had a rugged line of determination, his flesh a pink and ivory freshness, its outlines the firmness of marble.

Elgar flung open the mirrored door. Confronting him were a row of vials marked *Up, Down, Awake, Sleep, Stabilize,* and *Tranquilize.* With a single movement of his hand he swept them all into the trash can. What with his medicines, Marge's magic snake, and Fanny's white-fox fur (recently replaced by pastel mink), 709 Poplar Street would have some interesting trash to put out this week.

709 Poplar Street would also survive the coming holocaust. To let that foursquare brick front, those wide windows, that impressive door go under the wrecking ball would be a crime. So Elgar had decided to use his apartment as his business headquarters. Today was moving day. Clearing-the-decks-for-action day.

Incoming was a raft of office equipment: a double-winged desk, a conference table, chairs, typewriters, files. His business phones were already installed. There they were in a row: five squat, homely instruments in basic black, no nonsense about decorator colors or streamlined models. Checking each one in turn, he got five dial tones. All praise to monopoly.

Outgoing was his furniture, headed back to the Trejour, most of it earmarked for Borden. Except for one bed, one lamp, one chair, and one table which would refurnish Elgar's former cell.

Outgoing, also, were the boys, to their mother's quarters below, to be supervised by a custodian he had hired.

He had worried about the custodian, but she seemed capable enough. Motherly, yes, but no foolishness about her. From the looks of her, an able wet-nurse, too. Even more ample than Marge, who come to think of it was melting daily to a new svelteness. And, with it, a new sweetness, as if the gruff manner had been part of the outer layer.

Yesterday she had waltzed in wearing a snazzy little scarlet number. Oh, still by no means slender. But the first pounds had come from her face, which now emerged from its cocoon of flesh as delicate, even pretty. And radiant.

She'd whirled in the center of the room and curtseyed. "How do you like it, Landlord? First size 18 I've worn in eighteen years."

He'd kissed his hand to her. "Marge, you are a rose. A full-blown American beauty. May I ask what occasions this splendor?"

"A night club audition, Landlord. My agent is asking five hundred."

"A month?"

"What you mean, Landlord? I don't work for peanuts."

Well, that was that. For a brief moment back there somewhere, their needs had coincided. But now she saw nothing but her name in lights on a dazzling marquee framed in dollar signs.

At least he would try not to whine. "Forgive my selfishness, Marge. It is a far, far better life that you are beginning. Nevertheless, I shall miss you."

Marge promised contritely to make him a roast at her first opportunity. And admitted that tonight she had a date with a man. The night club owner, in fact.

"He's just what I like, Landlord. Fat, jolly, and a free spender." Lastly, she'd slipped a small, repulsive cheesecloth bundle into his hand. It was her most powerful charm, an all-purpose luck-attractor and evil-dispeller, concocted just for him.

Elgar took the distasteful object out of his pocket and fingered it thoughtfully. Five minutes after Marge had left, flustered as a prom-bound teenager, Phosdicker had called, cautious yet jovial. Elgar was now on familiar terms with the Authorities. Oh, not first-name terms as yet. But they knew his last name.

"I hope I find you well, Mr. Enders. Oh, splendid. Splendid. You will be glad to hear that your interesting proposal has elicited some very favorable comments in City Hall. Very favorable indeed. Not that I am at liberty to promise anything. As you yourself said, we must beware of hasty assumptions, Mr. Enders. Ha ha. But things look promising."

That nifty little alteration in the park plans had been the master stroke, he thought. That park had made Elgar uneasy anyway. All open spaces made him feel in danger of disappearing into the infinite. The point of cities, he felt, was that you never had to be too far away from the protection of roofs and walls. So in place of the wooded retreat which Phosdicker had so rapturously described, Elgar had put the campus of DuBois College. Or whatever it would be called.

When he had shown DuBois the plans, his tenant had given him a fishy, uncomprehending look.

"Why do you wish to do all this for me?"

Elgar had been embarrassed. "It's not so much, DuBois. With my contribution, and a little government money to match it, you can build one building. If you can raise some more funds, maybe two. One for administration and one for classrooms. Really a very small beginning, DuBois. But a beginning nevertheless."

Then, as DuBois' silent green stare was making him increasingly uncomfortable, he'd spluttered, "Hell, DuBois, I'm not doing it for you at all. I'm doing it for myself. So, for God's sake, don't go getting grateful on me. If there's anything I can't stand, it's gratitude."

"Then I will not burden you with grateful effusions. I will simply ask how I may be of assistance in this splendid and magnanimous undertaking."

"It's not a splendid and magnanimous undertaking. That's the whole point. —Look," Elgar had said earnestly, "I don't know beans about what I'm doing. But I do know one thing. I'm in competition with the monsters, and if I'm going to win, I've got to be as crass and hard-headed as they are. I've got to prove you can build decent housing for the low-income brackets and make it pay. Otherwise everybody will write this off as just another piece of rich man's madness. So this can't be a piece of crazy philanthropy, DuBois. It's got to be a paying venture. —And, yes, you can help."

"What will my assignment be?"

"To survey the neighborhood. Get me the straight dope on everybody's income, the size of their families, the rents they can afford to pay. I have a rough idea now, but that's not good enough. I have to have the facts."

"I know something about this sort of research," DuBois replied. "I once conducted new-product polls for the Comestible Foods Corporation, to determine consumer reaction to a new ice cream made of goats' milk and synthetic ingredients. Results were negative. But they marketed the product anyway. It failed, proving the accuracy of my research."

His point made, DuBois came back to the issue at hand. "I will prepare a very simple questionnaire. With a team of interviewers, I can cover the area in about two weeks."

This brought up a delicate matter. "Uh, about those interviewers, DuBois. I would prefer them to be guys who don't wiggle when they walk. And girls who do. No point in alarming the neighborhood any more than it's been already. I hope you understand."

"I do," DuBois said. "And more than that, I want you to know that I have been deeply moved by this generous gesture of yours. To the point of making a small gesture in return."

DuBois bent, reached beneath his bed, and retrieved a pair of items which he waved aloft with tactfully averted eyes: a pair of lacy black panties and a matching brassiere.

Elgar coughed discreetly. "Well, congratulations, old man. I hope you enjoyed it. I mean, that's the point, you know."

"One man's pleasure," said DuBois nobly, "is another man's supreme sacrifice." With a sigh he dropped the frilly garments to the floor.

Elgar felt a pang of envy. Personally, he had never carried a female to such heights of abandon that she left both items of basic undergear behind. Oh, one, occasionally. But never both. This fact generated a suspicion in his mind which was confirmed by a quick glance at the evidence, revealing a price tag fluttering from a strip of lace.

DuBois was, after all, a con man. But this time Elgar would let him think he had gotten away with it.

"You once said I was a fool, DuBois," he said. "Do you still think so?"

"At this point," DuBois said, "I might initiate a long philosophical discourse on the subject of innocence. A quality which I regrettably lost at the age of three. Innocence is extremely rare, and therefore very refreshing. For instance, only an extremely innocent American could be free of the taints of certain prejudicial notions. As you seem to be."

"Not quite," Elgar admitted. For instance, he thought, I've always balked at the prospect of marrying a colored girl. Until recently, that is. "But generally speaking, I've always been too confused about who I was to decide who I was better than."

"Perhaps," DuBois speculated, "the very rarity of innocence accounts for the amazing feats it is sometimes able to perform. In short, yes, you are a fool. But a fool I am proud to know." He waved his hand at the plans. "Because only a fool could accomplish all of this."

DuBois was due to report in at three o'clock with his preliminary findings. Also due were Elgar's lawyer, his accountant, two city planners, the boys' nurse, and the moving men. Everything depended on proper organization and the most precise sort of timing. Otherwise, when the time rolled around for Elgar's appointment with the Mayor, he would still be babysitting, and the Mayor would have to come to him.

Elgar returned to the clipping, an ad from the book pages, which he had been studying before the architect's arrival.

WHY ARE YOU WASTING YOUR LIFE?

From beneath this headline the author, one Manfred J. Master, stared out at him accusingly.

If you will just stand before your mirror and do TEN LITTLE EXERCISES A DAY, *I promise you a fantastic increase in your executive abilities, a surge of* DYNAMIC POWER *that will amaze you!*

Here is the first exercise. Stand before your mirror and say, "Enthusiasm!" As you say it, concentrate on the word. Let every part of your mind, every muscle in your body, every vein, every fiber, every atom be concentrated on producing enthusiasm.

Elgar returned to the mirror.

"Enthusiasm," he said.

His image stared back at him, lips stretched back, eyes expressionless. "Enthusiasm!" Elgar bellowed.

This time he felt it swelling his veins, bursting through every pore to radiate from the surface. Now for Exercise Two.

Ah, but the ad was a cheat, a come-on, like so many things in this fake world.

For Exercises Two Through Ten, see Pages 30–35 of my book, Develop Your Dynamic Executive Power. *Order today, $7.95* c.o.d. *Only $7.50 if check or money order enclosed.*

Elgar balled up the piece of paper, tossed it into the trash along with his tranquilizers, and leaped energetically across the room as four of his five newly installed phones began to ring simultaneously, failing by some miracle to awaken Willie Lee and Walter Gee. But from the depths of Elgar's chest of drawers a faint wail of discomfort arose.

"Coming," Elgar said to all five noises at once. Coming. Dynamic Executive Power to the rescue.

"No, Levin," he said into the first phone, "I have not changed my mind. Not, as you put it, recovered my sanity. I am proceeding with my plans, and I am not interested in buying any more Consolidated Coast-to-Coast or Allied Preferred. But be patient, Levin, and maybe you will get to compile that pretty little portfolio after all. Meanwhile you will await further instructions from me. Check? Check."

Plunging the receiver down, he proceeded to the next. "No, Nimmo, of course I do not wish an interest in any of the Seven Branches. Why do you propose such a ridiculous notion? What? My father is proposing it in lieu of the loan he promised me? Ye gods. Hold on a minute, Nimmo."

With a little thrill of power, he pushed Nimmo into limbo by pressing the *Hold* button, and answered the next call. "Hello, McMenamee, what's *your* problem? . . . I see. Before you undertake any more work for me, you want your fee. Well, that sounds reasonable but I resent the implications. My word's as good as my name. Haven't you ever heard of J. P. Enders? What's that? You say you don't like their style of building? You couldn't possibly work that way? Splendid. That's the best recommendation you could have. Have your lawyer see my lawyer in the morning."

He released the *Hold* button and said, "Look, Nimmo, that offer is just a trick of my father's. His last attempt at dominating me. Reject it unconditionally. What? Yes, of course I realize the Seven Branches is profitable, monstrously profitable, but I am not interested in making monstrous profits. I am interested in creating beauty and sanity, and for that I need cash, do you understand? C-a-s-h, cash. Fluid assets, Nimmo, not frozen, and the quicker you can thaw them, the better. Am I making myself clear? Good, Nimmo. Keep smiling."

A twinge of remorse pinched him as he recognized the awkward accent of the next voice. "Oh, Borden, I'm sorry I've been too busy to keep my last four appointments. What? You're *not* sorry?—Well, of course not, you shiftless phony, this is the easiest hundred dollars you've ever earned in your life. Oh. You mean you're glad I'm working out my problems in the world instead of in your office. You guys have an answer for everything, don't you?—No, of course, continue to bill me. That's our little arrangement, isn't it? I want to keep my appointments on your books in case I need them. Sort of a safety valve. —No, I don't begrudge you the money, and what's more, the names I call you are merely my quaint way of expressing affection. I have the fondest affection for you, Borden, and the highest respect, and the deepest loyalty. In proof of which expect delivery of a few small items this afternoon. —What? You mistrust me when I pay you compliments? You feel better about me when I insult you? I see. Very well. In that case, Borden, I'll see you—" Elgar flipped the crowded pages of his calendar pad "—next Tuesday. No, that's no good, I've got a conference with the Mayor on Tuesday.

I'll see you the *following* Tuesday, the twenty-third. Usual time. Got to hang up now, Borden. The baby is crying."

Elgar hurried to answer the urgent summons from his dresser drawer. Wesley Free's little fists were clenched, his feet thrashed the air. Elgar, by now an expert, picked him up with one hand and felt his bottom with the other. It was dry. But the howling continued. Across the room Wesley Free's brothers, two restless mounds, stirred, then burrowed deeper under the covers.

"Shhh," Elgar said, carrying the baby into the living room, walking him up and down. The wailing increased in intensity. Elgar's panic grew. He was competent now to deal with lawyers, stockbrokers, Mayors, Authority-Figures of all kinds. But still helpless before this tiny source of inexplicable sound.

"Shhh," he said, shifting the baby to his shoulder, adding a gentle rocking motion to his walk. "Help me a little, Wesley Free. You haven't got a mother any more, and it's my fault. So you'll just have to put up with me instead."

Hard to picture Fanny as a mother these days. Hard to picture her as having ever been anything but a successful businesswoman. The Beauty Saloon's doors had not stopped swinging since they were opened, and Fanny was now all business and no nonsense. No more eyelash flutterings, no more surprise unbuttonings, no more agonizing tussles with indecision. Last night she'd come home outraged by a customer. The nerve of that hussy. Threatening to sue because she'd been burned by one of Fanny's bleaching preparations.

"Hush, son. Believe me, I'm doing the best I can." Pat, pat on the tiny bottom, the tiny shoulder. Wesley Free went into a sudden, alarming convulsion, hiccupped, and released a small, moist burp. Contented silence followed. "There, there, soldier. You'll be O.K. now."

After the successful resolution of *that* crisis, it seemed the day could hold nothing to dismay Elgar.

24

Puffing on one of the large cigars he had recently begun to smoke, Elgar paced Borden's office. He was much too keyed up to lie down. Much too busy, really, to spare the time to be here. Today he had to call Nimmo, get him to draw up the papers for incorporation. Call Phosdicker and see if approval on his final application was coming through as fast as it had on his preliminary one. Check with DuBois on the survey results and start getting his costs in line. Confer with the architect again, get some variety into those floor plans. Read through approximately five tons of official charts and documents. And give his father the go-ahead on that deal to bring in a shopping center which would include the eighth of the Seven Branches.

Elgar had balked on that at first. But the more he thought about it, the more it made sense. People had to shop somewhere. Prices had to be in line with their incomes. And Poplar Street people loved J. P. Enders merchandise.

"It makes sense," he said aloud.

"What was that, Elgar?"

"Nothing, Borden," Elgar said with a start; he had forgotten where he was. "Just a business deal I'm considering. I have to make a phone call about it right away. As a matter of fact I have a lot of phone calls to make. Dynamic executive habits, Borden. Getting things done. I pick up a phone and people start scurrying. About my business, not theirs. It's an exhilarating feeling, Borden, one I recommend to you. Do you mind if I run out and make a few phone calls now?"

"I would prefer that you postpone them, Elgar," Borden said. "Yes. I think, now that you are here, I would prefer you to stay."

237

Disappointed and petulant, Elgar perched on the edge of the couch. "Well, I don't know what for, Borden. I can't think of a thing to talk about today."

"Nothing at all? No associations? No dreams?"

"Dreams? Sorry, Borden, I hate to disappoint you, but I don't dream any more. I work sixteen hours a day and fall into bed like a ton of rocks."

"A sixteen-hour workday. Hmmm," Borden said. "An interesting schedule for someone who once wanted to be a playboy."

Elgar's voice went up four notches in the scale. "Well, I still mean to enjoy myself. Why shouldn't I?—Hell, Borden, I'm a rich man. I'm going to be even richer. I should be sailing my yacht on the Mediterranean. Zipping along the Azure Coast in my sports car. Having a different woman every night, blondes, brunettes, redheads, all nationalities."

"Well, why don't you do just that, Elgar? There is an airport in this city, and a plane leaving for the south of France at—" Borden consulted his watch "—two P.M."

"You know I can't go, Borden," Elgar said sadly. "I have to give the baby his four P.M. feeding."

"And after that?" Borden inquired. "There is an evening plane also, Elgar."

"I have to give the baby his *eight* P.M. feeding, too. At nine my architect is coming by to go over some plans. And after that I have to see my lawyer."

"These flights," Borden said silkily, "are on a daily schedule. What about tomorrow, Elgar?"

"Tomorrow is the hearing on my Urban Renewal proposal." Elgar hesitated. "I wasn't going to admit this, Borden, but I called my old man again. And this time I got through to him. He's putting up the money I need to develop Poplar Street." He looked up guiltily. But Borden was not frowning. He was beaming.

"I suspected that this was coming. It is a significant breakthrough, Elgar. A sign of real movement."

"How do you know, Borden? I haven't even told you what happened."

Borden put his fingertips together. "Let me see if I can reconstruct the situation, Elgar. You were full of indignation about something." He held up his hand for silence. "Never mind what. You were full of anger. Yes. So you called up your father and told him off. You gave him hell. And to your surprise—" he spread his hands "—the old man unbent from his rigid position and became agreeable to your wishes. For the first time."

It was spooky. Borden, too, had the Powers. Elgar looked at him fearfully. "That's exactly how it was. Exactly. But how did you know?"

Borden shrugged in self-deprecation. "Predicting behavior is not difficult when you know the people involved. Your father is an authoritarian type. Yes. The only thing such types respect is a stronger authority."

Was Borden talking about *him?* Elgar could not believe it. He would have to think about that one for a while.

"So you are now engaged in many active projects, Elgar. You are very busy. Yes. It seems you do not really wish a sybaritic existence."

"Hell, yes, of course I wish a—what you said. It's just that I can't take off right now. I have too many responsibilities."

"And who made you take on all these responsibilities?"

"Well, uh, you see, uh, it was like this, Borden. Uh—" Though Elgar began in this halting way, he waxed eloquent as he talked. "Uh, it was more in the nature of clearing up confusion, Borden. How could I get my bearings, when everything around me kept shifting? My tenants were in a constant state of flux. They were Creoles, Indians, tribal chieftains, college presidents, anything but what they were. It was like dealing with a houseful of Missing Persons."

"Only you were the one who was missing, Elgar. Until you began to take things in hand."

Elgar looked up hopefully. "Do you see me more clearly now, Borden? Am I beginning to appear?"

"Yes, Elgar," the doctor said, smiling. "You are coming across more and more clearly."

"Tell me what you see, Borden," Elgar begged.

"Not yet, Elgar. The clues are shaping up very nicely, but I do not wish to jump to conclusions. Also, I would prefer you to make the identification for yourself. Yes. Because at that point, you will be ready, Elgar."

Elgar gave a sigh. "Well, all I can say is, it's the height of absurdity when a bachelor has to hire a baby-sitter in order to keep his appointments."

"I have often noticed," Borden said thoughtfully, "that patients tend to say the opposite of what they mean. You, for instance, complain loudly about the nuisance of children. Yet there is much in your tone and your manner that suggests contentment with your present circumstances."

"Contentment? You're crazy, Borden. My life has nothing in it even remotely resembling contentment. Listen. Walter Gee wakes up every night with nightmares, and I have to calm him down. Wesley Free is teething, poor little guy, so he cries all the time. Willie Lee is down with the flu, and keeping an active boy like him in bed is like trying to chain a tiger. Oh, I tell you, I have my hands full, Borden. Morning till night, nothing but problems."

"That's the way real families tend to be, Elgar," Borden said, smiling broadly. "But I have never seen you looking better."

Elgar was bewildered by the compliment. He had been afraid to look in the mirror since his last crisis with Fanny. Convinced that masturbation made one haggard-looking, he expected to see deep creases and furrows in his face, dark rings of depravity beneath his eyes.

"How could I look good, Borden?" he demanded. "I haven't had a good solid meal in weeks. I haven't had a decent night's sleep, either, what with the baby crying. And I can't even tell you how long it's been since I got laid."

"Amazing," Borden said, "that you appear so healthy. Perhaps a Spartan regimen really suits you, Elgar."

"Never," Elgar said, leaping up in agitation. "Never. I had enough of that Puritan crap while I was growing up. 'Take cold showers twice a day, work hard, be thrifty.' Where do you get off, Borden? You're supposed to help me get rid of all that."

"Oh?" No one else could invest a single syllable with so many complex meanings as Borden.

"Yes. Guilt, morals, restrictions—I'm here to get rid of all that excess baggage."

"But perhaps these things are a part of you, Elgar. Perhaps you *are,* at heart, a Puritan."

Elgar remembered that he had once used that term to describe himself to Fanny. Nevertheless he threatened, "You better prove that statement, Borden. And you better prove it fast."

Borden proceeded to do so, with devastating effect. "Well, Elgar, if pleasure without responsibility were what you really wanted, you once had the perfect set-up. By your own description, Paradise. A lovely and willing mistress unavailable for marriage. A generous mother-figure to supply you with home-cooked meals. And in the background, for diversion, a chorus of carefree darkies."

"Carefree darkies," Elgar said grimly, "are a myth, Borden."

"Of course," the doctor agreed. "They are a useful myth, which allows the typical insensitive man to see the world as a pleasant, charming place in which he has no responsibility. But you, for some reason, were unable to see the world in this way, Elgar."

"How could I, Borden? The people around me were as desperate as I was."

"So," Borden said, "your tenants no longer pose such a personal threat to you. Having outgrown your dependency needs, you are beginning to see that they have their own problems."

"Problems. What a pretty understatement, Borden."

"It is a general term we use in psychiatry," said Borden with an apologetic sniffle, "to cover a multitude of conditions."

"How about psychosis? That describes the conditions better."

"When reality is grim," Borden said, "people often develop fantastic adaptations, grotesque performances and masquerades. But they are not the most effective ways of coping."

"You said it, Borden," Elgar agreed. "Copee's way of coping landed him in the crazy house. DuBois' disguise was collapsing, that's why he threw that disgusting party. Picture it, Borden. More gorgeous girls in one room than you ever saw before. Only every one of them was a man." He looked up indignantly. "Naturally I had to break it up, Borden. I couldn't allow such goings-on on the premises."

Borden wheezed excitedly; he was on the track of something. His accent also grew more prominent as he said, "Listen, Elgar. You have told me repeatedly that you wish to have no truck with conventional morality. All that sort of thing represents your father, and his rigid rules. Yes. All your life you have been in flight from moral codes and restrictions. How is it, then, that I detect in your tone a note of righteous indignation?"

"Well, of course," Elgar said. "It's different now, Borden. Fun is fun. Sure. Live and let live is my motto. But, like I told DuBois, I have three boys to raise."

"Elgar," Borden said with a sniffle, "think back now, and try to remember. Who else had three boys to raise?"

No answer was required, and none was given. Borden allowed Elgar to stare at the abyss for several awful seconds, then swiftly steered him past it.

"It is rewarding to see you become so active, Elgar, recalling the days when you were a passive ping-pong ball, bouncing between Hell and Paradise."

"What else is there, Borden?"

"Don't you know, Elgar?" the doctor's voice teased. "Don't you know where you are now?"

Elgar sat up indignantly, tired of these riddles, preferring the concrete and immediate. "Of course. In your office, you idiot!"

Though, when he looked around, he barely recognized it. From its former barrenness, Borden's office had sprung into lavish bloom with Elgar's chairs, his couch, his rugs, and his fancy lamp assortment. Elgar might almost think he was back in his own apartment if Borden had not been there to remind him, lanky and graceless as ever in cheap, rumpled corduroy. Elgar's own suit was mohair, brand-new and custom-made. —But cheaply, a little side-street tailor he had found.

"No, on earth, Elgar. Where, as all good Puritans know, one must labor in the vineyard."

"To hell with that, Borden!" Elgar cried. "I want to have fun."

"So," Borden said, "you still insist that you want to be a playboy."

"I suppose you're going to tell me to go in for hard work and clean living instead. Is that the formula, Borden?"

"It seems," Borden said, "to be the formula you have found, Elgar."

Elgar had no stomach for that sort of statement. "Well, I don't like it. It sounds too much like my father."

"Yes, all your life you have been in rebellion against your father, Elgar. Being a playboy, having no fixed occupation or identity, was part of that rebellion. The rebellion seemed to cease when you became a landlord. But for a while it turned out to be more playing. —And more rebellion, since you had chosen a forbidden playground."

"—I have observed, however," Borden said with a sniffle, "that it is amazing how all our paths of rebellion tend to lead us straight back home."

"Never, Borden," Elgar said. He would never turn out like his brothers, solid citizens with hollow conversations. *Hi, Moe, how's the family?* Oh, can't complain, Shu, can't complain. What's new? *Nothing much. Pretty good dance at the club last week. Cy Baxter's wife got a little tight, took her shoes off. Nothing scandalous, though. Nothing scandalous ever happens to People We Know. What's new with you?* Oh, nothing much. Wife picked up a nice chest at the country auction last week. Bird's-eye maple, handmade dowels. *Better watch out, Moe. She may be planning to bury you in it. Ha ha.* Could be, Shu, could be. I ought to fit pretty good in there by now. Getting squarer all the time, you know.

"Never," he repeated emphatically.

Uncannily, as if he had followed Elgar's thoughts, Borden said, "When we take the roundabout route home, Elgar, we find we are the same as we always were. But we are also somehow different from those who have never left. Different, I think, and better. Yes."

Elgar was thinking that his reconciliation with his father had made rebellion somewhat pointless.

"And your tenants, how are they doing these days, Elgar?"

Elgar thought about that. His tenants had lacked working capital; until Elgar came along, no one would lend them a dime. But like all Americans they had a rich fund of dreams. Lacking real capital they had drawn heavily on their fantasy accounts. But now they were proving that they could be as realistic as anyone else.

In spite of Levin's dire predictions, Elgar's investments were being paid back with interest. Business at the Beauty Saloon was booming. So were sales of Marge's record, *Revengeful Woman Blues and Other Lonely Laments by Marge Perkins*. Late at night he played it, and thought of Lanie.

The night club owner had asked Marge to marry him. So, it seemed, had a well-known band leader and a prosperous banker from Copenhagen. Marge was in no hurry. She had lost fifty pounds. She was radiant. She was playing the field.

She had her wigs styled, her nails manicured, her flesh pounded and her makeup applied regularly at Fanny's Beauty Saloon, as did every other singer, actress, and model in town. Out they trooped daily in a gorgeous, giggling, giddy stream, each from five to thirty-five dollars poorer, but not caring after the free Martinis.

That girl, he thought for the hundredth time, was no dummy.

She still found time to visit Charlie regularly at the hospital. He recognized her these days. He was calm. He kitchee-kooed the baby, listened solemnly to Walter Gee's space fantasies, and advised Willie

Lee to read more books and swat fewer baseballs. He was friendly with all of the 5,000 inmates. He had signed up more than half of them for Pan-Humanity-Solidarity, which was shaping up as the newest craze in religions. It was good, Elgar thought, to know where next year's tax deduction would be coming from.

"Pretty good, I think, Borden," he said. "I've been helping them to get stabilized."

"What is interesting to me," Borden said, "is that it seems to have been a two-way process. Your tenants seem also to have stabilized *you*, Elgar."

"But I hardly see them any more," Elgar protested.

"So," Borden said, "in this scheme of things, you have become a sort of engine of centrifugal force. Pushing your tenants away from you. Out on their own."

"I guess so. Though that's not what I meant to do."

"Don't apologize, Elgar. It is the best thing you can do for anybody," Borden said. And added ominously, "Soon, I hope, I will be able to do it for you."

Elgar panicked. "Oh no, Borden. You don't mean that. Not the end of treatment. I've only been seeing you for two years." No, three. No, hmmm, four.

"I do mean it."

"But you've been saying yourself, I'm still full of guilt. And Puritanism. The job isn't finished, Borden. I'm here to get rid of all that."

"Well," Borden said in a kindly manner, "I think soon, after all your hard work is finished, you should be able to allow yourself some pleasure again, Elgar."

"Yep, I was thinking about that," Elgar said. "I saw an ad for a hunting lodge the other day. Up in Canada. Thought I might go up there and have a go at some deer."

"Good," Borden said. "But I must correct certain mistaken assumptions, Elgar. You are not here to overcome all inhibitions. No. That is not our main purpose."

"What is, then?"

"You are here," Borden said, "to become yourself."

In answer to the unspoken, half-hopeful, half-terrified question on his patient's face, Borden threw open a closet door, revealing a full-length mirror. In which Elgar, rising, saw himself in his new suit of conservative cut and sober color: the very vision of a tycoon. Hard-working. Frugal. Moral. Austere. A commanding figure. Even, one might say, an Authority-Figure.

"Oh, no," he moaned.

"After rebellion," Borden said gently, "comes recognition, Elgar. We are all the sons of our fathers. Yes. It is destiny."

"But Borden," Elgar pleaded, "maybe this isn't the *real* me either."

"Elgar," Borden said wearily, "everybody has to stop sometime."

"I'll sue you!" Elgar raged. "I'll get my money back. Every cent, you fraud, you cheat, you phony! This is outrageous! There ought to be a law against quacks like you. And if there isn't, I'll have one passed. I have influence in the government these days, you know."

Borden only gave a slight, diabolical chuckle at this tycoonical tirade. And said mildly,

"By the way, Elgar, since you won't be coming in any more, would you mind if I got my old things back? My old leather couch, and my swivel chair? I miss them. I am not accustomed to all this luxury.

"—You see," he said with an apologetic shrug and a sigh, "I too am a Puritan."

25

Memo to Lanie:

  You are right. (You are always right, admirable and adorable woman; I suspect I shall never find your equal anywhere.) Playing God has its pitfalls. Because when God made people, He put in free will, just to make the game more fun. . . .

After this afternoon's events, my impulse was to purchase two airline tickets to the south of France, and say, "Darling Lanie, while the last fading garlands of youth still cling to our graying hairs, let us go kick up our heels on foreign shores. Perform a *plié* at Marseille, an *arabesque* at Antibes, etc., etc. . . ."

But duty intervened, in the form of an emergency conference with my contractor. I will not bore you with the details (I promise never to bore you with business details if you promise never to serve me liver), but I solved the difficulty with my usual dynamic decision-making power, and proceeded to the next challenge, a request from Walter Gee to correct an engineering flaw in one of his roller skates (Fanny's third baby-sitter having quit three days ago).

As you said, people are perverse. Daily I gain more respect for your wisdom. Though I still disagree with your description of my role as Great White Father, I know now that I can only count on the kids to make it worthwhile. As for the rest of my tenants . . .

You know that my diet has been both meager and erratic since Miss Perkins resumed her career as a tragic chanteuse. Therefore you can probably imagine my surprise this afternoon when I looked up from my desk and saw her wheeling in a meal consisting of:

One rosy roast beef accompanied by rich gravy,
A mountain of mashed potatoes,

A bowl of potato salad,
A bowl of *macaroni* salad,
Turnip greens seasoned with bacon,
Homemade applesauce in which substantial chunks of apple floated, and
Two dozen homemade rolls.

I noted without comment that her garb gave her the appearance of
a pallbearer—hair pulled back into a dreary little Olive Oyl bun, and
a loose, drab Mother Hubbard garment that brushed her ankles but
did not conceal the fact that she was putting on weight again. No,
having just anticipated my daily decision-making exercise (items 1
through 9 on the D-R's unvarying menu) without joy, except at the
prospect of seeing you, sweet, I did not question my luck. I simply
said, "Lord, what a feast, Marge. I can't eat all this myself. Pull up a
chair and join me."

She did so, and unfolded her napkin. Then shot me a look at once
shy and commanding.

"Shall I say the blessing, Landlord?"

I nodded, unable to speak because of excessive activity on the part
of my salivary glands.

"Lord make us truly thankful for this nutriment which we are about
to receive to invigorate our bodies in the name of . . . "

I reached out with my fork and took a stab at that luscious roast. But
the expected "Amen" did not come.

". . . and in remembrance of His suffering for our sins make us ever
thankful and mindful . . ."

Discreetly, I wiped a bit of slaver from the corner of my mouth with
my napkin.

". . . and make us strong against temptation, though the flesh be weak.
Be our rock and our fortress, our rod and our salvation, our comforter
and our mattress . . ."

Fortunately, Marge ran out of breath then, and I leaped into the happy
breach with, "Amen. Lovely, Marge. Pass the roast."

She looked at me mournfully, and inquired, "Landlord, have you
given much thought to the condition of your immortal soul?"

"More to the condition of my mortal stomach at this moment, Marge.
The roast beef, please."

" 'Egypt is like a very fair heifer,' " she quoted as she passed the meat, " 'but destruction cometh; it cometh out of the north.' Jeremiah 46:20."

"Marge, no one can make rolls like yours. Ambrosia."

"Enjoy them while you may, Landlord. Worse times are coming. 'Thus saith the Lord, Behold, I will bring evil upon this place, and upon the inhabitants thereof.' II Kings 22:16."

"This gravy, and these mashed potatoes. Delicious. —What the hell?" In my innocent zeal, I had bitten down on a piece of resistant metal lurking in my mashed potatoes. I retrieved it from my throat and gave it an inspection. *Blessed St. Christopher,* it said. *Pray for us.*

"Marge," I said, "I thank you for your solicitude, but in future please direct it only to my stomach, and let my soul go to Hell in its own way. I do not need religious booby traps in my food. Or artifacts of witchcraft, either, and as far as I am concerned they are the same thing."

"They are not the same," she reproved me, and quoted, " 'For rebellion is as the sin of witchcraft, and stubbornness is as iniquity and idolatry.' I Samuel 15:23. I have given up my black arts and idolatry along with all other rebellions, Landlord." She nodded toward my filing cabinet. "I promised the Lord I would give up conjuring if He would just let that baby be born safely. Well, He's kept His promise, so I've kept mine."

"Good," I said, though to tell the truth I was feeling a bit uneasy, a reaction I always have around fanatics of whatever variety. I attempted a bit of casual conversation. "How's the career, Marge? Did you get that night club job you were after?"

"I have given up worldly ambitions," said she, "since I met the Reverend R. Jamison Galsworthy, on the day when his choir, the Soul Refreshers, was recording in the studio next to mine. 'Woman,' he said to me, 'shun the evils of this world. Sing no more wicked songs. From now on, make a joyful noise unto the Lord.' "

"But think of your career, Marge. The joyful noise of applause. Fan letters, bouquets, telegrams. Hollywood calling. Your figure restored."

That last comment hit home; Marge's beatitude was marred by a sigh. "The Reverend R. Jamison Galsworthy," she said, "is against worldly vanity. He likes good home cooking."

"Well," I said with an indelicate belch, "that's one point in his favor. Another roll, Marge, and some more of those pungent turnip-tops."

"The Reverend R. Jamison Galsworthy," she said, "is a Traveling Elder in the Lilies of the Field International Gospel Mission. I have devoted all my future worldly profits to his missionary work. In return he has made me a Traveling Evangelist and Soloist. From now on, I will sing only hymns. Starting tomorrow, I will be on the road, bringing the gospel to the heathen. Only the sanctified will stand in the kingdom. The wicked and the unbaptized will perish together. Because I believe you are not wicked, only unsaved, Landlord, I came to cook you this last meal, and to ask you, 'Have you been baptized?'"

I tell you, Lanie, I almost choked on my roll. While coughing I reflected that I should have known this was coming, witches and saints being two sides of the same coin, the coin of fanatical faith. "R. Jamison Galsworthy," I said unwisely. "What a phony name. Sounds almost as phony as P. Eldridge DuBois."

"This morning," Marge informed me, "the Reverend R. Jamison Galsworthy and I were married."

"Uh, congratulations," I said. "Number fifteen, isn't it? That's a nice round number, Marge. A good sign. Augurs well." And other bits of inane babble, until I was distracted by an urgent summons from my upper left-hand file drawer. (Did I mention that the third baby-sitter quit three days ago?) Order is All, as my father used to say; Wesley Free was filed under "B" for Baby. I picked him up, expertly ascertained the cause of his distress, and proceeded to the middle drawer, where, under "D," I had prudently placed an emergency store of diapers.

While I was thus occupied, Wesley Free's brothers arrived home from school and, with their usual hearty directness, proceeded to set up an elaborate war-game on the floor around my feet.

Their appearance was followed shortly by that of my architect, McMenamee, a young man whose considerable gifts are restrained only by a trace of stuffiness, which promises to be relieved by continued association with me.

(Darling Lanie, at moments like these, I am more grateful than ever for having at last been allowed in your bedroom, which is such a contrast to the rest of your apartment. You too adopt flippant poses, such as *la vie Bohème,* to hide your sweetly conventional heart. But now I have found you out. And when chaos descends, I think of that fragrant bower of satin and flowers, the place where the *real* Lanie lives, and I'm reconciled, knowing a haven from chaos exists somewhere. You will never know how much I need such thoughts.)

For my architect found me seated on the floor, surrounded by troop movements, model planes, and electric trains, with Wesley Free on my lap and the diaper-changing operation in progress.

"Don't just stand there, man," I said sensibly. "Come in. What are you staring at?"

McMenamee displayed an odd, rocking sort of motion, as if trying simultaneously to retreat and move forward. "Nothing, sir. I dropped by because I promised to show you these revisions. But I see you are otherwise occupied. I can always show them to you at some other time. Next week," he said, moving back hastily as Walter Gee charged, dive-bombing him with a model B-17.

"Mother. Jumping. Son of a bitch," I said sincerely (I had stabbed my thumb with one of the pins). "Don't be silly. What's wrong with right now? Sit down. Sorry the floor is all I have to offer you."

McMenamee is a tall, slender, not ungraceful young man. He navigated the electric trains neatly, then stumbled on another booby trap. For a magnificent moment he stood poised on one foot, his arms flapping like the wings of a giant bird, until Walter Gee's skate rolled out from under him and he crashed to the floor.

"Sir," he gasped, "usually I prefer to confer with my clients in a less confusing atmosphere."

"I don't see what's confusing about it," I said around my wounded thumb. "I already had a lawyer here today, two city planners, one accountant, two councilmen, and the Mayor. They didn't have any complaints. Now, if you want to withdraw from the competition, I'm sure I can find an architect with more enterprise—"

"Oh no, sir," McMenamee protested. "If you will just look at the drawings here, and let me know whether you agree that the single-family units should have overhanging diapers—"

"Well, here's your client right here," I said, unrolling the drawing for Walter Gee's benefit. "Let's see what *he* thinks. Walter Gee, how do you like these houses?"

"Cool," said Walter Gee (he is learning to talk a little better, but not much). "Real cool. Plenty of places to play hide-and-go-seek in."

"Yeah," Willie Lee said over his brother's shoulder, "but no place for a guy to play baseball."

"Does that suggest anything to you, McMenamee?"

"A play lot," the architect said, scribbling rapidly on a large pad. "A baseball diamond."

"You see, McMenamee," I said, "this is a golden opportunity for you, an opportunity not many young architects have. A chance to observe your future clients in action. Now, when you go back to your drawing board, you will work with the *real* raw materials. Not pencil and paper, McMenamee, not brick and stone, but life. Real, active, squirming life."

At that moment, the smallest unit of life in the room began squirming. He also did something else. Like a man shot, I clapped my hand to my right eye.

"Man," Walter Gee said admiringly, "did you see that? If Landlord hadn't got in the way, he'd of hit the moom."

"You got to be fast," Willie Lee observed. "Once that diaper's off, you got to slap on the other one like lightning. It just ain't no time to be fooling around."

What is love, Lanie? You continue to insist you don't know. Marge, as she expresses herself in song, seems to feel it is a tragic emotion. Borden says it is something very rare, very difficult for human beings to achieve even under optimum conditions.

But I say *I* am making progress. If I can sustain the emotion even when its object pisses in my eye, there is hope for me. For us. For the world.

To continue, I had just succeeded in making Wesley Free comfortable when his mother arrived, bristling with pent-up maternal energies. Perhaps it will relieve your irrational jealousy if I describe her appearance on this occasion. As I have had to tell you too many times, Fanny lost all allure for me after she became a career woman. But today she was even less attractive, with her face devoid of makeup, and the rest of her covered by a limp gray garment (Muu Muu? Mau Mau? I cannot spell) which she had not worn since her Early Hausfrau period.

Giving me the sort of look which mothers usually reserve for kidnappers and dirty old men, she snatched her youngest from me and announced, "I sold the Beauty Saloon, Landlord. I'm staying home from now on. Charlie's coming home, and my babies need me."

Did you say I should not expect gratitude, Lanie? To prove how right you are, let me tell you Fanny's parting remark to me. At least I hope it was her parting remark, because, I swear, I never want to see her again.

"I've been away from home too long already. If they grow up with complexes on account of it, I'll sue you, Landlord."

After Fanny had left with her noisy brood, Mrs. R. Jamison Galsworthy sighed and remarked, "I guess I put on fifteen pounds this week alone, Landlord." Tears formed in her eyes as she reached for her fourth helping of potato salad.

And I, feeling the ominous rumblings of an approaching storm in my stomach, said with equal sadness, "I thought I was through with indigestion. Forever."

But there *was* that enormous meal to be consumed. So together we chewed, and swallowed, and stuffed ourselves, and cried.

Urp. I tell you, Lanie, that meal, delicious though it was, made me homesick for the comforts of the D-R, sterile though they are (except, of course, for you). I want hamburgers tomorrow. Extra dry.

Elgar.

26

Elgar, crouching, spread his hands over home plate and the skinny boy who had just slid there in a pinwheel of dark limbs and red-brick dust.

"Safe!" he cried.

From the field, a chorus of young voices was raised in protest.

"Jeeesus!"

"No fair!"

"He missed it by a mile!"

The third baseman threw his glove on the ground. "I'm going home, and taking my glove with me!"

"Me too!" cried the shortstop. "They can't play without me. It's my ball."

"It's my bat," declared the center fielder.

"It's my field!" Elgar shouted.

That settled the matter. "Play ball!"

I am getting older, Elgar thought sadly as he went into his crouch again. Thirty-five. No, thirty-six. Soon I will be too stiff to umpire.

It was the top of the ninth, and the Royal Rocket Men had just moved ahead of the Poplar Street Panthers. Seven to six, with two outs and two men on.

"Batter up!" cried the pitcher, a scrubbed pink bonbon of a boy. The daily game on the newly bulldozed lot had begun to attract players from surrounding neighborhoods. This one, in addition to a platinum thatch, had an arm that swiveled as if mounted on ball bearings.

Up to the plate came Willie Lee, lean and nervous, his bat on his shoulder.

"Ball one!" Elgar called as the sphere wobbled past the left of the plate. And added, under his breath, "Move your wrists down an inch or so, Willie. Loosen up. Go for the long ball."

"Easy there, Willie. Easy," he crooned as a high one floated up from the mound and Willie Lee laid into it with a sudden twist of his shoulders. The ball shot out over right field, crossed the street, and crashed through one of Elgar's third-story windows. Under the blue sky, tiny figures rounded the bases and kept rounding them, like riders on a carousel. One run. Two runs. Three. It was beautiful.

Elgar, jumping up and down in his enthusiasm, did not care about the window. He had bought his house back from the city for half of what they had paid him for it, anyway. These days, all he had to do was look up at the sky, and it rained money. Advance deposits on apartments, not yet built, but already three-quarters full. And the city was bulldozing all of his construction sites free.

"Deductions!" Levin exhorted him almost daily. "Find more deductions, Elgar."

Elgar complied, pouring money into Julius Pride Enders College as fast as he dared, building a science lab, a library, dormitories, a stadium. This month he hoped to get a theater past the trustees, though he had reservations about DuBois' wish to establish a Department of Mime and Male Dancing.

No, he decided as the game ended with the third of three easy outs and the small fry, the ones who were too little to play, poured onto the field, he would not help to mold these midgets into a future chorus line. His own youth had been plagued with too many uncertainties, too many *pliés* and *grand jetés*. DuBois would have to settle for a Department of Speech and Dramatic Arts. Balanced by a rugged athletic program.

Led by Walter Gee, the midgets trooped forward. Elgar greeted them all individually.

"Hi, Roger, William, Darrell. Hi, James, hi there, Freddy. Well, if it isn't Jeffrey. And LeRoy. And Tyrone, too. Hi, Tyrone, how's the model airplane business? Hi, Melvin, hi, Johnny, hi, Charles, hi, Paul, hi, Jerome."

One and all they answered, "Hi, Landlord." And presented for inspection their treasures—a pure, translucent green marble, a gory new comic book, a magnificent new cast on a broken arm. As well as their requests—broken flashlights, yoyos that yawed, wind-up toys that didn't wind.

"Hi, Nathaniel, hi, Carl, hi, Eddie. What ho, Chauncey, a new bike?"

"I don't ride so good yet, Landlord. I smashed in a fence today."

"Hmmm. From the looks of that fender, I'd hate to see the fence. But you'd better show it to me, Chauncey.

"—Later," he added, for Walter Gee was tugging urgently at his sleeve, asserting rights of prior acquaintance and proprietorship. "What is it, Walter?"

Walter Gee pointed to a swaggering redhead, left fielder for the Panthers, and a sore loser. "That boy over there, he called me a name."

Elgar bent so that Walter Gee could whisper it in his ear. Then felt the tension of the worst crisis ever stiffen his spine and burden his shoulders with an awful weight.

"What does that mean, Landlord?"

"Well, now, Walter Gee," he said, "I'm going to tell you a secret. This is just a secret between you and me. Other people wouldn't understand, so you mustn't ever tell them. But you mustn't ever forget it, either."

Round-eyed and grave, Walter Gee promised.

"It means," Elgar said, "absolutely nothing."

"Hey, kid," the bully called across the field. "Hey, you there. Is that your father?"

Small, strong fingers gripped Elgar's firmly, pulling him forward. "No, don't be silly," a clear voice sang out. "He's my friend."

And all at once the burdens and the stiffness slipped from Elgar's shoulders, along with plaguing questions of identity and role. You knew me all along, Walter Gee. Not your Great White Father. No. Your small, scared pink friend.

Then he was skipping lightly across the field, turning occasionally to catch a fly and toss it back into the warm-up. Life was both simpler and more complicated than he had imagined. One did not, after all, change one's skin or one's society. One was given both, along with one's identity, at birth. And all things ossified as one grew older. But within the rigid framework were loopholes of possibility, spaces in which small miracles might occur.

Someday he might be a crusty old tycoon, living elsewhere and cursing the liberals. Someday there might be a landlady who would complain about the high cost of household help.

But first the Landlord had fences to mend.